CAVE MARIE

Perfect Chemistry

A Second Chance Romance

To the love of my life, there is no one I love to annoy more than you. Thank you for always supporting me, no matter how unconventional our path has been.

To PPP, gaining you as friend and co-conspirator has been the best part of this adventure.

And finally, for the bottom feeders who like to pirate and profit from others' hard word...
Get out a bit, try not to choke on the vitamin D you obviously need.

Chapter 1

Katie's Point of View

August 23rd. Today was my *last* first day of school. I couldn't wait to leave this place and see the world. *I hated this town.* Everyone knew everybody here, and there were no secrets to be kept. Every year I did my best to avoid the drama and bullshit, and just hope that something better would happen for me next year.

Knowing I still had one more year before I could leave made me grumble quietly as I dragged the brush through my hair for the umpteenth time before I headed into school.

I hated this school too. Biggest school in the state. Biggest gathering of assholes was more like it. Everyone here was so judgmental and critical about every little thing. Who was wearing what brands, or how you did your hair. Not to mention, who you dated said so much about your worth.

And here I was, finally a senior and had never had an actual boyfriend.

I had never been on a real date in my 17 and a half years on this planet.

I never had a guy pour his heart out to me. I just *existed* in this state for 17 years. Walking to my first class, my thoughts drifted to Kai. If Kai didn't have a girlfriend this year, I would tell him how much he meant to me. I would tell him how much I liked him.

But that would never happen because he seemed to be dating all of my friends. This was what sucked about this town. As big as this town was, as big as this school was, we all knew each other. So, I was prepared to sit and pretend I cared about how great his relationship was with Alison. *I didn't.*

Just like I pretended that I cared when he was dating Michelle. *I didn't.* I didn't care if he was happy with Jennifer, Janet, or Kimberly. I wanted him to be satisfied with *me*. I pretended that we were better off as friends. I told him about whatever random boy I had a crush on, but they didn't hold a candle to my Kai. He was perfect for me. I just wished that he would see me as something other than one of the guys.

Imagine my elation when I arrived to second period and Mr. Tinneson paired me with Kai for chemistry labs! I had to keep calm and not squeal as we walked back to the lab benches. I didn't know what was wrong with him today. He had seemed like he was distracted or upset about something since the class started. I didn't know what happened over the summer, but I was sure I could get it out of him.

"Hey," I whispered as we set everything up. "Are you okay? You don't seem like yourself."

I watched as his hands paused for a split second before continuing with the directions for the experiment. He looked at me from the corner of his eyes before he whispered quietly back.

"There's this girl that I liked, but she doesn't like me like I like her," he confessed to me, and I heard my heart break as the test tube I held shattered on the floor.

"Shit! I am so sorry, Mr. Tinneson. It slipped out of my hand," I apologized as I walked to the back of the room to get the dustpan, broom, and another test tube for the lab.

"Just clean it up, Katie. Thankfully, it was empty and didn't have white phosphorus. But, be more careful," Mr. Tinneson scolded me.

I returned to our lab bench and did my best to seem normal. I couldn't cry in front of him again. "What were you saying?" I whispered to Kai, "about this crush you can't have?"

His blue eyes sparkled, and then they looked into my big dull brown eyes. I wished he could look at me the way he saw the possible girlfriend. At least as someone other than one of the guys.

"It doesn't matter. She doesn't see me like that, so I decided to just let it go," Kai whispered back to me as we observed the apparatus at work and took our notes.

"Is it someone I know?" I asked. "Maybe I could help you out?" Why did I offer to help him hook up with some other girl?

I watched as his body stiffened for a second. She *was* someone I knew. I only had so many friends in school, and he'd already dated most of them.

"Yeah," was all that he responded to me with. He didn't say anything else to me during the rest of the lab that wasn't related to the experiment. It was the longest and most agonizing hour of my life.

When we had finally cleaned everything up and the bell rang, I grabbed my bag and left for my next class as quickly as possible. Thank God, I only had two classes with him this year. My eyes watered up as I lost myself in the crowded halls. It didn't matter. I was leaving this town next summer.

Whether my mom signed my contract or not, I was joining the military when I turned 18. I couldn't stay here and watch him live happily ever after with someone else.

I found Andie at lunch and we grabbed a table together. She was going on and on about this person and that class, but I just felt like crying. I had been so excited to see Kai, and hoped even just a little, that maybe there was *something* more than friends possible.

"Hey, are you listening?" Andie asked, pulling me from my thoughts.

"What? Sorry, I didn't hear you," I confessed.

"I was saying that my sister invited me to go dancing Friday. Do you want to go?" She asked, her eyes twinkling with all kinds of evil thoughts.

I looked over to where Kai sat with all of the other jocks and sighed. What did I have to lose? "Sure, I'll go. Sounds like it could be fun."

Andie squealed loudly, and began hugging all over me which drew a bit of attention. I didn't want to look to see if he noticed. I didn't want to look and be reminded once again that this was all a one sided love.

By the time we were headed to our next class, I was engrossed in whatever crazy shit Andie was planning for Friday night. She was amazing and had me laughing to the point of tears in no time at all.

The last first week flew by. I successfully avoided Kai when we weren't in classes together to minimize the strain on my heart. By Friday night, I was excited to go dancing. Andie convinced me to wear a pair of cut-off shorts and a cute knitted tank. I loved the outfit. I did my make-up light, like always, and out the door we flew.

I couldn't stop laughing at Andie's reaction when her sister pulled up to a fire hall. "What are you doing here?" Andie asked her sister.

"Um, dancing, dummy. Did you think I was going to take you into a club in the city? Come on. You'll have fun!" She promised, smiling ear to ear. Laney was two years older than Andie, and was home on leave from the military. Hearing her tell stories about that kind of life was what sold it for me.

"But what kind of dancing is in the fire hall?" Andie asked.

"Line dancing, duh!" Laney chuckled.

I pulled Andie's arm as we followed Laney into the massive hall. "I don't know how to line dance, Andie!" I whispered loudly.

Laney sighed, and took each of us under an arm. "Look. Think of this like dance classes. We're going to learn a routine, and then have fun. I have seen you two dancing enough to know that you'll be just fine. It'll be fun!"

Three hours later, Andie and I were drenched in sweat, laughing our asses off trying to keep up with the people around us. I wondered if Kai would ever agree to go dancing with me. He wouldn't. He wouldn't even go with me to a dance in eighth grade, why would he ever agree to line dancing. Andie grabbed my hand, pulling me out of my thoughts and back to the moment. I needed to enjoy the now and forget about my what-ifs.

One Friday led to another, and before I knew it I was being dragged to the mall by my sister to pick out a dress for the homecoming dance.

"Well? Are you getting it or not?" Fiona asked, staring at me in the full-length, green, satin, body-con dress that I contemplated buying for Homecoming. "You look hot as hell!"

I rolled my eyes at her. I could be daring and adventurous in my own way. This dress just screamed *sexy,* and I wasn't comfortable with that yet. I had hoped Kai would maybe ask me, but some chick from another school asked him to *our* homecoming. I would wear this if Kai were taking me, but he wasn't.

Instead, my slightly younger sister was trying to convince me to go with her boyfriend's brother. Because nothing screamed pathetic like the senior who couldn't get a date to her last homecoming dance. I would have been just as happy going stag, but now I was the unofficial chaperone of my Irish twin and her horndog boyfriend.

"I'm just going to borrow the black maxi dress from mom. There is no way in hell I am wearing this around someone that I don't like," I sighed as I closed the dressing room curtain.

Despite my protests, Fiona was not deterred. She felt that it would be *'great'* if we double dated brothers. There was no way in hell. First she was barely sixteen, and her boyfriend was 18. His older brother was supposedly only 23, but he looked like he was 30.

I couldn't do this. I had to stop obsessing over a guy who saw me as a perma-pal and just move on. I just wasn't moving on with a 30 year-old.

I stopped listening to whatever my sister was rambling about. I stopped thinking about any of it, because it didn't matter. Nothing I wanted in the past came to be, and my future gains weren't looking too optimistic either.

"I'm going by myself. I'm not taking a set-up date, and I am not going to be your plus anything," I told her as we arrived home with our purchases two hours later.

She looked genuinely upset. "That's so sad, Katie-"

And for a moment I genuinely thought she was worried for *me*...

"What do I tell Ray? He has a suit and everything already!" She yelled, looking clearly distraught.

I stared forward at our house for a moment, willing myself not to lose my temper. "I never asked Ray to go. I did not buy a ticket for Ray, I only bought a ticket for me. You want him to go to Homecoming so damn bad, he goes with you. Just stop trying to hook me up. I'm not like you. I don't need a date to feel validated," I sighed, hating how exhausting it was to be around her.

Homecoming arrived before we knew it, and I made sure to get ready and leave from Andie's house instead of mine. I couldn't put it past my sister to spring a date on me. She had found a way to purchase a third ticket, but I destroyed it when I found it.

When Andie and I arrived, the gym took my breath away. They had stretched long sheets of fabric across the gymnasium's ceiling. The smoke and dancing lights made the billowing fabric look like clouds floating over our heads. The effect was amazing. The theme was "Somewhere over the Rainbow," which meant half of the girls here were wearing sparkling red slippers.

I chose to wear black and white striped stockings, paired with four-inch heels decorated with a prominent buckle across the toe box. The effect was a sexy witch's shoes. Not that anyone saw this, because my dress dusted the floor as I walked.

Andie disappeared as soon as we checked our coats. I

would find her later, but for now I just wanted to dance and have fun. I found several girls I knew from class and we hung out together dancing and laughing. We joked about life and the monotony of school. The night was nearly perfect.

Until I saw Kai.

He looked so good in his suit. He was so fucking gorgeous to look at. Unlike the majority of guys at school he kept his hair short with an almost flat top. When he smiled, it filled his eyes and lit up his whole face. I couldn't help the smile that broke across my face. I waved and started walking toward him, but stopped suddenly when I remembered he had a date.

His arm was around a girl I had never seen before. She was a pretty brunette with bright blue eyes, and looked pissed to see me looking at him. I watched as she pulled his face to hers and started kissing him.

I stopped looking when he didn't pull away and kissed her back. I wanted to throw up when I remembered I would never be his type. I needed to stop doing this to myself. Kai was never going to give me the time of day. That's all there was to it. I found Andie, made an excuse about not feeling well and left the dance.

I walked the mile home in my four inch heels. My feet would be destroyed tomorrow, but that didn't matter. I couldn't feel anything beyond my broken heart. By the time I walked in the door of my house, the bottom of my dress was frayed from dragging on the pavement, and my make-up was smeared from crying.

I was thankful that my parents were not home to see me like this. I had no doubts that my mom would have seen me and assumed I had been attacked by feral animals. I needed

8

to stop getting emotional about someone who didn't want me. I was just torturing my own heart by getting my hopes up, only to have them crushed in my face.

As I cried myself to sleep, I swore it would be the last time I ever cried over Kai Rayburn. He was a friend. He would never be anything more than just a friend. No matter what I thought, his actions were resoundingly clear: *I was not his type.*

October quickly rolled into November, and Kai was out of school during yet another chemistry lab. Mr. Tinneson assured me that I would be fine and let me pair up with another group to do the experiment. The two sophomores looked scared shitless to see me suddenly standing in front of their table. I just shook my head at their weirdness, and proceeded to set up the apparatus for the lab. They eventually got the hint, and joined in.

I was distracted half of the class, barely listening to what they were talking about until one of them bumped into me. "Sorry," I mumbled and shifted out of his way.

"No, it was my fault entirely," he apologized blushing.

"It's okay. I won't bite," I said. "Unless you want me to, Taylor."

The guy's jaw dropped and his eyes looked like they were going to fall out of his head. The look on his face had me laughing in seconds. I couldn't stop, even after Mr. Tinneson scolded me for distracting the other students.

"I'm sorry. That comment was inappropriate," I whispered as we were leaving class.

He looked around him to make sure no one else could hear him, then leaned close. "It's only inappropriate if I was offended. I'm not," he said and then walked away.

I felt my face flush. Cheeky monkey.

Wait.... Did he just flirt with me? No. I needed to get through this year. Just get through the year and then off to the military.

Things never progressed with Taylor, and before I knew it the whole school was counting down the days until Christmas break. Unfortunately, midterm exams came right after vacation, so I would be studying the whole time.

Thirteen days remained but Kai was finally back at school.

"I told you not to mess with her. That's what you get for playing with cra-" Bradley stopped talking as I took my seat in Chemistry. I didn't know what he and Kai were talking about and I didn't care.

I hadn't really talked to Kai like I used to. He hadn't been himself since Homeceoming, and it felt like I had lost my best friend. I began to wonder if that girl was something more? He used to talk to me before but now things were strained. He always seemed to miss classes when we had labs, and when he did come to class he barely spoke to me. I wasn't paying attention to their heated whispers, then I heard someone mention my name. I lifted my head up from my work to see Taylor smiling at me.

He was one of sophomores I had been partnered with the numerous times Kai wasn't in class.

"Sorry, did you say something?" I asked.

He actually blushed. That was new.

"Um, I was asking if I could borrow your notes from the labs?" he asked, eyeing me like I was going to vomit rainbows.

"Yeah, sure. Just give them back when you are done," I said, pulling the lab notes and calculations from my binder.

Taylor. He was a beautiful guy, and I knew for a fact that

half the girls in the senior class were after him. Somehow they found out I had labs with him, and they peppered me with questions about his likes and dislikes. I couldn't tell them anything. I just never paid attention because of Kai. I suddenly felt bold, and took the papers back for a second and scribbled my number on the top.

"If you get stuck, or need anything explained just give me a call," I smiled at him.

His eyes lit up, and that gigawatt smile of his actually got bigger. He leaned across the aisle toward me, and I instinctively leaned toward him.

"What if it's not about the labs?" he asked quietly, eyeing my every facial twitch.

I thought about everything that I had endured waiting for Kai, and decided to be brave. "Taylor, I am happy to help with *any* chemistry problems you have," I whispered back.

His face flushed bright red and he sat up straight at his desk. He was really cute, but I felt like I was soliciting a child. Yes, Taylor was beautiful and built like a young Norse God. He was 6 feet 2 inches tall, and just pure eye candy. But he was also 15.

He turned 16 soon, but I would turn eighteen shortly after that. This was never going to happen. I decided I would let him down gently whenever he got the courage to call me.

Notes passed over, I directed my attention back to my assignment, and repeatedly cursed Kai in my head for being a blind twat. Why couldn't he just *see* me?

To my surprise, Taylor did call me that night. He stuttered at first but then we got to talking about the notes and he relaxed. He was stressed about his grades, because of baseball. It was a well known rule in our school that if any grade fell to a C, the athlete would be benched for probation. Getting a D or an F, could have them removed for a season.

The more we talked the more I learned about him. He was hoping to get a sports scholarship to an Ivy League. I was jealous of his dreams and ambitions. I just wanted to go away, and this guy was planning his whole life at 15.

* * *

January, why do you hate me? Not only did we get way too much snow over the weekend, but because of the numerous holiday weekends, midterms were moved up. Normally, the whole school took exams during the same two week period. This year, they crammed it all into one.

Annnnnd because I was repeating chemistry as a senior I really couldn't afford to fail this class. I had spent a lot of time studying with Taylor and a few other classmates since winter break, so I wasn't as stressed as I thought I would be. It didn't mean I could relax. I rocked the labs, but sucked at exams.

I looked over at the clock and realized it was later than I thought. I stood up from my notes and stretched. When I heard the phone ringing, I smiled. Taylor was such a spaz about study time.

"Katie, it's for you!" my dad yelled through the house.

Midterms were next week, and I needed to do well. I had turned off my phone and made sure there were no distractions while I studied. Leaning over to grab a cordless phone sitting near the bed, I answered the call, covered the mouthpiece, and yelled back, "Got it!"

I listened and heard the main house phone disconnect from

the call before I responded, "Hello?"

"Hey," a deep voice said back. One syllable and I knew who it was.

"Hey," I repeated. "I wasn't expecting *you* to call me…. What's going on?"

There was shuffling on the other end of the line, followed by a thump noise and whispered cursing. I couldn't help but laugh.

"Um, this a bad time?" I asked, giggling.

"Shit, yes. I mean no! Ugh! I need help damnit," Kai admitted over the phone.

"Yeah, ask your girlfriend taking the AP honor classes at the private school to help you," I sneered into the phone and started to hang up.

"Stop! I broke up with her right after Homecoming. Please! I really need your help to pass this class," he whined through the phone.

"Seriously, Kai? You called me now? Where the hell have you been during labs the past two months? Suddenly, you can talk to *me* because you dumped *her*?"

There was a long pause before he said anything. "Can you just meet me at the library? I can tell you about it if you care, if not, I still need your help to pass this class. Please, please, please," he pleaded through the phone.

"Fine," I agreed. "But you owe me a coffee and an explanation, butthead!"

"Deal!" he agreed. "Meet you in about thirty minutes?"

I looked at the time. It was already seven o'clock. "Yeah, I can meet you in thirty."

We said goodbye and I stared at the phone for a few moments. He broke up with her? I didn't even notice the

13

smile that crept across my face as I packed up my study materials.

Kai was single...

It took me fifteen minutes to get to the library, but Kai was already there waiting with what I hoped was a steaming cup of coffee. It was freezing cold outside.

"Come on. Let's get this over with," I said with as much detachment as my screaming heart would allow. We stayed there until the library closed, reviewing everything I could think to cover with him.

"You'll be fine, Kai. Just review the labs and remember the formulas, and you'll do fine," I encouraged him, packing up my stuff.

"Hey, Katie," he called as I walked to my car.

I turned around to find him just behind me. My breath caught for a second before I remembered that Kai didn't *like* me. I was just his tutor.

"Yeah?" I asked.

He was quiet for a moment, studying my face. "Thank you. I really appreciate it," he finally said, patting the pile of papers I had given him.

"Oh. Yeah. Sure. No problem. I'll see you Monday in class," I mumbled and got into my car. I refused to look at him. I refused to see something that didn't exist. *Just friends.*

* * *

Staring at the calendar on my phone, I realized it was already March. *Three months left until graduation.*

"Happy birthday," Kai whispered from behind me.

I turned to find him standing there in the hall, a small gift bag held at eye level. "What did you get me?" I asked him, knowing that my smile betrayed me and smeared itself from ear to ear.

Kai *always* got me the most ridiculous birthday gifts. Last year was a "*hot for Bevis*" t-shirt that I refused to wear because Bradley was Bevis. The year before that it was a key chain with a small black cat dangling from it. They were corny gifts but they always made me laugh.

In return, I would give him some outrageously girlie gift on his birthdays, like a pink unicorn keychain or a hello kitty pencil bag.

I started to open the bag, but he stopped me.

"NO!" Kai almost shouted at me before he composed himself. He looked around the hall at the strum of students passing us. "Not now. Just wait to open it. Like when you get home. Ok?" he smiled at me, and I found myself nodding and agreed to whatever he said.

"Can you tell me what it is? Is it something I can wear to school and show off?" I asked, looking at the pretty gift bag. I was so busy staring at the bag, I almost missed the crimson hue that covered Kai's face.

"Yes. You should wear it to school tomorrow. If you like it," Kai told me. His eyes danced with mischief. Whatever this was, it had to be good.

I couldn't wait to see what he bought for me, and peeked inside the bag on my way to class. He had wrapped everything up and attached a note that read, 'No Peeking!'

I laughed abruptly, startling several people walking near me. "Sorry," I apologized, biting my lips. I carried that gift bag around the rest of the day like it was a prized possession. I could have opened the gift during lunch or study hall, but after the warning message, I decided to just wait. It was the longest wait of my life.

I ran straight up to my room when I got home and dropped everything but the gift bag on the floor. I sat on my bed and stared at the bag for a solid ten minutes before opening it.

What the hell was this?

Chapter 2

Kai's Point of View

First day of school senior year. *This was my last chance.*

"Dude, are you going to actually make a move this year or what?" Bradley, my best friend, asked, hitting me in the chest as we took our seats in chem. He was tired of listening to my whining about the same thing year after year.

I was about to answer him, but I looked up to see *her* walking into the classroom.

Kat *"My Goddess"* Preston.

She was gorgeous. She had this amazingly easy personality, and could talk to anyone. I didn't know a single person in our senior class who disliked her. To the contrary. I couldn't count the number of guys who had the hots for her, myself included. Unfortunately, for me, Kat had zero interest in me outside of friendship. She had no idea how bad I had it for her.

In fact, I had spent the last seven years of school fantasizing about her. But to her, I was just one of the many guys surrounding her and she never gave me a second glance. The guys that she liked were all older. I knew, because she would tell me about them. Jocks. Tall, pretty boys.

Then there was me. I wasn't much taller than Katie. I wasn't built like a brick shit house, and the only thing I had in common with her *type* was being a jock. *Fuck.* She was even older than me by like a month, a fact she made a point to note every year since the eighth grade. I didn't know who was more pathetic: her gaggle of would-be's or me? Fuck, I hated those guys flocking around her. *Every. Single. One.* I hated them all.

I looked over to lock eyes with Bradly, and quietly shook my head. I had to be content with another year of smelling her perfume and leaving class with blue balls. I'd admit it. I'd listened to her stories and pretended that I was a friend when I told her all of the dirt, rumors, and bullshit, I could dig up on every guy she liked. *FUCK!*

"*Hey, Kai.* I didn't know you and Bradley had Chemistry, too." Kat winked and smiled as she took the seat in front of me like always. Sometimes, I played with her hair when it fell back on my desk in the few classes we shared over the years. She smelled like vanilla and strawberries. Her smile always lit up her whole face. You couldn't help but want to smile with her. Then there were her eyes. I couldn't look at another girl with brown eyes and not think of *her*.

Bradley leaned toward Kat and shamelessly flirted, "Are you interested in some experimentation...."

Kat leaned toward him. "Only if you're taking notes..." she purred.

Bradley went to comment further but Mr Tinneson closed the door loudly and interrupted their weird flirting. He eyed Bradley and Kat, and then shook his head like he wanted to unhear everything they just said.

"Kiki, your lab partner will be Bradley. Help him pass so I don't have to see him ever again," Mr. Tinneson mumbled under his breath as he walked around passing out the class syllabus and assignment packets.

"Katie, your lab results were excellent, if I recall. I have paired you with Kai. Hopefully, between the two of you, you'll pass and be gone as well," he continued.

"Mr. Tinneson, did someone steal your parking spot or something?" Bradley asked.

Mr. Tinneson looked confused for a moment, then shook his head. "No, I just can't stand repeating myself or wasting time. Yet, here you five are, repeating this class. Try not to piss me off any further this year."

This was a sophomore level class, and five of us were repeating it as seniors. Bradley never turned in his final project which automatically failed him. I had been too distracted by the opposite sex to pay attention, and blew up more labs than I completed.

Kat barely passed the final and had failed the midterm. She couldn't graduate with the D in Chemistry, and that's how we ended up in class together. *Again.*

I just smiled like I always did and hoped to hell that this year would end my obsession and fascination with Kat Preston. I needed to just get over her. I was not dating anyone. I ensured that I wasn't even talking to anyone just in case she came back from summer break single.

But watching her flirt with Bradley, just reinforced what I knew deep down. She would never see *me* like I saw *her.*

Why, why, *why* was I torturing myself? Because I had had a crush on her since the sixth grade. I had liked her since before she even knew I existed. If I hadn't asked her friend Michelle out in the eighth grade, I never would have gotten into her circle of friends.

If it didn't work out, I needed to move on and pretend to be another friend like I always had.

The first week was awkward as hell. Everytime she looked my way, or brushed against me walking to labs my traitorous dick twitched. It got to the point where I just couldn't even make fucking eye contact with anyone in class. I have never focused so hard on classwork before. I just needed to stay focused and not think about Kat Preston's juicy ass squeezed into her jeans.

"I'm going to fail," I whispered to Bradley as we headed to lunch.

He looked at me like I had confessed to being an alien. "Dude! You have the smartest fucking lab partner in the damn class. Get a fucking grip," he scowled at me.

"That's not the point and you fucking know it!" I growled back. "Does she even know I can see down her jeans when she wears that shit?"

"Tell you what. I'm going to a party with Alex and a few of the guys. Maybe we can find you a distraction for a night… Eh??" he asked, wiggling his eyebrows up and down.

I couldn't help but shake my head and chuckle. I had slept with two of my previous girlfriends, and it wasn't good for any of us. Since then my hand was the only intimate partner to touch my dick in months. I don't know why Bradley thought meeting someone else would change that.

September was another torturous month of blue balls being around Kat. She had to know that I was getting a front row view of her ass every time she leaned forward in class. Her jeans just didn't quite fit around her small waist, leaving me a perfect view to stare at her underwear. Thankfully, Bradley kept dragging me to parties with Alex each weekend, so I wasn't stuck home stewing about who Kat was out with. A few beers could always help to keep my thoughts off of Kat.

Alex's cousin went to some snooty private school two towns over. It was a pain in the ass to coordinate shit with him, but he had pretty big parties. I had gone to a couple with Bradley and ended up talking to the same girl, named Kristin, two or three times. She seemed nice enough, but I wasn't really interested in flirting with anyone there. My head was constantly circling back to Kat. Unfortunately, Kristin heard Bradley talking about homecoming, and asked if I had a date.

Somehow that turned into me *agreeing* to take her as my date. I couldn't remember when I agreed to bring Kristin to Homecoming. She had asked me while I was drunk at the last party, then called me the next day to coordinate our outfits. I couldn't remember even talking to her. She was pretty, but super high maintenance. *Not my type at all.*

Bradley and I agreed to ride together so that I wouldn't be stuck with Kristin by myself. I picked up him and his date before we picked up Kristin. She talked nonstop the entire way to the school. By the time we got to the gym, I couldn't help looking for Kat. I was certain that her date would be some jock or dude she met at work. There was no way that she wouldn't have had a line of guys waiting to ask her out.

I was standing there under the billowing canopy, my ears ringing from the blaring music, regretting coming with the wrong date. I was so fucking annoyed. I honestly didn't think it would be this bad. Kristin was a mean girl.

From the moment we walked in, she began bad-mouthing every other girl in here. Who was fat, whose makeup was wrong, who she thought was ugly.... Then she stopped

21

talking, and I couldn't help but sigh with relief in my head.

I didn't hear what she said, but it sounded like, "I don't fucking think so." The next thing I knew, she had grabbed my chin and was kissing me. I returned the kiss without thinking.

Then I remembered Kat.

I pulled away and tried not to be obvious about wiping my mouth. Nothing about that kiss did it for me. Even as desperate as my dick was, it wasn't interested in anything Kristin was offering. "That's all you get," I told her, trying my best not to cause a scene. "I told you, we're here as friends, Kristen," I whispered in her ear.

She just laughed and said, "We'll see about that. I can be very persuasive."

At that moment, Bradley's pointing finger caught my attention. I turned my head to see Kat Preston. She looked amazing. Her dress hugged every curve when she moved, and she danced like she didn't care who was watching.

My date must have seen me staring and followed my line of sight. "She knows her place," Kristin muttered, wrapping her arms around me.

I didn't understand what she was talking about, and I wasn't comfortable with her touching me. I put some distance between us, and did my best to ignore the bullshit that came out of her mouth. I wasn't feeling it at all and made an excuse about feeling ill so that I could leave early. I took Kristin home first and didn't wait for her to get to the door before I was pulling away from her house.

By the time Monday rolled around, I was fucking exhausted. Kristin had messaged and called me all weekend. I didn't know how many ways a guy could say he wasn't interested, but it felt like I had used them all. I finally got to the point that I just asked her to stop calling me and blocked her number. When she started calling from an unknown number, I shut my phone off.

Now I had to sit behind the girl of my dreams, and be content with the fact that smashing my head into the desk was the closest I was getting to her. She was cordial with me when she sat down which meant she was seeing someone new. She always distanced herself when there was a new guy. I'd have to find out who and put an end to that shit.

Unfortunately for me, the nightmare that was Kristin kept me busy for weeks after Homecoming. I wasn't sleeping, my grades were slipping, and Kat was giving me the cold shoulder.

* * *

"Kai! Get down here right now!!" my mother yelled from the bottom of the stairs.

After yet another night of shit for sleep, I wasn't sure what I had done or forgotten to piss her off. To be honest I hadn't slept well in weeks. My phone would go off at random times with various messages or calls from Kristin, the homecoming nightmare from hell.

I tried to break things off amicably, but the chick was a psycho. When did she fucking sleep, because she called and messaged all fucking night long. Last night was the worst. I finally shut my phone off at 3 am just so that I could sleep a couple of hours before school, only to be woken by my mother screaming downstairs.

I sat up and rubbed my face. I don't know what I did to get

her this fired up, but I'm sure it would be funny when she calmed down. Trudging down the stairs, I looked past the railing to see both of my parents standing in the living room with *two* State Police.

What the fuck? I stopped walking and just stared, my eyes darting between the cops and finally going to my parents.

"What's going on?" I asked, still not moving from the stair I stopped on.

"The car was vandalized," my mother informed me.

I didn't understand what that had to do with me, so I walked down the remaining steps to peek out at the car. I immediately felt like I had been punched in the gut.

The windows had all been smashed, and the sides of the car painted with bright red letters: **R-A-P-I-S-T.**

"Do you have any idea who would do this to your vehicle?" One of the cops was asking.

I shook my head, trying to keep down the sparse contents of my stomach. I hadn't been with anyone since Alison last school year, and she would never….

"Kai, go get your phone. I'm done with this," my father barked at me.

My head jerked up to look at him, obviously confused. "I didn't *rape* anyone!" I shouted back, feeling like I was being accused of the worst thing possible.

I watched their expressions soften, and my mom quickly crossed the room to hug me. "We know, sweetie. That's not what we meant. Go get your phone so that we can turn it over to the police as evidence."

I jerked back from her hug, becoming more defensive. "Mom! I didn't do anything wrong!" I kept shouting my innocence, making the two officers nervous.

"Kai-" my dad's voice broke through my shouting. "We're not accusing you, son. The police need your phone to press charges against the person who did this. It contains *evidence*."

Until my phone was in the cops' hands, I had no idea what they were talking about. It never occurred to me that my parents had been shielding me from a lot of crazy. We ended up spending the entire day at the police station giving statements.

By the time we got home, I realized I had missed my chem lab. "FUCK!" I yelled, startling my mom.

"Kai Rayburn! Do not cuss like you have no manners! I know this is a lot of stress on you, but we'll help you get through this," she consoled me.

"I missed class today," I mumbled back as she pulled me into a hug.

"Don't worry about that. Your dad is contacting the school to get your missed assignments. Until she's arrested, you're staying home," she informed me.

I went back to my room and crashed. I couldn't even think about the world outside right now while I was living in a fucking twilight zone.

When I woke up the carousel of crazy continued. I just wanted my fucking life back. Just one thing that I could control, but there was nothing. After the second week, I stopped counting the days I had missed, and just holed up in my room to complete missed assignments.

Suddenly, it was December and I could move forward from the worst experience of my life. I wanted to talk to Kat, but I didn't even know where to start. There was so much I couldn't talk about until now, but now.... I didn't want to talk about it. I wanted to forget it, to be honest.

"How'd it go?" Bradley asked, as we sat down in the cafeteria to eat lunch.

"It's done," I muttered. "I still can't believe she did that shit."

Bradley shook his head. The last three weeks had been nothing short of some crazy wild ride in some alternate universe.

"She confessed to messing with my parents' car, stalking, communicating threats," I shuttered, remembering all of the details that I did not know about.

"First stalker, *my man,* right here!" Bradley tried to make a joke. "Your parents ask for the restraining order?"

"Oh, yeah!" I chuckled. "500 yards, from me, my house, my school, no contact whatsoever or she gets tried as an adult for, and I quote *'exploiting a minor.'*"

"*Shut up!*" Bradley choked on his soda. "Seriously?!?"

"Dude, I feel…." I paused as my eyes drifted over to see Kat leaving the cafeteria with two of her friends. "so fucking filthy."

We didn't talk about it further. Kristen was a psycho. She stalked and harassed me for two months. Left dead animals on our doorstep, and finally destroyed my parents' car when I shut my phone off that last night.

I had to take time off from school for the hearing at court, and before that there was the behavioral therapist evaluations, social workers, and police statements.

I wanted to tell *Kat,* but she hadn't even looked at me since Homecoming. I could only imagine what she thought of me. Bradley and I got quiet as Kat sat down in front of me before chem class started. She was so focused on school this year that we barely talked.

I saw a guy from the baseball team lean over and ask her

something. I wanted to interrupt whatever he was trying, but then she passed him her lab book. *Thank fuck for that.*

I didn't want to be the ball blocker, but I'd do it if that kid thought for even a second he was going to have a shot with her.

* * *

Preseason started in January. We had selections for the varsity team, and were practicing every day for our first game in February.

The guys were laughing and joking when I entered the locker room. Baseball season had finally started, and I was ready for it. I wasn't team captain, but I was a Senior who had earned their place on this team.

There were a few freshmen and sophomores who showed promise, but they were not focused on the training this early in the season. Not like the seniors looking for scholarships.

"Way to go, Taylor!"

"Yeah, bro! Bagging a senior!"

"Hell, yeah! That's what's up, Tay!"

The underclassmen's banter slowly filtered in. *Good for him,* I thought.

"I can't believe you made a move on *Preston*, and she went for it!"

I slammed my locker shut and clenched my fists. No. *NO.* I needed to calm down. I waited until most of the guys had left the locker room before calling out.

"Hey, Taylor, you got a sec?" I asked without moving from my locker.

Taylor was a big guy. Not that I was small, but he was much

bigger than me. I wasn't sure that I could take him in a fight if he went all in, but if it came to it... I'd kick this kid's ass to keep him away from Kat.

Taylor came around the lockers smiling. His smile dropped as soon as he saw me. *So he knew he fucked up.*

"I'm not going to tell you what to do," I started. "But you're not going there. You might win in a fight with me, but you won't get what you're hoping for."

He stared for second, his jaw clenching and unclenching as I leaned down to grab my gear.

"You cock blocking me, Kai?" he asked, looking surprised.

"Yep," I replied, popping the p.

"Seriously?"

"Try me," I responded quietly, taking a step in his direction.

I honestly thought he was going to punch me, but he just tipped his head back and groaned.

"I hate you so much," he growled, turning to leave.

I didn't realize I was holding my breath until that second, but I called out to Taylor before he could walk away.

"Hey, Taylor?"

"Yeah?" he asked, looking every bit as angry as I was just minutes ago.

"Thank you."

His face relaxed and he nodded. "Yeah, yeah."

By the time I got home, I couldn't sit still. I had no idea what the fuck I was going to do, but it needed to wait until after midterms. First, I needed to pass my exams. Then, I could plot how to get my girl.

By seven o'clock, I couldn't stand it anymore. I didn't understand half the notes because I had missed so many labs back in November. I needed help, and I couldn't put shit off any more. Midterms were next week.

I paced my room weighing the options. I didn't just need help with the labs. I needed to know if there was a guy or not. Kat wasn't talking to me, but I knew the key to getting her to open up. I was on my way to the coffee shop before I called. Thank god she agreed to meet me at the library. I needed to graduate to get my scholarship, and I had to pass chemistry to graduate. Having Kat as my study partner filled all the gaps I had. It was the perfect excuse to see each other.

Not only did I pass the midterms thanks to Kat's amazing notes, but I found out she wasn't seeing anyone. I wanted to tell her everything about Kristin, but there was no way I was opening that wound up. I did tell her that I was involved in a criminal case, and my parents pulled me to give witness statements. It was enough to explain why I was quiet, and not enough to show how fucking stupid I had been for not taking *her* to our last homecoming.

This season's baseball team was solid. We won our first three games and tied the fourth. Before I knew it, February was over and March was upon us.

I was sitting with Bradley watching TV at his place. I had to tell him. I was nearly bursting and I just needed to tell *someone.* "I did it."

He was quiet for a long while. Didn't say a word until the show ended. Then he looked over at me, and I had no idea what he would say.

"Sooooo, you finally lost your virginity?" he asked, looking at me for a minute before adding, "Again."

I couldn't help but laugh. This guy was such a dick. He knew exactly what I was talking about but was going to make me say it.

29

"I let Kat Preston know how I feel about her," I told him as I jumped off the couch and grabbed us a few drinks from the kitchen.

Bradley's jaw dropped, and I knew he was shocked that I finally made a move. He had been sick and tired of listening to me talk about my crush since we met in our first year here. He was going to ask her out, and I stopped him with some bullshit excuse as to why he shouldn't. He immediately called me on my crap and said, "Dude, if you got a thing for her, all you had to do was say so. How can I help you?" We've been best friends ever since.

"Kai!" He ran after me to the kitchen smiling. "What did you say? What did she say? You aren't asking to hit my parents' minibar, so it couldn't have gone bad... What happened?"

I leaned against his counter, and laughed. I knew he would be happy for me. "She hasn't said anything. *Yet.*"

Bradley's smile slowly calmed down. "Ok. Did you *actually* make a move on Kat Preston, or do you still hope she understands your weird way of flirting, *aka cock blocking*, as some sort of interest?" he asked with one raised eyebrow.

I just smiled as I took another drink of my soda, "She can't misunderstand this one."

Chapter 3

Katie's POV

I stared at myself in the mirror, debating whether I could do this or not. How the hell was I going to face Kai today in class? I had become used to the corny gifts over the last few years. I was expecting another corny gift this year....

Imagine my shock when my gift went from a Bevis and Butthead t-shirt to three lace thongs. Everyone knows that a gift of lingerie means the person hopes to see you in said garment. But when the hell did Kai *ever* see me like that? Was he desperate to get laid? Was his hoping to make me his end of school *slum* fuck?

No. I couldn't think like that. But fuck if my heart wasn't pounding in my chest. What if he *did* see me as someone he liked? What if he liked me for me? *Yes.* That was it. Kai was telling me that he liked me. This had to be it. That or he was really fucking confused and gave me the wrong gift.

I walked into chemistry class and took my seat as usual. I was not sure how to show off the birthday present for Kai shy of dropping my pants and parading through the halls. I didn't want to draw any more attention to myself, but I wanted him to know that I really liked it. A lot. I honestly didn't think that he knew my preferences so well, cause they were super comfortable. Maybe he had been paying more attention than I thought.

I sat with my back straight at my desk, one leg crossed, and began reviewing my notes before our Chemistry test. I saw Kai come in just before the bell and moved past me to take his seat. I leaned forward in my seat and heard him trip. His breath caught as he walked past me, but I pretended I didn't notice.

Mr. Tinneson began to explain the test, and we all cleared our desks. As I bent over to put my books in my bag, I heard Kai whisper to me.

"What the hell are you doing?" he asked, almost growling.

Was he angry with me? I couldn't turn around to see him, so I decided to play innocent, "I don't know what you mean? I am just putting my things away."

"What the hell are you-" his next question was silenced as Mr. Tinneson dropped a test packet on each of our desks.

"There will be no talking. If you finish early, you may bring your packet to me and step to the back lab tables while the others complete their test. You may not use your cellphone's calculator. If you need a calculator, there are several on the front table. You may begin now."

I walked up and grabbed a calculator. I was great with algebra and what I would call normal math. But the decimals and fractions in chemistry always threw me. It was better to err on the side of caution. I flipped through the packet and recognized many questions from my sophomore year when I failed this class. I did great with the labs, but struggled with the tests.

Thankfully, I kept my notebooks and homework from back then so that I could study my ass off and pass this year. It didn't take me long to get through all of the questions. I finished my test, turned the packet over, and placed it in the box on Mr. Tinneson's desk. Kai was working on the last page as I walked past his desk to sit at our lab table in the back of the room. He still looked furious.

His face was flushed red, and he kept flexing his jaw like he was trying to break his teeth. I watched as he flipped through each page once more before turning his test over to Mr. Tinneson. He stalked toward the back of the class staring directly at me. My heart began thudding in my chest again, because I couldn't tell what he was thinking. He paused behind me, and I would have sworn I heard his breath hitch.

I was freaking out in my head, even though I smiled at him. He sat next to me and stared down at the lab table, his jaw clenching tightly while his hands balled into white knuckled fists. I moved to ask him if he was okay, but he turned my body back to face the front of the room.

I felt his breath on my cheek, and I couldn't breathe. "Take a hall pass," he whispered in my ear, and I nodded. My face felt flushed, and I knew it had to be cherry red. I had butterflies in my stomach from the feeling of his breath on my skin.

I quietly went to the door and took a wooden block that read 'hall pass, Tinneson.' I held it up and Mr. Tinneson nodded to let me leave.

Closing the door quietly behind me, I walked down the hall to the water fountains and leaned over to take a drink while I waited to see what had Kai so damned upset. I couldn't think of anything that I did wrong. Maybe he got dumped again, and was pissed and wanted to vent. Then a thought occurred to me. What if my gift was not actually *my gift?*

Before I could dwell further down that depressing rabbit

hole, I was pulled from the fountain and dragged into the girls' toilets. Kai shoved me into one of the stalls, and followed behind me before closing the door and locking it. His eyes were radiant, and he studied my face like he was trying to find the right words.

"What are you doing?" he asked. His voice came out in a gravelly whisper.

"I don't understand," I admitted softly.

"What are you *wearing?* I could see straight down your fucking jeans, Katie."

Noooo. I felt like throwing up. I had completely misunderstood every fucking thing…

"Was I not supposed to wear the gift you got me? Or was I mistakenly given the wrong gift for *my birthday*, Kai?" My voice trembled as the words came out. I was torn between humiliation and rage because of him. *Again.*

I watched a thousand emotions flash across his eyes. He stood so close, but then turned away like he'd been caught and didn't know how to respond. I felt my heart shattering. I honestly thought he was using passing this class as an excuse to be with me. I was wrong. Again.

"I'm so fucking stupid," I whispered, trying to hide the tears burning my eyes as I reached for the stall door.

Kai grabbed my hand and pulled me roughly into his chest. There wasn't room to move around, so I bounced into him before I smashed back against the side wall. His lips caught mine in the barest of a kiss.

My eyes widened as I stared at him. Kai just kissed me. Kai. MY KAI. His eyes watched me; took in my every reaction. Was he waiting to see if I would lose my shit or become angry? Why did he keep toying with me? *Fuck it,* I thought.

If I am going to lose his friendship anyway, I might as well take it straight to hell.

I jerked my hands out of his, grabbed his shirt, and kissed him with everything I had felt for years. I parted my lips and was surprised to feel his tongue plunging into my mouth. This kiss was heart-stopping, but I just couldn't stop. *This. Oh My Heaven!*

He took my hands from the front of his shirt, held them over my head, and pressed his body against mine so I could feel how hard he was. His lips devoured mine, sucking on my bottom lip before his tongue explored my mouth again and again.

I whimpered into his mouth when his hips rocked so subtly against mine. It felt like every sensation in my body had just pooled deep in my stomach and soaked my panties. He wanted me. *Me. Holy-*

We stilled when the outer door to the restroom creaked open. *Fuck. How long had we been in here?* He quickly stood up on the toilet seat, and squatted down as he grinned at me. I couldn't think. I just stood there staring at him, while he stared back at me. The butterflies in my stomach were revolting, because of all the questions I wanted to ask. What the hell did this mean? For *us?*

"Katie?" a girl's voice called into the restroom, breaking me from my thoughts. I recognized the voice of Kennedy from our chemistry class. I immediately went from nearly hyperventilating to trying to hold my breath. I bit my lip and closed my eyes. I needed to get myself under control. She was one of the many sophomore underclassmen in chemistry with us. She had a crush on Kai and thought no one realized it. Kennedy was a nice girl, but she annoyed the shit out of me every time she batted her eyes at him.

Kai flushed the toilet and nodded for me to leave the stall first. I was flipping between grinning like a cat that stole the canary, and wanting to be sick when I slipped out of the bathroom stall and washed my hands. I saw how flushed my face was in the mirror and looked over to see Kennedy staring at me from the door.

"Is there something wrong?" I asked her as I dried my hands.

She looked nervous, and I wondered if she had caught us. "Um, no. I- You were gone a while, so I said I would check on you," she admitted, though it didn't seem like that was it.

"Yeah, sorry. I wasn't feeling right so I needed some air. I appreciate you looking out for me though, Kennedy," I said as I wrapped an arm around her shoulder and forced her to walk out of the bathroom with me.

She turned, attempting to look down the hall behind us, but I wouldn't let her in case Kai was sneaking out. "I'm sorry, Kennedy. Did you need to use the bathroom?" I asked her, hoping that I honestly looked concerned.

Kennedy's face flushed and she looked embarrassed. "Uh- um... I. Um- Kai also left with a hall pass, so I didn't know if he was out here."

She was looking over her shoulder toward the fountains searching for Kai. I wanted to laugh, and tell her, *'Not today, little girl.'* But I couldn't risk

"*Ohhhh.* Did you want to help him in the bathroom, too? Were you hoping to lock yourself in a stall with Kai during the exam and test your *chemistry?*" I asked her bluntly, knowing that I had just done *exactly that.* And the chemistry was.... *Explosive.*

"Good thing you came in, Bradley. I was stuck with no teepee," Kai told Bradley as they walked past us to return to class.

Their voices immediately changed over to mimic Bevis and Butthead, "heh heh heh. You said teepee."

"I needed teepee. Teepee for my bunghole. heh heh heh."

Kai's eyes locked with mine for a split second, and I knew he was not done with me. My thighs clenched together as thoughts of his kiss played through my head, and everything unknown swirled through my mind. Then I caught Kennedy staring at him. Again.

"Really? You wanted to get it on with the *butthead* taking a dump?" I asked her. I walked back to the classroom and left her to stand alone in the hall. As we took our seats, Mr. Tinneson looked up from his desk and seemed confused.

"Are you missing someone?" he asked me.

"I didn't take a friend to the bathroom, so I don't know who I would be missing, Mr. Tinneson," I told him, doing my best to look confused by his question. "Kennedy was looking for Kai, but he is here, so I am not sure what she is doing," I explained.

Was it right to air that tiny bit of laundry to the whole class? I didn't really care at that moment. I couldn't be bothered to spare her feelings, not after I had just kissed him myself. I wanted to turn around and talk to him, but the bell rang and Kai was out the door before me.

He gave me a quick look over his shoulder, but then disappeared with Bradley into the swarm of students flooding the halls.

It took everything I had not to touch my lips. They were still tingling. How the hell did I end up making out with Kai

Rayburn in a stall of the girls' toilet?

* * *

I couldn't stop thinking about that kiss. Did he kiss me because he wanted *me*? He was definitely turned on by the kiss, but I didn't know if it was me. Like, was he turned on because it was me? Or was he turned by the thought of someone else, and I just happened to be the one throwing myself at him.

I huffed and went back to work. I worked for a car repair center that my mother's family managed. As one of a few women working here, I had more attention than I ever wanted. I learned at 14 to ignore the guys in the service bays, and not to make friends with any of the drivers or lot runners.

The guys must have thought I was crazy. I was mumbling to myself as I argued whether Kai liked me or not. I wanted to just call him and ask, but I couldn't use my phone at work. Thankfully we were slammed tonight, so I was busy cleaning rental returns and preparing contracts and cars for the customers who would come in the morning. It allowed me to not obsess the *whole night* about Kai.

The problem was, every time I did think about him, I blushed crimson red. It was drawing too much attention and I was running out of excuses as to why I kept blushing. I stuffed my cell phone in my back pocket and stepped outside to get a breath of fresh air. I leaned against the wall and just let out a long, deep breath.

"You alright, Katie?" a deep voice suddenly sounded through the night air.

I looked over to see one of the mechanics outside smoking. "Hey five-speed," I smiled.

Five-speed's real name was Jason, but he earned the name 'five-speed' when the other mechanics found out he couldn't drive a manual. Specifically, he didn't know manuals had a fifth gear, and he nearly destroyed a transmission delivering a car to a customer.

"You seem preoccupied tonight. You doin' alright?" he asked again.

I stared down at my feet, and debated on how much to say. Five-speed wasn't that much older than me, and had been my guy guide when I didn't understand shit. I went back and forth in my head before finally deciding, *why not ask?*

"There is this guy I like," I started. "I've liked him for a long time, and we kissed, but I don't know if it means anything. I thought the feeling was mutual, but then he basically ran off and messaged that we needed to talk," I confessed quietly.

Jason's eyebrows shot up, then he composed his facial expressions to look more serious and less shocked. "Wait, which guy are we talking about, Katie?" he asked me.

"The guy," I said, feeling my face burning up again.

He dropped his cigarette. "Whoa! What did I miss? Wait, I take that back!. We don't have time for the whole story. Tell your mom I'll drive you home, so you can tell me what happened!"

I started laughing. He was just as bad as my best friend Andie when it came to any gossip pertaining to me and a guy. "Yeah, sure, but we can't stop for coffee cause my dad is on days, and he times how long it takes me to get home."

Jason rolled his eyes. "Got it. Call your mom, I'll message your dad so he knows it's me taking you home, and not one of these other perverts," he said, gesturing toward the rows of open garage bays.

"Sure thing," I said smiling. "Thank you."

"No worries, baby girl. You're like my kid sister. I have to look out for you," he smiled back and pulled me into a side hug as we walked inside.

I used the office line to call my mom so that she would know I was calling from work and not somewhere else. Of course she had no issues with Jason driving me home. And, since Jason *manned up* and called my dad, dad was fine with me getting a ride home and even agreed to let us stop for coffee.

My parents were super strict. So much so, that I referred to them as the wardens. It wasn't that they were religious or conservative. They were just super protective. It was the one downside of having parents who grew up under rough conditions, they were strict as hell because they grew up in hell.

On the way to grab coffee, I told Jason everything that happened. Well, almost. I didn't tell him about the three thongs that Kai got me for my birthday. I just said I flirted a bit more than usual to get his attention.

Jason listened without saying a word through it all. By the time he was passing me my medium latte, I was done with story time.

"He likes you," he said.

My jaw dropped open. "How do you know? What if he wants to talk because it was a huge mistake?" I asked quietly.

Jason shook his head and chuckled. "He'd be crazy not to like you, Katie. But you make guys nervous," he explained. "Give him a chance and just let him find his courage, okay?"

I nodded my head, then stopped; feeling like I missed something.

"Wait. What do you mean *I* make guys nervous? I'm not even one of the popular girls, Five-speed." I was confused.

"Katie, you don't care who is watching when you enter a room, and it makes people notice you that much more. You laugh like it is your favorite job, and you are a genuinely nice person. That's so close to perfection, it scares the shit out of guys," he explained, laughing at my still confused expression.

"That's ridiculous. I'm not even that good looking, Jason."

This time he looked at me seriously. "Katie, I hope you never realize how incredibly beautiful you are. It'd be like unlocking an evil superpower. Stay ignorant. Ignorance is safer for the rest of us mortal men."

At that point I started laughing again. He just watched me from the corner of his eye as we drove the rest of the way to my house.

I thanked Jason for the talk, coffee and chauffeur services, and promised to let him know how things progressed.

I still didn't know what to say to Kai, so I chickened out and said nothing.

Chapter 4

Kai's POV

After confessing to Bradley last night, I came home and slept like the dead. I had finally let Kat Preston know how I felt. Then I woke up this morning and remembered that I had given my crush, the Goddess of my dreams, the biggest fucking banner announcing how I felt. I wanted to throw up, if I was being honest.

Then I walked into chem class, and almost choked on my own saliva. Kat Preston was leaned forward over her desk and all I could see was a bright red lace thong.

I could see down the back of her jeans when she sat straight forward. I mean all the way down. Then I caught Taylor and some other dick named Ryan also checking out her ass, and I wanted to fucking snap. I leaned forward to ask what the hell she was thinking, and she played fucking coy.

She had on a thong that *I* bought. I spent the whole class staring down at her plump ass spilling out on either side of a red lace thong *I picked out*. But I wasn't alone. Oh, no! Every other guy in our class was trying to get a peek down her jeans.

I just wanted to know *why* she did that. Had she known this whole time that I could see her ass when she sat like that?

Was she showing off for me? Or did she just not care about my feelings? No. She wouldn't do that. She wouldn't show *that* off for other guys.

I couldn't even concentrate on the fucking chem test. I flew through it as quickly as I could, just so that I could talk to her before she left. I handed over my test to Mr. Tinneson and walked back toward her. I honestly couldn't tell if she was toying with me. Was she smiling like that for me? I had to stop and shift myself in my jeans just to sit down.

I wanted to ask her questions, but I couldn't. Then she leaned over, and asked if I was okay. *NO. I was not okay!* This was not a discussion we could have in the back of chem class.

I told her to take a hall pass, and then I followed a minute later. I came down the hall to find her ass bent over the fountain. When she stood up, her tongue flicked out to catch a drop of water on her bottom lip and I almost came. I didn't even think. I grabbed her and dragged her into the bathroom, and locked her in a cubicle with me.

I had no idea how to even word what I wanted to say. Did she want me? Or was she mocking me? What came out was, "What are you doing?"

Suddenly she was fucking angry and asking if I had given her someone else's gift by mistake. I had never bought another girl any gifts. Only her. But I couldn't get the words out. When she tried to leave, and I was still trying to find the right words that didn't sound like, 'you're so fucking hot.' Then...

Then my lips touched hers... I didn't mean to kiss her but I couldn't pull away from the feeling of how her lips felt. I just wanted to talk, but then I was in fucking shock. Her lips were so soft. I was honestly waiting for her to slap me, but then she grabbed my shirt and *really* kissed me.

What could I do? I kissed her back.

Sweet. She tasted sweet.

I pulled her hands from my chest and held them over her head. I wanted to feel as much of her body on mine as I could. I wanted to devour every whimper that came out of her. When someone came into the bathroom, I pulled away and made sure that only her feet were visible. I just kissed my crush, and I didn't want this moment ruined by people gossiping about her.

I wouldn't have stopped if Kennedy hadn't come in when she did. If I closed my eyes, I could still hear her whimpering and feel her writhing against me against the stall...

Feee-fi -Fuuuuuuucccck.

It was seven o'clock at night and I was still hard from this morning. From a single kiss. The worst part wasn't that I was hard. It was that I had already showered and 'relieved' the pressure three times under ice cold water. This boner wasn't just an uncomfortable situation, it was becoming stubborn as hell.

I hoped to talk to her after class, but Bradley had caught me sneaking out of the girls' bathroom. As soon as the bell rang, he dragged me out the door for gossip hour. I didn't know what to say, so I said nothing. I didn't tell him a fucking thing about that kiss. I told him I had tried to sneak in to talk to her, but Kennedy came in. It wasn't entirely a lie. Just not the whole truth either.

I picked up my phone to send Kat a message, but chickened out again. What if she didn't mean to kiss me like that? What if she kissed every guy like that?

No. She meant that kiss for me.

Right?

God, that was hot though. We had talked about so many dirty things over the years, but she never made a move until this morning. Did she want me? Was that even a possibility all this time? How much time had I fucking wasted?

I finally decided to bite the bullet, face whatever this was, and sent her a text.

[We need to talk]

Straight to the point. She couldn't misinterpret that.

An hour went by before I heard my phone ping with a message. I quickly grabbed it off my desk, but it was just Bradley reminding me about a weekend party.

I said that I would go if he drove this time. I really hated these things, but I promised that I would. So I called him back and confirmed that I would go. Then he dropped the bomb; Kat Preston was going too.

This could go really well or blow up in my face. I wouldn't see her again before the party. Fuck. I couldn't get drunk if she was going to be there. I needed to be clear-headed.

"How about I drive on Friday instead?" I offered him.

"You sure?" he asked back.

He knew I hated being the sober one when we went out. I couldn't stand most of the assholes that showed up, but I could never bring myself to talk to *her*. Whenever she was there, I couldn't be myself. I couldn't speak to her like I wanted to, so I got drunk and made it all go away. Bradley knew this.

I sighed, "Yeah. You have fun. I will be the responsible one this time."

Bradley laughed some more. "So how was your move received?" he asked, changing the subject.

I hadn't told him anything about what happened in the bathroom yet. I hadn't even told him about the actual gifts, let alone the kiss. I usually told him everything, but this time I kept it all to myself.

It wasn't that I didn't want to hear his advice, but I just couldn't stand the look he would give me if this all went south. I needed to figure this mess out on my own. Then I could tell my best friend how royally fucked over I was.

"Earth to Kai!" he yelled through the phone.

I snapped out of my fog.

"Sorry. What were you saying?" I asked.

"I was asking if you wanted to go to Alex's or that other kid's. Alex is a known element, the other kid I am not too sure of."

I thought about it for a minute. Like there was ever really an option. Kat wouldn't go to an unknown place.

"You know what, let's just go to Alex's. It may be the last time we all get together before we graduate. Besides, that kid Nate is a sophomore," I answered.

"Alex's it is then," Bradley agreed. "You still okay with driving?"

I smirked, not that he could see it. "Yeah, man. I'll be the DD."

"PAAAAARRRTYY!" he sang into the phone.

"Dude, I'm gonna let you go. See you tomorrow."

He laughed. "Yeah, yeah. See you tomorrow."

I threw my phone down on my bed and went to get showered before bed. A cold, cold shower.

* * *

I couldn't help looking for any sign that I was being avoided, and I have to say, the results were mixed. I went home after school completely depressed and no less confused than the day before.

I checked my phone again, but there was still no response. I didn't want to text her again and seem needy, so I just put my phone away and sat down to do my homework.

Why hadn't she messaged me yet?! I could see that she read the message. Why was she avoiding me? Fuck. I couldn't continue like this. I needed to call Bradley, and ask his advice.

I slammed my head into my pillow and growled. I needed some kind of answers or I was at risk of pulling a crazy stalkerish move, and I didn't want to go there after the time I had with that crazy bitch last year. I decided not to call either of them and wait it out.

Thank fuck, the rest of the week flew by.

My parents agreed to let me borrow their minivan. Unfortunately for me, it was not nearly as cool as the Mystery Machine (aka the Jeep Cherokee) and instead looked like a total soccer mom-mobile. Because it was.

My mom called it the best "anti-chick" device. She swore that no girl would ever get pregnant by her sons if we drove her van. I just shook my head at Bradley as he walked out to the van on Friday night.

"Dude! Your brother wouldn't let you borrow his Jeep?" he asked, climbing into the front seat beside me.

"Just shut up," I muttered.

Bradley laughed and thumped me in the arm, "You are so not getting any tonight!" He continued to laugh until tears were streaming from his eyes. "Shit, Kai. How much do your parents really hate you?" he asked, still laughing.

He knew this was the only vehicle I was allowed to borrow when we went out. It had been my parents' rule since I got my license nearly two years ago.

I looked over at him while I drove toward Alex's farm through town. "You can always walk," I told him pointedly. I didn't know if he got the point I was making or had just laughed this one out to its end. But he finally stopped chuckling, and we talked about normal school shit for the rest of the drive.

The music was already going when we got to the dirt road leading up to Alex's place. Alex's family owned about 130 acres outside of town, and his parents let him throw one massive party each year. Alex had the best birthday parties when we were kids because his family always did hayrides or haunted mazes through a corn field. When we got to High School, he moved his annual party closer to the end of each school year.

His parents didn't care if we drank; so long as no one got stupid, and we *had* to have designated drivers. The last rule was broken only once. Alex's dad had caught one of the designated drivers drinking two years ago at one of Alex's older brother's parties. That kid woke up in a horse stall covered in shit the following day. No one broke that rule again. Not one of us dared to.

I parked the van in a cleared field next to all the other vehicles, and we made our way to the barn where the party was. As we walked up, Bradley reached over to a table and passed me a red solo cup filled with beer. I looked at him, confused, but he grabbed the van keys out of my hand and nodded to the cup.

"I don't know what you have going on, but I know you

need this more than I do. You don't have to tell me today. I know you have your reasons for keeping shit quiet. So I got the cock-block-mobile," Bradley said, jingling the van keys at me, "and you have a beer, and go get you some!!" He patted my chest before walking into the throng of dancing people.

"Wooooo! Hellllooooo, Ladies!" he shouted as he shimmied into the crowd.

I chuckled to myself and took a swig of the beer. Bradley had his hands in the air and danced his way into a group of girls. He was a known flirt, but he always respected their boundaries. He never touched without permission, and I had even heard him ask a girl if she was flirting with him. So I wasn't surprised when they welcomed him into their group laughing at his antics.

I never understood how he just got people in a way that I didn't. Then again, that's how we became friends. Dude was super nerdy on the outside, like a young Rowan Atkins. But he fit in with every crowd at school like a damned chameleon.

I walked around the inside of the barn, stepping around hay bales and kissing couples, looking for Kat. My heartbeat sped up each time I saw a blonde making out with a guy, then it calmed back down when I realized it wasn't her.

I finally found a place near the back of the barn where I could see the doors and the whole interior of the barn. Maybe she wasn't coming after all. I scowled at the thought.

No, she was going to come to this party. Bradley had talked with a friend of a friend, or some such bullshit. But he assured me that she would be here.

My phone vibrated in my back pocket, and I took it out to see who was messaging me. I almost choked on my beer. There was only one "*hot Kat*" in my contacts.

📱💬⬛: [Why do you look so angry one second and then fine the next?]

She was here. I looked up, my eyes scanning the room, but I didn't see her. I texted her back, still looking around the barn.

[Where are you?]

📱💬⬛: [Right where I can see you. Can't you see me?]

I laughed and found a bale of hay away from everyone else, and sat down.

[What about now?]

📱💬⬛: [This is the best view yet. All alone and vulnerable in a dark corner...]

There were only so many places that she could be and still see me. I swore as I leaned back and looked up to make sure that she wasn't up in the loft. I quickly finished off my beer and sat the cup on the floor next to my feet.

[We need to talk. You haven't said a word to me all week. What's going on with you?]

She didn't respond. I looked around the room but still didn't see her anywhere. Finally, I looked back at my phone and started to type another message. My attention was suddenly drawn to a pair of feet standing in front of me.

My eyes trailed up from the open-toed sandals to the long legs that disappeared into a colorful skirt. I wanted to appreciate the view a bit more than the exposed skin at mid-thigh. Truth be told, I was afraid to look up at the face. I didn't want to face the sadness of an inevitable rejection.

"I'm here, Kai. So talk."

Chapter 5

Katie's POV

Andie was coming to my house in 30 minutes so we could attend this party at Alex's. Alex and his friends had never been my sort of crowd, not that I really had a crowd. I was friendly with just about everyone at school, but my parents were so strict that I never got to attend these. Now, however, I was 18. As much as they wanted to keep *protecting* me, they couldn't use that as an excuse any longer.

I jumped in the shower and got dressed as quickly as I could. I shaved my legs and pits and then stopped short of clearing the whole hedge. I had tried shaving myself bald before, and I did not like it. I kept everything trimmed and tidy, but bald it was not.

I rubbed down every inch of my skin with my vanilla lotion, and pulled on one of the few matching sets of underwear I owned. I had a colorful layered skirt and plain white shirt laid out on my bed. Andie bought me the skirt for my birthday and insisted I wear it tonight.

I generally didn't like to show off this much leg because I was super self conscious. After four years of soccer, my legs were thicker than any other white girl I knew. Hell, they were *thicker* than most girls in school. *But I loved leg days...and never missed an opportunity to build my ass.* So, sighing to myself, I continued to get ready and began the process of taming my wild mane of blonde hair.

I applied a little bit of eyeliner, mascara and my strawberry lip gloss. Then I swiped my fingers through the cream blush and gave my cheeks a slight sun-kissed look. I gave myself one more glance in the mirror before running down stairs with my open-toe wedges. I had just gotten my shoes on, when I heard a car horn outside.

"Is that Andie?" My dad asked from the living room.

"It is," I confirmed running through the kitchen to find my house keys.

"You all going to Alex's tonight?" he asked, giving my outfit the once over.

"Yep. You have his parents number if you hear sirens, otherwise I call mommy if I need bail money," I said, leaning over to give him a quick peck on the cheek.

"Love you, see you sometime tomorrow!" I called behind me as I ran out the door.

Andie had been sitting in her little red Geo Storm, waving up at me. She had an infectious smile that made other people want to be around her. I couldn't remember how we became friends, but I couldn't imagine getting through High School without her in my life.

As I walked down the driveway, she stepped out of her car and leaned up against it before whistling at me.

"*Girrrrrrl*, that outfit looks so good on you!" she squealed, stomping her feet.

I felt my face getting warm, a sure sign that I was crimson red.

"Do you think I should change the skirt?" I asked her, still nervous about the amount of leg I was showing.

She shook her head, "Absolutely not. I don't know how you made a white t-shirt look so fucking hot, but you are totally rocking the shit out of it with that skirt."

I couldn't help but laugh, my face felt even warmer as I climbed into the passenger seat of her car. "Should I have put on more make-up?" I asked while looking at myself in the mirror of the sun visor.

Again, she shook her head as she glanced quickly at me and drove off through my neighborhood. "You look perfect, Katie. Now tell me what the plan is."

I felt my stomach turn over, and nausea built up at the back of my throat. I had broken down and told her everything after I talked it out with five-speed. Andie fucking called Bradley.

Who knew that Kai hadn't said a word about the kiss to his own best friend.

"I have no idea what to do, Andie. What if it was a mistake? What if he only kissed me because I kissed him?" I rambled off question after question.

She shook her head again. "No. Nope. Not buying that. Look, I know you are not as experienced as you let people believe. Believe me, I know. You would rather people think you're a slut than admit to being the only virgin in our senior class," she chided me. "But you must, at some point, take a leap of faith. If it doesn't work out, then so be it. You're leaving for the military after graduation anyway."

"What if it *does* work out?" I asked my voice barely a whisper. I didn't want to hold on to hope for anything. My entire life had been in chaos because of Kai. Because of that kiss.

53

"Then you take that bridge when you get to it," she said without batting an eye.

That was Andie. Always an optimist, and yet so grounded. She was the oldest soul I knew.

When we got to Alex's farm, the field was crowded with cars. My eyes scanned over the area and found his blue van. He was here. I wanted to throw up.

My door opened and I jumped, startled to find Andie standing next to me. I was so lost in my own world that I didn't realize she had gotten out of the car.

"Let's go," she said, pulling me out of the seat as soon as my seatbelt was unbuckled.

We walked up to the barn arm in arm, and she handed me a beer.

"Andie, I can't drink that. I'll be sick as a dog," I said, scrunching my nose.

"Oh, yeah... You're the weirdo who is actually allergic to hops and barley," she reminded herself while cackling at me. She put the beer back on the table, grabbed a cup with soda instead, and then dumped her pocket flask into it. "There you go, one rum and coke!"

I laughed with her this time. She came prepared for me. I accepted the cup and started drinking it slowly as we wove through the throng of people from school. I found a spot to sit away from everyone else and look around for Kai. It didn't take long before I spotted him scowling at all of the couples sitting together.

[Why do you look so angry one second and then fine the next?]

I watched as he pulled his phone out to read the message. His head shot up, and he looked around the barn for me. I ducked behind a stack of hay next to me and watched as he typed a message on his phone.

A second later, my phone vibrated and I saw his message.

♥Kai♥:[Where are you?]

I smiled and typed back.

[Right where I can see you.]

He started to walk toward the corner where I was standing, and my heart skipped. He was going to find me. He sat on the other side of the stack I was standing behind and looked down at his phone.

My phone vibrated again.

♥Kai♥: [What about now?]

I smiled and texted him back, giggling quietly to myself. I didn't want to ruin our friendship. If he rejected me- I couldn't even think about that.

[This is the best view yet. All alone and vulnerable...]

His eyes were scanning the barn. I watched him down the rest of his drink, and I did the same with my rum and coke. Liquid courage and all that. While he was looking at his phone, I walked over to stand in front of him. My phone vibrated, but I didn't even look to see what was written. I didn't want to know.

His body tensed when he noticed my feet standing between his. I watched as his head slowly lifted, his eyes taking in my legs but then stopping at my waist.

I reached down and tilted his head back to look up at me. I had been in love with these blue eyes for as long as I could remember. They darkened when he was angry and turned pristine and clear when he laughed. I had seen everything, yet they had never looked at me like they were now. I didn't know what this was, and I was too afraid to ask.

"Here I am, Kai. Talk."

He stood up and I felt like my chest was going to burst. I didn't know what to say to him. I took a step back, but he followed me. I took another, trying to increase the space so that I could breathe and think clearly, but he followed step for step until my back hit a solid wall, and I could run no further.

"Why- What do you want to say?" I barely whispered the words; my voice was cracking under the thrum of emotions pounding in my chest. I stared into his eyes, waiting for him to speak.

When he finally tried to say something, I didn't want to hear it.

"Ka-" I stopped his words with a slap of my hand over his mouth.

I took a deep shuddering breath, grabbed his hand, and guided it to my thigh. I kept watching his eyes, searching for the moment of rejection and his repulsion at touching me, but it wasn't there. Instead I watched his pupils dilate as I guided his hand under my skirt until it covered my ass cheek. It was now or never.

I leaned into his body and whispered against his ear, "I loved my birthday present, Kai. I hope you like yours." Then I kissed his neck, nibbled his ear, and waited for any reaction to confirm that he *didn't* want me. I couldn't be any clearer to this man. I was throwing myself at him.

A moan left his throat, and his left hand squeezed my ass *hard*. His right hand grabbed my hair and forced my head so that I was staring up at him. He was breathing hard, and I had never seen his eyes look so dark and stormy.

"Kat- Don't mess with me. I am begging you. If this isn't

what you want. If you don't want *me*," he said, as his eyes stared into mine.

I felt my face getting warmer. I knew that I had turned cherry red under his gaze.

"Is this what you really want? I don't want to be some guy from school, it would break me, Katie. Do you really want *me?*" he asked again, his voice low and gravelly.

I couldn't breathe. I wanted to run, hide, and never say what was in my heart. I wanted to keep this small part of me in love with Kai a secret and carry it with me. But instead, the words poured out of me in a breathy confession, "It's always been you, Kai."

His mouth crashed into mine, and it felt nothing like the kiss in the bathroom. Instead, this was violent, needy, and filled with every unsaid word between us. I wanted to feel every part of him against me. I wrapped my arms around his neck and pulled myself closer to him. He pulled my right leg up to his waist. Then, pressed his body into mine, forcing my back back against the wall.

A moan escaped my lips, but he gobbled it up with his kiss. If I had to die, I wanted it to be after tonight.

My heart was racing so fast, I felt like I was drunk. I could feel how hard he was in the way he was rubbing up against me. He started to grind his hips against me, and the friction against my clit made me feel like my entire body would shatter any second. I kissed him harder, afraid to make a sound. I didn't want him to stop. I didn't want him to realize it was me and regret this.

My breath hitched when I felt his fingers glide over the outside of my thong and caress my clit. No one else had ever touched me. Of course, I had gotten myself off, but it had never felt as good as what his fingertips were doing to me at that moment.

"Which one are you wearing?" He asked, breaking our kiss to trail kisses up and down my neck. "Did *I* buy this for you?" he asked as his finger slid under the lace thong. He pulled it away from my soaking wet lower lips, and when I couldn't answer him immediately, he let the fabric snap against my clit and growled in my ear, "Tell me."

"Aaah, th- the black," I barely stuttered the words out and whimpered quietly as his fingers slid under the material again and stroked me from the top of my clit to the bottom of my slit, spreading all of my pooling wetness.

"I don't want my first time with you to be against a wall in a crowded barn, Kat," he whispered, staring into my eyes with our foreheads pressed together. His mouth twitched up into a grin as he watched me react to the sensations that he was creating with my body. His fingertips were dancing around the opening of my - *Oh my god, his fingers felt so fucking good inside me.*

I could not even think what to ask him. My brain had stopped working, and all I did was feel. "Please, Kai," I begged in a hoarse whisper, as I felt him push a finger into me. My body shuddered uncontrollably from the pleasure, and my eyes rolled back and closed, as I let every sensation and emotion wash over me.

"Jesus, Kat. You're so tight," he whispered, gently biting my ear and dragging his tongue down my throat.

Any thoughts I had at that moment were gone. Kai's finger was still pumping in and out of me as he kissed my throat before biting my collar bone.

"Take me out of here, Kai. I need more," the words tumbled

out of my mouth without another thought. My whole body was thrumming already, and I wanted more. If Kai was a drug and I was getting my first high, and guaranteed to get addicted.

He looked behind him and pulled away from me to unzip his jeans. I did not stop my wandering hands from trailing down his chest to his stomach, before I grasped him through his boxers. He was so hard and much bigger than I thought he would be.

I reached inside the elastic band and lowered it so that I could feel him. His breath hitched this time as I wrapped my hands around his velvety smooth shaft. I watched his face contorted in pleasure as he bit his bottom lip, thoroughly enjoying what I was doing to him.

His voice was raspy, "Is this what you want, Kat?"

"Yes," I whispered, cupping his face again and ensuring he saw *me*. "I want you. I just want you all to myself," my voice sounded as raspy as his. I didn't know if I was just caught up in the moment. I didn't even know if I cared anymore. I just knew that I wanted whatever could happen tonight to happen.

"Kat, I don't have a condom," he whispered with his forehead against mine again. He cursed under his breath, and rubbed his dick against my soaking wet underwear.

"Pull out, Kai. I trust you."

I said that. Those words just left my mouth, like I had no idea how precum swimmers were just as effective as the last to leave the '*shoot*'. I told him to pull out, and then his mouth was devouring mine again.

59

Chapter 6

Kai's POV

"Kat-" my chest was heaving. "Don't mess with me. I am begging you. If this isn't what you want. If you don't want me," I stared down at her.

Her face was flushed, and her breathing had picked up. I needed to be sure. "Do you want me?" I asked.

I watched as her breath caught. "It's always been you, Kai," she whispered, staring into my eyes.

That was all I needed to hear before my control snapped. My mouth crashed onto hers, and it felt like electricity was storming through my body every place our skin touched. Her arms wrapped around my neck, and I pulled her right leg up around my waist and grinded myself against her.

She was so quiet; I wanted to make her whimper and moan and scream my name. My hand trailed back up her thigh until my fingertips were grazing the lace of the thong she was wearing. The more my fingers slid against the material covering her clit, the wetter they became.

"Which one are you wearing?" I asked against her neck as I trailed my lips kissing every bit of exposed skin I could. "Did I buy this for you?" I asked as my finger slid under the material. I pulled it away from her skin, then let it snap against her. I enjoyed feeling and watching her shudder from the sensation. "Tell me."

"Aaah, th- the black," she whimpered quietly as my fingers slid under the material again and stroked her wetness.

Whatever thoughts I had before this moment were gone. All I could see was her. I couldn't hear the music or the people behind me, I only heard the soft whimpers and moans that escaped her lips, and I wanted more. She kissed me hard and rubbed herself against my cock, which was now so hard it felt like it could break.

"I didn't want my first time with you to be against a wall in a crowded barn, Kat," I whispered. Touching our two foreheads together as I stared into her eyes and tried to regain some semblance of control.

She stopped grinding against me, but my fingers were still teasing her, sliding back and forth between her clit and her opening. Each time I touched the edge, her body shuddered against me. She was looking at me with glazed eyes, biting her lip. My lips quivered into a faint smile. I was the only one turning her on. She was like this because of me, for *me*.

"Please, Kai," she begged as her eyes rolled back when I pushed a finger inside her.

"Jesus, Kat. You're so tight," I whispered into her ear, biting it gently before I trailed my tongue down her throat and licked down to the base of her neck. My finger shallowly pumped in and out of her as I kissed the base of her throat and bit against her collarbone.

"Take me out of here, Kai. I need more," she whimpered.

I looked behind me and realized that no one could see us. She led me to the one spot that no one could see from any other point in the barn. I pulled my body away from hers

61

so that I could unzip my jeans. My breath caught when her hands reached down and massaged me through the fabric of my boxers before they slid the elastic band down and grasped my bare cock into her warm fingers.

"Is this what you want, Kat?" I asked, barely holding onto my sanity at the sensation of her hands on me.

"Yes," she whispered. One of her hands cupped my face and tilted my head to look at her. "I want you. I just want you all to myself," she whispered, her voice cracking again.

I realized she was waiting for a rejection. She thought I didn't want her, but there was no one I wanted more than her. Never had been.

"Kat, I don't have a condom," I finally admitted to her, so that she would understand my hesitation.

She looked at me for a moment and said the words that destroyed all of my resolve to do this right. "Pull out, Kai. I trust you."

My lips were on hers again, kissing her like I needed her lips to breathe. I pulled the fabric of her thong roughly to the side and pushed the tip of my cock against her opening. "Tell me again, Kat."

"Yes," she whispered, rubbing her wet folds against the head and coating it with her slick. "I want –"

I pushed into her before she could get another word out. I felt her body tense and her breath hitched when I pushed into her. She was so fucking tight; it almost feels like she was a v-.

My whole body stiffened. "Kat," I was looking at her face scrunched up in pain. "Please tell me this isn't your first time-"

Her eyes told me everything I needed to know. She had

never been with anyone else. All of the stories, rumors, and gossip were bullshit. I was her first. Right now, months before graduation, against a barn wall, I took Kat Preston's virginity. I tried to pull away, but she'd wrapped her leg behind me and forced me to push back in. Her head tipped back and she sighed.

"Don't turn me away, Kai. I couldn't breathe if you walked away from me right now."

She thought I wanted to reject *her*, because she was a *virgin*. I shook my head, sighed against her hair and kissed her temple. "Wrap your arms around me," I told her.

I picked her up then and turned us toward a bale of hay off to one side. We were still connected, my cock buried deep inside of her. Her legs wrapped around my waist as I moved us, causing me to groan when her weight shift had pushed her further down on my cock.

I lowered her down until her back was against the bale. I leaned my left elbow against the hay, my arm bent next to her head, and pulled slowly back. She was mesmerizing, experiencing this for the first time. When I pushed back into her, her whole body tensed against me and tightened around my cock. She felt like fucking heaven.

My mouth found hers again when she began to feel good, small whimpers and moans escaping her lips. With one hand bracing her head from the hay, the other hand slid under her shirt. I ran my hand under her bra to cup her breast and pinch her nipple between my fingers.

I continued to watch her reaction to every stimuli I introduced to her body. I felt her begin to tighten around me with each thrust into her if I squeezed her breast too tightly. So I did it over and over to drive her wild.

She was gorgeous lying beneath me. I could come right now, but I wanted to make this count for her. When I felt her start to relax again and she started to push her hips up to meet mine stroke for stroke, I almost came. *"Jesus*, Kat."

"Ahhh... ung... Kee- Keep going. M-Make me come," she whimpered as she clutched onto me. I grabbed one of her legs behind the knee with my free hand and opened her up further so I could move deeper into her.

"Like this, baby? Hmm? Is this what my *KitKat* wants," I whispered to her as I started to pull back further and push into her. Each time, I tilted my hips up at the end to hit her in a spot that made her gasp with every thrust

"Ahhh, yesssss-" she mewled under me.

I covered her mouth with my own again and swallowed her moans. I kissed her as she felt everything that I was doing to her body. I felt her start to tighten around me. Her body stiffened and shuddered, but I couldn't stop. She was going to come on my cock. Her back arched up, pressing her chest against mine as she came undone beneath me. She was squeezing and pulsing so tightly around me; it was the last push needed to make me come.

I rocked my hips and pushed into her a few more times before I pulled out and pointed my dick away from her so that I shot everything into the hay bale. The orgasm hit me so hard I could barely breathe, and let out a growl of relief at my own release. I looked down at Kat, and saw her staring wide-eyed back up at me.

"You could have told me sooner, you know," I shook my head smiling.

She looked defensive and I realized that she completely misunderstood me when she started speaking, "What should

I have said? Hi Kai, I am a virgin. *Please,* help me, sir?"

I chuckled and lowered my body against hers again. "No, Kat. You should have told me sooner that you had feelings for me. We wasted all of this time that we should have been together."

Her eyes softened and she kissed me. It was different this time. There wasn't any need behind it. This was sweet and vulnerable.

"Can I take you out?" I asked her.

She looked confused for a second, "Like on a date?" She squeaked at me and made me laugh.

"No. Not *like* on a date. An *actual* date, Katie," I corrected her.

She nodded her head smiling, "Okay."

We fixed our clothes out and found a place to sit and just talk. I didn't know how long we had been sitting in the back of the barn holding hands and talking about stupid shit we had both been through. We realized that the music had stopped and the voices started to die down.

"Um, do you think they will notice us sneaking out of the barn?" Katie giggled, pulling me up to my feet.

My phone pinged at that moment with a message from Bradley.

[Dude, I am in your van. Are you still here?]

"Shit," I chuckled. "Uh-Bradley is my ride home. Do you need a ride?" I pulled her against me again to straighten her clothes. I was not ready to part with her.

"You want to give me a *ride*, Kai?" She asked with one eyebrow arched up.

"Yep, but for tonight just a ride *home*," I laughed as we walked out of the barn into the night air. We weren't the last

65

ones to leave from the looks of it, but definitely the most sober of those still left behind.

Kat walked beside me, occasionally bumping her shoulder into me. I knew her, she had something on her mind that she needed to work out.

I stopped walking and pulled her into my chest for a hug before we got to the baby blue van. "I have to tell you something, and-" I took a deep breath, "I need you to not get weird about this, ok?"

She pulled away from me and looked up at me suspiciously. She looked so vulnerable, and I could see the start of a seething anger bubbling behind her big brown eyes. She was waiting for me to finish speaking, expecting the worst of me as always.

"Your ride this evening is a powder blue mini-van. Please don't hold that against me. Ok?" I asked, doing my best to look as serious as possible.

Her face flushed cherry red before she exploded. "Are you kidding me?!" She screamed. "We're done. I can't do this. A *MINI-VAN??*" She stomped off toward the field leaving me speechless.

When she was about 10 yards away, she stopped and looked at me over her shoulder. "Gotcha!" She sang before laughing hysterically as she ran toward the van on the other side of the field.

"You better run!" I yelled and sprinted after her.

"Open the door, Bradley! Let me in!" She yelled, still laughing.

Bradley jumped in the driver's seat after opening the back door. "You're not gonna make it, Kat!" He heckled.

She slowed down to look over her shoulder, and I closed

the distance and grabbed her around the waist. I spun her around as she squealed.

"You *got* me?" I asked her. "You think that's *funny*?"

"Oh, God. Soooooo funny," she laughed while turning in my arms to wrap her arms around my waist. "Did you see his face, Bradley? I said it exactly like you told me to," she giggled into my chest.

My eyes darted up to see him red-faced and laughing. "You bastard," I muttered at him before looking back at Kat. "And you… I think my heart stopped beating for a solid minute there. You can't joke with me like that. Not now."

She looked up at me and batted her eyelashes. "Yes, sir. Whatever you say, sir!" She purred.

Fuck. Kat couldn't talk to me like that. Now I wanted to tie her up and watch her beg and call me *Sir*.

Chapter 7

Katie's POV

I woke up feeling like my heart was crushed. Kai and I talked for hours last night. We talked about all of the things we did to sabotage the other's relationships, and laughed about how blind and stupid we were. I had had no relationships and he was an idiot.

But then this morning, I woke up and felt like maybe it was my wishful thinking. Kai had so many girls and never paid any attention to me. Was he with me because he thought I was easy?

He obviously didn't know that I was a virgin, so that said enough about what he thought of me before last night. I needed to call Andie. I needed my girl. I couldn't talk to any of my guy friends about this.

I didn't even know what time it was. I had been lying here staring at the ceiling for who knew how long. I rolled over to grab my phone and winced.

My legs, my abs, my….were all feeling it. No one told me my legs would feel like I had done a work out. *Oh my god.* I had sex.

I, Katie Renee Preston, had sex last night. WITH KAI!! Oh my god. I had UNPROTECTED sex with Kai. Shit.

I called Andie. It was almost ten o'clock in the morning, but I knew she had off today.

She answered on the fourth ring. "So, how'd it go?"

"I don't have time to explain. This is an emergency. Come get me, I need you!" I said as dramatically as I felt.

Of course, Andie immediately understood. "You have five minutes to have your ass outside. I already grabbed coffee and we can run to the pharmacy near my place."

"Shit! Andie, I need to shower!" I yelled.

This of course only spurred her laughter. "What happened to my neat nick, Katidid?!? You lost your cherry in a barn, and you didn't even shower when you got home?!?" She squealed through the phone.

I just groaned. "I know. Just give me fifteen, ok?"

Andie laughed, "Yeah, I figured as much. That's why I bought coffee for your dad, too. I'll be downstairs when you are ready."

I hung up and jumped out of bed. Well, attempted to. My girlie bits were a bit tender and I felt it when I sat up. I ran to the bathroom and jumped in the shower.

Thirteen minutes later I was showered dressed and walking down the stairs. I didn't have time to dry my hair, so it was twisted up into a bun on top of my head.

I didn't wear any make-up, because honestly, I couldn't be bothered today.

"There she is!" My mom called from the kitchen as I came through the house.

Andie looked at me like she was going to burst. She just wanted gossip, and I was surprised she didn't tell my parents everything.

My dad walked up to me and gave me a kiss on my temple

as he walked by. "Morning, sweetie. What time did you get in last night?" He asked.

I couldn't help but lean into the quick embrace. "Morning, daddy. I got in just before two. I'm sorry if I woke you up," I apologized.

"No. We didn't hear you, so we weren't sure. I know that you are 18, but I appreciate that you still met the curfew," he sighed and walked away.

I caught my mom looking over at me, and I couldn't help but seem confused. I mouthed my question, 'What did I miss?'

Mom shook her head and smiled. "We're glad that you are still being responsible, and being *safe*," she said.

I couldn't stop the blush that crept up my face. Thankfully, I could control my facial expression and tried to look serious for her. Then my mouth opened, and I couldn't help but rile her up.

"Well, I didn't want to go too hard this first weekend, so I'll be keeping it light with just sex and booze. *Lots* of booze," I emphasized, dramatically. "But *next* weekend, I plan on testing a line of blow. Nothing says adulthood like taking a leap with the good ole Columbian marching powder... Oh, and I was asked about jumping a local gang! So, there's that too. My first tattoo will be whether I get in or not."

I heard Andie choking on her coffee, my dad coughing from the next room, and then watched my mother explode.

"Katie *Renee* Preston!" She yelled my full name. "You are still my child! Don't think I won't beat your ass just because you turned 18."

My serious expression broke, and I started laughing. "Seriously, mommy? You need to calm down. I am not as crazy as you two were in high school. It was a joke," I laughed at her reaction.

"That's not funny!" She grumbled.

Andie and I left shortly after assuring my mom that I was not actually joining a gang. Sometimes it felt like my mom had no idea who I was. She always assumed the worst about my character and my intentions.

Once we were in the car and away from my place, Andie turned down the radio and gave me the side eye.

"Ok. Spill."

It wasn't a suggestion. It was an order.

I couldn't help but giggle and blush, telling her everything that had happened. I told her everything that Kai had said, from the birthday gift, to the bathroom make-out session, and then last night in the hay stacks. I put it all out there.

She was quiet and let me talk, laughing at my innocence in some situations and boldness in others.

"So, have you talked to him since?" She asked as well pulled into a strip mall the next town over.

I shook my head. "He hasn't messaged me either," I whispered, staring down at my phone.

She just nodded in understanding. "He will. He's in shock," she explained, giggling.

"What does that mean?" I asked.

Andie rolled her eyes at me as we walked into the shopping center. "I swear you both are so dense. Katie, he has had a thing for you for years. *Years.* Now, you not only confessed to each other but even knocked boots. Give him time. He's probably trying to make sure that it wasn't a dream," she chuckled, seeing my shocked expression.

Finally, we stopped and looked through the glass windows

to the people inside. "You sure you want to do this today? We can always do this another d-"

I cut her off, "No, I'm sure. This is happening today."

* * *

Kai's POV

I had crashed when I got in this morning and then immediately woke up at seven when my alarm went off. We had an away game this afternoon, and the whole team had to meet at the school by eight. I didn't have time to think about anything else other than getting cleaned up, grabbing my gear and rushing out the door.

I heard a couple of the guys on the bus whispering, but I just ignored them. I was replaying everything from last night because it really had not sunk in. After we dropped Katie off, I told her I would call her later.

Kat knew we had an away game, and it wouldn't be until later that we could talk. Coach never allowed us to use our phones on game days. In fact, he collected them in a box as we boarded the bus. It was to prevent us from losing focus before a game.

I didn't need my phone to lose focus. My mind was replaying last night. Over and over and over. Kat Preston was *mine.* She hadn't been with anyone else. *Just me.* I leaned my head back against the seat and tried to not think about everything that happened. The last thing I needed was getting hard with a bus full of guys. I felt my dick twitch.

"Fuuuuuuucck," I muttered under my breath, trying to find something else to think about.

We had a two-hour drive, and I needed a distraction. I

called out to a couple of the other guys and started talking about the other team's line-up, strengths and weaknesses. Before I knew it we were there, and filing off the bus.

The game was not our best, but we managed to eek out a win with two runs in the ninth inning. Considering they were ranked as a top team in the State, it wasn't a bad outcome. The coach still railed us about our discipline and poor communication the whole way back.

By the time I was back home and finally able to think about everything clearly, it was almost six o'clock at night. I had sent Kat a message saying that we were back. Asked how her day went.

I wanted her to come over, but I wasn't ready to share this news with my family. I *needed* to see her.

[Have you eaten dinner yet?]

Kitkat ❤:[Just finished. Why?]

Shit. Dinner date was out of the question. I had to find some reason to see her. Anything. I was laying on my bed, and bit the bullet. We promised honesty.

[I want to see you.]

Kitkat ❤:[Ok.]

I sat up. She said, 'ok'?

[Can I pick you up at seven?]

Kitkat ❤:[I'm with Andie. Can we meet somewhere?]

Of course, she was with Andie.

[Just tell me where.]

Kitkat ❤:[So eager, huh?]

[Honestly? Yes. I have been thinking about you all day.]

Kitkat ❤:[We are at the mall. I can meet you at the theater?]

I didn't waste another second. I grabbed my wallet and

convinced my brother to let me borrow his jeep.

[On my way]

It took everything I had not to break every speed limit crossing town. I parked and walked toward the theater. I saw her before she had a chance to notice me. Watching her made my chest tight and I couldn't breathe for a second.

What if this wasn't what I hoped it would be? What if I wasn't enough for her? What if she didn't feel for me the way I felt for her?

My head was filled with thousands of doubts every second that passed. Then she looked up and saw me, and my brain shorted. She was smiling at *me*. I watched her say something to Andie, and the two hugged before Andie left Katie alone to wait for me.

"Hi," she whispered as I finally got close enough.

I pulled her into my arms, wrapping my hands around her waist. "Can I kiss you?" I asked. My stomach knotted with nervous energy.

She nodded, and I didn't hesitate. I brushed my lips against hers and sucked on her bottom lip. I tried to keep it PG13, figuring that any public affection would make her uncomfortable.

I pulled away from the kiss and saw her face flushed crimson. I couldn't help but smile at her. She was so cute.

"Did you want to stay here? Or, we can go somewhere and talk," I offered.

I didn't need to guess what she was thinking because her face immediately turned bright red. It made me laugh and I hugged her against me.

I tucked my face into her neck and whispered against her skin, "I really just want to talk, Kitkat. I need to make sure that I'm not dreaming. I feel like my heart is about to come out of my chest. My stomach is all kinds of twisted up."

I felt her melt against me, "Me too."

We went to the park on the riverside and found a bench to sit on. She laid her legs over mine, and I pulled her body into my side so her head rested on my shoulder.

"Are you comfortable?" I asked.

"Yeah," she whispered.

"I really like you, Kat. A lot," I confessed.

"I like you, too," she whispered back. "Is this happening? Is this a thing," she asked, leaning her head back to look at me.

I let out an exaggerated exhale, "God, I hope so."

Kat giggled and snuggled back into me. We sat there for a while just content to finally be together. It was perfect.

We eventually started talking, and it was cute seeing how awkward she was asking questions.

"Was, um…. Was it, you know, ok?"

I wasn't quite sure which *it* she was referring to so I asked her to elaborate. I was rewarded with her blush deepening in her cheeks, even her ears turning deep red.

"You know… the sex…. I'd never….. so I wasn't sure…if it was like…ok?" She stuttered.

God, could she be any more adorable than this? The girl that I had known and seen since sixth grade was so confident and open; and now she was cuddled against my chest, stuttering nervously.

I tipped her chin up so that she would have to look at me, "Last night was the best night of my life, *Kitkat*. Never doubt that."

She seemed to relax into me again. Then she asked the question I was *not expecting*.

"So how come you're not trying to have sex with me again?" Whispered from her lips.

My head fell back and I started laughing. I tipped my head back down and kissed her. "Are you for real? Katie, I am trying so hard to be a gentleman. I don't want you to think this was just about sex," I explained.

"Oh," she responded.

"I would bend you over this bench, if I knew I wouldn't be arrested. Or have you riding me in the back seat of the Jeep," I whispered against her hair, as I pulled her to sit on my lap.

"It's been hard since I laid eyes on you in the mall, Kat," I confessed, rubbing her ass against my erection. "But you're not some random girl. I want our next time to be in a bed so that I can show you what it should be like."

She was almost panting in my lap.

"Do you need me to help you with anything, *Kitkat*?" I asked, nibbling on her ear.

She shook her head. "N-N-no. I was j-just asking," she stuttered again.

I tsk'd at her for lying. "Tell me what you want, Katie," I sucked on her ear lobe. "You can ask me for whatever you want. I'll give it to you, if I have it to give."

She twisted in my arms so that her arms wrapped around my neck and her lips were next to my ear. "Even if I ask you to take me somewhere less public?" She whispered.

I hugged her tightly to me and already regretted the words about to leave my mouth. "I am going to hate myself for this, but no. Please don't rush this, Katie," I pleaded with her.

She sighed and relaxed against me. This was a test and I just passed.

Chapter 8

Katie's POV

Kai and I had been together for nearly two months, and it was amazing. I didn't have to pretend to be something that I wasn't. I could just be myself, and it felt like I could breathe.

We kissed and made out, but he hadn't tried to sleep with me since that first time in Alex's barn. At first, I thought that he was not that into me, but he said that he wanted us to date properly instead of us just being about the sex.

It just made me want him that much more, but we agreed to wait until prom. Prom was the middle of May this year, and I had my dress made rather than going out and spending an unnecessary ton of money. My mom knew a lady who was a seamstress, and she agreed to make my dress for the cost of material and help with her gardening over the next month.

Honestly, I felt like it was a fair trade. I had met her at the fabric store to select a pattern and material. I chose a sleeveless maxi dress with a square neckline that showed off my collarbone and neckline without exposing my cleavage. Jody, the seamstress, selected a beautiful pearlescent sateen material that changed colors under different lighting.

Jody surprised me by dragging me to the lingerie store

to buy a bra and panty set for the occasion. She explained that certain material would 'catch' the fabric or show my panty lines. Both of those were no-no's. I ended up buying a matching set of nude satin bra and panties, and thigh-high stockings that did not require a garter belt.

My shoes were a set of violet Mary Janes with silver buckles. They complemented the dress so well. Kai was getting a matching tie to wear from the excess material used for my dress. Prom was going to be a night to remember.

I kept my hair looking natural. Large looping curls fell down my back and my make-up was soft and shimmery looking. There were eight of us sharing a limousine to prom. Andie's date was a guy she met in shop classes. He seemed nice enough, but was just arm candy. Bradley's date was a girl from chemistry class, a sophomore named Kiki. He didn't have anyone that he liked and thought he would take Kiki as a thank you for helping him pass the labs and midterm exam.

Then there was the final couple that Kai and Bradley invited from the baseball team, Matthew and Christine. I had known Matt since the first grade; his date, I had met our freshmen year. Matt was nice enough, just really misunderstood. As for Christine, I hated her and she hated me. I could only imagine how this was going to go down.

Just after six o'clock, the limousine pulled in front of my house. Andie, Kiki, and I had decided to meet together at my house as the last stop for pick-ups. Of course, Christine had a fit, but we didn't care. The guys climbed out of the limo and we all posed for pictures in the garden.

Nearly thirty minutes later, we were all giving our parents hugs and running to the limo. Unbeknownst to me, my mom thought it would be sweet to have *all* of the parents over for pictures before we left and now she was stuck with them.

Unlike homecoming, prom was held at the nicest hotel in our area. Hart Castle was a gorgeous hotel built in the early 1900s to look like a European castle outside. Inside, it was completely modernized and very glamorous. I never understood how the school could afford to rent such a luxurious venue, but I wasn't complaining.

The grand ballroom was decorated with twisted shimmering branches, dangling stars and muted vines. The whole room looked like a dining hall for fairies. There were soft silvers, golds, pinks and purples around the room, and twinkling lights that made it seem like fireflies lit up the ceiling.

Kai held my hand as we walked through the grand entrance and found our table with Andie and Bradley. Thankfully, Christine was sitting on the other side of the room. The food was amazing, but I spent the whole night afraid that I would spill something down my dress. Kai went to get us drinks and I walked around to speak with friends I knew.

I cleaned up nice and dressed girly, but I was a tom-boy at heart. Aside from Andie, my closest friends were guys I met working around cars. I understood that shoes, pads, and the need for a bigger C to get a job done, referred to changing brakes. What's more I could hold my own in any conversation that pertained to motorcycles, high end cars, or classic roadsters.

Thankfully, most of the girls accompanying my friends knew me and just saw me as one of the guys. That was until I bumped into Matthew. He smiled and asked how things were going, and we proceeded to chitchat. Then, he asked if

I had ever made a decision and I knew that he was referring to the time Andie and I ran into him at the strip mall.

"I did," I replied, smiling.

"Any regrets yet?" Matt asked, eyes looking around the room.

"None. You?" I asked back.

"Not really sure yet. My secret hasn't seen the light of day yet. Yours?"

"Same. Are you going to let your date know?" I asked, wiggling my eyebrows at him.

Matt laughed. "No. Not this weekend at least," he sighed.

"I won't know about what?" A nasally, high-pitched voice asked from behind us.

We turned to see Christine glaring at me. Matt shook his head and waved it off. "Nothing, Chrissy. Just an inside joke," he attempted to explain it away as he pulled her into his arms.

Christine, however, had decided that she needed to make a scene out of this moment between friends. *"Bullshit.* What does *she know* that *I don't? I'm* your girlfriend!" She started to yell.

"Matt, I will talk to you another time. Have a good night," I said, attempting to make my departure, but Christine had other plans.

"Oh, no, bitch. You tell me right now what the hell you were talking about!" She screamed.

Matthew's face flushed bright red with embarrassment, while I stood still in shock.

"Chrissy, you need to apologize right now. You have no idea what we were talking about!" Matt seethed, pulling the other girl away from me while I simultaneously took a few steps away from her.

My eyes began to search the room, looking for Andie or Kai or anyone who could help diffuse this situation. I didn't want everyone to find out my personal information. My decisions were my own, and I wasn't ready to share them.

Christine's voice began to scream above the music and chatter, "NO! NO! You don't get to tell me to calm down, when you cheated with this SLUT!!"

The music stopped. I looked over at Christine as she huffed in rage. I couldn't help but laugh. It started small, and then grew until I was laughing loudly at her face.

I shook my head at her, "You are so stupid." I watched as her mouth opened to say something more but then snapped shut when Matt whispered something in her ear. I looked at him and smiled. "It was nice running into you. I hope you get to enjoy the night."

I turned and started to walk back to my table. The music had started back up, but it did nothing to conceal the now arguing couple on the other side of the room. Andie and Bradley finally made it through the crowd of spectators to walk with me back to the table. "What the hell was that about?" Bradley asked.

"Matt joined the Marines, and hadn't told his girlfriend yet. He was planning to propose this weekend, hoping they could get married after he finished bootcamp, but he may be rethinking those plans," Andie said quietly.

Bradley's eyebrows shot up and his jaw dropped. "Holy shit, that's a lot to unpack."

I laughed, "Yeah, but he says that she's it for him. I'm not getting married anytime soon. There's too much world to see."

"That so?" Kai's voice whispered from behind me.

81

I leaned back into his arms and nodded, "It is."

"What if you found the love of your life?" He whispered in my ear.

I smiled, "Then we would see the world together."

"Will you dance with me, Kitkat?" He asked.

I nodded and Kai pulled me to the dance floor. I wrapped my arm over his shoulders and felt his arms pull my body flush against his. The sheer fabric of my dress made it so that I felt every contour of his body and he mine.

I had no idea which song was playing, because I was lost in our own little world. His cheek rested against mine as he whispered in my ear while we swayed to the music.

"We have the limo to ourselves the rest of the night. Matt is taking Chris home early, and Andie and Bradley both have rides home. The driver has our bags and he is going to take us to the beach tonight," he explained.

"I'm ready to leave whenever you are," I whispered back.

Kai smiled and began leading me back to our table. I grabbed my small handbag and said good night to our friends. Andie winked at me, causing me to blush. She knew how nervous I was to be alone with Kai.

As we walked out into the night air, our driver was already waiting outside the hotel. "I hope you had a wonderful evening. Are we going to the final stop next?" He asked.

Kai nodded, and helped me into the car as the driver opened the rear door for me. "Thank you," I murmured, as Kai sat down beside me.

Once the driver had pulled away from the hotel and confirmed the address for the beach house, Kai closed the glass partition and privacy shield separating us from the driver.

Then he dropped onto the floor and knelt between my legs. His hands started at my ankles and slid up my legs bunching my dress up higher and higher as they went. My breath was heated and panting and we hadn't done anything yet.

I tried to lean forward but Kai stopped me. "Be patient, Kat. Let me enjoy this." His voice sounded deeper and huskier.

I leaned back instead and spread my knees further apart for him. I knew he could see how wet I was for him. Satin did not hide a thing.

"Is this for me?" He asked as his fingers caressed up the insides of my thighs, and his thumb stroked the wet spot on my ruined panties.

"Yes," came out in a whiny whisper.

Kai smirked and leaned away from me. "Come over here and lay down," he said, patting the long seat behind him.

I shifted so that my head lay toward the driver's compartment and my legs bent toward Kai at the rear of the vehicle. He knelt between my legs again, running his hands up the outside of my thighs. His fingers hooked into the sides of my panties, and pulled them down.

I lifted my butt as he removed my underwear and tucked them into his pocket. His blue eyes looked so dark; his pupils blown open with lust.

"May I?" He asked, leaning forward to kiss the insides of my knees. I nodded, unable to speak.

We had never done anything like this, and I had no idea what to expect. I felt his breath on my most intimate parts and couldn't help but whimper. Kai chuckled, causing another warm breath to flush across my lady bits.

I didn't know where to place my hands, so I just held the seat on either side of me. Then I felt his lips kiss my clitoris.

Oh My God! The shot of electricity that went through my body had my back arching off the seat.

Kai chuckled, repeating the action a couple of times before sucking my little sensitive nub between his lips and then swirling the tip of his tongue over it, over and over and over.

I came just like that. He had barely touched me and I was seeing flashes of white and my entire body pulsed with euphoria. I gasped for air and tried to open my eyes to look down at him between my legs.

Kai had lowered his pants, and was rolling a condom down his shaft. "Come here, Kitkat. I want you to ride me," he whispered, sitting back in his seat facing toward me.

I sat up and moved across the floor space to straddle his lap. My hands wrapped behind his neck as my lips found his. I tasted myself on his lips. His hands grabbed my ass and pulled me up until his tip was positioned against my entrance.

I lowered myself slowly until I felt the stretch of him filling me. I had only ever had sex the one time, so this was an entirely new position for me. Kai seemed to understand. He lifted and lowered me until I was fully seated and filled to the hilt with his cock.

We both let out a contented moan. "Rock your hips, baby girl. Show me what feels good for you," he whispered against my lips. One hand was caressing my cheek while the other gripped my ass and demanded I move.

I rotated my hips slowly, forward then back, raising and lowering myself as I did. "Jesus, Kat. Just like that," he moaned quietly against my lips.

I felt so full and nervous, I had no idea what I was doing. Suddenly, the vehicle hit a bump and I dropped down hard.

A moan tore out of my throat as he hit a spot that I had forgotten existed. Kai smirked and ground my waist against his so his tip rubbed the spot repeatedly.

"Aaaaah, sto-stop," I whimpered breathlessly.

"No, you're going to come," he whispered back, continuing the ruthless assault on the magic spot.

I felt myself building up again and ripped his hands off of my hips, raising myself on my knees before slamming down again.

"Oh, god. Kai, Jesus," I panted as I chased my orgasm.

He slammed his lips into mine and hugged me against him as I rose and dropped harder and harder. "Just. Like. That," he panted.

I suddenly felt my body burst into starlight and shuddered as I fell backwards. Kai laid my back on the seat I was on earlier, and proceeded to thrust into me harder than I could manage while riding him.

I didn't think my orgasm had stopped when everything behind my eyes flashed white, and I came again to the sensation of Kai's cock twitching inside me as he came in the condom. I held onto him and giggled.

"Is that normal?" I asked breathlessly.

Kai smiled down at me and kissed my nose. "If this is normal, you may have ruined me, Katie."

His lips trailed kisses down my jaw to my neck. He sucked on my collarbone before continuing further south down my chest. My dress slid down my arms to expose the tops of my breasts in the satin bra. Kai's hand lifted my right breast out of the cup and his mouth descended on my pebbled nipple.

My back arched into the sensation, another moan escaping my lips. I felt my core clench and Kai finally released my nipple with a pop sound. "I know I promised our next time would be in a bed, but I don't think just a bed will be enough," he whispered against my jaw as he tucked me back into my bra.

I couldn't help but blush. This was going to be a very long weekend.

Chapter 9

Kai's POV

After spending three days with Kat at the beach, I knew I was in deep. Waking up that first morning with her tucked against my body was… *Fuck.*

I didn't even have words to describe how fucking content my heart felt. It was getting a glimpse of what our future would be like. I wanted it, all of it, *with Kat.* I knew 18 was too young to get married, but I couldn't imagine there being anyone else.

By the time the weekend was over, we were inseparable. My brother had met Katie a few times over the years, and they got along well. Katie came to every baseball game and cheered me on, and I was on the sidelines cheering when her soccer team went to the State semi-finals.

Like that, the three weeks after prom flew by. We finished our exams one week, and had meetings with counselors to discuss our final grades the next. Basically, they pulled us in one by one to let us know if we were graduating or not.

Then, there was that final week of graduation rehearsals before we left this chapter behind. We had finished the last rehearsal and were leaving for the day when Christine decided to start a fight with Kat.

Matt had gone over to congratulate Katie on the soccer team taking second at State, and Christine lost her mind.

"Can't you leave my man alone? Stealing Kai from my friend wasn't enough?" She yelled across the gymnasium.

Katie was completely blindsided and looked for me. "Again, Chrissy, not after Matt, and two, I don't hit on guys who are taken. That's your thing."

I was damn near running across the gym to get to Katie. Matt was trying to pull Chrissy behind him, but she punched and pushed him out of her way.

"So you weren't hooking up with Kai all this time? You weren't sitting back filling his head with bullshit, sabotaging his relationships?" Chrissy accused her.

Katie smirked. "No, I supported every single one of them, and gave him advice on how to make them work."

Chrissy was not deterred. "Yeah, right!! So, you're telling me you never had a secret hook up with Kai when he was taken?"

"*That's* what I said," Katie drew out.

"Oooooh, so it's just *my* man that you secretly hooked up with since Alex's party?" She screamed at Katie.

I finally elbowed my way through the crowd and pulled Katie into my arms. "Chrissy, she never met up with Matt after Alex's party. She was with me the whole damn night."

Chrissy snorted at me. "You're an idiot, you know that, Kai? While you were down state for your baseball game, she was meeting Matt in Southend!"

I went to say something more, but Katie stiffened in my arms. There was truth to what Chrissy was saying, and Katie was holding something back.

Chrissy looked vindicated when Kat didn't respond. "See?

Can't talk now that you are caught?" She pointed at Katie.

Katie looked at Matt and sighed, "Just tell her dumb ass."

Matt shook his head, smiling sadly. "It doesn't matter any more, Katie. Tell her the big fucking secret."

I felt Katie's body shift and she chuckled, preparing to receive whatever Christine was going to throw at her.

"It wasn't just me, Chrissy. There were three of us that day. We all met up at Southend, two devil dogs and a witness. And when it was over, we went and picked out rings." Katie laughed.

Chrissy lunged at Katie, nails out, screaming. I already had Katie in my arms, so I turned my back and pulled Katie away from the fight. Matt jumped in and finally lost his patience.

"What the hell is wrong with you? I never fucking cheated! Why do you keep going after Katie? Huh? She's been in love with Kai since we were 10!" He yelled at Chrissy as she struggled to free herself.

"She saw me picking out a fucking engagement ring for you and gave me advice on how best to propose. You fucking satisfied?" He screamed.

The entire area stilled and the spectators became commentators.

"He's going to propose!"

"Um… no. Who wants to marry crazy?"

"She had been after Katie since January, for no reason."

"January? It was Chrissy's friend from Saint Augustine that he took to Homecoming!"

"The stalker!?"

"What stalker? Didn't she lose interest?"

"Ha! Because of a restraining order!"

Chrissy had turned to face Matt, ignoring all of the chatter surrounding them. "You want to marry me?" She asked, seeming shocked and contrite with tears filling her eyes.

"No." He replied, letting go of her. "I did. But marriages are built on trust and it's obvious you don't fucking trust me. I've tried, Chris. I can't do this," he sighed.

"Katie and I enlisted in the Marines on the same day. That was it. All of our *secret meetings* were about getting ready for boot camp with other enlistees and the Gunny, and Katie asking when I was going to pop the question," he explained.

"'Cause unlike you, she was happy for *us*. She didn't try to sabotage us. *You* have done that. I've known Katie my whole life, and if anything was going to happen, it would have. She's one of my friends, whereas you are nothing to me." The last words came out so low I almost didn't catch them.

Chrissy's head jerked from Katie to Matt. "What?!"

Matt had let go when she stopped trying to attack Katie through me, and now he was physically distancing himself from Chrissy. His voice was quiet, but there was no mistaking his words this time. "I'm done, Chris. I can't keep doing this. I'm fucking exhausted, and I don't deserve to be treated like a creep when I have never done anything to deserve it. I treat you like a queen, and you treat me like shit. Find someone else to be your punching bag."

With that Matt turned and left his stunned 'ex' in the sea of classmates. Katie looked over at Chrissy and frowned. Pulling from my arms she walked over and slapped Chris across the face.

"Go after him, dumbass!" She seethed.

Chrissy's head whipped back from the slap, and her eyes glared at my girl. Katie's voice lowered, "Go *after* him. Don't prove him right by not fighting for him. *Fight* for him," she urged her.

Chrissy pushed Katie back, mumbled a quiet thank you and ran after Matt. As things settled down, Katie turned to me. Her eyes looked uncertain. I don't know what look was on my face, but it did not reassure her. She didn't tell me she had enlisted already.

"Kai?" Her voice was so soft and insecure.

I didn't know what to say. I didn't know what any of this new information meant for us. We needed to talk but this wasn't the place. "We need to go, come on."

She took my outstretched hand, but for the first time it didn't fill me with energy. I was overtaken by an overwhelming sense of dread. Would she choose to chase me? Would she be faithful to me, so far away from everything here? Was I supposed to just sit around and wait while she went off and did her military thing and left me behind? We didn't talk about any of it that night. Katie was off with her family preparing for graduation, and I was home looking at my college acceptance letter for the huge university two towns over.

It wasn't a full ride, but it was damn close. I couldn't afford to follow Katie if it meant passing up this scholarship. I needed to talk to her, but I had no idea how to do it. Would she see it from my perspective? Would she be willing to give up the military for now so that we could start our lives together?

* * *

Katie's POV

Graduation day finally arrived and I didn't know if I was happy or scared. Things had been off between Kai and I, and I didn't know how to fix it. I tried talking to him about it, but he always found some way to change the subject.

My date was set for two weeks from now. Matt had convinced them to let him report later so that he could get married. I was happy that he and Christine talked through their shit, but it left me in the lurch. It wasn't like I hadn't told Kai, I had. Repeatedly. I told him that I decided to be a Marine after High School. How was it my fault that he understood that as 'someday'?

As we filled the football field seating in our caps and gowns, I felt absolutely alone in the sea of red and black. My friend had managed to contract mono and wouldn't walk for graduation, and my boyfriend would barely talk to me. I tried to get Bradley to talk with me but he seemed reluctant to get in the middle. I didn't blame him. I just wanted some insight.

I walked across the stage and smiled when I accepted my diploma, and then shook hands with each of the senior class faculty.

"Oooh-Rah, Preston!" Mr. Henry, our World History teacher, barked at me.

The other teachers jumped, startled by the outburst, but it managed to put me at ease. "Ooooh-Rah, Sir!" I responded just as emphatically.

"You won't regret it. I promise. Get out of here and see the world before you settle for one of these idiots," he patted me on the back and pushed me to the next teacher in the line.

Finally, the last name was called and two-hundred seventy-five graduates cheered and threw their caps in the air. I held onto my cap, at my mother's request, and just waved it in the air. I followed the crowd off the field and filtered through the crowds of smiling families to meet with my parents and sisters. I was done. This was my last day.

I called Kai that night, but he didn't answer, not that I expected him to. I knew that he would be at his grandparents' house celebrating his graduation and scholarship with the university in Southend. It wasn't an Ivy League college, but they had a ton of who's who as alumni. Their sports programs were among the top in the nation, and it was exactly what Kai had wanted since we were freshmen. Getting into that school was all he wanted.

I was happy for him. Genuinely happy. I didn't understand why he couldn't be happy for me too. I was really excited to be a Marine. They had opened up so many jobs for women in all of the services, and I wanted to try. Maybe I wouldn't make it, but then again, a lot of the guys wouldn't make it either. Didn't matter to anyone here except my history teacher, but it meant everything to me.

When the call went to voicemail, I was going to hang up but decided to just put it all out there. "Hey, it's Kat. I know you are busy with family, but I wanted to tell you that I was thinking of you. I know things have been weird. We need to talk, Kai. We promised no more secrets or not being honest with each other. I have done that. I have been an open book with you. Please. Just talk to me. I lo- I really want this to work out. Bye."

I hung up and stared at my phone. Just then it pinged with a message from Andie telling me to come over and visit with her. She wasn't contagious and her fever had gone down enough that she was allowed visitors. I threw my phone on my bed and changed into my pajamas. I decided to spend the day with Andie tomorrow. Tonight, I just wanted to be alone.

I shut my phone off and crawled under my blankets. Gunnery Sergeant Thompson said that I could back out at any time if before I reported. I didn't want to back out. I was getting a chance to do something for me, and I wasn't giving that up. Just like I would never ask Kai to give up the school program of his dreams, he couldn't ask me to give up this dream.

It was a few days later before I got a message from Kai. His grandparents had surprised him with a trip for graduation. He needed time to think. He would call me when he got back. It made me feel a little better that he was willing to talk.

Chapter 10

[Kai. Please answer me]

[You said you needed time to think. You haven't answered my calls or messages in nearly two weeks.]

[Is this how it is? You're ghosting me?]

[I gave you all of my firsts, Kai.]

[My love. My kiss. My virginity. My heart.]

[You took all of my firsts. My first broken heart is yours too]

[Did you ever care?]

[Did you mean anything you said?]

[I am leaving today. I won't come back for you.]

[You did this. You broke everything because you're selfish.]

[Goodbye, Kai.]

* * *

I looked down at all of the messages I had sent him, all of them left unanswered. I turned off my phone and threw it into the bottom of my bag. I wouldn't do this to myself anymore.

I dragged my small duffel bag down the stairs to the front

door. My mom was in tears, but what else was new. My recruiter was coming here in less than two hours to take me to the military processing station.

Andie followed my sisters out of our kitchen and hugged me. "Come on, we should sit outside and enjoy your final moments of freedom."

I wanted to laugh, but I felt like I was being suffocated. Fiona smiled sadly and made some excuse about needing to call someone and left me after a brief hug. My older sister, Candace, had to get to work and nearly cried hugging me. We had a five year age gap between us which meant we weren't super close, but she always made it a point to show up for me.

"I love you. Don't forget about me," she whispered.

"Not possible," I whispered back.

Andie and I stepped out into the summer heat on the back patio of my parent's home, she offered me a cigarette. "Want one?"

I shook my head, my eyes burning from the utter sadness I had been holding back. My older sister leaned over and gave me one more hug. Both of my sisters knew that I was struggling, and had hugged me while I sobbed in my bed the night before.

Andie lit her cigarette and took a seat at the picnic table. "Ok, it's just us. So spill it, Katiedid."

I smiled at the nickname that she had always used when we had serious talks. Then, finally, I let out a staggered breath and told her everything.

Kai wanted me to give up the military. He wanted me to stay here and go to college with him. Kai wanted to start our lives together, and when I said I wouldn't back out, he broke it off. Kai hadn't said a word to me this last week. He stopped answering my calls or responding to my texts, and Bradley wouldn't talk to me either. So I was leaving with all of these words unsaid. My heart was completely and irrevocably broken.

Andie pulled me into her arms and hugged me. "It'll be okay," she cooed while rubbing my back. "I don't know what will happen after this, but it will be okay. You are stronger than you know, Katiedid."

We sat there and talked until my mom stepped outside to tell me that it was time. I walked through the house to a waiting Gunnery Sergeant Thompson. With my bag in hand, I trudged out the door. I gave my mom and dad hugs and then burst into laughter as my sisters jumped out of the next room together to bear hug me.

"I thought you left me!" I yelled, laughing.

"Never! We just let you have a little time with Andie," Candace explained, wiping a tear from my cheek.

"You ready, Private Preston?" Thompson asked, interrupting our small moment.

I nodded and followed him to his small sedan. As I climbed into the passenger seat, he put my bag in the trunk. I looked down the road hoping to see Kai's car, but there was no one. He was not coming for me this time. I wiped the tears from my eyes as Thompson climbed in and started the car.

"Don't worry about this stuff. It's hard to leave home. We've all done it. This is a great start for your future," he reassured me as we drove off.

I sat waving goodbye to everyone until my house fell out of sight. Then, staring ahead at the road, I promised myself to be stronger. I wasn't enough for Kai, but I was enough.

And someone would love me for me one day.
I was 18 years old and had barely started my journey.
I had a long road ahead of me, like Andie said.

* * *

"All right, recruits. Line up, single file. You will proceed through the processing depot to obtain your identification card, health check, and finally your uniform and equipment issue. Do not assume that these Marines know you have clown feet. Sound off with your information when asked. Is that clear?"

"YES, DRILL INSTRUCTOR!" a group of sixty other recruits responded with me.

This was everything that I hoped it would be, with the added bonus of being in southern California. I didn't get Lejeune for training, but left for Pendleton instead after basic training.

"Name?"

"Private First Class Preston."

"Says Infantry, that correct?"

"Yes, Gunnery Sergeant!"

"Follow the yellow line for your uniforms and equipment issue."

"Yes, Gunnery Sergeant."

"Next!"

* * *

"Congratulations, Marines!"

"OOOH-RAH!"

The parade field was soon overrun with the families of the newly graduated Marines. It had been almost a half a year of training, but I did it. I was in beautiful California far from all of my worries.

I searched the field for my family. I didn't have to look far before I saw Andie bounding across the field squealing.

"GIRL!!! You look so fucking HOTT!!!" Andie screamed as she jumped in to hug me. "My goodness, I may go gay for you after all, Katiedid."

I laughed at the looks other Marines gave us as we giggled and hugged. I didn't realize how much I had missed her. We stopped when a voice cleared behind me. I turned slowly to see a man staring at us expectantly. He looked familiar.

I looked at Andie's blushing cheeks and it all clicked. "JONAS?!?" I squealed. "YOU HOOKED UP WITH JONAS?!" I laughed so hard I couldn't stop the tears from falling.

Jonas was four or five years older than us. His parents lived near Andie's and we would see him when he stopped by to visit. He was shy but Andie would tease him relentlessly. I knew she liked him, but she always denied it.

"HA!! I KNEW IT!" I squealed, hugging her again. "Spill! Tell me all about this secret affair!" I ordered them looping one arm through Jonas's and wrapping the other around Andie's waist.

We gathered my gear from the barracks and loaded it into Andie's car as she told me all about her seduction of the sweet and innocent Jonas. She was going to drive with me to my next assignment on the East coast. I had been worried about her driving to California alone, but now I understood why she told me not to worry.

I couldn't help but laugh each time she referred to Jonas as sweet and innocent. Andie didn't keep sweet *and* innocent men. She was a man eater. Jonas had to be a closet Dom to keep her this enthralled. I won't lie and say I wasn't interested to know, but there was no way in hell I would ever ask either of them. She was happier than I could ever remember seeing her and that was all that mattered to me.

"Did you want to get right on the road? Or should we put our feet in the Pacific before we go?" I asked when we got to their hotel. I was signed out on leave for the next ten days, giving us plenty of time to drive to my next assignment in North Carolina.

Andie leaned back one of the two Queen beds in the room. "Let's get on the road! I want to spend a day or two in Arizona."

Jonas and I agreed. Arizona had always been a dream destination for Andie and I, and she had not stopped on the way to pick me up in California. With the car packed and the hotel checked out, Andie drove the first stretch. We drove until we reached the Arizona state line and found a campsite for the night. Thankfully Andie brought two tents. I slept alone and I was okay with that. The trip went by so fast with the three of us laughing and sharing stories.

We stopped in Tombstone and Bisbee, then drove north to see the colored mountains around Flagstaff and Sedona. It was so freaking cold that we opted to get a hotel rather than camp out again. I could ignore my heartache when I was in training, but not now.

With every mile closer we drove to the East coast, my heart ached a little more. I didn't want to go back home and see anyone and had declined the option for hometown recruiting. My parents had come to my boot graduation, but

I still didn't have a car, so driving up to visit them was not an option. I would request leave in the summer and see them then. I didn't need to bother them with the move to my first assignment.

Andie knew me so well. "Do you want to talk?" she asked quietly while Jonas slept in the back seat.

I shook my head looking out the passenger side window. We were somewhere in Oklahoma or Texas.

"Kai-" she started, but I didn't let her finish.

"Stop. I don't care. Not any more. I know I said I left my phone, but I didn't. He never once tried to contact me. Did it matter how I felt? What about what I wanted all this time? Huh? I had no fucking say before, and now he doesn't either. He wanted to end it, it's ended." I whispered out harshly.

Andie glanced over at me as she drove. "Ok. I won't bring it up again."

We spent two days in Memphis, visiting Graceland and eating some of the best barbecue I had ever tasted. Jonas also had a bucket list for this road trip, and it involved a food crawl through Memphis. We laughed and ate until the meat sweats set in.

"No more. Please," I cried when Jonas pointed to another barbecue shop further down the road. Andie laughed at my pain, but convinced Jonas to save the last stop for their honeymoon. Jonas blushed and stopped pushing for more restaurants.

I couldn't help but watch the two more closely. Andie always said she didn't want to get married young. She wanted to 'sample the seven seas' before settling down. Now, she was talking about honeymoon plans with Jonas.

"Um... Something I should know?" I asked Jonas while

Andie ran into the gas station to buy drinks somewhere near Nashville.

He chuckled and shook his head. "She is something else. If she wants to marry me, I'll marry her tomorrow. If she says this is all we'll ever be, I would take that too. She's amazing, Katie."

I couldn't help but smile. "She is amazing."

We detoured south from Nashville to Chattanooga to visit the Tennessee aquarium and tour some caves that Andie had read about. I didn't care, I was enjoying the ride seeing all of the sites with my best friend. Before driving the final stretch to Lejeune, we stopped in Wilmington, North Carolina to walk along the beaches. It was cold as hell in January but another experience that I would not trade for anything.

Andie kept her word and hadn't mentioned Kai the rest of the trip. When we finally stopped outside my new barracks to unload my gear, she still didn't bring him up. I didn't know if I was relieved or disappointed that she didn't mention him again. Over the months that followed, Andie and I talked about everything under the sun, but Kai was not mentioned once.

Chapter 11

Kai's Point of View

"How long has he been like this?"

I couldn't understand what was being said.

"Since Friday."

Everything sounded muffled and distant.

"Jesus Christ. Get him in the bathroom. If he doesn't get his shit together, he'll lose his scholarship."

"What the hell happened?"

I felt like I had been hit by a bus. I tried to move but everything just felt heavy, so I drifted back to oblivion. It hurt less there.

"It's been over a year, this needs to stop."

I jolted awake when the cold water soaked through my clothes. "Ugh, fuck! Stop. Stop!" I grumbled.

"Get your shit together, Kai. Do you think you are the first dumbass to muck something up?" My mother yelled while she hosed me down with ice cold water. "You messed up and broke that girl's heart. Why are you self-destructing? HUH?!? *You* feel bad? GOOD! You *should*, but messing up the rest of your life is not the way to move forward.

"Now get your ass cleaned up and come out when you don't reek of booze, vomit and rotten gym socks. Your dad and I need to speak with you, and this will not wait while you pretend to take exams and skip more classes."

I had no idea how long it took me to stand and get myself stripped and cleaned up under the ice cold water. When I finally came out of the bathroom, there were clean clothes laid out on the bed. I got myself dressed and went out to find where my parents were. I thought crashing at Bradley's would keep me off of their radar but that was not the case.

"Kai, sit down."

I looked up to see mine and Bradley's parents seated at the table in the dining room. My mom was stone faced and my dad wouldn't even look up at me.

"What's going on?" I asked, knowing damn well this was an intervention.

"You're about to lose your scholarship due to poor academic performance, Kai." My dad was quiet. I was waiting for him to yell or threaten me, but he didn't.

"We know that you have been hurting, but killing yourself like this is-" he stopped talking, his voice choking up. "What can we do to help you?" he asked.

I wasn't expecting this. I was mentally prepared for yelling. Threats to cut me off, even violence, but seeing my dad like this broke me. It broke me in a way that I didn't know could be broken. I finally hit the bottom of whatever hole I had been digging for myself. "I messed up," I whispered out.

"How can we help you move forward from this, Kai," my mom asked.

"I don't know what to do," I said honestly. I had no idea how to move forward. I felt like my heart was shattered when I realized how badly I had fucked things up with Kat. It made me sick to think of how I made her feel. I drank to numb that nausea.

"How about we start with speaking to each of your professors about getting your late assignments caught up. You won't make the Dean's list, but you may actually keep from failing. Do you need tutors?" My mom was the one to plan shit. She was the organized one in the house, and she would have me on a tight schedule from here on.

"You will also attend substance abuse counseling until cleared otherwise," my dad said. I had been staring at the floor up to this point, but he had my attention.

"Dad, I don't-" but he wasn't hearing it.

"It's not a fucking request. You *will* attend substance abuse counseling, or you will lose your scholarship," he finished.

For the second time since sitting down, I felt like I had been punched in the gut. The university knew how fucked up I was. My parents weren't just trying to help me with school, they were trying to save my future.

"Can we go home?" I asked.

"Yeah, we can go home. But you can forget about using Bradley to cover for you anymore. If you show up here drunk again, you can forget about staying in school. You can forget about playing baseball, you can just forget about all of it," my dad was calm again.

I watched in shame as he apologized to Bradley and his parents for my conduct, and then thanked them for keeping me alive when I didn't value my own life. I couldn't look at Bradley or his parents when they pulled me in for a hug and wished me well. It was almost Christmas break. I had drunk away my sorrows for the last year and a half. It was time to get my shit together and move forward.

* * *

"How much do you have left?" my brother asked, looking over my shoulder as I typed away on my laptop.

"Um, I think this one is about done. Just need to run through and double check it, but then I can submit it and that's it," I said. "Why? Do you need help with something?"

My brother smirked, "Yeah, I'm gonna ask Sissy to marry me at Thanksgiving. If she says 'Yes', I was hoping you would be my best man."

I slammed my laptop shut and jumped up to give him a hug. "Holy shit, bro! Congrats, well not yet, but holy shit."

Reggie laughed. "Yeah. It's crazy right? I mean we've been together for a year, but I feel like she is it, Kai."

I knew what he meant. It had been three years since I let Katie get away. "Well, what do you need from me? Is there anything that I can help with?" I asked, giving him another hug and patting him on the back. "I'm really happy for you, Reg."

My brother told me about how he asked Sissy's dad for his blessing and even taken Sissy's mom to pick out the ring. I couldn't believe he was ready to get married.

"When do you think you'll tie the knot?" I asked.

"Honestly, I am going to let her decide," he chuckled.

We went out to dinner and talked about how he was going to pop the question after dinner. I offered to help in any way that I could, including hiding the ring. He started laughing when I offered.

"Thank God!" he exclaimed, rummaging in his coat pocket. "This thing is like carrying the ring of the nine around." He handed me a small black box as we finished eating.

I put the box in my jacket pocket without even looking at it. We talked for a bit longer before he dropped me back at my apartment and went home. There were two weeks until Thanksgiving, and four weeks until my end of term exams.

I had six months until graduation. I had managed to recover my grades with two summer semesters and a lot of hard work. I would start my practical as a physical therapy assistant in January, and hopefully qualify for the doctorate program in the fall. My life was finally getting back on track.

I heard a buzzing noise and found my phone still jammed in my jacket pocket. Bradley.

"Hey, man. What's going on?" I asked.

Bradley had transferred universities last year, so contact had not been nearly as often as it used to be. "Hey. What are you doing for Thanksgiving?" he asked.

I told him how Reggie was proposing to his girlfriend and the two families were in on the whole thing. Bradley laughed and asked a few questions about how Reg planned on popping the question.

"That's awesome. Tell him we said congratulations."

I paused for a second. "Who's this we?" I asked.

Bradley took a deep breath and then left me stunned with his next words. "I asked Amy to marry me and she said, 'yes.' We're getting married the Saturday after Thanksgiving, and I was calling to ask you to be my best man."

"Seriously?" I asked, stunned at this news.

"Yep."

"In two weeks? How long have you been engaged?" I asked, feeling like everyone was getting their happy ending except me.

"Well, I asked her last night, and we decided to keep it small and just ask a few witnesses. We'll have a real wedding after graduation."

"Yeah, yeah. I'd be honored! Just tell me when and where, and I will be there for you!" I chuckled, truly happy for him.

I had only met Amy a handful of times, but she was a great match for him. They balanced each other out and they were happy together.

I needed to get my shit together. I hadn't dated since. Well, it had been a while. There were a couple of women who I had asked out, but nothing really continued beyond the first couple of dates. There was no chemistry.

"So Alex is hosting a party. He said something about having big news, and invited the whole damn class for an impromptu reunion this weekend. Would you be interested in going?" Bradley asked.

I laughed, "Are you asking me out on a date?"

This time Bradley laughed. "No, Amy is asking for a double date, so you won't be this awkward third wheel when we go."

"Shit-" I exhaled like he had punched me in the gut.

"Sorry," he muttered into the phone.

I smiled realizing what was going on, "She's listening to this whole conversation isn't she?"

"Yep," he said, popping the P.

"Yeah, I'll take the plus one. But, I am begging you. Please. No more fucking crazy bitches. I know Amy is super chill, so can she *please* stop trying to hook me up with super high maintenance women?" I whined into the phone.

I heard a gasp in the background, "That was ONE time! Can't he let that go already?" Amy was hollering.

Before I could say anything Bradley called her out. "One? You really want to stick to that? What about the Blonde

Barbie? She was literally branded with LV. Then there was the Roller Derby Queen. She needed *constant* contact. And not just with Kai, she couldn't keep her hands off of *you!*"

I listened as Amy tried to explain some of the quirks of the women she had attempted to set me up with, but Bradley kept going. "Then there was pre-law Laurie. Thank god, Kai had Lacy and Val with him, or she would have been another psycho with a restraining order for his repertoire. Why don't we let Kai find his own date at the party," he concluded.

I felt like I should be in counseling after hearing the horror stories of the women that Amy had introduced me to over the past seven months. Don't get me wrong, they were all really good looking. They were just equal parts crazy to the hotness, and it was a huge turn off.

I decided to interrupt their bickering. "Alex already called to invite me. I will see you guys there. Bye!" I hung up before I could hear any more details about my sorry dating life. I sat back down with my laptop and ran another check on my paper before submitting it to my professor.

Alex's farm was packed as usual. It was great seeing a lot of the folks from school who had traveled back to town for the holidays. I ran into a couple of the guys from the baseball team and we talked about the upcoming professional season. There were only a couple of us still playing. The biggest surprise was Taylor.

He had gotten a full ride to a school in North Carolina, and there was talk that recruiters from New York were looking to pull him to the majors. It didn't surprise me. He had an arm like no one I had ever met. The guy was just naturally gifted when it came to the game.

Alex had pulled out all the stops. There were tables set up

around the barn, people sitting on hay bales while servers mingled through with trays of food, asking everyone to sample this and that. The food was great, but I didn't understand what this was all leading up to.

Finally, Alex called everyone's attention. "Thank you everyone for agreeing to come and celebrate with us. Unfortunately, this will be the last party like this in the barn."

There was a quiet murmur of whispers as we tried to figure out what was going on. "Is your family selling the farm?" one of the guys asked from the other side of the barn.

Alex looked over at his family, who nodded to him in support. "They have sold it," he said.

Before the whispers could get any louder, Alex continued, "to me. I bought the whole place. I wanted you to be the first to sample the new menu for *Alex's*. The first totally green restaurant in the state will be right here."

"Shit. Congratulations!"

"Congrats!"

"That's so awesome!"

"Oh, man! You're really doing it? Congrats!"

Alex had not only bought the family farm, but was converting it into a destination restaurant. *The Barn* would become a carbon neutral fine dining experience. They had already converted the main house and outbuildings to solar and wind power, and the food circling the guests was the tasting menu.

There were plans to source their own produce and only purchase meat from local farms also moving toward green initiatives. It was crazy how much work he had done in the short amount of time since high school. Alex was 21, and already looking to start his own business.

"Damn. Congratulations, man," I patted him on the back

as he made his rounds around the barn.

"Thanks. I appreciate you all coming tonight. I hope that you will come back here when we open."

Bradley stood and pulled him into a hug, "Congrats. When is the big day? When do you open?"

Alex blushed a bit. "Two years."

"Two years? Why so long, if you don't mind my asking."

"I need time to finish the green houses, and converting the not so sanitary barn into a fine dining fixture is going to take some time. I applied to have the barn put on the historical registry and it was approved. So, now I have extra funds to ensure the building is preserved for the foreseeable future," he explained.

"That's a lot of work. When did you start all of this?" I asked.

Alex laughed, "Actually, after senior year. I went to culinary school out west, but I missed the east coast fare. I am a homebody. I love cooking, but I want to be home. You know what I mean?"

We nodded. We understood. It was why I chose to attend a local university instead of traveling further from home. This was where our roots were deepest.

"Then I ran into Katie and she suggested I just open my own place."

My heart stopped in my throat. Bradley didn't even think before continuing the questions.

"No shit? When did she get back in town? I haven't seen her since graduation."

Alex laughed, and looked over at me. "I ran into her when I was out in California. Katie hasn't been back here since she left. She's doing great though. I heard she deployed in

August, but should be back stateside sometime in May or June."

This time Amy joined in my torture. "She's in the military? Which service?"

"Marines." Bradley, Alex and I answered at the same time.

"That is so cool. What does she do?" Amy asked.

Alex looked unsure now. "Honestly, I'm not really sure. I know that she got promoted to Sergeant last month, but they had her training to work with females overseas. That's all I know. Her sister didn't really give me a lot of details when I spoke to her."

"When did you talk to her?" Bradley seemed curious now.

"Oh, we talked back in the spring. I called to ask how Katie was doing and her sister kind of gave me a run down. Well, I need to get around to a few more people. It was great seeing you all again. Thank you for coming tonight," Alex shook our hands and walked off.

I knew I had no right to feel anything for Katie. I really didn't any more. She was my high school sweetheart, and I was the idiot who let her get away.

Bradley looked at me as if to judge whether I was going to spiral out of control again. I smiled and reassured him, "I'm good. Just took me by surprise."

I left shortly after that. Although I did not agree to meet with Amy's blind date, I did have plans with my other wingman, Lacy. Lacy and I were in the same science classes together. She was totally hot, and we had the same tastes in women. The benefit was that she had a better radar for keeping crazies away than Amy did.

Tonight, we were going to a new bar that had opened in Southend. I had no hope of finding anyone but Lacy seemed convinced that between her and her new girlfriend Val, they would find someone for me.

By the time I got to the bar, it was packed. I had no idea where Lacy or Val were, and they weren't answering their phones. I waded through the crowd of people and ordered a coke from the bar. I had a designated driver bracelet on, so it let me have free nonalcoholic drinks at any bar in the state.

If I got caught drinking while wearing it, the state would pull my license. I didn't think it was a bad program, to be honest. The law passed last year, and had already made a significant impact on the number of incidents involving alcohol. Suddenly, our state had one of the lowest indices for drunk driving in the country.

I was taking a sip of my drink when two arms wrapped around me. I turned expecting to see Lacy, but instead looked into a pair of brown eyes framed with long blonde hair.

The stranger smiled up at me and kissed me on the cheek. "I need you to pretend to be my boyfriend, so the creepy guy at the end of the bar will stop following me," she whispered in my ear.

I nodded and pulled her into my arms. "What's your name, fake girlfriend?" I asked, pretending to nuzzle her ear.

She laughed, "Jenny. You?"

"Kai."

"Do you want to dance?" Jenny asked.

"What the hell. Why not," I smiled back, and followed her to the dance floor. She wasn't breathtaking, but she was cute and it was fun talking with her. Best of all, she was not crazy.

Chapter 12

"If that's an eight, tens don't exist. You are out of your mind."

"She might be hot, but she's cold as fuck. Have you tried holding a conversation with the *Ice Queen*?"

"Don't let Gunny hear you calling her that. He'll have your ass."

"At least then somebody would be getting some action."

"And what *action* were you hoping for Sergeant Beliago?"

The two marines smoking outside the tent city never heard the man walk up behind them. The deep gravelly voice caused them both to choke.

cough cough cough "Fuck, Gunny. You scared the shit out of us!" The marine named Beliago answered.

Gunnery Sergeant Tyson Johnson stood behind them. His soft brown hair was buzzed and faded high and tight. His green eyes stared down at the two men in front of him, jaw clenched, as he waited for either of them to answer his question.

"You can tell me, or explain it to the CO," his voice drawled out like a growl.

Before either could answer a woman's voice interrupted. "Apparently, my *sparkling* personality is preventing me from experiencing all that your *Sergeant* has to *offer* me, Gunny."

The three men turned to see the subject of the two's conversation. Staff Sergeant Preston stood at parade rest before Gunny Johnson. The color drained from Sergeant Beliago's face, realizing that the object of his lewd appraisal had not only heard what was said, but also reported it to their Gunny.

"Apparently my disinterest in your two idiots warranted a lowered ranking on their *'who's fuckable'* scale," Katie stated matter of factly, as if she were discussing whether to purchase a new pair of boots.

"What did you just say?!" Gunny Johnson asked.

"I'm sorry. Was the language too vulgar to be clear? What was the wording you used, Beliago? *'I might be hot, but I'm cold as fuck'* or did I mishear the same conversation the entire motor section was listening to when you called me an *Ice Queen?*" She asked the now speechless Sergeant.

Beliago stared wide eyed at his platoon sergeant. "Gunny! Shit, I didn't mean for anyone to hear!" He stammered.

Gunny just shook his head. "Go see the C-O. *Both of you,*" he directed to Beliago and the Corporal he had been speaking with.

"Staff Sergeant Preston, if you would like to file a formal complaint, I will be your witness," another NCO walked up to join Katie and the Gunny.

Katie smiled at the support, but waved them off. "Don't worry about it. Gunnery Sergeant Johnson heard them. I appreciate the offer though," she thanked them.

Time quickly flew by. Before she knew it, Katie's third tour in the desert was coming to an end. The unit would fly back to North Carolina on Wednesday. Her bags packed and loaded onto the pallets with the rest of the platoon's gear. The relief in place was complete, so there wasn't really anything for her to do.

She found a book in the morale, welfare, and recreation tent, and sat outside to read for a bit. This was downtime that had not really been possible before now. It wasn't long before a shadow loomed over her.

"Hey," the deep voice of Gunny Johnson called her from her book.

Looking up at him, Katie smiled, "Hey, yourself, Tyson."

Hearing her call him by his name made him smile. He couldn't help it. They had started dating before this deployment, but he had no idea how hard it would be to keep this professional. Sitting down next to her, he leaned in and nudged her with his shoulder.

"What are you reading?" he asked.

She smiled, pulling the book to her chest. "It's called, *Amidst the Storm.*"

Tyson smiled, "What's it about?"

"Well, it's a story about second chance love," she explained.

Tyson chuckled, questioning further, "Annnnd?"

He watched Katie's face as she formulated how to answer. She could be stoic and stone faced when she tried, but she couldn't control the blush that tinged the tips of her ears or cheeks.

"A soldier returns from deployment, and his wife leaves him because she was cheating. He signs up for another tour, and is wounded in combat and discharged. His ex-mother in law convinces him to take a security job overseas, and I just got to the part where the new partner confessed their feelings," she explained.

Tyson nodded again. "Why are you embarrassed about a

military love story?" he asked her quietly.

"I am not embarrassed about the story, or any military love story," she refuted.

"Uh-huh," he chuckled, leaning closer to her. "Then why are you blushing so hard, baby?" he whispered quietly.

Katie snorted, "I am sunburnt, not blushing!"

Tyson let out a barking laugh that came from deep in his chest. "Ok!"

"STAFF SERGEANT PRESTON!" Their commander called out as he ran toward where the two were seated, causing them both to jump to their feet.

"Sir?" Katie responded, moving to meet the man halfway.

"I know you fly out on Thursday, but the new folks just lost one of their female engagement NCOs due to a health issue. Staff Sergeant Holmes is being taken to Headquarters for further evaluation from the Division Surgeon. Until then, I need to know if you'd be willing to lengthen your tour to cover her missions?"

Katie looked over at Tyson, and the two shared a look not missed by the CO. "Gunny here was tasked by the Sergeant Major to clean up the last flight, so he'll be on ground to ensure your dates aren't pushed once we leave," the Captain continued.

"Yes, sir. That shouldn't be a problem," she paused, recalling that her gear had all been palletized for the return flight. "But my gear was taken with the rest of the company. Is there any way to pull it back?"

Their commander nodded. "Yes, they're already sorting the bags according to chock manifests. So, you'll do it?" he asked again.

Katie smiled, "Yes, sir."

117

"Excellent. Go see the second battalion's ops team for your mission brief. You roll out tomorrow with Charlie Company" the commander informed her.

Katie's eyebrows shot up. It wasn't exactly last minute, but she would definitely need to get moving in order to be prepared. "Thank you, sir. Excuse me, Gunny," she addressed the two men before running to gather her gear and receive the mission brief.

The commander watched the normally gruff and stoic Platoon Sergeant, Gunny Johnson, watch Staff Sergeant Preston run off. "You are so fucking done for," he laughed thumping Tyson in the chest.

Gunnery Sergeant Tyson Johnson cleared his throat, "Obviously. That's my future wife right there."

The commander laughed and pulled Tyson along with him to hear the upcoming mission brief as well.

* * *

Katie's Point of View

Charlie Company seemed pretty squared away based on the mission briefing presented. The plan was to drive one of the outer roads away from the airfield to visit some village elders in one of the more remote areas. The mission would take three to four days to complete. I had been there a few times, so I was familiar enough with the route to let my vehicle take the lead.

My vehicle had a young Private First Class driving and a newly promoted corporal manning the turret. Listening to the two of them shit talk each other for two hours was honestly the funniest shit I had heard in a while.

I had no problem with their bickering back and forth, but the area we were traveling through was not always the best for safety. Intell had come in that several Warlords were attempting to exert pressure on smaller villages in order to restart drug trade routes that my unit had all but quashed.

Terrorists were one thing, if not predictable. Those involved in the drug trades were anything but. I couldn't believe how quickly money could change someone's beliefs. This was my third tour, and it broke my heart to see community pillars turn their backs on their own tribes for drug money.

"Weren't you supposed to be headed back in two days?" My driver asked during a lull in their banter, quickly glancing over at me.

"Yeah, but I volunteered to help you guys out until all of your people were on ground and ready to go," I answered, watching the roads for anything out of place. "Hey, Corporal? Be on the lookout for any trash collection points ahead," I directed the gunner.

We were now in a fairly remote area. While some wouldn't think anything of a pile of trash on the side of the road, I knew for fact there weren't any houses close enough to generate it. Not to mention, most people burned their trash because it wasn't like there was a garbage company to collect it up.

"How long did it take you to make Staff Sergeant?" He asked.

"Four years," I responded, feeling an uneasiness in the pit of my stomach.

"Shit. That seems fast. How long have you been in?"

"Just over five years. Hey, concentrate on the road," I advised the nosy Norman, playing twenty questions with me.

There was silence in the vehicle for ten minutes. I called in our next check point, and then he started up again.

"You gonna make Gunny?" He continued questioning me.

"Hopefully. Hey, Corporal? Be on the look out for any trash or debris on the road ahead," I shouted up to the gunner.

"I don't see any trash but the-"

The world shifted in red and white.

Shit. Shit. "PULL UP A PERIMETER!" I yelled from beside my truck to the Marines running toward me.

"MEDIC! WE NEED A MEDIC!"

"HELP!"

"PLEASE! I'M PINNED. DON'T LEAVE ME HERE!"

Fuck. My ears were ringing. What were they doing? Why weren't they securing the perimeter? This wasn't how we did shit.

"SET UP THE DAMN SECURITY PERIMETER!" I screamed again.

They were panicking with their first IED contact rather than doing what needed to be done; how they were *trained* to respond to such a situation. I watched as my words finally registered, and the panicked scrambling bodies suddenly stopped and took up their proper positioning.

The sound of gunfire started up behind somewhere to my right, but it was muffled because of the incessant ringing in my ears. I looked over to the next vehicle now moving to block the wreckage that my vehicle had become.

"WHERE'S THE RTO? CALL IT IN AND SEND UP THE NINE-LINE!! TELL THEM WE NEED AIR. NOW!" I continued to bark orders at the top of my lungs.

I felt a pair of hands pulling me away from my vehicle, but I tried to fight them off. "Stop, I am not the priority. Get the other two first!" I barked, pointing to my driver and gunner.

"Staff Sergeant, you're bleeding out. I need to get you stable. Can you feel your legs?" The medic questioned me as I tried to swat him away in order to keep my eyes on what the others were doing. Why did he look pink?

"I'm fine. I need you to save the other two! Please," I attempted to divert his attention back to the two junior Marines who had been in the vehicle with me.

"The others are taking care of them. You're the priority right now, do you understand. They might lose a limb, but I'm looking at your insides, Preston. So, shut the fuck up and stop moving so I can save your fucking life!" the medic, Lieutenant Corry, growled at me.

I heard him, but it didn't register. "They're going to lose a limb? *Shit.* I promised them I would look after them!"

"Preston? Preston?" Someone was calling my name.

Wait. My organs are hanging out?

I looked down to see the red mess that was my abdomen. "Oh, shit," my voice sounded so quiet as everything went black. *Tyson, I'm sorry.*

"PRESTON! *SHIT, I NEED EXTRA HANDS! WE'RE LOS-ING HER!!*"

Chapter 13

Kai's Point of View

I was slammed with work at the clinic this week. I thought I could swing working full time while attending night classes, but I barely finished my assignments for the physical therapy assistant certification. I had no idea how hard it was going to be juggling the two, but I needed the money if I was going to pay for the doctoral program.

My phone pinged, but I couldn't stop to check it. I had three more patients today, and then I needed to finish charting before I ran home to eat and change for class.

It took me two hours to finally clear the patient list, clear my charts, and get out of the office. I didn't have time to change before classes, so I just went straight to class. I was walking back out to my car at eight o'clock when I remembered to check my phone again. There were a ton of missed calls from Jenny and a few texts asking me to call her.

She was never the super clingy type, so this was definitely throwing up some red flags. I waited until I got into my car before giving her a call back. Driving toward my apartment in town, I dialed Jenny's number. When she didn't answer I left a brief message apologizing for not taking her call while I was with patients, and laid out what my schedule had been for the night.

If she called back, she called back. Otherwise, I would see her tomorrow when we had our next date. Could I call it dating? We'd been seeing each other off and on for nearly six months, after we hooked up that first night. We just didn't label what we were.

She seemed down to earth, just stressed from the crazy shit we all dealt with in life. Who didn't have their own stories of heartbreak? She knew all about my shit. We got along well enough and the sex wasn't bad. Not to mention, she was super low on the drama scales.

As I pulled up outside my building, I thought I saw Jenny's car leaving the parking lot. She hadn't shown any signs of crazy over the last month, and I was hoping that she wasn't going to end up like the stalker in high school.

I grabbed my bag from the back seat once I parked, and my phone rang as I walked into the building. I shifted everything in my hands and answered.

"Kai?"

I couldn't help but chuckle a little, "Last time I checked. Sorry I couldn't answer earlier, we were swamped at the clinic." I explained as I reached my apartment.

"*Shit!* I completely forgot you had the clinic today. Oh my god, I am so sorry. You must think I am crazy," she quickly apologized.

A part of me relaxed, realizing that it was just a mistake of scheduling, and kept talking as I sat on the sofa to talk. "It's okay. I was worried something had happened, and you weren't able to get a hold of me."

She chuckled lightly, and I could hear her starting to relax. "I did need some help earlier, but it's all- Well, things aren't as dire as I thought they were."

I furrowed my brows, because she sounded like she was speaking in riddles. "You okay, Jen?" I asked.

I listened to her sigh, and then there was a long moment of silence. "Not really," she finally admitted. "Is it okay if I come over?"

I looked around my apartment, seeing what needed to be tidied up before she came over. It wasn't bad, so I agreed. "Sure, I was just going to order a pizza tonight. Do you want anything in particular?"

"Cheese pizza?" she asked.

"Cheese pizza it is," I agreed and hung up the call. I ordered the pizza while I walked around cleaning up the living room and then straightened up my bed. Not that I was hoping to get laid, but just in case we ended up in my room, it should look neat.

Jenny showed up five minutes after the pizza was delivered. We sat down on the sofa, a baseball game playing in the background and ate our food.

I waited until she was done eating before trying to pry any information out of her. When she wouldn't eat any more, I cleaned up our plates, and put the leftovers in the fridge. Worst case, I would take a couple slices with me for lunch tomorrow.

"Alright, what's going on?" I asked, sitting down next to her on the sofa.

She passed me a piece of paper, but refused to make eye contact with me. I didn't know why I thought it was cute, but I chuckled, thinking of passing notes to girls I liked in school.

I leaned back and started to read over the sheet. It was

discharge paperwork from the hospital. I felt like I was reading a foreign language, because my brain completely shut down at some point. Jenny finally spoke up and pulled me out of my stupor.

"Surprise! I'm pregnant." Her voice sounded hoarse. She had to be fucking terrified, because I knew I was.

"I was not expecting that," I admitted, tearing my eyes from the lab report to look at her. She looked nervous as hell, and on the verge of crying. "What do you want to do?" I asked.

I watched her face process my words. She went back and forth between red and white, like she was alternating between rage and fear, but she didn't say anything. I kept talking instead.

"I'll support whatever decision you make, Jenny. It is your body, and we haven't known each other that long, but I will support you and the baby if that is what you're worried about."

Jenny burst into tears at that point. "I was so worried that you would hate me!"

I pulled her into my chest and hugged her. *Fuck. We were having a kid!*

"You aren't mad at me?" she asked.

I couldn't help but laugh a little. "I think we both messed this one up equally," I admitted.

Jenny relaxed against me. "I don't know what to do, Kai. I never wanted to be a single mom or raise a child in a broken household. It's horrible," she sniffled.

I couldn't agree more. She said everything that had already rushed through my mind in the past two minutes. Neither of us were ready for this. Neither of us planned for this.

Yet, here we were. Expecting the unexpected. "Move in

with me."

Jenny pulled back and stared at me wide eyed. "What?"

I realized that I had said that out loud rather than just thinking it. I took a deep breath and repeated, "Move in with me when your lease expires, or we can look for a bigger place. We get along well, and we're going to be raising a baby together. We might as well cut the travel time down."

Jenny looked quiet for a minute. "Kai, my job is across the state line. I can't commute from here every day. I would go broke."

I nodded. I hadn't thought of that. "Ok. My lease is up in two months. How about we find you a bigger place in between our two jobs, and when my lease expires, I move before the baby is born."

Jenny's eyes were wide, staring at me. "Oh my god, you're serious."

There was a moment of silence again before her eyes watered up and she started to cry again. "Oh my god, you're *serious?!*" she asked.

I just nodded, lost for words because I couldn't keep up with her mood swings. Should I have asked what she wanted first? Was she upset that I was making plans without asking what she wanted? Before I could ask if it was alright, she threw herself into my arms and hugged me.

"I thought you would leave me or demand I get an abortion. Oh my god, Kai. I have been scared shitless to talk with you about all of this," she finally admitted.

I just held her in my arms and rubbed her back as she cried. We were going to be parents. Didn't matter how we got here, what mattered was that the child that we were having together would be taken care of.

"How does your family feel about children out of wedlock?" she asked after she had calmed down.

"Honestly?" I asked.

Jenny nodded against my neck, where her head was resting.

"They're *Catholics*. Should we go to Vegas?" I asked.

She leaned back and looked at me seriously. "That's not funny."

"I wasn't trying to make a joke of it. We're already having a child together. Let's go all in."

I had no idea what the hell came over me. Two hours ago I thought she was a crazy stalker. An hour ago, I offered to move in together. Now, I was asking her to elope. *Fuck. This was not what I had planned.*

"*Okay.*"

"*Okay?*" I asked her.

"Okay," she repeated.

Shit. She agreed.

"We're going to sneak off and tie the knot, move in together and have this baby," I repeated the plan like we were planning a daily itinerary.

Jenny was quiet for a minute. "Kai, I can't believe how calm you're being about all of this. Think about it until this weekend. If you still want to do this.... *All of it.* I will agree with whatever you decide."

←ᑭ←←※→→ᕼ→

We got married at the courthouse, with two strangers for witnesses, and decided to wait until after her first obstetrics appointment to announce the pregnancy. The month delay between the two had given us time to scout out new apartments, and get all of our legal shit in order. I added Jenny to my insurance, and she added me to hers.

Neither of us were ready for joint accounts, but we did set up one shared account to pay our future bills from.

My phone hadn't stopped ringing for three days. We decided to rip the band-aid off and just put it all out there. Jenny and I posted the same picture on our social media accounts and tagged each other. It was just our left hands holding the first ultrasound picture. The wedding bands were super prominent, once you got past the shock of seeing the image we were holding. The caption read, "Welcome to the family."

Now everyone knew that Jenny was pregnant and we were married. My grandmother was beside herself for the first day, but after that she was really happy for us. Once she realized that this would be her first great grandbaby, she really got excited about the whole thing.

Then my brother announced that they were also expecting. His wife was due one month before Jenny. They decided to follow our steps and married in the courthouse over the weekend. Our parents were all thrilled with the prospects of two new babies in the family. I was still scared shitless, but it was something I could only admit to Jen.

There were so many things that had changed suddenly. I made the decision to put off the doctoral program until we could afford it. Jenny, being who she was, tried for weeks to talk me out of it, but our new family was more important. I was 22, and there were no age limits for getting a doctorate in physical therapy.

When Jenny would start to get stressed about what I was giving up, I would just remind her that it was about *us*. We could only take this one day at a time, and hope like hell that everything worked out.

Chapter 14

"How was everything last night?" the doctor asked after entering the hospital room.

"Rough," Tyson grunted, trying to sit up from the small bed.

"Fever?" the doctor asked.

Tyson shook his head, and looked to the other side of the room. "No. No fever. Just nightmares."

The doctor nodded. "It's to be expected. I can put in a prescription for something to help with the sleep, but it may slow the recovery."

"Let me think about it," he grunted.

The doctor nodded again. "I'll let you get to it then. Just page if you need a nurse to help this morning," he offered before slipping back out of the room.

Tyson stood slowly and stretched. He hurt all over. He had barely slept last night, and the bed they had given him was uncomfortable as hell and way too small for his massive frame. Grabbing his hygiene bag, he walked into the ensuite bathroom to shower and clean up.

Twenty minutes later he was clean shaven, showered, and dressed for duty. "Time for physical training," he said, walking to the opposite side of the room.

Katie was in a coma for nearly a month, but was finally out of danger. Although she still hadn't spoken a word in the two weeks since coming out of it, he could tell when she was conscious versus when she slept, even if her eyes never opened for more than a few seconds.

Her body was still too weak to do anything, so Tyson made a point to move her limbs for her every day. The physical therapists had shown him how to massage and move her arms and legs to prevent muscle atrophy. He followed the same routine each morning. He started with her arms and shoulders, then worked down to her legs. Once they were done with what he referred to as Preston Pilates, he would give her a sponge bath, wiping down her entire body. He even had a soft rubber cap that went over his finger to brush her teeth.

As he was finishing work with her legs, he thought he heard her grunt. Normally, he would talk constantly about what a beast his girlfriend was to get through PT each day without a single complaint. He talked about the unit's redeployment, and read aloud the cards that were sent from friends and family.

He met Katie's parents and sisters shortly after Katie arrived at the military hospital, and Tyson convinced them to go home after the first two weeks. Her mom still came down every weekend, and that was when Tyson would travel home to check in with the unit.

"You finally going to start talking back?" he asked, chuckling at her. "You think a month of Preston Pilates, and you have what it takes to come at me? Come on, baby girl. Show me how tough you are," he taunted as he continued her therapy.

He watched her eyes flutter a bit, but they couldn't stay open. "Kept me up all night moaning, now you want to challenge me, huh? I'm waiting, Preston. Show me what you got!" He said more forcefully, though his hands continued the same gentle massage and stimulation to her muscles.

She was quiet for the remainder of the therapy and massage. As Tyson began to pull back the blankets to wipe down her skin the blankets caught. He looked down and saw that Katie held the blankets in two tight fists at her sides.

His heartbeat picked up, as he looked from her hands to her face. "Baby girl, it's Ty," he cooed softly, and brushed her cheek. "It's just me and you. I won't let anyone else touch you, baby. I've got you."

Her eyes fluttered again, and he watched her try to open them. "What's the matter, baby girl? You shy on me now?" He teased her.

He watched her cheeks blush, and almost barked out a laugh. "You better open those beautiful brown eyes, Katie. Look at me. I know you've been waking up. I know you're in there. Open your eyes. Look at me, Katie."

The nurses heard Tyson's voice becoming raised. In the time that he had been by this woman's side, he had never once raised his voice. He had always spoken low and calmly, but now he was almost barking orders at the unconscious women in the bed.

Tyson heard the door open behind him, but he couldn't pull his eyes away from Katie. What if she opened her eyes and he missed it. "Damnit, Preston. Open your eyes, or I won't go easy on you. It's time to get to work, Marine!" he yelled.

"Gunnery Sergeant-" the nurse approached and started to

pull Tyson back. "This is not how we do things here!" She was going to remove him from the room.

"OPEN YOUR EYES OR I'M LEAVING!" He yelled. "THEY'RE MAKING ME LEAVE! OPEN YOUR EYES, KATIE!"

Three orderlies had come in to help the nurse, each assuming the caretaker had finally lost patience with the extended convalescence. It wasn't the first time a caretaker had lost their fight and the frustration took over. "Let's go. You need to leave *now*."

"duh"-

Tyson couldn't pull his eyes away. "Shut up!" He yelled at the noisy nurse and orderlies now trying to pull him away.

"That's it-"

"Damnit, SHUT UP!" Tyson bellowed. "My wife is talking to me!"

The chaos and noise in the room stopped, as five sets of eyes suddenly turned to the woman on the bed. Two brown eyes peeked out from heavy lidded eyes. Katie blinked slowly.

"Duh-le" the hoarse whisper came out.

The nurse sucked in a breath and ran out of the room. "I'll page the doctor!"

The orderlies released Tyson and stepped back.

Tyson stood in the middle of the room and watched her struggle to open her eyes and speak. Finally, her eyes opened and fixed on him. "Don lea m"

Tyson exhaled a shaky breath. "Say it again, baby girl." His voice was hoarse as tears threatened to fall at any second. She had been unconscious for nearly two months. "You can do it. Say it one more time."

"d-don lea me," the small voice whispered again.

Tyson took three steps to the bed and shakily took Katie's hand. He caressed her cheek and kissed her forehead. "I'm not leaving you, baby girl. I promise, I won't leave you."

The doctor rushed in with the nurse hot on his heels moments later. "She's awake and speaking," one of the orderlies reported.

The nurse looked wide-eyed from the orderly to Katie, then to Tyson. "I'm so sorry, Gunny. I misunderstood."

Tyson shook his head. "Don't be. My girl's quite jealous. Aren't you, Preston? Perked right up when you saw someone putting their hands on your man, didn't you?" He teased.

Katie tried to roll her eyes, and only succeeded in exhaling a huff. For Tyson, she might as well have stood up and danced. She was still in there, and she was fighting for him.

The doctor finished Katie's exam, and confirmed that she was finally on the path to real recovery. "These are excellent results, Staff Sergeant Preston. You're out of the woods, but there is still a lot of work to be done. Gunny, may I speak with you for a moment?"

Tyson nodded and tried to follow the doctor out of the room, but stopped when Katie squeezed his hand. "No," she huffed out in her hoarse whisper.

Tyson looked down at their clasped hands and smiled. "If it's alright with you, Doc, Katie would like to be present for this conversation."

The doctor looked over at Katie as her eyes moved to him. He nodded in acceptance. "Very well. Let's have a seat and discuss the next few steps of the recovery plan. Although Staff Sergeant Preston is awake and responsive, I will recommend that Gunnery Sergeant Johnson retain the medical power of attorney. Do you understand, Staff

Sergeant?"

"Uh," she grunted.

Tyson nodded, smiling.

Over the next hour the attending doctor reviewed several options for the next phase of Katie's recovery. Katie fell asleep after ten minutes but woke up periodically to grunt when she liked something. Tyson remained by her side holding her hand the entire time.

"If you have any questions or issues, just give me a call," the doctor informed them before leaving the two alone in the room again.

Tyson sat still for a moment, and then stood up. He walked over to the door and locked the bolt. "Ok, baby girl. There's no one but us, and I have to tell you something." He paused for a moment as he gathered a few things from around the room, keeping his hands low where Katie couldn't see what he was holding.

"You stink, Marine. Who does PT and doesn't conduct proper hygiene after, huh?" he chided lightly.

Katie grunted and the corner of her mouth twitched.

Tyson chuckled and caressed her face again after placing everything on the small tray table beside the bed. "Seriously, though. Are you ok with me being here? I have seen every inch of you, baby girl, but you're awake now and you have all the power. If you want me to grab a nurse, I will step outside while you get cleaned up."

"Stay. me."

Tyson smiled. "Okay. I'm going to start with your face, and then we work our way down. Ready?"

"uh."

When Katie was finally cleaned up and had sipped a bit

of lukewarm water, she fell asleep again. Tyson arranged the room so that the two beds could be side by side and laid down to rest as well.. He kept one hand in Katie's as she slept, and drifted off to sleep.

* * *

Katie's Point of View

"Hey, mommy," I whispered into the phone. "I'm just letting you know that I am home again. If you and daddy want to come down this weekend, Tyson's cleaned up the guest room."

I listened to my mom gush and rave about Tyson and all that he had done for me. I smiled, looking at the man sleeping next to me. "He is amazing, isn't he?" I agreed.

Tyson never left my side in the four months that I was hospitalized. Before we had deployed, I had listed Tyson as the person to escort should anything happen. I hadn't even told Tyson, so I couldn't understand how he and the commander had worked it out so that Tyson got temporary orders permitting him to remain by my side until I could come home.

I had gone back up to the military hospital a few more times, but now I was finally home for good. No more doctors, therapists, rehabilitation, or extra checks remained to be done. When I first left the hospital, Tyson moved all of my stuff into his apartment, insisting that I still needed a caregiver while I was convalescing. I knew he was amazing from the beginning, but the last year only confirmed just how truly amazing he really was.

When I hung up with my mom, I lay back down in bed and

135

snuggled into Tyson's body. His arms pulled me close and held me. All of the stress, worry, and doubts disappeared from my mind. We hadn't said the words yet, that I could remember, but I knew I was completely in love with Tyson Johnson. We had been together for a year and a half of hell. What couldn't we get through after this?

Tomorrow would be my first day back to regular duty since the attack. I was nervous and excited to be back amongst my military family. It had been a long recovery, but I was finally cleared as fit for duty and taking on a new platoon of marines.

"Go to sleep, or I will make you pregnant," Tyson threatened in his sleepy voice.

I couldn't help but giggle. That had become his new thing. He had taken me up to visit Andie, and I helped deliver her son. Now, all he talked about was how much he wanted to marry me and knock me up.

I honestly thought I would have been opposed to the idea, but life with Tyson was more than I ever imagined. He was wearing me down with his love and devotion.

I closed my eyes and fell asleep with a smile on my face.

Chapter 15

Our unit had been so busy these last four months preparing for another deployment. Between training rotations in the field, technical certifications, and everyday training, it felt like a roller coaster finally nearing the end of the ride.

I cinched down the straps on my pack and hefted it onto my back. This morning we were going to conduct a range, and the companies were rucking out and back after qualifications were complete.

Tyson's platoon was running the range, so I had packed some extra snacks and a thermos of soup in my pack for him. It was early fall, and the air held that crisp cold that always came before a snowstorm.

I tightened everything up and then moved to check over my marines before we stepped off. The march out would take less than two hours. If my marines dug in, every last one should be at the range within ninety minutes.

"Sound off, Marines!" our platoon commander shouted as he began roll call.

"Anderson."

"OOO-RAH"

"Anthony."

"OOO-RAH"

Each marine stepped off to begin the march as their names were called off. The commander had organized the list by squads so our folks could maintain their unit integrity and report back, just as we had always trained.

The sun was barely crested over the horizon when I reached the range. I grounded my gear at the assembly area and retook the roll for the firing orders. One of the range cadre was standing by to give the safety brief as soon as my checks were done. I stood back and watched my platoon move in an orderly fashion between stations.

I didn't need to fire today because I had qualified with the rest of the regiment leadership the day before. This would be my second day in a row marching twelve miles. Tyson promised to spoil me the whole weekend for my efforts.

A deep voice broke me out of my thoughts. "What are you smiling about, Marine? Were you given the authorization to look that happy?"

I realized that I had been smiling at the thoughts of Tyson spoiling me. So I chuckled and turned to see the man who occupied my thoughts. "I got my chit signed this morning, Gunny!" I replied.

Tyson's solemn expression broke, and he started laughing. "Of course you did."

We walked together behind my platoon, observing them. I evaluated the range cadre's efficiency and organization, and Tyson saw how good my Marines were with marksmanship. Unfortunately, our regiment was on orders to deploy in three weeks, so we didn't have more time to train and correct deficiencies.

"They look good, Preston," Tyson admitted, nodding at the first group's initial qualification marks to come off the firing lanes.

"They worked really hard," I said, proud of how hardworking these marines were. "Are you nervous?" I asked without looking away from the firing line.

"Why would I be nervous?" Tyson scoffed. "When you lose, you just remember what you promised, Preston."

I scoffed. "I have never broken a promise, Gunnery Sergeant Johnson. You better hope your marines are better than mine, or you're in for a freezing night."

The CO walked through the range murmuring with our folks. There was a pause between firing lines, and he pulled my platoon in to speak with everyone. I hadn't planned on joining the huddle until suddenly, every set of eyes turned to look at me. Their expressions were so severe I needed to know what had happened.

I took a roundabout path to get close enough to hear the CO. "- I know this is asking a lot, so I won't ask for more than one shot from six Marines."

Six of my marines raised their hands. Everyone was so focused, but their eyes were dancing with a fight I knew very well. He was challenging them.

"Ok. You six, pull one shot. If Gunny Johnson can't get his wife after this, he's just not putting in the effort. Agreed?!?"

"OOOOH-RAH!" the marines sounded off.

I choked. *What the hell? How the hell did the commander know about our bet, he even recruited my own people to sabotage my win!*

"Sir!" I called out and watched his back stiffen. He knew he was caught.

"Staff Sergeant Preston."

"Are you conspiring with the other party?" I asked, raising

one eyebrow.

"Haven't you got other shit to do, Marine?" he huffed and walked off.

I couldn't help but laugh and shake my head. I followed behind my troops and started yelling. "Third Platoon, you better think really hard about where your loyalties lies. Semper Fi, Marines. Don't help cheaters!"

"It's community service to help our elders!" one of my guys yelled.

"WHO SAID THAT?!?" Tyson suddenly hollered. "SIR, GIVE THAT MARINE A THREE-DAY CHIT!"

My jaw dropped as I stared at the line of marines now cackling and guffawing about how shameless Gunnery Sergeant Johnson was to win a bet.

I had never felt so loved. These marines were family. They were Tyson's and my family. They wanted to see us succeed as much as we pushed for them to succeed. They wanted us to be happy as much as we hoped for their happiness.

"SHAMELESS!!" I yelled back, laughing and red-faced.

Tyson winked at me and returned to business mode as the next group prepared to walk onto the firing line. I helped keep my Marines moving through the lanes until the last group finally came off the line. As they prepared to ruck back to the unit, I remembered to grab the thermos and food from my pack for Ty.

"Gunny, where's your gear?" I asked.

He glanced over to where I stood and smiled. "Tower base."

I walked over to the range control tower and found his pack. I opened the top and put the food and snacks away. As I stood up, I felt a presence behind me. I didn't need to turn around to know who it was.

"What'd you pack me, baby girl?" he whispered when we were close enough.

"Hot soup, some fruit snacks, that jerky you like," I whispered back.

I watched him look around to make sure no one would see before he pulled me toward him for a kiss. "You should marry me, Katie," he whispered.

My breath caught in my throat, and I could feel my face heating up. "What did you just say?" My voice sounded hoarse as I fought back the emotional reaction.

Tyson pulled me into a hug and repeated it. "Katie Preston, I am hopelessly head over heels in love with you. From the first day we met, I knew I wanted to marry you. So... You need to take responsibility." He was so adamant.

I heard a whistle behind me and pulled back from Tyson's hold to see who had caught us. Tyson pulled my hands so I could face him again, but he was no longer standing before me. I felt like everything in the world had disappeared, except for the Marine kneeling before me.

"Staff Sergeant Katie Preston, will you take responsibility for this old man? You've been my work wife for nearly three years. Can we make it official? Will you marry me and be my lawful wife?" he asked, pulling a ring out of his pocket.

I had to blink back my tears because this was Tyson. "You cheating, bastard," I swore under my breath.

He laughed, and his eyes danced with joy. "Is that an *ooh-rah*?"

"Oooh-rah, Marine," I whispered breathily.

"WOOOOOHOOOOO!!!!!"

"OOOOH-RRAH, GUNNY!!!" All of the Marines were standing around us, cheering.

"No take backs, Preston." Tyson stood, pulled me into his arms, and kissed my temple. He knew me better than I knew myself most days. I couldn't imagine my life without him.

"I love you, Ty," I whispered against his chest. I felt his breath catch. It was the first time I had said the words to this remarkable man. I couldn't say why I held them back before today, but I just couldn't bring myself to tell him before this moment. I decided that he should hear them daily for the rest of our lives.

"Ok, love birds. Congratulations," the company commander came over to shake our hands along with our platoon commanders and the other marines. "Now get back to work, slackers!" He yelled, laughing.

We laughed and got back to business. I waved goodbye once I had all my gear on and began the ruck march back with my platoon. I looked down at the ring on my finger and smiled from ear to ear.

* * *

It had been a long week. Tyson had been busy on the range all week, and I rucked back to back 20km. My whole body felt like it had been worked over.

I lay in bed snuggled against his body, my head resting in the crook of his shoulder. My left arm and hand rested on his chest, and Tyson kept caressing my hand.

"Do you want a big wedding, baby girl?" Tyson asked.

I thought about it for a moment. Did I really want a big white dress and people staring at me? *No.*

"No. I like things that are simple, Ty."

He was quiet for a moment more before rolling to face me.

"Let's elope."

"What?" *Where was this coming from?*

"Let's run off next weekend and get married. You know they let married couples cohabitate now, right?" Tyson whispered, kissing my nose.

I lost it and started laughing. "Is that all you think about Tyson Johnson?" I smacked his chest.

He caught my hand and smiled at me. "I don't want to waste any more time waiting. Marry me, Katie. Let's get married next weekend. You, me, a few witnesses."

I stared at him in disbelief. He was serious. What would it change to be his wife? Truly. I loved this man more than I ever thought possible. We lived together and shared a bed every night. *Hell,* he had been my person longer than I was willing to admit.

"Ok. You've twisted my arm long enough. I will make an honest man of you, Tyson Johnson, and make you my lawful hubby, hubby," I sighed out the words.

Tyson didn't miss it. He jumped onto his knees and pinned me beneath him, whooping and laughing before smothering me with kisses. "Hot damn, I love you so freaking much, baby girl."

Needless to say, it was a long night between us, and I woke up the next morning sore and smiling from ear to ear. Tyson laid beside me, sound asleep, and I was near bursting with happiness. I needed to call Andie and tell her to drive down if she could.

I started to shuffle out of bed, but Tyson pulled me back against him. "I already told Andie. She's coming down with Jonas and the kids."

I turned to stare at his sleepy face smiling at me. "How?"

"I know you, baby girl. I got you," he grinned and kissed my forehead.

"When?" I asked.

"As soon as you said, 'yes,'" he chuckled.

"What?" I was staring at him with my jaw hanging wide open.

Tyson looked at my face and started laughing. His laughter, hoarse and deep in his chest, rumbled through his body and echoed into my own held against him. It was joy, elation, love, contentment, hope; everything warm and fuzzy.

"I knew you wouldn't want to deal with planning a wedding. You don't like big girlie fancy wedding dresses, let alone going to try on clothes. You like options, but you let me make decisions. So I gave you options, and I planned for both." Tyson explained while caressing my face and tucking my hair behind my ears.

My breath caught and came out a staggered exhalation as my eyes teared up. "How are you so perfect?" I croaked.

"You make me want to be the best man I can be, Katie. I'm only this amazing for you," he whispered back.

"I haven't even met your parents, Ty!" I gasped as the realization set in. Tyson loved his parents more than anyone else. He was a devoted son and still sent his parents money every month to help with their bills, even though they didn't need it. He was just a good man through and through.

"Don't worry about them, Katie. They will love you because I love you," he coaxed.

"Are you sure?" I asked.

"Positive. Annie and Tom Johnson will love you."

I didn't need any more convincing. Ty was it for me. He was my world. I didn't want to wait another week, let alone two more days. "Marry me on Saturday, Tyson Johnson. I don't want to wait."

Tyson smiled at me. Tears brimmed his eyes. "Ok, baby girl," he croaked out before kissing me until I was lost in his arms.

We were going to be late for work.

Chapter 16

Kai's Point of View

It's been almost three years since Jenny and I married. The shock of suddenly being a couple, let alone welcoming a child into the family, put strains on us that I never considered. From Heather's first week of life, Jenny became this obsessive and controlling parent.

She freaked out when I tried to take Heather to her six month appointment alone. I wasn't allowed to travel with our daughter without Jenny. At first, I chalked it up to first time parent jitters, but it never stopped.

Poor little Heather was prone to upper respiratory infections which had developed into pneumonia on three separate occasions before her second birthday. While other toddlers were starting to run, even if a bit clumsily, Heather was still shaky standing, as if her legs were jelly.

I brought it up to Jenny, and she told me that it was unfair to compare Heather to other kids. The pediatrician wasn't worried, so I shouldn't be either.

It wasn't that Heather wasn't developing normally. I had done my research, and it didn't add up to me. We fought, I don't know how many times, about Heather's health.

I made an appointment to take Heather to the doctor without Jenny, but Jenny found out and canceled the appointment. She kept assuring me that everything was taken care of, but, in all honesty, I couldn't shake the feeling that something was seriously wrong.

I spoke with my colleagues in the physical therapy office about what we could do at home to strengthen her legs. They had gotten so tired of listening to me worry that one of the doctors offered to give her a look. We did occupational therapy for kids and adults in the clinic. They trusted my gut enough to offer this favor.

Jenny wouldn't let me bring Heather to work with me. I would be alone with our child, and that could never happen. It finally worked out that Jenny came with Heather to pick me up from work because my car was in the shop.

While Jenny ran into the bathroom, I played with Heather in our pediatric occupational therapy suite. She loved the colors, and tried so hard to move from place to place, but her coordination just wasn't there. I disguised it as playtime so that Jenny would not suspect or become upset that I was having our daughter assessed.

It didn't take long. I watched Doctor Lee's expression change as he observed her. Finally, he came over with a few bright colored sponges and began playing with Heather. Her arms shook with a lack of strength. Her legs were not able to hold her up for more than ten to fifteen seconds before collapsing.

I heard Jenny come out of the bathroom, but before she could reach us, our daughter collapsed entirely in my arms. She wasn't breathing. Lee called an ambulance and we began attempting to resuscitate her. Jenny ran over and attempted to collect Heather into her arms, but I shoved her away.

Our child was dying. I had seen all of the signs, and let my wife convince me otherwise. I was so disgusted with myself, I couldn't breathe.

"Kai, what happened?!?!" Jenny screamed.

"Stay back!" I yelled, as I began chest compressions. "You can follow in the car, or you can go home. I don't care. But if you attempt to touch our child before we get to the hospital, I will have you arrested for endangering her life!" I growled.

Jenny's face paled. She stumbled back and stared at me in shock. It felt like I was looking at a stranger. How the hell had I let her take it this far?

The ambulance arrived with a quickness I couldn't believe, and we were enroute to the hospital within fifteen minutes of Heather's collapse. The emergency medical team had to intubate her to keep her breathing, as her body was no longer doing it, and I couldn't stop chest compressions or her heart would stop.

Somewhere between my office and the hospital my brain disconnected from my heart. I stopped looking at her as my baby girl in order to focus on helping her live.

The ambulance stopped and a doctor pulled open the back doors. Seeing me doing chest compressions, he jumped in and took over. "Are you the father?" he asked.

"Yes."

"Let's go, people!" he barked at the other medical staff as they began to unload the gurney. As soon as the wheels were on the ground, the doctor was on the gurney and continuing chest compressions while they wheeled my daughter into the hospital.

I was suddenly stopped by a nurse, "This is as far as you go, sir."

I started to protest, but one of the EMTs from the ambulance interrupted her on my behalf. "This is the father of the child. Come with me, Kai. I will take you to where they are treating Heather."

The nurse, to her credit, looked embarrassed and saddened. I had rendered chest compressions on my child for a total of thirty minutes. I followed the EMT like a mindless zombie, unable to talk.

"Blood type?" Someone asked.

"Ah, O positive, I think."

"Says here your wife told the EMT the baby is B negative?"

I didn't understand. "We're both O type blood. That's impossible," I corrected.

"Well, we'll type her out just to be certain. It's rare, but mutations can change a baby's blood type from that of the parents. What can you tell me about her symptoms before she collapsed?"

I began retelling everything that I had observed over the past year. I told the nurse about the conversations with Jenny, what she had relayed from the pediatrician... I even told them how Jenny stopped me from taking our daughter to the doctor's on several occasions.

"Sir, I need to ask. Is it possible that your wife could have harmed your child and attempted to cover it up?" the nurse asked.

I opened my mouth and nothing came out. If anyone had asked me before today about Jenny as a mother, I would have immediately defended her. She was always loving, doting, and protective of Heather. Now, however, I was sitting in a hospital wondering if this protected child would even live through the night.

I had no idea how much time had passed. I sat in a windowless corridor outside of the pediatric intensive care unit, across from an emergency operating room. The same EMTs had come and gone from the hospital a couple of times with other patients, but stopped to check on Heather's progress each time.

As the time grew on, I felt myself becoming more and more bitter. I messaged my parents and asked for the number of a lawyer. I couldn't tell you what possessed me, but I began proceedings to block Jenny from interfering with our child until she was out of the woods.

I requested an emergency protective order as the father, and had a nurse from the PICU forward all of the records to social services and the state police. The lawyer called back several hours later and informed me that the request had been approved, but I would need to appear in family court in two days to petition the case in person.

I agreed and hung up. The doors opened just then, and the doctor came out. I stood up and watched as he walked toward me. He looked as haggard as I felt at that moment.

"Well, I have good news and bad news," he started.

My knees buckled, and I dropped back into my seat. He took a seat next to me, and began to explain everything that I didn't know about my own daughter's health.

"The good news is that we have her stabilized. Your daughter was born with a genetic defect. I had them pull the records, and saw that you and your wife were informed of this and encouraged to get tested for any other genetic anomalies that could affect her prognosis."

I shook my head, "I was told everything was normal by the pediatrician."

This time the doctor furrowed his brows. "That's impossible. The pediatrician on file confirmed the newborn screening results at the child's two week appointment, and both parents signed."

My brain was a fog. "Fuck...." I exhaled. "May I see the test referral and results?" I asked.

The doctor pulled up the information on his tablet and showed me everything. Jenny had been taking Heather to a different pediatrician for her well-baby exams and lab work. I realized it wasn't my signature as the father on the consent forms. I felt bile coming up the back of my throat, and choked to keep from vomiting.

The doctor ran over to a nurse's station and grabbed a vomit bag, in which I promptly threw up. Two years. Jenny had kept me in the dark about Heather's health for two years by having someone else impersonate me.

"I don't understand, I thought this was treatable," I murmured, sipping some water that a nurse handed me. "I read about this when she was pregnant, this is completely treatable."

"It normally is, but the decision was made to pursue... What did she write? Oh, here it is, 'my husband and I do not believe in the practice of torturing children, and we have decided to pursue holistic measures for our daughter's treatment.'"

"I would have never agreed to that. This," I pointed at the doors to the PICU, "this is inhumane treatment of a child."

At that moment, everything that I had been holding back boiled up, and I sobbed. With my head in my hands, hunched over in a chair, I sobbed for my daughter. I was devastated that her chance at a normal life had been taken away by my wife, Heather's own mother. I was devastated that Jenny had denied me the right to have any say in our daughter's well-being.

"How-How bad is it?" I asked when I had composed myself enough.

He looked grim. "That's the bad news. I'm so sorry. You need to be prepared to say goodbye. If you have any family that you can call, you need to do that."

I choked back another sob. "Shit."

I did my best to call my parents. It was four o'clock in the morning. I couldn't tell them everything the doctor said on the phone. I said it was bad, and they needed to come in. If they saw Jenny, they weren't to give her any information.

Twelve hours later, I was standing next to Heather's bed holding her hand, and whispering to her how much I loved her, as they prepared to withdraw her life support. Despite our best efforts, she had gone too long without oxygen, and the neurologists confirmed there was zero brain activity.

She would never wake up. She would never look at me with those big blue eyes. I would never again get to hear her grunting laughter. I felt my parents put their hands on my shoulders to comfort me.

No parent should ever have to see their child die before them. I nodded to the doctor, and the life support was stopped with the push of a button. They had told me to expect a slow deterioration, but it didn't happen that way. As soon as the machines stopped forcing life into her, she died.

I dropped to my knees and cried, pulling my daughter to my chest. "I'm so sorry, baby. Daddy loves you so, so much. I'm so sorry," I whispered into her hair.

It was another three hours of paperwork with the hospital, a social worker from the state, and arranging for Heather's funeral. I hadn't slept in two days, and I felt like I was dead inside. All of my emotions were numb.

As we walked through the hospital's central waiting area, I heard a woman screaming, but didn't connect it to me until Jenny was standing in front of me. She had grabbed my shirt and was shaking me, while screaming, "Where's my baby? Where's my daughter!?!? WHY WON'T YOU LET ME SEE MY BABY?!?"

I smacked her. I smacked her across the cheek, and she stopped making noises. "You don't deserve to be a mother," I gritted out between clenched teeth. Jenny stood there staring at me without saying another word.

"How many times, Jenny? HUH? HOW MANY TIMES DID I TRY TO TAKE TO OUR CHILD TO THE FUCKING DOCTOR?!? HUH?? TELL ME!" I screamed in her face.

"YOU WANT TO SEE YOUR BABY? SHE'S IN THE MORGUE! *YOU* KILLED OUR CHILD! *YOU* KILLED *MY DAUGHTER, YOU HEARTLESS BITCH!*" My voice broke, and I began sobbing again. "You killed her, Jen. She could have been treated and lived a whole life, but you killed her."

I felt my mother pull me into her arms. Someone else moved Jenny away from me, but I couldn't be sure who it was. It couldn't get any worse. My world went black at that moment as my own body shut down.

Chapter 17

I felt numb when I opened my eyes. The past three days felt surreal, but I knew that everything had happened. Social services had demanded an autopsy to confirm Heather's cause of death, because of Dr. Lee's statement to the EMTs after she collapsed. It made me sick to my stomach.

I rolled out of bed and ran to the bathroom, dry heaving over the toilet. There was nothing by bile left in my stomach, and I was sure even that had been emptied out. I rested my head on my arm as I slumped over the porcelain. The court hearing for the protective order was today, not that it mattered, but the social services' appointed case worker was presenting the unofficial autopsy results.

The original hearing should have been four days ago, but they postponed it for the results. I hadn't spoken with Jenny since the hospital. Her messages all went to my old phone that my lawyer held as evidence. My brother got me a new phone with a new number, so I wouldn't have to deal with her.

I gave the lawyer every penny I had in savings to file for immediate dissolution of our marriage following today's proceedings. There was nothing she could say that would change how much I hated her.

"Kai?" my mother called from outside the bathroom. "Can I get you anything?"

I shook my head. There was nothing she or anyone else could ever give me that would make this better. "No," I barked.

Standing up, I started the shower. I needed to keep moving forward. I needed to get past today. I choked back another sob, as I stepped into the shower. All I could see was Heather when I closed my eyes, and hear Jenny's lies when I tried to sleep. I was a fucking mess.

Thank god for my family, or I would have shot myself already. I didn't want to live like this. I couldn't. It hurt so fucking much. I failed to protect my daughter. As a health professional, I failed to advocate for her health. I hated myself.

I didn't know what I was expecting from this hearing, but it felt more like a mediation than an actual hearing. My lawyer and I sat at one side of a conference table, with my family seated behind us. Across the table were Jenny, her lawyer and two other men. One looked familiar, but I couldn't place where I knew him from. The second was suited up and obviously a lawyer.

When the judge came in, her face looked grim. Behind her was the social worker, Dr. Lee, and the doctor from the hospital. They nodded politely at me and took seats along the wall where my family was seated. It occurred to me that none of Jenny's family had shown up to support her. I sneered at her before turning to face the judge.

"Mr Kai Rayburn?" the judge asked, looking at me.

"Yes, your honor," I responded.

"Mrs Jenny Rayburn?" she asked, looking at Jenny.

"Yes, your honor," she whispered.

"I have the two primary parties to this case seated at my table, may I ask who you are, Sir, and why are you here?" the judge stared down the man next to Jenny.

Before he could speak, his lawyer stood up, "Your honor, my client is Timothy Moreland, the father of the deceased child."

I jerked to stand up and saw Jenny flinched, like I would ever lay my hands on her.

"Your honor! This is outrageous!" My lawyer shouted.

Timothy's lawyer smiled politely, "Your honor, these are the paternity test results conducted at the child's two week well baby check, at which my client was present as the father."

I felt the bile rising in my stomach. I was a fucking green hat wearing idiot. "You are the cruelest fucking woman I have ever met in my life," I whispered, staring Jenny in the eyes.

"Your honor, I want to file a criminal complaint for fraud against my estranged wife," I stated calmly.

My lawyer patted my hand and passed the red folder down to the judge. "Your honor, attached are the appointment notes for every well-baby check of Heather Rayburn. As you can see clearly, *Mrs. Rayburn*, clearly wrote the name of the child's father as my client, Kai Rayburn. The insurance was billed to my client's plan, as you can see here," he paused, passing another dossier to the lawyer.

The judge reviewed the two files, then placed them in the pile with the stack she had carried into the room. "Clear the gallery," she ordered the bailiff.

The uniformed man by the door began ushering my family and the others out of the room. Before the door closed, she looked at Timothy and his lawyer, "That includes you. Get out."

Timothy looked like he wanted to say something, but was stopped by his lawyer. When the door closed the judge was quiet for a moment. "I have seen all that I need to see in this matter. Council, are your clients prepared to hear my findings?"

My lawyer looked at me and I nodded, "Yes, your honor."

He had warned me that something like this would happen. It was not uncommon for a female judge to side with a mother without hearing the father's side of the story.

Jenny's lawyer answered for her as well, looking more hopeful than I was. "She is, your honor."

"Quite frankly, I don't even know where to begin with this onion. Mrs Rayburn, you knowingly went against medical advice to the detriment of your child's health. You withheld the paternity of the child from your legal husband, and the listed father of the child according to state vital statistics records. You fraudulently presented another man as your husband, and allowed him to sign as your husband for medical decisions pertaining to the child, Heather Rayburn.

"In addition, when your legal husband, Mr Kai Rayburn attempted to seek treatment for the child, you blocked his every effort by use of psychological abuse, emotional blackmail, and physical barriers," the judge stopped when Jenny's lawyer interrupted her.

"Objection, your honor. That is speculative hearsay," he opined.

The judge slid a file down to Jenny's lawyer. "This is a transcript of messages between the Rayburns for the past two years and three months. Mr Rayburn relinquished his mobile device to law enforcement as evidence in the wrongful death of his child. Forensics confirmed the messages from 'Wife,' originated from your client's device."

Jenny and her lawyer flipped through the records. Her face paled significantly as they neared the last page. I had no idea what she had sent in the last few weeks, and I didn't care.

"My decision is for the plaintiff, Mr. Kai Rayburn. I am upholding the no contact order, and ordering Mrs Rayburn to 10 days in holding for violation of the no contact order she received eight days ago. In the matter of dissolution of the marriage, I am finding for the plaintiff, or the condition of irreconcilable differences."

She went on to say that she would be forwarding everything to the district attorney's office for criminal charges against Jenny and Timothy. I had to serve 20 hours of anger management training for slapping Jenny in the hospital. I didn't want to sit in that room any more. I was struggling to breathe, and I needed to get away from here.

"Your honor, brief recess?" my lawyer asked as I bolted out of my seat.

"Yes, we'll reconvene in…thirty?" she asked.

"Yes, thank-"

I didn't hear the rest, because I was stumbling out the door. I needed to breathe. I was having a panic attack. I felt two arms grab me, and I swung to fight them off.

My brother's voice immediately filled my ears, "I got you, bro. Let it out. I got you."

I hugged him and the flood gates just broke. I sobbed. I sobbed for the woman who betrayed me. I sobbed for the child I thought was mine. I sobbed for myself, the broken man who was duped, lied to, used, and betrayed by the person closest to him. I let it all out.

I was officially a broken man. I had nothing left in me when I returned to the courtroom. My eyes were so puffy from crying, I could barely see. I felt empty at that moment. I didn't hear any of the remaining judgments. I didn't listen to anything that Jenny or her lawyer had to say.

It didn't matter to me anymore. Heather was never my child. Jenny only married me to raise another man's child. She had never been faithful. She had never been in love with me. The past three years were all in my head. I might as well have imagined all of it.

"Kai," my lawyer broke through my thoughts.

"They want to seal these records. Do you agree?" he asked calmly.

"No. I do not concur. I want them publicly available, according to state law in the matter of divorce proceedings," I deadpanned.

"Kai," Jenny spoke up.

I couldn't look at her.

"Kai, please. Our personal grievances shouldn't be put out for the whole county to read. I know I hurt you, but-"

"Shut your mouth." I didn't yell. I didn't growl. My voice was quiet and calm because I had no emotion left. "You cheated. You used me. You killed a child through gross negligence and selfishness. You defrauded my insurance and aided in another person committing identity theft. You don't get to decide what I do or don't do anymore. You don't get to tell me, sorry, or make up stories for your circle of friends. If they choose to seal the court records, I'll buy a two page spread in the Sunday Post and print my copies of everything. So shut up.

"What's the longest I can keep the no contact order," I turned to ask the judge.

"Two years," she responded.

"What do I need to file criminal charges?" I asked next, making Jenny gasp.

"The matter has already been turned over to law enforcement," the judge explained.

"What about insurance fraud?" I asked.

"The charges for the medical appointment billing were forwarded as well," the judge confirmed.

"I understand that, but she totaled our car a year ago, claiming that she was the driver but her injuries were consistent with her as a passenger. I would like that investigated as well, seeing as how my insurance was billed to cover medical expenses for my then wife and *'her friend.'*"

"Your lawyer can escort you down to the police desk on the first floor to make a report," she informed me.

"Thank you, your honor."

"I'd offer you a beer, but I don't want to see you spiral again, dude," Bradley said, sitting next to me in my parents' backyard two days later.

Heather's funeral was today. Jenny was not allowed to attend because of the restraining order against her. I didn't need to do anything about Timothy because he was arrested for identity theft and a few other unrelated warrants.

It was a simple graveside service. She was buried with Jenny's maternal great grandmother. I may hate Jenny, but her family had been good to me while we were together. Jenny's parents paid the cost of having her name engraved on the family stone with a small angel next to her name.

I didn't have any tears left to cry. I could only replay every interaction with the child I thought was mine. She was loved and happy while I had her. It was the only thing I could hold on to.

Now, I was sitting with my own family and coming to terms with the loss of everything I thought I had in my life. I didn't have a loving wife. I didn't have a daughter. I wasn't a family man.

I was a ship adrift in life, and no idea how the hell I had gotten here. I wasn't even thirty and my life had imploded.

"I think one beer will be okay," I replied to Bradley.

He nodded and passed me a nonalcoholic drink. I stared down at the labeling. "You're a dick."

He nodded, taking a swig of his beer. "Don't feel bad. No one is drinking if you're not."

That's when I realized that Bradley and everyone else were drinking nonalcoholic beers or sparkling grape cider. I felt a smirk twitching at my mouth. "Thank you."

"You don't ever need to thank me for being your friend, Kai. You're like my brother; only more dysfunctional so it makes me feel superior being around you," Bradley continued in his platitudes disguised as insults. This was Bradley.

I couldn't help the laugh that erupted out of me. "Dude, you're such an asshole," I wheezed, laughing. Bradley smiled and tipped his bottle to me. "Thank you," I whispered when I could stop laughing.

"No 'thanks' between friends," he replied and gave me a hug.

I would move forward from this too.

Chapter 18

Katie's Point of View
knock knock
"Give me a second. I think the pizza guy is here. Shit! Ty is going to call any minute! I will see you when you get here, Andie!" I hung and ran through the apartment looking for my wallet.

* * *

"Hey, Ty, your dad's trying to call you," I said passing the phone as he came into our bedroom.

He grabbed the phone and answered, "Hey, pop. What's going on?" Ty leaned over and gave me a quick kiss on the forehead before walking out of the room.

I went into the bathroom and stripped down. We were going to the Justice of the Peace tomorrow, and I wanted to be cleaned and shaven for our wedding night.

I laid back in the tub to soak, listening to bits and pieces of Ty's conversation with his folks as he paced outside of the bathroom.

"You don't even have to ask."

"-No, don't even worry about me, pop. Ma comes first-"

"No. No, I get it. I do. Let me know if you need any help-"

"Ok. Give ma a kiss and hug from us grunts."

"Ok. Love you too, pop."

I heard the sound of clothes dropping to the floor and peeked from the tub to see Tyson in all of his naked glory. I couldn't help but giggle and scoot forward so that he could climb in behind me.

"Everything okay?" I asked him.

"Just perfect," he sighed as I leaned my back against his chest.

"How do you want to spend your last night as a free man?" I asked him as his hands began caressing my arms.

"The same way I plan to spend the next fifty years.... Buried so deep inside of my woman, she can't see straight," he whispered against my hair.

I couldn't help but giggle. "What if she has plans for her last night as a free woman? There are wild oats to be sown!"

Tyson's arms wrapped around me and he growled, the sound vibrating through my back to my chest. "Are you messing with me, baby girl? You think I won't put you over my knee and spank your behind for messing with me?"

I laughed, wanting to keep egging him on. "But there's this man I want to use as I see fit for one night, before we are married. You wouldn't allow me to do that?" I ask.

"Tell me about this man, and I will consider it."

"He's been after me for years, to be honest. I used him as a personal trainer and masseuse a while back, and I never could shake the memory of his hands on my body," I confessed.

Tyson's hands began to wash my arms and chest. "That so?"

"Mmmm. Yes." I mumbled, enjoying the feeling of his hands caressing and massaging my breasts.

"So he was your trainer?" he asked.

"Mmmm. Never had anyone make me as wet as he did... Sweaty, hot...." I sighed.

I felt his chest rumble as he chuckled. "Tell you what. How about you let me get you ready and then if you still feel like you need to sow your oats, I'll make sure the field is plowed."

I started laughing. "You can't even pretend to be jealous?"

"Maybe if you hadn't told me that no one makes you cum like I do." His voice was husky and low as he peppered kisses on my neck.

* * *

I opened the door, fumbling through my bag to my wallet. "How much do I owe you again?" I asked, never looking up.

"Staff Sergeant Johnson?"

* * *

"Hello, handsome," I cooed breathily into the phone.

"Jesus, Katie. You can't answer the phone like that," Ty grumbled, his voice sounded deep and husky. "You get me in a kind of way and it's uncomfortable."

I giggled. "I'm so sorry, Gunny. I thought you were my husband calling. I guess I got all excited."

"Say it again," his deep voice urged me.

"Say what?" I asked, playing stupid.

"Don't make me beg, baby girl. Say it again," he whined.

"What did you want to hear, Gunny? That I was sitting here all alone, waiting for my man to call me? That I was getting worked up thinking about talking with my husband who is deployed?"

"Fuck, baby girl. Let me see you. I need to see you, Katie. Turn on your camera," his voice was a growl as he begged.

I couldn't help but chuckle as I crawled into our bed, and set my phone on his nightstand before turning on the video. "This what you wanted to see, hubby?" I asked as I stretched out on the bed.

"When are you getting here, wifey?" he asked, his eyes raking over my body. "I can't stand sleeping alone. I need you," he confessed as he loosened his belt.

"I'll be there in five days," I answered, shifting closer to the phone. "That your new hooch?" I asked, gesturing to the new quad container room he was in.

"This is OUR hooch, as soon as you get your sweet ass on this side of the pond," he growled again, and gestured around him.

I couldn't help but laugh. No one saw this side of Tyson except me. This man was serious and stoic with everyone, but a needy whipped mess with me. "You are so whipped, Tyson Johnson." I tsked.

"Hell, yeah I am. Have you seen how smoking hot my wife is? I would crawl through regimental headquarters barking like a true devil dog if she told me to!" He swore, shaking his head in earnest.

I laughed so hard I had tears in my eyes. "I love you so much," I confessed.

"I love you so much, it hurts," Ty whispered back.

I bit my lip hearing him tell me he loved me. "Show me how much you miss me," I whispered back.

Tyson smirked and then took off the t-shirt he was wearing. Jesus, he was getting so cut. I memorized every inch of the man's body the night before he left with my tongue and lips. The 'V' cut in his abs showed how hard he had been working out since he got in country.

He did not miss my breath catching or the lustful look I was giving him through the camera. He chuckled, and it melted my panties. This was the deep laugh that was like a calling on my very soul, demanding I submitted and did what I was told.

165

"You got a little something on your chin," he told me, implying that I was drooling over him.

"If I were there it would be your nuts, wiping it away instead of my hand," I retorted.

* * *

"Staff Sergeant Katie Johnson?"

* * *

"GUNNY!!" my platoon commander yelled from his office.

"Gunny deployed," one of the marines responded back.

"Gunnery Sergeant!" he hollered again.

"Sir! Gunny deployed last week!" another marine informed him.

"Gunnery Sergeant Johnson, get your ass in here!" he hollered.

I ran into the office, swearing. *"Sir. Ty is deployed. What are you fussing and hollering for him for?"*

The man jumped up, and then bear-hugged me. *"You were selected, GUNNY!"*

I was confused for a second before it clicked. *"No shit?!?!"* I squealed.

"No, shit! List just posted! Congratulations, Gunnery Sergeant Katie Johnson!"

"Hell yeah, GUNNY!" our marines congratulated me.

I squealed again. *"Oh my goodness! I can't wait to tell Tyson tonight!"*

They all congratulated my selection for promotion before we started talking about operations. This MEU was originally a security force mission, but, after earthquakes rocked Syria, Turkey

166

and parts of Iraq, it became a humanitarian relief mission.

The runway of the airport that Tyson's folks had landed on three weeks ago, was now a refugee camp for those displaced due to the destruction of so many buildings.

The earthquakes were the reason that my flight was delayed. They couldn't risk getting us there until the aftershocks had died down, due to the mountainous terrain.

"Go. Your gear is already on the pallet for tomorrow's flight, I'll see you here at 0900!" The acting commander dismissed me.

"Ok. Wait! Do you want me here early for manifest, sir?" I asked pausing before I ran out the door.

He laughed. "Be here at 0900. That's early enough. If our time changes, I'll send someone to pick you up."

I smiled. "Thank you, sir. I appreciate you!"

"Leave already! Everyone else who is deploying tomorrow is already gone for the day!" he yelled at me as he returned to his desk.

I didn't wait around to be told again and ran out of the building. I jumped in Ty's truck and headed home. Tomorrow, I would be on a flight to the Middle East and Ty. I couldn't wait!

* * *

knock knock

"Andie, you are the first person I called!" I squealed.

I listened to her cheer and congratulated me on the other end of the line.

"No, I am telling him tonight when he calls. How far out are you?"

She described a few landmarks and I knew exactly where she was.

"You're only about 45 minutes out. I ordered a pizza, so it'll still be hot by the time you get here." I told her as I paced through my apartment.

Andie was coming to take the keys to the apartment and then she and Jonas were going to take my car back with them and leave it with my folks. Ty and I had both left Andie powers of attorney to handle our apartment and our vehicles while we were deployed.

knock knock

"Give me a second. I think the pizza guy is here," my eyes wandered over to see what time it was. "Shit! Ty is going to call any minute! I will see you when you get here, Andie!" I hung and ran through the apartment looking for my wallet. I was fumbling through my bag to my wallet when I opened the door. "How much do I owe you again?" I asked, never looking up.

"Staff Sergeant Johnson?"

"Yep. You guys got here fast!" I replied without looking up as I finally found my wallet.

"Staff Sergeant Katie Johnson?"

"How much did I owe you, I missed it?" I asked, finally looking up to see two Marines standing outside my door.

The Sergeant Major looked at me and repeated his question, "Staff Sergeant Katie Johnson? Wife of Marine Gunnery Sergeant Tyson Johnson?"

My brain didn't understand what was going on. "Did our chock get moved up, Sergeant Major? Shit, I am so sorry. I have been on the phone with my best friend. I didn't even realize the unit was trying to contact-"

My words dropped off. The two men before me were in

168

their Alphas, hats in their hands. The Sergeant Major who had been talking to me, watched my face, recognition slowly dawning on me. The second marine beside him was a Major, a chaplain more specifically.

"Staff Sergeant Johnson, may we come in for this?" the Sergeant Major asked.

I don't remember walking into my apartment or sitting on the sofa.

"The Commandant of the Marine Corps has entrusted me to express his deep regret that your husband, Tyson Johnson died in Kazkheli, Turkey on 13 February. Gunnery Sergeant Johnson's platoon was helping a family free three trapped children from a partially collapsed structure. An aftershock caused the building to collapse as they were about to exit to safety. Gunnery Sergeant Johnson pushed his marines and the civilians from harm's way, but sustained fatal injuries when the structure collapsed behind him. The commandant extends his deepest sympathy to you and your family in your loss."

I sat staring at my phone. "No, I just talked to him. We talked yesterday. He's going to call any minute."

"Katie, is there anyone we can call for you?" the chaplain asked, seated beside me on the sofa.

"I -" my voice choked.

The Sergeant Major said something to the Chaplain and left the apartment. "Katie, I know this is a lot. Sergeant Major Gray is going out to meet with Master Gunnery Marie Gonzalez. She's going to be your CAO. Is it ok if she comes in and talks with us?" he asked calmly.

"I-" my words stopped as a realization dawned on me. "Oh my god! Ty's parents! They don't even know we got married!

169

Have you told them? Do they know?"

I was shaking and as my mind reeled with the thought of his parents finding out that not only had their son died, but he was married to a woman they knew nothing about.

I heard more voices talking, but I couldn't hear them. My ears were ringing.

"Katie?"

Andie. I heard Andie's voice, and my knees buckled. She was here. The Marines were still in my apartment. I wasn't dreaming. My heart shattered and the most gut wrenching wail left my body. "No. No. God, no."

I sobbed in a ball on the floor. My soulmate. The love of my life was gone. Tyson left me alone. Everything around me ceased to exist in my sorrow. My chest felt tight, and I couldn't breathe.

"I - I - I…. No," I stuttered repeatedly as arms wrapped around me. "No. *Not Ty*, Andie."

I don't know how long I lay in Andie's arms sobbing. At some point the Sergeant Major and the Chaplain left, and it was just Andie and this Master Gunnery Sergeant assigned as the casualty assistance officer to a widow.

I started to retch, but I couldn't move from the ball I made on the floor. Andie pulled my hair back and a small waste basket was put in front of me as I retched again and threw up stomach bile.

"I've got you. I'm not leaving you, Katiedid," Andie's voice cooed as she continued rubbing my back.

When the retching turned dry-heaving finally stopped, I collapsed on the floor. *He was my sun. Without him I would wither and die. If Tyson wasn't in this world, I didn't want to live it in either.*

Chapter 19

Kai's Point of View

I demonstrated the stretching motion for the patient in front of me. "Just like that, Grace," I encouraged her.

Grace rewarded me with a million dollar smile. She was by far one of my favorite patients since I started working with this clinic.

"I need a new therapist!" she exclaimed, continuing to repeat the stretching motions with the pulleys. "I can't concentrate with your flirting and strutting in front of me."

I barked out a laugh. I loved this woman. Grace was almost 90, and just as sharp as any one I knew at my own age. She was recovering like a champ from an accident that limited the mobility of her shoulder.

"Grace, I think you have that all wrong!" I chuckled. "These men are going crazy in here with you doing all these Jane Fonda poses."

Grace peeked at several of the older men working through their own therapy sessions. She nodded slightly, "Can't seem too available. I have to make them work for it, you know."

She changed arms and then whispered quietly, "If they think a young stud like you has my eye, they'll try harder to impress me."

I staggered back with my hand on my heart like she had just wounded me. "Are you using me, Grace?"

She giggled like a young girl. "You are shameless, Dr. Rayburn!"

I laughed with her and we continued her stretches before I set her up on the ice massage. "So which one has your eye? Do you need me to be your wingman, Grace?" I asked her as she was sitting with her head back in a chair.

She didn't even open her eyes, and just smirked. "Young man, if I ever get to a point that I need a young man like you to help me, I have lost the game," she confessed, chuckling.

I sat with my mouth agape.

Grace opened her eyes and looked at me, then started laughing. "Don't look so offended. You have done enough. I have two dates this weekend thanks to you," she admitted, wiggling her eyebrows.

My face actually flushed. "Holy sh-"

Grace's eyebrows shot up. "Don't you swear at me!" she scolded.

I could feel the heat in my cheeks. She actually made me blush! "Grace, you *minx!*" I whispered out.

She laughed. She had an infectious laugh that I enjoyed. She made me hope for my own future. "What's your secret?" I asked her, smiling.

When she finally stopped laughing, she sat quietly for a moment with a gentle smile on her lips. "When I married Henry, I knew he wasn't the love of my life. We met when I was 19, but I just knew. I met the love of my life when I was 15, but walked away from him. Henry was mine for thirty years, and filled my youth with so much joy and stability, I thought it was what I needed."

She had never shared stories about her youth before. I couldn't help but ask, "Did Henry pass away?"

Grace snorted, "Not then. The pig got caught cheating with his secretary and we divorced. Made me realize that one-sided love was not enough," her smile was sad now.

"I'm sorry," I apologized quietly. "I didn't mean to pry."

Grace shook her head. "Don't apologize. I have spent the last forty years loving myself. It's been the greatest romance story, filled with wild nights and passionate weekends," she winked.

My face heated up again.

"When I learned to love myself, the love of my life walked through the door. Klaus and I were together for three decades before he passed two years ago. We never married, but I never doubted his devotion to me," she smiled brightly.

"So don't give up hope. She's out there. The love of your life is waiting for you to get your shit together."

My jaw dropped open. "Grace! Did you just curse?"

She laughed and her eyes danced with mischief. "Young man, I am a lady first. Never curse in front of a lady. And if you are lucky enough to get a lady's attention, don't muck it up!" she said seriously, patting my hand as I walked with her to the front door of the clinic.

As she was about to leave, I remembered that she never told me who she was going out with.

"Grace, you never told me who-"

She turned and winked at me before going out the door. "A lady never kisses and tells!"

For the fourth time today, Grace left me speechless. I chuckled and turned to head back into the clinic. Grace was my last patient of the day, and I needed to finish up my charts before heading home.

"Kai," one of the other physios called as I walked by.

"What's up, doc?" I asked, mimicking Bugs Bunny.

Doctor Jones shook his head. "I am going to pretend you didn't just say that."

I just chuckled and leaned against the door to his office. "Sorry, I couldn't help it. Did you need anything?" I asked.

Jones shook his head. "I was just wondering if you had heard anything back yet?"

This time I shook my head. "Not yet. Should be this week though," I said, showing him my crossed fingers.

He smiled back at me. "You'll get it. You're too good to be bypassed," he encouraged me.

"Here's hoping," I said before walking to my desk and the stack of patient journals waiting to be updated.

* * *

"What are your plans tonight?" Bradley asked as I stepped out of the office. I knew he was calling to get me on some blind date his wife Amy had set up.

"B, I am not going on a date," I huffed, as my ass dropped into my car. "I logged 10 hours today, 10 yesterday, and tomorrow I work from eight to five, and then I have classes with the other PTA. Unless you are offering to feed me and let me sleep, I am not available." I explained.

Bradley laughed. "No strings. Amy made lasagna and garlic bread, and the guest room is set up. We didn't know if you had gotten your results yet."

I couldn't help but smile. "No. Nothing yet."

"Well then this will either be a celebratory dinner or your

pity party," he deadpanned. "Results will be posted today, right?"

I chuckled. "Yeah. It's today. Let me run home and get cleaned up. I can be there in about an hour, hour and a half?

I waited while Bradley relayed information to Amy.

"She said make it an hour and you have a hot meal. Hour and a half, you may be eating burnt toast," he laughed.

I couldn't help but chuckle. Amy may have thought we were laughing at her threat, but it was more that we both knew she couldn't stand to let food burn.

"Ok. I'll be quick," I promised and hung up as I drove home.

It felt good to have everyone's support. I thought they would be more critical when I told them I had applied for a doctoral program in Physical Therapy.

It was another three years of schooling, and I would have to foot the entirety of this bill myself. Thankfully, my living expenses were fairly low, so I had saved up quite a bit in the last few months.

In April, my grandmother asked me to take over her house after she moved into an assisted living community. That meant no rent or mortgage, just upkeep and utilities. I tried to decline, but she insisted.

Then there was the restitution from the suit against Jenny and the douche for. The State pursued felony fraud charges against Jenny and her douche boyfriend after our divorce was finalized. I was shocked when I received a check for twenty thousand dollars. My lawyer had accepted settlement money from the doctor's office who *"treated"* Heather. He cleared all of the medical, funeral, and burial expenses, and zeroed out what I owed for his services.

The money was restitution for the wrongful death of

my acknowledged child. The pediatrician's office hadn't followed proper protocols, or something like that. It made me sick to receive it. Still made me sick to think about it.

My parents had advised me to set the money aside, and forget about it. When I applied for the program, Val suggested that I use the money toward my tuition. I started to argue against it, but then she made a counter argument that made me rethink things.

Val thought I should treat the funds as a grant from Heather. I could use this portion of settlement money to fund my education, and, in return, donate time to treat the elderly and children and adults with congenital defects or birth defects. In this way, that money would enable me to help those most at risk of being overlooked.

I talked to my bosses, Doctors Lee and Jones. They were thrilled when I told them what my plan was, and began adjusting my patients accordingly. It was how I came to meet Grace, and, to be honest, provided me the final push needed to move forward.

I was in and out of my house in under twenty minutes. Given the travel time between work, home, and Bradley's place; I made it to their door in just under fifty-seven minutes.

Amy smiled from ear to ear when she saw me. "You made it just in time!" she said, giving me a hug and pulling me in the door.

I heard several voices coming from the dining room, and couldn't help but laugh when I saw the mess. Bradley was next to his and Amy's daughter, Hannah. On the other side of the table were Lacy, her wife Val, and their newly adopted son Xavier.

Xavier and Hannah looked like they were competing to see who could wear the most red sauce. Val and Lacy were embracing the chaos, and Bradley was losing the fight against his two year old.

"Su-pize!" Xavier yelled when he noticed me. His hands shot up in the air and sauce went flying.

I knew I was smiling ear to ear. These were the people nearest and dearest to my heart. "Hey buddy!" I greeted him back.

These were my best friends and my life lines when I didn't want to live for myself. They kept me going, and helped me through the never-ending grief. It only made sense that they would be with me to celebrate a victory too.

"Is there anything left?" I asked, as I sat down in a empty seat next to Bradley. Amy and Bradley always ate with Hannah seated between them. Didn't matter where they sat at the table. On any other day, I would have given everyone hugs, but tonight I could only shake my head at the messes they were wearing.

"Don't worry, Kai. There's plenty of food for us. Kiddos are eating pasta noodles," Amy explained as she sat down.

"When do the results get posted?" Val asked.

I gave a polite shrug. "I just know they will notify the applicants today before midnight."

Lacy's eyebrows shot up. "Midnight?!? Why the hell is it so damn late?" she asked, covering Xavier's ears.

Amy answered before I could. "They have applicants from both coasts. It's some weird timed thing about making sure their call center is closed so no one can call to complain."

I had never heard that and furrowed my brows. "Seriously?" I asked.

Amy shook her head, "I have no idea. But it sounds more professional than, 'Because they forget to send the email before leaving work.'"

There was a second or two of silence before Bradley, Val, and I started laughing. Amy's super power was the ability to spit out an answer to any question or problem, and it was plausible every single time.

We sat around talking until the kids were done eating and cleaned up. Once Hannah was down for the night, and Xavier passed out on the sofa, the adults could eat and drink a couple of beers.

I hadn't planned on drinking anything but they convinced me to stay over. Val and Lacy had already planned to take the guest room, so Amy had prepared blankets for me to crash on the sofa.

"You all really kept this whole plan hush hush," I complimented as we finished eating.

Bradley didn't say a word. Val and Lacy looked down at their empty plates awkwardly. Amy was the only one who laughed.

"Tell him, babe," she giggled.

Bradley looked pained. "Can't we just let this one go?" he whispered to her.

Amy's face took on the most sinister smile I had ever seen her make. Her top lip arched on one side as one eyebrow also raised. "Just this one?" she asked sweetly, turning her attention from her husband to Val and Lacy.

Lacy dropped her head on Val's shoulder, pretending to hide. While Val bit both of her lips.

"Hmm?" Amy asked, taking a sip of her beer.

Bradley finally dropped his head in resignation or surrender. "No."

I watched this power play, and I knew exactly what had happened. I started laughing. "You blabber mouths didn't remember, did you?" I asked them.

Amy immediately started laughing with me.

"Fuckers!" I chided them.

"To be fair-" Lacy started, but was cut off when Val put a hand over her mouth.

"Accept your fate," Val advised.

"They knew it was this week, Kai. I just couldn't trust them not to run their mouths," Amy explained.

"I figured."

"I told Bradley we needed a quiet night home, so he left work early. Lacy and Val were invited for a girls' night, and I told them Bradley would babysit if Val volunteered as a designated driver," Amy continued.

"She confiscated our phones when we got here!" Lacy blurted out after pulling Val's hand away.

Val shook her head laughing, "That doesn't help your case, babe."

"How is that?" Lacy asked.

I couldn't stop laughing at this point. "You are a big mouth, Lacy! You would have called or texted me as soon as you figured it out."

"I can too keep a secret!" Lacy exclaimed, looking indignant.

At this point Bradley was happy to keep the attention on someone else. "When? Name one time you have kept a secret," he demanded, wiping his mouth with his napkin.

Lacy looked around the table like she was looking for a life line. "I haven't told anyone about Amy being pregnant!" she

179

gloated.

Several things suddenly happened at once. Amy, who was drinking a glass of water, sprayed it back out of her mouth. Bradley nearly dropped his beer, but caught it as the bottle bounced on the table. Val dropped her head in her hands to hide her face.

I took all of this in. Amy and Bradley were expecting baby number two, and Bradley had no idea yet. Val didn't even know, which was, to Lacy's credit, an amazing feat.

"Um... Congrats?" I offered.

"You're pregnant?" Bradley asked, eyeing his wife. "When?"

Amy's face blushed red. She looked so shy looking back at her husband. "Yesterday. The doctor confirmed it yesterday. I wanted to tell you tonight after dinner. I was saving it for the good in case of bad news," she explained to him in the sweetest, softest voice.

"Get out," Bradley said, quietly never looking away from his wife.

I grabbed my beer and ran out of the room with Lacy and Val scurrying behind me.

"You are SUCH a blabbermouth!" I barked out laughing when we were outside in the back garden.

Lacy looked so ashamed, while Val was doing her best to not laugh at her wife's blunder. We sat there for a half hour before Bradley and Amy joined us.

Bradley held Amy in his arms and smiled. "WE'RE HAVING A BABY!" whisper-yelled so as not to wake the children or disturb the neighbors.

As I stood to congratulate them, my phone pinged. I opened up the message and just stared.

"Is everything okay?" Val asked.

"Did someone die?" Lacy asked.

Bradley scowled at Lacy, "Don't tempt me."

"Kai?"

"I got in."

Chapter 20

Katie's Point of View

"No! We-we just got married!" I cried.

"Sir, tell them they are wrong! Tell them!" I shouted at my platoon leader.

His lips trembled as he held back his own sorrow. "Pres-I'm so sorry-"

I didn't want to hear their apologies. "NO! NOOO! Not him! We just got married! I haven't even met his parents! Do they know? Do they hate me?" I sobbed.

"They know, Gunny," Marie whispered beside me.

Oh god. "What-What do I do?" I cried, my voice cracking and breaking.

I couldn't breathe. I grabbed at my chest and struggled to breathe as the world around me went dark. Again.

* * *

"READY.........AIM.........FIRE!"

Boom* The volley of rifle fire filled the air.

"READY.........AIM.........FIRE!"

Boom again, seven rifles fired in synchrony.*

"READY.........AIM.........FIRE!"

Boom

"Present, ARMS!"

brrrr-brr-brrrrrr

The sound of Taps played, the somber whine of the bugle echoing across the cemetery where Tyson was laid to rest. I sat awkwardly at the grave, never taking my eyes away from the casket that was slowly lowered into the ground. I didn't even register the man who presented the folded flag to me.

Ty's parents hated me. His mom couldn't stand to be in the same room as me. His dad declined any thought of hosting anything at their home, and closed the car door in my face when the funeral was over.

Tyson died three weeks ago today, and was buried in the middle of the country in the same cemetery as his grandparents. I couldn't even visit his grave when I missed him.

"Katie? Come out and eat," my sister called through the bathroom door of my apartment.

"I'm fine," I said from my position in the bathtub. I sat there with my head leaned back, recalling the times Ty and I sat right here and planned our futures together.

"Katie, do you want to come home," she asked.

"I am home."

"Katie, you need to get help. You need to grieve."

I snorted and began coming out of the tub. *I needed to grieve? Had I not cried enough for them? Was my grief not harsh enough?*

I ripped the door open and stared at my sister and Andie. "Get the fuck out of my house," I told them and slammed the door shut again.

I stopped listening to whatever the fuck they wanted to

say, and opened the bottle of rum sitting next to the tub. I held the bottle up to the air, "To Tyson Johnson, the liar who broke his promises and left me anyway."

I took a huge drink from the bottle, too numb to feel the burn as it went down.

My phone buzzed on the floor beside me, but I ignored it. I didn't deserve their worry. *I deserved to suffer. His parents were right to despise me.* I lost every piece of their son I had to protect.

Andie: [Katie, call me.]

Mom: [Katie, are you okay?]

UNK: [I'm so sorry for your loss.]

CAO Marie: [Katie, I will see you at 9am for your appointment with social security ~MSG G.]

Andie: [Katiedid, if you don't answer me I am breaking into your apartment with the police!]

[Katie....]

[Katie...]

* * *

The pain in my stomach was insufferable. I hadn't felt pain like this since... Since I was gutted in the desert. Tyson's parents were seated across the table as our casualty assistance officers finalized the funeral arrangements with us.

I felt myself break out in a sweat, and I must have grunted louder than I realized. Suddenly, everyone was staring at me.

"Gunny? Are you ok?" Maria whispered to me.

"I think I need some air," I whimpered as another wave of pain ripped through my body.

'Ugh,' I grunted and fell to the floor when I attempted to stand

up.

"Call an ambulance," Maria advised the others.

I didn't know what was happening to me, but I hoped I was dying. "Let me be with Ty," I whimpered.

I was delirious for another day before my world crashed again. I was pregnant.

Was.

I had been pregnant with mine and Tyson's baby, and miscarried. I was so wrapped up in my grief that I lost our child. My last connection to him.

* * *

I choked back a sob, as I remembered the doctors telling me that I had lost our baby. I took another swig from the bottle.

My phone rang. I looked over but refused to answer. I had another two weeks of leave before the Marine Corps got any of my time or attention. I wasn't allowed to die, but I didn't have to pretend to live.

For now I could sit in my tub with my memories of my husband and drink to him. "To you, baby-" my voice crackled again. "Take care of our baby. I'm sorry I failed you both. I am so lost without you," I cried.

* * *

I woke up in my bed. I looked over at the clock and saw that it was nearly two in the afternoon. I didn't want to get out of bed, so I pulled the covers back over my head and went back to sleep.

I woke up covered in sweat, shaking. The room was pitch

185

black. Someone was holding me, rubbing my back and trying to soothe me as I whimpered

"Shhhh. It's okay, love. I've got you," my mother's voice cooed against my hair.

Another sob broke from my chest as I shook and cried. I lay cocooned in her arms until I succumbed to exhaustion again.

When I awoke again, someone else was in my bed holding me. I jerked when I realized a man was in my bed.

"It's just me, Katie," my dad murmured, and held me against his chest. "You're not alone."

"He left me, daddy," I whimpered, barely above a whisper.

"Not by choice, and you have to know that. Tyson was one of the most honorable men I have met-" my dad's voice broke.

"If he could have stayed with you he would have. You will never know how grateful I am that he brought you back to us, Katie. We all are. Tyson loved you so much. Don't lose that in your grief," he urged me.

I shook my head and nodded off again.

When I awoke again, I was in a hospital room. The sound of machines quietly beeping with my heartbeat and whirring of the oxygen confused me. For a moment, I thought I was back in the military hospital after the bombing. I couldn't keep my eyes open then either.

I looked around expectantly, hoping to see Tyson on a cot next to my own bed. Instead, I was alone. This was not the military hospital, and Tyson was still gone.

I closed my eyes and willed myself to die. I didn't want to live without him.

Some time later, I faintly heard voices talking around me,

but I couldn't open my eyes again.

"The procedure was a success. I can't imagine how she held out this long. If you hadn't got her in when you did, I don't know that we could have saved her. Your girl's a fighter," a woman's voice praised me.

I wasn't a fighter. I lost my will to fight when my sun was extinguished. I let sleep take over again, hoping I wouldn't wake again. *Ever.*

* * *

"How do you feel today?" Doctor Carson asked, looking me over.

Hers was the voice I heard when I was coming out of anesthesia. "I feel like shit."

She nodded. "That's to be expected. Can you tell me what you remember?" she asked.

My mind flooded with the memories of Tyson. His funeral. Losing our baby. Drinking in my bathtub.

"I didn't try to kill myself," I deadpanned.

She smiled sadly. "No one thinks you did. That's not why you're here," she said.

"Then why am I here?" I asked.

"When you miscarried two weeks ago, did the hospital give you a complete exam? What did they tell you about your condition?" she asked.

I closed my eyes, trying to forget the condescension that poured out of the doctor who had treated me. "I most likely lost the pregnancy due to stress, malnutrition, exhaustion, or any combination of other factors including excessive alcohol consumption," I stated quietly.

Her breath sucked in, and it prompted me to open my eyes to see her. She looked mortified, and then her face flushed with anger. "That damned hilly-billy, back woods, quack!" She yelled.

She paced the small room, and then stopped at my bedside. "You had an ectopic pregnancy, Katie. Do you know what that means?" She was seething and trying not to take it out on me.

I remembered back to health classes, "Something to do with an egg latching on a tube instead of the uterus?"

Dr. Carson nodded. "That's exactly it. Ectopic pregnancies are never viable. They are aborted by the body, naturally, or terminated artificially to save the mother's life. They cannot go to term without killing the mother."

I nodded, but felt confused. "What does that have to do with me?" I asked.

"Yours was an ectopic pregnancy, Katie. If they had scanned you when you were miscarrying they would have seen that your body was not able to flush everything," she explained.

I must have looked as confused as I felt, because she sighed and sat down in the chair next to my bed.

"Basically, your body recognized that you couldn't carry the pregnancy and tried to abort. *You miscarried.* You were in forced premature labor, for all intents and purposes. The problem was your body couldn't flush the tube, and so the nonviable fetus was still there."

At first I didn't understand why that caused me to be hospitalized, but she continued to explain.

"The nonviable fetus began to break down, but because it couldn't go anywhere, it was rotting in place for lack of an easier way to explain it," she continued.

"Oh my god, that's disgusting," I whispered, clutching my stomach.

"You had toxic shock due to early stage sepsis. When the ambulance brought you in, you had been lethargic for at least three days, and had a fever of 104 at the time you were admitted.

"A series of scans and blood work confirmed what I suspected. We couldn't do a dilation and curettage because of the location, so we went in laparoscopically. The surgery was a success and you have responded well to the antibiotics and post operative care."

I felt my eyes watering up. "I didn't- *hic*," I tried to force the words. "I *-hicc- I didn't kill my baby?*" I finally wheezed out the question.

Dr Carson's expression softened and she leaned forward to take my hand. "There was nothing any of us could have done to save the pregnancy, Katie. This was not your fault."

I leaned my head back and sobbed. It felt like an enormous weight lifted from my chest and I could breathe for the first time in weeks. *I didn't kill our baby, Ty.*

* * *

Unknown Point of View

"*Is she home? I thought you were driving her home?*" Her mother's voice questioned.

"I didn't see her. I looked everywhere and couldn't find her. Can you call her phone again?"

She was holding the phone between her ear and her shoulder as she knocked on the door.

"*Can you hear it ringing in the house?*" she asked.

The young woman could hear it ringing from inside. "Yes!! Shit! She's not answering. Where's the key?"

"*Look under the mat. There should be a black key.*"

"I'm looking but I don't see it-" She overturned the welcome mat, and dumped out the flower pots. She was panicking and opted to ring the doorbell incessantly.

ding dong ding dong ding dong

"Katie!! Katie! Answer the door, Katie!" She started shouting and banging on the door.

"*Calm down. You freaking out is not going to help right now. Are you sure it's not under a brownish-blue flower pot?*"

"No. NO. I'm telling you it's not he- WAIT! I found it, hold on I'm unlocking the door. Katie? Katie, where are you?"

"*Is she there? How bad is it?*"

"No I don't see her any- OH MY GOD! Call an *AMBULANCE! KATIE!! KATIE? WAKE UP, SWEETIE.*"

"*What's going on? What happened?*"

"CALL AN AMBULANCE! She's ice cold!"

"*OK! Stay on the call with me. Call an ambulance. Give them Katie's new address.*"

"*KATIE? LOOK AT ME, KATIE! OPEN YOUR EYES. COME ON, PLEASE DON'T DO THIS! Pleeeease, Katie!*" She cried, pulling her sister's body to her chest.

* * *

Katie's Point of View

"Am I getting discharged now?" I asked as my parents walked into the hospital room.

"Katie, you can't continue like this," my mom whispered.

"Like what? What, mommy? I didn't take any drugs. I wasn't drinking. My system was clean!" I yelled at her.

"Katie, you were hypothermic and unresponsive when Fiona got to your place," my dad interjected.

"That doesn't mean I tried to fucking kill myself!" I shouted.

"Katie, look at me," my mom spoke quietly. "We're worried, and we don't know how to help you."

I shook my head. This was fucking unbelievable. I chuckled sarcastically. If my sister hadn't left me at the race to find my own way home instead of going out to lunch with a guy she had met cheering, I wouldn't have frozen my ass off.

"My husband died. The other half of my soul was taken from me. I'm sorry that I can't bounce back fast enough for everyone else's comfort," I growled at my parents. "Get out of my room. I don't want you here," I dismissed them, and hit a button to call a nurse.

The door to my room opened and a middle-aged woman in teal scrubs came in. "Can I help you?"

I looked at my parents again, shutting down all of my emotions. "I don't want any visitors, and they're refusing to leave."

The nurse looked between us awkwardly, before quietly ushering my parents out of the room.

I was discharged four hours later and found a cab to take me home. I called a locksmith and scheduled to have the locks changed on my little house. I was done.

I was tired of my family constantly butting in, and telling everyone that I was a risk to myself. I went to grief counseling that Maria had set up for me, and joined a gold-star family support group. I showed up to work on time every day. I did my job to the best of my abilities, and hadn't been reprimanded once in the year since Tyson's death.

My family said I wasn't grieving, but I was. I just didn't want to talk about my future with them. I had my entire life planned beside Ty, and it was all taken from me. I needed to figure out who I was without Tyson Johnson, and it was *hard.*

I took up training for a triathlon with my therapy group. We were all widowed and used the training to get through the pain of loss. We met several days each week to either cycle, run or swim. The day I collapsed in my bathroom was after competing in the actual triathlon.

There had been a nor'easter the day before the race, and it dropped the water temps pretty significantly. Add to that the wind chill that set at barely 40 degrees and my exhaustion from exertion. Then, as if that wasn't hard enough, I spent nearly forty minutes looking for my sister, before finally finding a cabbie that would give me a ride home in my wet clothes.

The whole situation was a recipe for disaster. I was actually trying to climb into my warm tub when I passed out.

But this is about my grief. Because I am irresponsible with my health. Fucking hell.

[You know what you did, Fiona. You are no longer welcome here.]

Fi: [Are you seriously going to disown your own sister?]

[You almost killed me. Fuck you.]

Block Number? *Yes*

I needed a fucking break. I sent a request to Marine Corps

Headquarters and requested a transfer of duty assignment. I wanted to be closer to Tyson.

Chapter 21

Katie's Point of View

"Hey, Gunny! Sergeant Major is looking for you!" another marine called out in the office.

I was nearly done with everything anyway, so it was a good time to take a break.

"Tracking!" I yelled back, before logging off of my computer and clearing my desk. I was done for the day anyway.

I grabbed my bag and cap and made my way toward the Regiment Headquarters. I stopped by the first sergeant's office to hand him my chit requests, and to let him know that I had been summoned by the sergeant major. He just waved me off which meant he knew what this was about.

Entering the command suite I checked in with the secretary and stood by waiting to be called in.

"Gunnery Sergeant Johnson, come on in," Sergeant Major Ericson called from his office.

I nodded politely to the secretary as I passed her desk. "Sergeant Major," I greeted upon entering the office.

"Please," he gestured to a chair. "Take a seat."

I felt like I had been called into the principal's office for being naughty, but I had no idea what I had done wrong. So I opted for the fifth and waited for him to start talking before

I incriminated myself.

"Did Top speak with you yet?" he asked.

I shook my head. "No, Sergeant Major. He's been pretty busy today, and was still on the phone when I left to report here," I explained.

"That's alright. That gives me the opportunity to explain all of this directly. The new Commandant put out a call for protective service detail nominations. Specifically, she requested that the detail have at least three highly qualified females. You were one of the applicants selected to interview with the Commandant."

I felt like I had just been punched. "I don't understand, Sergeant Major."

"We had fifteen females who met initial screening criteria. After it was narrowed down to the top eight, we submitted the nomination packets up to the Commandant for final selection. You are in the final five from all of the MARSOC units," he boasted.

I clenched my jaw and thought about how to respond. "Sergeant Major. Though I appreciate the support and confidence in my abilities, I would like to decline."

This time Sergeant Major Ericson looked confused. "I don't understand. If you weren't interested why would you submit yourself for consideration?"

I bit my lip, realizing now why the first sergeant had been dodgy recently. "Sergeant Major, I am separating from the Corps. I submitted my packet today for terminal leave," I explained.

Sergeant Major leaned back in his chair and chewed on his lip a bit. "How much time do you have left on your contract? Would you be willing to fulfill one tour?"

I smirked and shook my head. "Sergeant Major, I have seven months left on my contract, and 90 days of accrued leave. I am grateful for the opportunity, but I can't continue to serve with all my heart when I have nothing left."

We sat there quietly for a few minutes before he changed the subject to my plans for after the Marines. I was honest and told him I had no plans. I had no idea who I was anymore. Everything I had planned became moot when Tyson died. If the Marine Corps was looking for a pound more of flesh, I had nothing left.

I lost my husband. I lost our child. I was blown up and gutted. There was nothing left to hold me. It all died with Ty. When I left, the first sergeant was standing by outside the sergeant major's office. He smiled and gave me a thumbs up so I returned the gesture, because I am petty. He was about to get blindsided and it made me smile.

* * *

"How are you feeling today, Gunnery Sergeant?" the therapist across from me asked me.

"I'm fine. I just needed a signature to finish my medical out-processing, so I am not sure why it required an appointment," I said honestly, smiling politely back.

"New requirements from Congress," she explained with a half shrug. "So how are you really doing? You've had a rough couple of years, why don't we start there."

I had no idea what the hell she was going on about. "I'm sorry, maybe I am confused. I just need a signature so that I can continue my out-processing from the Marine Corps. I didn't ask for therapy from you."

196

She continued to smile and neatly folded her hands in her lap. "I'm afraid that isn't how it works."

"Isn't how *what* works?" I asked, feeling my anger starting to rise.

The polite smile dropped and she became stone faced. "Quite frankly, until I have determined that you are no longer a threat to yourself, I am enabled by congressional mandate to hold you in service. Whether you like it or not."

My mind stuttered. "What the hell are you talking about? My record is fucking immaculate!"

She huffed, snatched a file from her desk and began reading. "Depression, Post Traumatic Stress Disorder, Panic Disorder, Attempted Suicide, Willful disregard for personal health and safety," she listed, pursing her lips at me. "If I think you may put your brains on a wall, I can admit you voluntarily or involuntarily. Your choice, Gunny."

"What the fuck are you talking about!? I'm done with you," I stammered, reaching to grab all of my things.

She didn't bat an eye. "If you walk out that door, I guarantee I'll have you committed before midnight," she threatened.

I snarled at her, "Fuck you. Do your worst." I stormed out of her office and heard the door slam behind me. I never closed the door, so she did that.

I stopped at the clinic's reception desk. I was starting to shake from the rush of adrenaline caused by my anger. "I need to file a complaint against a provider," I said.

"Katie?" a man called my name.

I looked up to see one of the organizers of my gold-star support group. Steven had lost his wife more than twelve years ago. Hearing him talk about how he still mourned her loss all these years later actually helped several of us in the group. Mourning was a process that took time. I didn't have to put a mark on the wall, because it would take as long as it needed to take.

"Are you okay? You look rattled," he observed.

"I-I need to f-file a complaint against provider, J-Jan-Jankowski," I stuttered, feeling my eyes begin to burn from unshed tears. Steven was a safe shoulder to cry on. I knew, because I had done it several times over the last two years since Tyson's death.

Steven walked up and pulled me into a hug. "It's okay to cry, Katie," he whispered. "Macy, can you cover the front? I need to handle a patient complaint."

The woman in pink scrubs named Macy nodded, "Sure thing, Steven. Take your time."

Steven guided me along the halls to a small waiting area. It was a few minutes before I realized that he brought me into the clinic's command suite. I sat up straight and almost started to panic when Steven emerged from a small conference room. I didn't realize that I was shaking my head at him until he started nodding.

"It's okay. Come on, Katie," he gestured for me to follow him into another office.

I lost all of my bravado. The tough as nails marine Tyson had fallen for was now just a shell. I could feel my legs shaking when Steven escorted me into the clinic commander's office. Seeing the commander went against every grain in me. This was not following the chain of command. This was the equivalent of burning down a building because the kitchen sink was leaky.

Steven asked me to sit down in one chair while he sat down in the other. My eyes were scanning every nook of the room looking for an exit. My breath hitched when I saw the name placard on the desk in front of me.

Colonel Kara Giancolo.

Colonel Giancolo was a role model for every female in this camp. She was a badass marine through and through. She entered the Corps as an enlisted private and worked her way up to Gunnery Sergeant before she finished her Masters in behavioral psychology.

She then took a direct commission and finished her PhD between deployments to the Middle East. Colonel G. was a beast at physical training, endurance, combatives, marksmanship, you name it. But what made her truly remarkable was her ability to mentor. She didn't just mentor females. She had a program to mentor the male leaders in her organization to be better mentors for their female subordinates.

Oh my god. I can't do this!

I couldn't complain to this woman. She would chew me up and spit me out. I stood up and turned to leave as the door opened again. There she was: Colonel Kara Giancolo; the Marine every female aspired to be like. Then there was me, the shell that no Marine should ever look up to.

She smiled and walked around me to sit down behind her desk. "Nice to meet you Gunnery Sergeant Johnson," she greeted as she began clearing paperwork off of her desk. "Please, sit. What can I help you with today?"

I sat there, tongue-tied. I looked over at Steven hoping he would be able to save me, but he just nodded encouragingly at me. I swallowed hard, and opened my mouth.

"I wanted to file a complaint against provider Jankowski. I just wanted to have my clearing papers signed. She said

I had to make an appointment to clear, so I did that. Then she accused me of shooting my brains out and threatened to admit me against my will if I didn't cooperate with her…"

My voice was raspy by the end, but I told her everything that had transpired with Jankowski. I didn't sugarcoat or glorify anything. My records were clean.

I was mourning the loss of my husband and child. That didn't make me a threat to myself.

I had PTSD from being blown up and watching another marine stuff organs back in my body.

I was sad. Every plan I ever dreamed to make was taken away the day I was notified of Ty's death. Everyone around me wanted to help, but no one listened to what I said.

Colonel G listened as I spoke, and wrote notes from time to time in a file. When I was done speaking she put down her pen and looked at me. She didn't smile or make platitudes; it felt like she was assessing my soul with her eyes.

"Do you remember March 8th?" she asked.

"Um, no?" I sat racking my brain trying to remember if it was a date that I should remember.

"When did you find out about your husband's death?" she asked.

February 14th

"When was his funeral?"

March 5th

When did I go back to work, April 8th.

I didn't understand why she was asking all of these questions.

"March 8th, Gunny. If you want me to help you, I need you to tell me what happened on March 8th," she stated firmly.

I didn't remem-

* * *

"You need to grieve, Katie."

"What am I doing wrong? Am I not crying the right amount of tears? What the fuck do you want from me?"

"Katie, you need to get help."

Katie.

Katie.

"She's not responding and the tub is overflowing."

"I can't open the door! Call 911! Dear God, KATIE!!"

KATIE!!

KATIE!!

"What's her name?"

"Katie, Katie Pres-Johnson. Katie Johnson."

"Call ahead and tell them it's suspected alcohol poisoning. They need to prepare the charcoal protocol."

"Oh my god, is she okay?"

"Right now she's alive, but we need to get her to the hospital. Are you her next of kin?"

"I'm her mother."

"Her blood alcohol was .39. We're going to admit her until we can detox her body."

* * *

Katie.

"Katie?"

I opened my eyes and looked up at Steven. Wait. *Why was I looking up at Steven?*

My eyes opened wide and I tried to move, but Steven held me still.

"Relax. You had a panic attack and hit your head. I need you to just focus on my voice, and bring yourself back down. Remember this drill?" Steven talked soothingly to me like he had when I first met him, and had attacks all of the time.

I listened to his voice and focused on my breath control, timing my inhales and exhales to the beats of my heart.

"That's it. This was a pretty bad spell, and you have a goose egg on your head from your fall. I don't want you to freak out again, so I am going to tell you what's happening," Colonel Giancolo's voice came from my side.

I realized that she was holding my hand.

"I need you to trust me, Gunny. I know it's hard. I know you don't want to let anyone else in, but I need you to trust me to help you." She spoke so calmly, it felt like my mom used to talk to me when I was little.

"Two emergency medical technicians are going to come in here and check you over. Then we are going to take you to the main hospital and get you checked over again", she continued. "I'm not leaving your side, ok. Let me be your advocate. Can you trust me enough for that?" she asked me and it nearly broke me.

I couldn't remember the last time someone stood up for me. When was the last time someone offered to be my shield so that I could be weak?

Tyson.

"*Ok,*" I whispered.

Just as she said, two EMTs came in and examined me before loading me onto a stretcher and taking me to the emergency department for examination and evaluation for concussion. No surprise, I gave myself a concussion. Colonel Giancolo was in the room with me for every lab, exam, and scan. She

202

never left my side.

When I was situated in a room, she took a seat next to my bed and started up a conversation with me.

"Have you ever heard of the expression 'hitting rock bottom'?" she asked.

I nodded, "Yeah. Doesn't it refer to people with addiction? They don't know how to get help until everything they have is gone?"

Colonel G nodded and then continued. "What if they already have nothing to lose? What happens when there is a loss of rock bottom?"

I had no idea, and I told her as much.

"They never stop spiraling," she explained. "Gunny, you lost everything important to you. You lost confidence in your physical body because of your injury. You lost your husband, your best friend and co-conspirator. You lost a child you never had a chance of keeping. What is rock bottom for someone like you?" she asked.

I didn't know the answer. I was just trying to make it through an hour, let alone one day at a time. I never thought of more than that.

"The brain is an amazing thing," she changed the subject. "It will force you to live, fighting for you until it can't. Sometimes it even does crazy shit like protecting you without you knowing it. Like creating a pocket around something unhealthy in the body. You know what I mean?" she continued.

I nodded. I had heard of people having cysts removed that turned out to be a foreign body, or a built up membrane to contain something infectious. It was an auto-response protection mechanism.

"Did you know the brain can do that with memories? Sometimes it's just a matter of repressing something so far into the subconscious that it is forgotten. And sometimes, in rare occasions, the brain creates a whole new identity to shield itself from traumas. Have you heard of that before?" she asked.

I had never heard of anything like that and told her as much.

"It's called dissociative identity. Basically, the brain tries to protect the original by creating someone else to do the dirty work," she explained and then changed the subject.

"I started a pilot program a few years back to help service members with traumatic brain injuries and PTSD. The intent was to provide access to the various treatments and therapies they needed to thrive outside of the military. What I found was that many of the patients presented signs of dissociation. It's why I took this assignment, in fact.

"I have a new pilot program that I would like you to participate in. You have all the hallmark indicators of dissociation. You have compartmentalized your traumas so much that you don't even know what you have really been through," she said.

"I don't have that," I said, shaking my head.

"Ok. What was the last thing you remember in my office before waking on the floor?"

"You were asking me about all of the dates. When Ty died. When his funeral happened. When I went back to work," I responded.

She smiled sadly at me. "Gunny, I never asked you any of those questions. I record every patient complaint interview that I take. I briefed you about the consent process for that recording and then asked for your statement. Do you remember any of this?"

I shook my head. "No."

She leaned down and pulled up a laptop from a bag on the floor. "We're going to watch this together, and if it gets too scary, you can squeeze my hand. Ok?"

There I was in her office. Pacing. Swearing. Threatening. Pleading.

"When? When did-" I tried to ask, starting to choke up watching myself become more and more unhinged.

"This is Katie you are protecting, Gunny. She's suffering and you are shielding her from everything," she explained to me. "I can't see a marine suffering and not help. It's not how I was wired. I want to help this young woman, but I need you to let me in.

"Can you do that, Gunny? Can you trust me enough to let me help her?" she asked, pointing to the woman on the screen who had collapsed on the floor before Steven could catch her.

* * *

It's okay.

"You're making great progress, Katie. We should be able to discharge you in the next week, at this rate."

"Call me if you need help, Katie. I'm here for you. This is my card. My name is Kara. You can just call me Doctor G."

* * *

"Did Steven know about this?" I asked her.

She tipped her head side to side. "He suspected, but you never tipped hard like today so I couldn't say for certain."

"We've met before, right? Today wasn't the first time."

She nodded. "We've met before, yes."

"Did you know Ty, too?" my voice cracked.

Col G bit her lip and nodded.

"Can you help me?" I whispered, afraid to hear rejection.

"If you'll let me."

"Okay."

Colonel Giancolo smiled from ear to ear, tears brimming in her eyes. "Thank you, Gunny. You can stand down now. I got your girl. I won't let anything happen to her."

Chapter 22

Katie's Point of View

"Do you remember the steps?" Kara asked.

"I do, Doctor G," I said smiling.

She moved over to me and pulled me into a tight hug. I was a little startled at first but I hugged her back.

"If you need me, you just call. If you feel like you are falling backward, use your support mechanisms. Tell me what they are," she encouraged me as we both pulled back from our hug.

"Talk it out. If my words are jumbled, I use running or another physical exercise to exhaust my brain so I don't spiral. No binging on cakes, chocolates, coffees or alcohol. Stay away from adrenaline-inducing sports or activities until I don't need to follow this list of shit," I repeated.

"And how do you know when that is?" she asked.

"When I stop repeating the fucking list every day."

"What happens if they aren't enough?"

"I use my support network and ask for help," I smiled shyly at her.

"That's right. There is *no shame* in asking for help. We're…..*what?*" she asked.

"Human. We're just human," I replied.

She nodded, tears welling up in her eyes. "We're human, Katie. We are fragile humans. It's okay to be fragile, remember that," she reminded me.

This had been the longest six months of my life. After having a complete dissociative breakdown in Colonel G's office, I was admitted for inpatient psychiatric care within a newly established military treatment facility called an Intrepid Center. They specialized in treatment of post traumatic stress disorders and traumatic brain injury rehabilitation and recovery.

I was poked, prodded, scanned, assessed, and questioned for two weeks as part of their intake procedures, also called Phase I. Once Phase I was complete, I was handed over to my "team" to begin Phase II. I had an assigned physical therapist, a neurologist, an osteopath, a counselor, a psychologist, a behavioral therapy specialist, a physical trainer, and a pharmacist.

It was exhausting keeping up with everything at first. Every minute of every day was strictly controlled and regimented for the first two months. What I ate, when I took meds and what meds I took was strictly controlled. From there, I graduated to Phase III. This felt more like a series of skills workshops. I learned archery and started swimming again. I attended a couple of fishing excursions with other participants, and learned how to cope with my grief and my traumas in a healthy way.

Andie came down several times to visit me, but I had declined my parents' requests to see me. I knew they were worried about me. I understood where they were coming from. But I didn't forgive them for the shit that I was subjected to in my time of crisis. Did I hold them responsible for the things they could not help? No.

But I did hold them accountable for the decisions they made with regard to my care. My wishes were repeatedly overridden by them. My concerns were not given attention, and my privacy violated. I blocked them on social media so I wouldn't see the year and a half of posts asking for prayers *'because Katie hit another rough patch.'*

I would heal my relationship with them eventually, but first I needed to figure out who the hell I was again. I would be officially released from the Marine Corps in three months, but I was using all of my unused leave to move to New England to learn woodworking and carpentry. I fell in love with turning wood during one of the many different skills workshops. It took some time and research, but I eventually found three schools in the country offering comprehensive woodworking courses.

I applied to all three schools with Colonel G's help with the application processes. She even sent a push letter to each school with pictures of my work to help me get a slot, I had been accepted into the only school on the East coast. The man who owned the school was a Master Craftsman, and had established it to keep his trade from dying out. After my acceptance, Martin, the owner, found a family for me to board with while I was attending classes.

The school was one year, and would allow me time to figure out what my next steps were. The family I would move in with seemed like a sweet older couple. Lucas and Mandy Black had a small mother-in-law suite above their garage that I would rent for the duration of my schooling. Lucas was a retired veteran, and a close friend of Martin's. They thought I would be most comfortable with people who "got" what I had been through.

Mandy wrote me an email with pictures of the small apartment, and even sent me a map of where everything was in town. She included the locations of the local VFW and American Legion, as well as locations for all of the VA hospitals and clinics within 100 miles. The last email included a request for power of attorney that would allow them to make decisions on my behalf in the event that emergency life-saving measures became necessary. As Mandy explained, the power of attorney needed to be very specific to the point it would be voided once my next of kin arrived.

The amount of care and consideration was overwhelming, to say the least.

"Have you finished clearing?" Andie asked as she and Jonas walked up to help me with the rest of my bags.

I nodded.

My sisters and parents had packed up my entire house while I was in the hospital. My dad drove a loaded moving truck *back home,* where they put all of my stuff into storage until I decided where I wanted to live next. I lost my mind when I found out.

I was so angry, I threw a tantrum and tried to destroy my hospital room. It wasn't that they had done it that bothered me. I had only been in the hospital for a month at that point, and spoken with them frequently. At no time did any of them ask what I wanted, or tell me what they were doing.

When I had finally calmed down enough to hear everything out, I revoked their visitations, and any powers of attorney they held were voided by a court order.

Andie and Jonas were the only people who cared enough

to ask what *my* wishes were. Since I turned 18, Andie was the only person who ever really stood by me through it all without judgment. Then there was Jonas. That man was a saint the way he spoiled Andie, but a fucking demon if you messed with his family. They were perfect together.

"Babe? Did you load everything up?" Andie asked Jonas, as he closed the back of the SUV.

"No… I thought I would open and close the hatch each time for the arm workout," he said, trying to hide his smirk.

She walked over and swatted him on the butt before laughing, and running a lap around the car to get away. I loved watching him rile her up. She might cuss and carry on, but I knew she loved it.

Maybe one day, I'll get a second chance at love.

"Alright, Katiedid! Let's get this party started!!" Andie cheered, breaking me from my thoughts.

I climbed into the passenger seat, and let Andie drive to the hotel she and Jonas had been staying in. Andie's niece had driven down with them to keep an eye on the kids while they were helping me to pack up my vehicle and clear camp. Now we needed to go check them out of the hotel and then get on the road.

Just like old times, there was a list of hot spots to stop in and sites to see. The added benefit this time was that Andie and Jonas's kids were going with us. Andie's niece had her own car, and decided to spend a week on the beaches of Virginia before going home. That left three adults and two kids trading between two cars.

Our first stop was a day's drive so that I could visit Tyson. Andie and Jonas let me sit at the cemetery, while they took the kids for a walk around Tyson's hometown.

211

"I miss you, Ty," I whispered. "I don't know if I have any faith left in me. I feel like everything died with you."

I caressed my hand over the engravings in the gravestone. "I tried to stop in and visit your folks, but they wouldn't even give me the time of day," I choked back my tears, as my voice cracked. "I wish I could have met them before you died. Maybe they wouldn't hate me so much now.

"I am so lost without you, Tyson. I-I let you in, and made you my whole world and- hic-" I covered my face to stop myself from sobbing. "I forgot how to do this without you. I forgot what living was like without you. It's so hard, Ty. So fucking hard."

I sat there for another hour, crying and telling Ty about everything that had happened in the two and a half years since his death. I told him about Intrepid, and getting accepted to a trade school up north.

"I have to go soon. It may be a while before I get back, but I wanted you to know why I wasn't here. I didn't want you to think that I had forgotten about you. You took half my heart and soul, Tyson Johnson. If you have any pull whereever you are, I'd really appreciate it if you could put in a good word.

"I promise, I will try. I will try to move on with you in my heart, even if I can't have you in my life. I loved you more than I loved myself, babe. But," my voice broke again.

"I have to move forward and learn how to love myself the most again. You wanted the world for me, and now I have to go and grab it. Look after our Angel. Tell them I am so sorry I never got to meet them, but I loved them fiercely and mourned them as much as I mourned their daddy. Thank you for loving me, Tyson Johnson."

I stood up from where I had been sitting, and leaned over

to place a gentle kiss on his name. "Let me be strong enough to live on," I whispered to myself like a mantra as I walked out of the cemetery.

Andie was standing by my SUV as Jonas strapped Aiden and Avery into their seats in their car. Originally the kids had been in my vehicle.

"You didn't have to do that," I whispered, as she pulled me into a hug.

"We got a hotel room for the night. Jonas is going to take the kids to grab food, and I am going to take you back and get you situated. They have a gym with a treadmill, a stair stepper, and a rock wall," she told me.

I snorted and then we both started laughing. "Why the fuck would I want to climb the walls?" I asked her.

"Hey! I was giving you options! You don't have to do it!" She huffed at me while still laughing.

Jonas waved as he drove off, and I went to the hotel with Andie. They had rented a suite with two rooms so that I wouldn't be left alone. It made me smile that they always thought this shit out. Andie shoved me into the bathroom and told me to take a shower.

By the time I got out, Jonas was back with the kids and dinner. I wasn't that hungry, and just picked at the burger and fries. "Can you just put this up for me? I'll probably eat it in a couple of hours, but I just want to sleep for now," I told them as a wave of exhaustion rolled over me.

Andie told me not to worry about anything, and shuffled me to bed. I was asleep before my head hit the pillow.

I woke up around two in the morning when little Aiden's toes went up my nose. I was confused at first but then I felt Aiden and Avery both snuggled up against me. I turned

Aiden so his head was up on a pillow, and stepped away to find my uneaten burger.

Jonas crept out of his room to use the bathroom and damn near came out of his skin when I stood up to throw away my trash.

"OH JESUS! You scared the shit out of me, Katie!" He screamed, patting his chest.

It started as a small giggle seeing him jump like he did, but the high pitched scream put me over the top. The giggle grew, and before I knew it I was bent over laughing so hard I couldn't breathe. Jonas hadn't seen me laugh like that, ever, and started laughing at me laughing at him.

Andie came out to see what the hell we were caterwauling about and couldn't stop herself from laughing at us. The three of us sat there laughing and crying for nearly thirty minutes. Once we calmed down enough to speak without wheezing, I thanked Jones for the food, and tiptoed back to bed giggling.

I snuggled in with Avery and Aiden, and whispered a quiet thanks to Ty. I hadn't laughed like that in years.

Chapter 23

Katie's Point of View

The rest of the trip was filled with small pockets of joy and laughter with equal parts of crying. Avery cried when she failed to mine a diamond from a bucket of rocks at a tourist trap.

Aiden cried when he thought he forgot a stuffed animal at a hotel. Two days later, Andie confirmed with her parents the precious dinosaur had never left little Aiden's bedroom. We had endured two days of tears, only for them to abruptly stop and turn into a giggle.

"Oh, yeah. I forgot he didn't come. Sorry, mommy."

At least he knew enough to apologize. Andie just jutted her chin, and added this to the list of things she hoped her future grandchildren would do to her children. I couldn't stop myself from laughing as she muttered under her breath about Aiden's nonsense, while Aiden cackled retelling the events and discussions that led up to the dinosaur staying home.

Jonas moved Aiden to his car, and said it was so they could have male bonding. I bit my lip and put my head in my lap to keep from laughing even harder.

"Shut up, Katie!" Andie muttered as we got back on the

road.

We had about six hours left to drive and we all agreed to just push through unless we found something to explore along the way.

"Avery, how is school?" I asked her.

Her eyes rolled, and I wasn't sure what kind of response I was going to get from her. Then the flood gates opened. I heard about her teachers, her classmates, her classes (ranked best to worst), and how 'oh sooooo gross' she thought boys were.

She told me how a kid had asked her to go out, and she in turn had lectured him on his 'priortees.' She had apparently dragged the poor boy by the ear back to his desk and stood over him while he completed his schoolwork. When he was done, he asked if she would go out with him then...

"But I tole him, 'no', cause I need someone who is jes' as smart as me, and can do their own work," she explained.

"Then what happened?" I asked, now invested in this mini drama.

"He asked Stella out instead," she huffed.

"Oh! I'm sorry sweetie," I said, but she threw up a hand and stopped me.

"I was so happy he stopped following me. They can go be dumb together. I had my own math sheets to do, Miss Katie!" she explained, sounding relieved.

My jaw dropped and I looked over to see Andie's reaction. She was biting her lip and struggling not to laugh. I thanked Avery for sharing *so so much* with me.

"You're welcome, Miss Katie!" she smiled.

I didn't have words. "You made that," I whispered to Andie. She nodded. "I know. And I should be correcting her, but

I just can't cause I'm so fucking proud!" She whispered back, trying to stifle her giggles.

* * *

"You must be Katie! It's so nice to finally meet you! I'm Mandy," a petite woman with a southern accent greeted me. She looked like she was barely out of college with the messy bun on top of her head, and the cut-off overalls. She was wiping paint off of her hands so that she could offer to shake with me.

I introduced Andie, Jonas and the kids, before Mandy insisted we get situated for the night. The "quaint" mother-in-law suite was a full sized apartment built over a three car garage. "This is so much space…" I gasped as we walked in.

"Lucas an' I were livin' up here for a bit while we built the rest of our dream home. That was so many years ago - Excuse me," she stopped, and pulled a water bottle from her back pocket and spit in it.

It was then I realized she had a cheek half stuffed with dip. I couldn't stop myself from giggling as she went through the list of things they did to spruce the place up for me. It was so much more than I could have hoped for.

"If there's anything, I mean anything, you need, you let me know an' we can go out tagether an' pick it up," she offered.

We stood there talking for a good twenty minutes before Mandy suddenly looked like someone lit her tail on fire. "Shoot! I'm supposed to have supper on the table! I have to run. Don't be shy!"

After she ran out the door, Andie and Jonas stared at me with their mouths agape. Mandy looked like she was barely

18, but I knew from her letters that she and Lucas had been married for more than 20 years already. She had the sweetest southern draw, and then spit a mouthful of chew into a water bottle. There were so many contradictions.

"I think I love that woman," Andie admitted, fanning herself.

"I think I may have developed my first girl crush," I laughed.

Jonas just shook his head and went to check on the kids playing quietly in the living room. From the pink on the tips of his ears, I think it was safe to say we all thought Mandy was too damn cute.

It didn't take long to bring all of the bags in. Still, the kids were asleep on the sofa before we finished.

"Why don't you two take the bedroom tonight, and I'll sleep out here with Ave and Aiden," I offered.

Jonas shook his head, and Andie thanked me for the offer.

"You sure?" Jonas asked his wife.

"She's not ready to sleep alone yet in a new place," she explained, pulling Jonas with her toward the bedroom. "Don't think she's being nice. *We are.* We are letting her use *our children* as a security blanket in the new place. Isn't that right, Katie? We're doing this for you…."

I laughed because she wasn't entirely wrong. I didn't answer and just waved them off. "Good night," I called over my shoulder as I pulled blankets out of a closet Mandy had pointed out during our tour.

I fell asleep with Aiden laid across my chest and Avery's legs tangled up with mine. I woke up to a 'shushing' noise, my head laid on Andies lap.

"I'm sorry," I mumbled as I started to come out of it.

"You didn't do anything. The kids got up early, and you

seemed like you were restless, so I came to sit with you and Jonas took the kids to find breakfast." Andie's voice was so quiet, as her hand gently caressed my hair. I wanted to argue, but I was overcome with exhaustion again. Her small reassuring gestures were enough to soothe me back to sleep.

When I woke up again, I was alone on the sofa. Avery and Aiden were sitting on the floor next to me watching a children's program, and Jonas and Andie were in the kitchen. "Morning," I whispered to the kids, and gave them each a peck on their head before getting up and shuffling to the bathroom.

I washed my face, brushed my teeth, and pulled my hair up. Feeling less like a train wreck, I walked straight to Andie and gave her a hug. "Thank you. I appreciate everything, but this only works if you don't lie," I whispered.

She hugged me back and nodded into my shoulder. "Aiden had a nightmare, and it triggered you. Jonas took him into the bedroom and I stayed with you and Avery. I didn't lie," she said.

"Now," she said with her bossy tone. "You need to go run. You have not done anything in days, and you need to be back on schedule if you are going to keep getting better."

I hadn't been for a run since we left the hospital. I did try a treadmill at one of the hotels, but it was a cheap model so it felt like I was bouncing on the machine as I ran. I could feel the concussive impacts radiating up my shins, and I had to stop. Breaking myself for a little dopamine was not an option.

I got changed and slipped out the door. I promised I wouldn't run that far, and left my phone. The morning air smelled crisp. I had lived in southern states for so long, I forgot how much I missed this.

I stretched lightly, rolling my shoulders and rotating my hips to loosen my joints. I was startled when Mandy's voice broke the silence.

"You run often?" she asked, walking up beside me in running shoes, a tank top and spandex shorts.

I nodded. "Yeah, it helps with the therapy stuff," I admitted.

"What's your pace?" she asked.

"Depends. Usually, it's a seven to eight minute mile, depending on distance, hills, playlist," I trailed off giggling.

Mandy smiled. "I'm doing five today. You up for it?"

I nodded and off we went.

"Stay with me," she encouraged as we hit one hill after another.

"Where did all of these hills come from?" I jokingly whined.

"Sneaky aren't they?" She huffed in agreement.

"This is shit," I huffed when we were half way up another hill.

"Great, isn't it?" She puffed back.

"Amazing," I agreed, nodding.

We ended up running closer to seven miles, but I felt amazing. We stretched in the driveway and I asked her about her run schedule. She admitted that she had not been running for a while, and quickly changed when she saw me outside.

I laughed, "Seriously?"

"I know, I had you thinking I was some kind of super woman. But seriously, if you want to run together we can, you just need to let me know your schedule," Mandy offered.

"Ok. I wouldn't mind the company," I admitted.

"Good. Now I need to go die in the privacy of my own

house," she told me before dragging herself to her house.

I shuffled up the stairs to my apartment. My legs were wobbly and face flushed red, but my mind was still. I hadn't had this kind of peace in my head in a long time.

Entering the front door, I was hit with the smell of french toast and bacon. "Oh, my god, that smells so good!" I exclaimed.

Andie laughed at the sight of me. "Good run, I take it?" She asked, passing me my water bottle.

I nodded as I chugged the water. "Yeah. It was good. I didn't remember us driving over all these hills though!" I exclaimed, closing the now empty bottle.

Andie laughed. "Seriously? The kids were squealing about the *'rollercoaster'* half the night!"

My eyebrows shot up. "Oh my god! They were talking about the main road coming in here? I thought..." I couldn't even finish my thought.

Avery and Aiden had talked non stop about the death defying drops and climbs of the road, and I assumed they were describing a rollercoaster. I started laughing when the two experiences finally overlapped: their descriptions with how it felt running those same hills.

"Now, go get cleaned up. You stink," Andie directed me.

"I *am* kind of ripe, huh?" I admitted, still chuckling.

"I can smell you from here!" Avery yelled from the dining table, pinching her nose.

I bit my lips to keep from saying anything more and ran to clean myself up.

When I was showered and dressed, Andie was waiting for me at the table with hot coffee, French toast sticks and bacon.

"Can you just stay here?" I asked, sitting down next to her.

Andie smiled, wistfully. "You and Avery both have school on Monday. I love spending time with you, but I miss my own bed."

I nodded in understanding as I took a sip of the coffee.

"I miss screaming out my orgasms. Having to bite my lip and hold it in is messing with my libido, if I'm being honest," she continued.

I choked and spit coffee across the table. "Andie!"

She looked at me like I was nuts, and stood up from the table. "What? At least now you know why we have to go home."

I shook my head, and went to get a wash rag from the sink, when Andie passed one to me. "Thank you," I mumbled and washed the coffee I had spewed off of the table.

When I was done, she pulled me into a big hug. "I love you Katiedid. I'm just a phone call away if you need to talk."

"I know. I appreciate everything you and Jonas have done for me. You will never know how much, Andie," I thanked her, my voice cracking.

Pulling apart from each other, we sat back down and I ate a second helping of the French toast and bacon. "When do you plan on leaving?" I asked, assuming it would be sooner than later, given the conversation topic.

"We're going to leave late tonight. It's easier on the road when the kiddos are asleep. Jonas already went back to bed, so he'll be ready to drive tonight."

"You made me French toast and bacon to pillow the bad news?" I asked, raising an eyebrow at her.

Andie didn't miss a beat and nodded. "Sure did."

"So smart…." I commended her.

* * *

I quickly fell into a routine once school began. I got up early and ran with Mandy four days a week. Sometimes we ran eight miles, others maybe three. Lucas eventually warmed up to me, and let me use his home gym.

Mandy and I decided to get buff together, and added a few gym routines into our workout schedule. It ended up being just as thorough and intense a schedule as I had in the marines, before the IED attack.

Lucas and Mandy together made me crack up. Normally, Lucas seemed quiet and brooding, but then he'd smoke a bit and suddenly be super chatty. No topic was off limits when he smoked. The contrast was hysterical for me. Lucas had pretty bad PTSD as well, and smoked instead of taking antidepressants and all of the other meds.

He convinced me to give it a shot, and I had to admit it worked better than the sleeping pills the military hospital had prescribed. I still dreamt when I smoked, but I wasn't a zombie the next morning like with the sleeping pills.

I also learned how to better identify and control my triggers after a couple of months. I enjoyed the routine of physical exertion and then classes. It was something closer to normalcy, even if only for the limited time I would be here.

I agreed to let my folks visit me at Christmas. I thought it would be so much worse than it was, but I smoked with my mom and we got through it. Neither of my parents had any idea that Fiona had used me as an excuse to get out of shit. I had to show them my phone, before my mom stopped trying to defend her.

My dad talked about his own experiences with me, and I explained that I hadn't known about the dissociative identity disorder.

"So, you have two personalities?" he asked.

"Not really. Not anymore. It's more like, I compartmentalized the civilian side of me and became just a marine. The marine side of me was stronger in my mind, and better equipped to deal with..... *shit.*" I explained.

"So what does that mean now?" My mom asked nervously. "Is it possible that you could relapse and spiral all over again?"

I didn't want to lie, so I just told them my truth. "It's always a possibility," I admitted and watched as they both tensed up. "But so is being struck by lightning, winning the lottery or carrying triplets."

My mom scoffed, "Don't even get me started about babies!"

I laughed and leaned into my dad's hug as we sat on the sofa. "I'm not a child, mommy. I had a lot of fucked up shit happen in very short order, and I couldn't cope. I know you both were trying to help me, but I'm not a kid."

My dad sighed, "We know you aren't a kid, Katie. We just did what we thought was best."

"I know," I acknowledged. "But you have to understand that, sometimes, what I need and what you want for me are not the same. *My needs* are the priority when it comes to my health and happiness, not your *wants...*"

Mom snorted, not happy with my wording, and walked to get herself another cup of coffee.

"Don't worry about your mother. She understands, even if she doesn't express it very well," he whispered against my temple.

I nodded. It was a start.

When mom returned, she was over the previous huff. "When you finish school in April, are you moving back?" she asked, not disguising the hopefulness in her eyes or voice.

I took a deep breath and sighed. "I haven't decided. Can I get back to you on that one?"

My mom bit her lip and nodded. I hadn't told her, 'No.'

Changing the subject, my dad asked about my trade schooling. "Have you finished anything yet? Can I see some of your work?"

My face must have lit up, because both of my parents visibly relaxed as I began telling them about the courses I was taking. I pulled out my phone and showed them pictures of the piece I was working on for my solo project as well as the group projects that my class worked on.

I gave my mom a wood and resin bowl that I turned. It wasn't perfect, but it was my first attempt. She got super emotional, "This is really for me?"

"I thought you could use it for your keys and wallets," I explained, watching her slide her hands over every surface.

"I think that would be a great place for it," my dad agreed.

"It's beautiful, Katie. Thank you," my mom said, pulling me into a teary hug.

"And thank you for not giving up on us," she whispered in my ear as she hugged me.

I squeezed her tighter and let myself cry in her arms. "I'm trying, mommy."

"I know, sweetie. We know, and you are doing everything right," she said, caressing my back as we held each other.

Hearing her acknowledgement and praise settled a doubt I didn't know I still harbored. It felt like a weight had been lifted, and I could breathe again.

"Thank you," I whispered back.

Chapter 24

Kai's POV

I was fucking exhausted. If I thought working as a PTA was a lot, being the doctor on call was so much worse. The work was amazing. I loved the patients and colleagues I had come to consider like family. It was just a lot, every day, and there was no one to share it with. I hadn't dated or even looked at another woman since my divorce. I buried myself in my work and focused on that to numb all the shit I didn't want to deal with.

In a rare moment of clarity, I accepted my parents' invitation to dinner. Reg and his family were coming up from down state, and they wanted the whole family together. It was a good visit, but it still hurt seeing how old my nephew was now. Heather would have been six this year. Just after eight, I made some lame excuse about an early shift and headed home. It didn't take long before the fuel light lit up on the dash.

I had forgotten to fill up on the way and had to stop at the Cumberland Farms to get gas because there was no way I was going to make it home from my parents'. I had always avoided stopping in this part of town because this was where Katie used to live. I hadn't heard from her since I fucked up and pushed her away, but it didn't mean I didn't think about her constantly.

After everything that happened over the last eleven years, I often wondered what my teenage self was thinking. Katie was perfect. She wanted the same things that I wanted: to get out of this town and do something *more* with our lives. Instead of following that dream, I pushed her away and hid like a damn coward.

I hoped to see her at our ten year class reunion last fall, but she never showed. I don't know why my heart always came back to Katie, but here I was. *Again.* I just wanted her to know that I did show up that day. I showed up at her parents' house to tell her I was fucking wrong, but she had already left.

Andie was there waiting instead and punched me in the face as soon as I got out of the car. Once she calmed down, she told me that Kat's phone had been disconnected. She couldn't take it with her, so her parents agreed to cancel the subscription. I still had her old number saved in my contacts under, *'What if.'* I never deleted it.

I looked up as an SUV pulled into the lane next to mine, the couple inside laughed as he stepped out of the passenger seat and she stepped out of the driver's side to fill up the vehicle with gas. I gave the guy a cursory nod as he passed me.

I looked up when I heard the woman yell over to him, "Grab me a green tea if they have it!"

My heart stopped beating. *Fuck. It was her.* Bradley wasn't pulling my leg last week when he said he had seen her in town. *My girl, Kat Preston.*

I didn't know what the hell compelled me. I stepped toward the rear of my car to get a better look at her. Bradley heard from Alex who still talked to her sister that she was thinking of moving back, but I never gave it any thought. Was she really here? I couldn't take my eyes off of her.

Katie was just as beautiful as she was in school. I hadn't seen her in more than a decade, but I couldn't mistake her for anyone. Her hair was shorter and darker, and she looked thinner without the baby fat on her face. But her eyes still sparkled when she smiled.

I was mesmerized. I finished pumping the gas and quickly closed up the cap. *I had to talk with her.*

At that moment, every doubt in my mind disappeared. For me, it had always been her. I didn't know who that man was to her, but I had to know if there was even a chance. I walked over and stopped just behind their car. There was a glistening ring set on her left finger.

She's married, and that guy's her husband. I've fucking lost her for good.

I felt like a stone was stuck in my throat, and my eyes watered up. I faced back toward my car as her husband walked past me again, and climbed into my driver's seat so I wouldn't hear him ask her about me: the creepy dude staring at his wife.

I grabbed my phone, and tried to blink away the fucking ache in my chest. I found Bradley's contact information and sent him a text.

[Dude, I need a DD tonight. I've lost her.]

* * *

Katie's POV

I finished filling up the SUV as Jonas came back from the

229

shop. He passed me a green tea and leaned against the back of the vehicle, blocking Kai's view of me.

"You know that guy?" Jonas asked me, subtly nodding his head toward the silver BMW two pumps over.

I had recognized Kai as soon as we pulled up. I should have kept driving, but I still stopped because I wanted to see what he looked like. If I were honest, my heartbeat picked up a bit when I saw him. When he stepped closer to my vehicle, butterflies erupted in my stomach. It took everything in me to pretend that I didn't recognize him. I wanted to turn and smile and talk to him. There was an unrequited joy seeing him again.

However, I quickly squashed that down when I remembered why we weren't together. He had his chance and abandoned me. Any hopes that I held once upon a time had long since been shattered. I had been happy and lost everything... *Twice*. And I had no say in the matter either time.

"Who? That guy?" I asked, feigning like I was happy beyond elation, tipping my head to the side smiling.

Jonas nodded at me, "Yeah, the guy you just reduced to near vomiting at the sight of you. If I hadn't walked out when I did, he was going to chat you up, wasn't he?"

"Yeah," I nodded with a brilliant smile. "That's the guy that broke my heart in high school. That man is Kai Rayburn," I whispered to Jonas.

Jonas got it. He had been married to Andie long enough to hear most of our stories. "Bugger for him, then. You are a happy woman!" He laughed loudly and kissed me on the temple before climbing into the passenger seat.

I appreciated the show of solidarity and *show* in front of

my ex. I finished pumping the gas and climbed into the Highlander I had bought myself the week before. Maybe it wasn't a BMW, but it was all mine. Kai was still sitting there in his car when I pulled away from the gas station to take Jonas home.

I was just moving back to town, so Andie insisted I stay with her, Jonas, and my gorgeous godson and goddaughter until I found my own place. Jonas and I were coming back from the storage unit my parents stored all of my stuff in. It was overwhelming seeing my entire life shoved into a ten by ten, so I had only grabbed four boxes and closed up the unit.

"You okay?" Jonas asked once we were on the road and my fake smile had fallen.

"I don't know, to be honest," I admitted. Seeing that man brought up shit I hadn't thought about in years.

"I know Andie is better at all of the advice stuff," he started.

I nodded and gave him a weak smile. I had known her longer so it was a given.

"But if seeing that man reduced to tears at the sight of you *happy*, doesn't bring you some modicum of joy, I don't know that we can continue as friends," he stated in no uncertain terms, smacking the dash for emphasis.

My jaw dropped as I stared over at him. I tried to say something, *anything*, but then he raised his eyebrows at me as if to challenge any argument I would make…. And I lost it. I laughed so hard, I thought I would have to pull over. "You're killing me, Jonas!" I wheezed.

By the time we got to his and Andie's house, I was still giggling. I couldn't even explain to Andie why I was laughing without losing it again, so Jonas leaned in and whispered what happened. Andie's eyebrows shot up and she smacked him in the chest.

"You can't say shit like that…. *out loud,*" she praised him. Jonas started laughing at that point.

We unloaded the boxes I pulled from storage and set them in my room. I didn't need anything in these boxes. I had enough clothes. I just wanted something from my life before everything went wrong. I opened one of the smaller book boxes, and pulled out two old notebooks.

The pages were filled with letters Andie and I had written back and forth to each other throughout high school. Most of the pages were filled with all of my thoughts about Kai before we had started dating. Rereading them after all these years made me smile a little bit for the unyielding optimism I used to have. Maybe Andie was right, and it was time to get on with my life.

I found myself caressing the wedding rings I still wore.

What should I do, Ty? No matter what we wanted for us, we *ceased having a future together when you died...*

I was a 29-year-old widow and a war vet. Maybe it *was* time to stop running from my life and start moving forward. I grabbed my phone from my bag and scrolled through my contacts.

There it was. The contact that I debated every day whether to delete or keep. I don't know why I saved it, but some part of me always held out hope that things hadn't been what they seemed back then. I bit my lip and typed out my message before hitting send.

[We need to talk.]

Chapter 25

"Dude, you ok?" Bradley asked his best friend of fifteen years. He hadn't seen Kai get this drunk since they were in High School. He was usually the responsible one between them.

Kai sent him the message asking for a designated driver, and then asked him to pick him up at the Stone Balloon in town several hours. It wasn't normal for Kai to get hammered like this. *Hell*, he hadn't seen him like this since right after high school when-

"*Shit,*" Bradley whispered, closing his eyes as he pinched the bridge of his nose. He must have seen *her* in town.

Looking at his best friend hunched over an empty glass he decided it was best to just get Kai home and sober. The last time Kai needed a DD he was drunk for a week. Amy, Bradley's wife, would leave him if he took care of a drunken Kai for a week like he did back then.

"Come on, buddy. Let's get you home," he said quietly, pulling Kai up from the bar.

"Noooo. Imm gooo-," Kai slurred out as he reached to stay at the bar.

"Come on, Kai. Amy is waiting for me to get back. Where is your phone?" Bradley asked ,looking around the bar top.

Kai seemed confused and looked around the bar top as

well, "Huh? no phone. I'll ged it frem my carrr-*hic*."

"Dude, you're drunk. Give me your keys, we can find your phone in the morning when you've sobered up," Bradley told him while pulling him successfully away from the bar. He nodded to the girl behind the bar, "He paid up?"

She nodded, walking over to clear the empty glasses. "Yeah. He cleared his tab just before you got here," she told him. The bartender was cute, and making eyes at his very drunk friend. Shame he was too blind to see shit like that anymore.

Bradley waved one hand at her, "Thanks." He got his arm under Kai's, and wrapped it around his chest before half dragging, half supporting Kai out to the street. His car was just two blocks down the road, but the walk would give Kai an opportunity to sober up a bit. He just hoped that Kai didn't throw up in it like back then.

"I'll tell you what, Kai. You throw up in my car and I will not talk to you again," Bradley warned him as they shuffled down the street.

Kai seemed quiet and just stumbled along, "Tell Amy it's ok. She can just do it," he whispered out like he was accepting a life sentence.

Bradley was confused. "What? Kill you if you chuck your guts in our car? Dude, she won't get a chance, because I will do it myself," he informed him.

Kai shook his head, "No. Tell her I'll go on the date with her fucking friend."

Bradley stopped walking and looked over at Kai, "Dude, you are drunk enough. So I, as your best friend and wingman of nearly 15 years, am going to pretend that you did not agree to that. I didn't hear it."

They continued walking the last few moments in silence

until they reached Bradley's car. The lights on the silver Volvo flashed as he unlocked it and opened up the passenger door for Kai to get in.

"Do *not* puke in my car, Kai," he warned him again before closing the door and walking around to climb into the driver's seat.

Starting the car up, Bradley drove off toward his house. He couldn't leave Kai alone like this. *Fuck.*

* * *

Kai's Point of View

Shit. My head hurts.

I felt like I swallowed a mouth full of dog hair. Trying to open my eyes, I realized that I was not in my bed as I looked around the room.

Shit. Bradley must have brought me back to his last night. I can't even remember what happened after I got to the Stone Balloon. I can't keep living like this. I can't keep waiting and hoping for something that I don't deserve.

I sat up slowly and looked around the guest room in Bradley's house. I had slept off many drunken nights here. On the night stand was a glass of water and two extra strength Tylenol, with a note from Amy: "Take these before you come down."

Grabbing the two pills and the water, I swallowed them down and finished off the water. I needed to get my life together. I can't keep crashing at Bradley's place when I have a shit day. I needed to just move on and settle down. *I'm too old for this shit.*

I shuffled to the bathroom across the hall from the guest

room and finally got a good look at myself. I had dark circles under my eyes, and I looked like shit. Turning on the shower, I stripped out the clothes that I had on and cleaned myself up. The hot water cleared my head up a bit, and allowed me to think clearly for a few moments.

I turned the water off and grabbed the fresh towel that Amy always left hanging on the rack. She always kept the guest room ready, and this bathroom stocked like they had guests coming over any minute. I wanted something like this for myself. I wanted to be married and have a wife who worried about this kind of shit.

I grumbled some more as I wrapped the towel around my waist and gathered up my clothes off of the floor. Amy let me leave a spare set of sweats at their house for nights like last night. Maybe that was a clue in itself that I never saw before now. I was so pathetic leaning on my best friend, that his wife let me keep clothes at their house.

I pulled a black t-shirt and gray joggers out of the dresser in the guest room and got dressed. I realized that I didn't know where my phone was. I'd ask Bradley if he had it when I went down. I folded up my dirty clothes into a bundle and returned the used towel to the bathroom rack.

Walking down the stairs, I could hear Amy talking in the kitchen; the smell of coffee filling my nose.

She turned to me smiling as I came around the corner, "Oh, good morning, Sunshine."

"Hey. Sorry about last night," I apologized to her, feeling my face heat up.

Amy smiled and nodded in understanding, then passed me a cup of black coffee. "I know you don't usually drink coffee, but you might want this when I remind you of what you did last night."

My hand paused as I accepted the mug from her, "Um, what did I do last night?"

Amy just looked at me and laughed, and went back to cleaning up the kitchen after making lunches.

Shit. Is that the time? I realized it was nearly one o'clock, looking at the time on the stove.

"You only promised to go on a date with my friend *Lindsey*. Don't worry, I haven't told her yet. Bradley told me not to make any plans before you sobered up," Amy winked at me while smiling ear to ear.

Fuck, I need to stop drinking. "Um, yeah. Hold off on that until I get my shit straight," I offered, smiling lightly. "By the way, have you seen my phone? I didn't see it upstairs."

Amy looked at me and furrowed her brows a bit. "No. Do you want me to call it?" she offered.

Can this day get any more embarrassing? "If you could?" I smiled at her.

I watched as she grabbed her phone out of her purse and started thumbing through the lock screen before passing me her phone mid call.

I took the phone as it began to ring. I couldn't hear it ringing in the house anywhere.

"Hello?" a woman's voice answered my phone.

"Uh, hey. My name is Kai. I lost my phone last night and was hoping you could tell me where it is?" *Who the hell just answered my phone?*

The woman on the other side chuckles. "Ah, cutie with the blonde hair and blue eyes from last night, right? Yeah, you left your phone at the Stone Balloon last night. You want me to leave it here behind the bar? Or I can meet you tonight

237

for dinner and give it to you then?"

I must have looked confused as hell, because Amy reached over and grabbed the phone from my hand.

"Hello?" she asked. "Who am I speaking with?"

"Uh-huh. Hi, *Katie.* My boyfriend left his phone there last night and I would like to come pick it up. *Mmmmhmmm...* We got into a bit of an argument and said some things, but we're all good now," Amy's sickly sweet voice cooed at the phone.

It made my skin erupt into goosebumps listening to her politely and succinctly tell the woman with my phone that she had no chance in hell. I wanted to laugh, but the more I listened the scarier she sounded. No wonder Bradley was so well behaved since they got married. She was scary as hell.

"Uh-huh...... Mmmhmmm. *Sure.* You do that. *Thank you so much,*" Amy told the woman before hanging up.

Looking at me like she was right now, I knew I was screwed. "Thank you?" I offered putting my hands together like I was praying to a goddess.

"I'll be back in about 30 minutes. There is a sandwich on the table for you, and you can help yourself to a soda or water. *I have to go meet with Katie,*" Amy informed me as she grabbed her bag and walked out of the kitchen.

Katie.

She was back, and I was a mess. I looked over at the table and saw that Amy had made me a grilled cheese sandwich. She was such a sweetheart. It made me feel even shittier that I was constantly crashing at their place when my life fell to shit. I choked down the food, realizing that my stomach was still not happy after my night out.

I cleaned up the dishes that I used and emptied their dishwasher while I waited for Amy to get back. *Shit.*

I had just remembered that my car was still parked outside the Stone Balloon when I heard the front door open. Amy and Ben came walking in, and I barely reacted in time when Ben tossed my car keys to me.

He smiled, one eyebrow cocked up, "Yeah, I got your car, too. Unless you wanted to do the walk of shame downtown?"

I couldn't even laugh, it was so embarrassing the way they took care of me. "No, I appreciate it. Really. You guys have done too much for me," I admitted, shamefully.

"Well, as long as you recognize that. I won't be too hard on- Did you empty the dishwasher for me?" Amy squealed, dropping her bag on the table as she walked over to the still open but empty dishwasher.

"Uh, yeah. I felt bad for everything so I wanted to make it up to you any way that I could."

Amy smiled at Bradley, "See? I told you! Men can be domesticated *before* you marry them off."

"What?!" I started laughing. "I am not getting married off just yet. But thank you again."

Amy walked to her bag, "Oh, yeah. That *Katie chick?*… You dodged a bullet with that one. You may owe me dinner, she was really cute…." she spoke as she passed the phone to me, "but a bit of a psycho. She '*accidentally dropped*' it."

As I took my phone, I looked down to see that the screen was completely shattered. I sighed. I needed a new phone now. One more thing on the list of shit for my day.

"Well, I am off to buy a new phone, I guess," I sighed still staring at the phone. "Thanks again for… *everything.*"

I gave Amy and Bradley a hug before grabbing my clothes and smashed phone, and walked out to my own car. I needed to get a new phone. I took off today, but I needed my phone in case any of my patients called in with an emergency.

Taking one more deep breath, I drove to the electronics store to get a new phone.

Chapter 26

Katie's POV

I sat on the bed in Andie's guest room and stared at my phone. *What the hell was I thinking?* I needed to have closure. I hadn't spoken with Ty's parents since I moved back here. They didn't know Ty and I had eloped before he deployed, and they didn't know that he had died until *after* I was notified: as his wife. They found out about me from the casualty notification officer.

It wasn't the way we had planned it. Everything was all wrong. I was no longer the woman their son had chosen, but the woman who had stolen and murdered their child instead. They didn't know that I left the military. They didn't know anything about me, nor did they try after the funeral. They just stopped accepting my calls.

I still messaged his mom every year on his birthday and the anniversary of his death. I didn't even know if my number was blocked, or if she saw them and deleted them. There was no one else to share his memories with. I had no one else to talk about our dreams with.

I sent another message with zero idea on what to do afterward. Would I get a response? *Probably not. Too little, too late, Katie.*

I sighed and threw my phone back down on the bed, and went to join Andie and her family for dinner. I needed to move forward and I couldn't do that sitting alone in a room.

"There she is!" Avery called from the table.

I couldn't help but smile. Andie and Jonas's kids were absolute sweethearts. Avery was just like her dad, quiet but very observant. When she did get to talking, she was quick as a whip with her comments. It was funny until you became her target. Their son Aiden was just a ball of energy. I had made it home for leave to see his birth.

When I had gotten back to post, I told Ty I wanted to have a baby. He proposed that night, but I turned him down. We didn't get married until two years later. We had dated for over a year before that. He always wanted to marry me, but I always found reasons to turn him down. *Too little, too late.*

I sat down at the table between Andie and Avery as Jonas started to pass the plates of food around the table. Aside from visiting with my parents and now at Andie's, I hadn't had real food in what seemed like forever.

I usually just snacked on whatever my stomach could tolerate, unless Mandy dragged me down to her place to eat a proper meal. One of the veteran groups had offered group counseling through excursions, but I had turned it down. I didn't need to fish for peace of mind. I needed closure. I needed my past to be put to rest, and I couldn't do that with a bunch of vets who seemed content to constantly rehash the worst experiences in our lives.

I picked at the chicken on my plate and ate a few bites of the potatoes and vegetables. I felt restless like I hadn't in a long time. Andie must have sensed it, because she reached over and took my plate.

"Go," she told me.

I looked at her confused. "What?"

"Go. Run it off. The trails are all lit up now, so it's not like it was when we were in school. I'll put your dinner in the oven to keep warm until you get back." She patted my hand and then nudged me to leave the table.

I felt my eyes burning with tears that wanted to fall. I just nodded my appreciation for her understanding and went to change into my running gear. This was all that I had right now. I could run.

I grabbed my phone and ear buds, and walked out the back door after I had changed. Seeing the looks that Andie and Jonas gave me made me feel like such a shit friend. They were so understanding and nice to me, and I didn't deserve their love and acceptance. I wanted to disappear and be forgotten, but they kept me tethered so that I would work through my shit.

I reached the start of the nature trails after a five minute walk. My phone was tucked into a band on my arm, and my ear buds began to play the same music list I always ran to. It was one of the music lists that Ty had created for my long runs. Every song carried a similar beat undertone. It matched my pace perfectly and let me just run on autopilot without thinking too hard or needing to concentrate on my speed. I could just run.

I set off down the trails as the first song began to play. The first and last songs were a bit slower, so that I could warm up and cool down. Ty always thought of things like this. He was always looking after me in the biggest and smallest ways. I ran through the woods and let the rhythm of the music lead my feet.

243

By the time I made it back to Andie's back door, it was nearly 10pm. I ran for three hours without batting an eye. Andie used to ask how far I would run, but I honestly couldn't tell her. I never kept track. I just ran until I started to feel tired, and then I would run back. Keeping track of the distance wasn't necessary to me. It didn't matter.

I snuck back into the house, and walked quietly back up to the guest room. I set my phone to charge and grabbed a change of clothes before going to shower. The kids were asleep, but Andie would sit up and wait for me to get back. She was still looking out for me after all of these years. I showered quickly, put on my pajamas and shuffled back to the kitchen to finish my plate of food.

Exhausted, cleaned up, and a belly full of food, I finally crawled into bed to sleep. This was how I slept. So exhausted that my mind couldn't keep pondering shit. There were no more what if's or regrets when my head hit that pillow. Like this, I could just crash and sleep through the night.

Sometime later I woke up to my phone ringing. *Who the hell was calling me?* I reached out to grab my phone and answered it.

"Hello?" my voice came out raspy and hoarse from sleep.

It sounded like someone was calling me from a bar. The noise of people in the background and music made it hard to hear if anyone was trying to actually speak.

"I think you have the wrong number," I told the unknown caller.

I hadn't looked at my phone when I grabbed it, and my eyelids were too heavy to look at it even now.

"Are you happy?" a man's voice asked.

I didn't know what to say, so I said nothing and the mystery caller continued.

"If you were happy, I could be happy for you. I could do that," the words were slurring. This guy must have drunk dialed me by mistake.

"I *could* be happy for you. I thought I could get a second chance. I know I messed up. I was an idiot, but I thought there was still *a chance*. I *hoped*. I really did. I wanted a second chance. But then I saw how happy you looked and I knew...... I was *fucked*," the man continued to ramble.

I had no idea who this guy thought I was. I was slowly falling back to sleep listening to this midnight confession. What would it hurt to let him pour his drunken heart out? At least one of us would have some peace tonight.

"I wanted my life with you. I did. I d-," he continued as I began to drift off to sleep. I couldn't hear all of his words over the noise of the bar he must have been sitting in. Poor guy sounded miserable.

I was almost asleep when his final words shook me wide awake.

"I saw you, KitKat, and I couldn't say a word. I saw you and you were so beautiful. I fucked up, Kat. I fucked up-" and then the line disconnected.

My eyes snapped open. *What the fuck was that?!?* I stared down at the number on my phone. *Fuck. Fuck. Fuck.*

I felt my dinner at the back of my throat as my stomach turned over. I was sitting up in bed staring at my phone. What the hell was that?

I dialed the number back and waited for the man to answer again. No, I was waiting for Kai to answer. But it wasn't Kai who answered, it was a woman.

"Hello?" she answered.

"Um- I just got a call from this number?" I pretended to be stupid like I didn't know who just called me.

She laughed into the phone, "Oh, sorry about that. He won't bother you again." Then the line went dead. *Again.*

What the actual fuck? Did he think I needed him to fucking torment me some more now that I was back in town? My eyes burned, but I let the tears fall this time. I shut my phone off, and turned back into the pillows to cry. I let out everything that I had been holding back, and I sobbed.

I don't know how long I had cried, or how long I lay whimpering. I vaguely sensed someone crawling onto the bed and holding me, and trying to soothe me. I was too lost in my despair and cried until I was too exhausted to cry anymore. Sometime just after dawn, sleep finally claimed me again.

I didn't dream of anything or anyone, it was just total blackness until I woke up to the sound of Avery and Aiden fighting outside of my room for the privilege of waking me. I heard Andie's voice and realized that I must have overslept. I slowly crawled out of bed and made my way to the bathroom.

As I got a good look of myself in the mirror, I realized that last night was not just another 'rough night.' My short hair was a mess of twisted snarls. My eyes were still red and puffy from crying last night, but there was nothing I could do about that. I just needed to get moving, and *keep* moving today.

Andie handed me a yogurt and a spoon as I entered the kitchen. "I need to run the kids to a party, but I won't be gone long. Do you want to go with me?" She smiled at me, but she was worried. I could see it in her eyes.

I nodded, "Yeah. Give me just a sec to throw on some

real clothes. I didn't sleep so well last night.," I confessed, knowing that she already knew. It was one of the conditions I had set for myself: acknowledging when I was struggling. I set the yogurt back down on the counter and ran up to my room to change.

Not your room. Don't get attached to things, because it won't last.

Returning back to the kitchen, I grabbed the yogurt cup and spoon and ran out the door to join Andie and the kids in her huge SUV. Buckling my seat belt, I had to ask her.

"Tell me again why you have this enormous vehicle when there are only the four of you?"

She smiled as she pulled out of her drive and onto the road that led out of her small community. "Well, the five of us will need space for road trips," she explained.

"What road trips? I am not going on a road trip with your family, Andi-" I stopped talking when I saw her face flushing crimson red. *Oh. My. God.*

"*OH MY GOD! ANDIE!*" I squealed startling Aiden and Avery.

"Shhhhh. Don't say anything. I mean do not finish your thought. We need to wait another three weeks before we say it out loud," she whispered. I could hear the joy and stress in her words. She always waited until she was past the first trimester to tell anyone that she was pregnant.

Too much could happen in those first twelve weeks. I was happy for her, but my hand still covered my own stomach. Grief involuntarily seeping into me again. I didn't know back then. *Too little, too late.*

I smiled at her and nodded. I would keep quiet and pray to whatever god she asked me to, to beg for their baby to be

247

healthy and happy like its older siblings. "Ok," was the only word that I could say.

Chapter 27

Kai's POV

I didn't need a new phone after all, but I would be without one for two days while the company replaced the shattered screen. I couldn't even remember talking to the bartender longer than ordering a drink. Sighing, I climbed back into my car. I needed to call Deedee at work to tell her I dropped my phone.

She would just forward my patients' calls to the reception instead of to me and then page me if I needed to come in. Takes a bit more time doing it old school, but I didn't really have much of a choice. This was what happened when you held out hope and it crashed down. I leaned my head back on the headrest and closed my eyes. Every time I closed my eyes I saw her. The girl I fell in love with growing up and the woman from yesterday interposed over each other.

Fuck. Get your shit together, Kai. I tapped the steering wheel a few times and decided to get on with my day. I needed to run a few errands and then stop by the store to grab a small gift for Lacy's son. I wouldn't stay for the whole party, but I needed to show up for my little man.

Lacy and I met in college and remained friends ever since. I liked to remind her as often as possible that if it weren't for my amazing wingman skills, she wouldn't have met her wife Val.

The memory of me striking out with the beautiful woman at a party still made me laugh. Lacy had convinced me that Valery was making eyes at me all night, so I gave it a go... And the woman laughed in my face. Turned out she wasn't making eyes at me, she was making eyes at Lacy.

I introduced them and the rest was history. They'd been together for six years now. When their adoption finally went through three years ago, they asked me to be their son Xavier's godfather.

I was honored. I still am. The shit that kid had been through in his short life, yet he acted like every day was a gift. I had never seen a kid wake up with a smile laughing before Xavier. He was just a magical kid. As silly as it seemed, he gave me hope.

I got home with a gift wrapped bat, glove, and ball. I promised Xavier I would teach him how to play baseball, and I was going to keep that promise.

Showered, changed and slightly more hydrated, I drove to Lacy's house to celebrate Xavier's sixth birthday. The yard was overrun with kids when I pulled up across the street. I parked my car and grabbed the gift bag from the back seat. It was time to join the chaos.

As I rounded the corner to the back garden I heard Andie's voice. Her son had been in the same kindergarten class as Xavier and the two were thicker than thieves.

"Lacy, this is my best friend since high school, Katie. She just moved back to town so you will probably see her a lot-" Andie's words filtered into my ears and my feet stopped.

"Xavier, this is my godmother I told you about!" Aiden was

excitedly introducing her to Xavier as well. *She was Aiden's godmother?*

"KAI!"

Everyone stopped talking as Xavier yelled my name and ran to jump into my arms. I barely had time to catch him before he knocked into me.

"Hey, birthday man. How old are you now? Ten? Twelve? You're getting so big!" I asked laughing as I hugged him back. I looked up to see Andie, Lacy, Val, and Katie all staring at me. *Shit.*

Val and Lacy were smiling. Andie looked pissed. And Katie. Katie looked like I had just broken her heart all over again. *What the hell?*

"Hey." That was it. That was all of the words that I could muster in that moment. There was a long moment of silence before Andie finally spoke up.

"You're an idiot," she directed at me. Before smiling at the kids and continuing, "Aiden, Xavier, why don't you boys go put the gifts on the table and go play. Ok?"

The boys smiled and ran off without a second thought. Lacy looked from me to Andie, looking confused for a split second before she realized something. Her eyes widened as she looked at me again mouthing, 'Ohmygod.' Her eyes darted over to Katie, and I knew that she had just connected the woman standing in her garden with every stupid confession I had made over the years.

Fuck.

"So, this is fuuuuunnnnn. Right?" Val cackled. "Andie, I had no idea that your best friend was *Katie.*"

Shit. Val had it all figured out too.

"Yeah. I've known Katie for what seems like forever. Kai,

251

you must have told some *great* stories about us from high school, huh?" Andie's tongue was as barbed as I remembered. She walked toward me and pulled me into a hug, and I flinched expecting her to knee in the balls or worse.

She whispered in my ear, "You fucking drunk called her last night, asshole."

What? I didn't-

My eyes closed as bits of memory passed through my head. I just assumed that when Amy told me the bartender's name was also Katie, I drunkenly confessed to a stranger. *No. I had confessed to Katie. My Katie.* I opened my eyes as Andie pulled away and looked over at the woman I could never get over.

"Hey," was all that she said to me.

"Hey. Um, you want to grab a soda and catch up?" I asked Katie, not wanting to see the looks the other three women were giving me.

She seemed uncertain, and looked at Andie. "We've got time, go ahead and grab something to eat too. You had a rough night," Andie said the last bit to her but she was looking at me.

I gestured toward the back of the house and walked with Katie trailing slightly behind me. I was nervous. Katie Preston was here and I was the asshole who drunk dialed her in the middle of the night. *I was an idiot.*

* * *

Katie's POV

I couldn't speak. First he called me last night while he was out with his girlfriend, and now he was just staring at me like I owed him something. I gave Andie one last look, hoping she understood how angry I was with her right now.

I followed him into the house. It was a beautiful home filled with bright colors, toys, and children's artwork. Once upon a time, I wanted this. With him. I pushed all of that back down and sat at the end of the sofa in the living room. Kai took a seat across from me and handed me a 7Up. Did he remember that I didn't like dark sodas? *No.* That was stupid. It was a children's party, so of course they wouldn't serve dark sodas.

"How have you been?" he asked quietly, staring down at his own drink.

"Ok," was all that I could manage. I was alive. That was *ok*, right?

"Um, I didn't mean to call you last night. I'm sorry if I disturbed you and your husband," he apologized.

Kai apologized for disturbing me and my hus- I started laughing. He had heard Jonas and I yesterday afternoon, and really thought *Jonas* was my husband. The more I thought about it, the more I found the irony of it funnier and laughed harder.

"You are apologizing for calling and disturbing me and *my husband,* when your girlfriend was taking care of you last night?" I asked him, my voice clipped with bubbling rage.

His head shot up and his eyes locked with mine. "Katie, I don't have a girlfriend."

My building anger crumbled with those words, "What?"

He looked at me honestly, "I said that I am not seeing anyone. There is no one in my life except for the people in this house and Bradley's family. I don't have a girlfriend."

Now I was confused. If he didn't have a girlfriend who the hell was answering his phone at one o'clock in the morning?

"Then who answered your phone?" I asked before realizing that I had just admitted to calling him back.

I watched his eyes, and knew that he was piecing things together.

"That was the *bartender* at Stone Balloon. Bradley was trying to get me out to his car and I left my phone on the bar. She was pissed that I wasn't interested in *her* and smashed my phone," he admitted to me.

Wait. Why was I sitting here listening to this?

"What do you want from me, Kai?" I asked him without any mixed messages or coy wording. Straight to the point.

"I want to take my friend out to dinner. That is if we are still friends?" he asked, looking at me like I could crush his heart at any second.

"I wasn't the one to break our friendship," I whispered. I could feel every single emotion in me bubbling up. Nervousness, anger, joy, curiosity, butterflies, and hope. *No hope.* I took a deep breath and tamped the hope out. There would be none of that.

"You can bring your husband," he offered and all thoughts in my head stopped.

I cleared my throat as I felt it getting tight. I willed myself not to cry. "Um, that won't be possible-" but he cut me off.

"Oh, yeah. You're right. Your husband would probably be pissed that I am asking to take you out to dinner. I'm sorry, I wasn't thinking," he apologized again.

"He can't come because he passed away," I whispered out. There. I said it. Out loud to someone else. I admitted that Ty was gone.

Kai's face paled and then flushed a bit when I said those words. I must have looked like I was about to crumble, because the next thing I knew he was sitting next to me and pulling me into his arms. There was nothing sexual about the hug, he just caressed my back and held me while I cried quietly.

"I'm so sorry for your loss, Kat. I didn't know," he whispered quietly against my hair.

I don't know how long we sat there, but I must have cried myself to sleep in his arms. I heard quiet whispers around me, but I had nothing left. I was thoroughly exhausted, and just let myself drift off again with my head leaned against a shoulder.

* * *

Kai's POV

I pulled Katie onto my lap and held her while she cried. I don't know what happened in the time we were apart, but whatever it was destroyed her. She was pure sunshine in school, so happy about life and everything that the future held. This woman in my arms was broken in ways that I couldn't understand yet. But I would hold her if she let me. I would hold her every night if she let me have the chance.

I listened to her breathing even out and realized that she had cried herself to sleep in my arms. I tucked the hair in her face behind her ear, and just looked at her. She looked so tired. Is this why she was so thin? I readjusted us so that she was cradled in my lap with her head resting against my shoulder. Her hands grabbed onto my shirt when I shifted our positions, but I shushed and soothed her until she relaxed against me again.

"Katie?" Andie's voice called through the house before she

came around the corner and saw me with my finger against my lips indicating to be quiet.

She came around the sofa and knelt in front of us, smoothing Katie's hair down in a motherly caress.

"She didn't want you to see her like this," Andie whispered to me, still staring at the woman asleep in my arms. "Do you want me to take her home with me?"

I shook my head. I didn't want to let go. Not yet. Not ever if I was being honest. "No, I'll take care of her tonight. I'll bring her to yours tomorrow. Nothing funny, I promise," I whispered as I stared down at Katie. "I won't let anything happen to her, Andie. I swear on my life."

Andie finally looked up at me and nodded. "Thank you for not giving up on her, Kai," she said before standing up and leaving a light kiss on Katie's temple.

As she walked out of the room, I leaned back into the corner of the sofa and gently adjusted our positions once more so that Katie was asleep on my chest, my arms holding her close to me while she slept. I closed my eyes and let my mind quiet down as I listened to her even breathing.

I opened one eye when I felt someone pulling a blanket over us. I mouthed 'Thank you,' to Val and looked down at Katie still sound asleep in my arms. I gently kissed her forehead, and closed my eyes to sleep as well. We would talk tomorrow or any day that she would let me in.

Chapter 28

Katie's POV

I didn't know how long I slept. But I knew that it was the best sleep I had had in years. As I woke up, I became aware of the fact that I was not in my bed but sleeping on a chest. I stilled my movements trying to recall the last memories before I fell asleep.

Oh god! Was I asleep on Kai? I fell asleep on Kai!

I jumped at the realization, flailing to get off of the sofa and put space between us as quickly as possible. My knee came up and hit something very hard as I fell onto the floor.

"Ungh! *Shit,* that is not a way to wake up," Kai grumbled, grabbing his goods that I had just damaged with my knee.

"Sorry. I was confused," I whispered and reached out to soothe him without thinking where my hands were *soothing*.

Kai's body stilled as his eyes fluttered open to look at me. "Kat, unless you plan on doing more than kicking me in the balls, can you not handle my dick? It sends a bit of a mixed signal," he whispered in a breathy gasp.

I stopped my movement realizing that I was in fact caressing his goods. I tried to jerk my hand back, but he grabbed it before I could get away and held it in place.

His eyes locked on mine, like he was trying to read my

thoughts or gauge my reaction. "I don't mind if you want to make it feel better," he smirked, his eyes twinkling with mischief like they used to. He guided my hand up his abdomen and pulled me back onto his body.

"Just stay here for now, Kat. I don't want to let go. Not yet," he confessed quietly against my hair as I lay down on his chest again. His arms wrapped around me and just held me.

I expected to feel anxious or nervous, but I felt safe. For the first time in years, I felt like I didn't need to be on guard. I let myself melt back into his embrace and exhaled the breath I didn't realize that I was holding. My ear was pressed against his chest when I lay my head back down, and I heard his heart starting to race. I still made him nervous.

I felt his lips press against my forehead in the lightest of kisses. "I don't know what happened to you, Katie, but I am here now. I don't want to pick up where we left off, because what I did back then was shit. I want to start from here and move forward with you. Can you let me in a little?" He pleaded with me.

His words were confident but his voice sounded so vulnerable. Like I held his life in my hands to lift up or crush at my discretion. I didn't know what to say, so I said the only thing that came to my mind.

"Ok."

"Ok," he repeated back. "Then can I make you breakfast? Take you to my house and make you breakfast?"

He must have felt my body tense ever so slightly, because his hands soothed and caressed my back until I relaxed against him again.

"We did sleep together. It seems only right that I take you

258

for breakfast," he continued.

I couldn't stop the giggle that escaped my lips. This man was just as brazen, twisting shit to make it sound indecent.

"Not to mention you groping me so early in the morning," he continued in his serious whisper.

I reared back to look at him, and he finally broke and started laughing. Seeing him laugh made me laugh. He pulled me back against his chest and I felt the vibrations of his laughter through his chest. "I missed this," I whispered out so quietly, I thought maybe he had not heard it.

He tipped my head up to look at him. His eyes searched over my face and stared into my eyes. "Can I kiss you, Kitkat?" he asked me.

I just stared back at him, wide eyed and nervous. I think I nodded, because his lips came up so gently and kissed mine. He lay a second kiss against my lips, then a third before sucking my bottom lip between his. The change surprised me, and he took that opportunity to explore the kiss further. It was not a greedy kiss. It wasn't crazy or passionate. It was a sweet kiss that gently stoked whatever small ember still remained between us.

I had to admit it…. There was still some chemistry.

He pulled away first and looked at me again. "Can I take you home, Katie?"

I nodded again, afraid to say a word or make a sound. We got up and straightened the sofa, and folded the blanket that someone had pulled over us. I didn't say a word, as Kai left a note on the counter for our hosts Lacy and Val, and then guided me across the street to his car. The same car that I had seen him in at the gas station.

He opened the passenger door for me and waited until I

was fully situated before gently closing the door and running around the car to climb into the driver's seat. Neither of us said a word during the fifteen minute drive to his house. He pulled up in front of a gorgeous two story colonial on the outside of town.

"This yours?" I asked him, looking up at the beautiful brick home.

"Mostly," he admitted turning the car off after he parked in the drive.

I looked at him and waited for him to finish explaining.

"I own most of it. It was my grandmother's and she left it to my brother and I. He already had a place down state, so I pay him rent every month until his half is paid off."

"How many more payments do you have?" I asked him curious about how this worked out for them.

"Mmmmmm, about 10 years," he chuckled. "His half came out to a little over seventy thousand, so I pay him six hundred a month. He was fine with me just taking it, but it didn't seem right. We worked it out between us. My payments every month go into his kids' college funds. It works out."

I nodded as we walked into his home. It was not the bachelor pad I was expecting. The walls were warm colors, and the furniture made the space feel inviting and homey. He grabbed my hand and pulled me behind him into a spacious open kitchen and dining area.

"Sit. I'll make us some coffee and some breakfast," he instructed and went to walk away.

I didn't let go of his hand though. My heart raced and I wondered if I would have the courage to tell him everything. Would he still look at me like a treasure if he knew that I was damaged goods? Would he still want me if he knew just how fucking broken I was?

He turned to look at me when I wouldn't release his hand. Did he know what I was thinking? What I was worried about?

"Yes, Kat?" he whispered as his mouth smashed against mine. His hands braced either side of my face as he kissed me like he wanted to convince me to stay. When the reality was the opposite. Would he run away from *me* after this?

He whispered small affirmations to me, between kisses "Yes," he wanted me.

"Yes," he would stay forever if I let him.

"Yes," he still loved me.

I didn't realize that I was crying until he wiped away my tears, kissing my eyes, nose and lips again.

"Jesus, Kat," he swore with his forehead resting against mine. "I wanted to take our time, but I don't think you understand the words. I want to worship you, Katie."

His mouth trailed kisses down my neck to my collar bone. His hands came under my ass and lifted me to sit on the island countertop so that my legs were spread to either side of his body. One hand grabbed one of my breasts and massaged it, while the other pulled my ass to the edge of the counter, where he ground his stiffening cock against me.

The friction against my clit was sending ripples of need through my body as I held onto him. I moaned quietly, which seemed to encourage him even further. "Katie, I want you. I need to hear you say that you want this," he stopped kissing me and looked into my half lidded eyes.

"Please, Kai. Don't stop," I whimpered, pulling his neck toward me to kiss him again. He grabbed under my ass again, lifting me off of the counter and wrapping my legs around his waist.

"Then we are not going to fuck on my counter," he told me before stopping and reconsidering his choice of words. "I *will* fuck you with your delicious ass bent over my counter, but first I want to tell you everything you need to know. *In my bed.*" He continued to carry me through the house kissing my throat and sucking on my ear lobes.

My mind stopped processing any rational thought. I couldn't think past that moment and every sensation I experienced under Kai's hands and lips.

* * *

Kai's POV

I couldn't believe that I was carrying Katie through my house. When I finally got to my bedroom and laid her down on the bed, I continued kissing every exposed inch of skin that I could. I looked up to her eyes to see if she was still okay with this.

She responded by pulling my shirt over my head and running her hands down my chest. "I'm okay, Kai," she whispered, pulling me back to kiss her again.

My hands ran under her t-shirt and lifted it over her head. I threw it onto the floor and stared down at the woman beneath me. She was still a goddess in my eyes. I ran my hands over a noticeable scar that ran across her abdomen and chest. I watched as her body tensed, her eyes panicked. Did she think this would scare me away? I bent over her body and trailed more kisses across her skin, licking and sucking the scar until I reached her breasts.

I slid the straps of her bra down her arms and then pulled

her bra further down her chest. Taking one nipple into my mouth and sucking hard, I rolled the other between my fingers pulling on it gently. I loved the sounds that she made when I did something that she liked.

Her hands dug into my hair, and pulled me closer to her. I used her moans and whimpers as the guide for whether she liked something or not. I would relearn every spot on her body until there was nothing left to learn, and then I would worship her until she begged me to stop.

Her hands reached for my pants as she unfastened them and pulled down the zipper. She reached into my boxers, grasped my cock and caressed it from the base to the tip. Her hand tightened around me and I had to release her breast from my mouth to suck in a breath. *Fuck, that felt really good.*

I grabbed either side of her waist and pulled her shorts and panties down her legs. As soon as I had them off of her, my mouth was trailing kisses down the inside of her left thigh. I watched her face as I continued to the point at the top inside of her thigh and I sucked hard. Her body arched off of my bed and she moaned.

She was so wet already, and would always be wet like this for me. I wanted to devour her but I was so hard it was painful. I moved back up so that I could grind my erection against her wetness and watch her writhe under me. I kissed her again, but slowly this time. "Are you sure, Katie?" I asked one more time as I pressed my tip against her opening.

"Yes, please, Kai," she whimpered, wrapping her legs around my hips and pulling me into her.

"Fuck," I gasped as I slid into her.

She tensed as I pushed all the way in until I could push no further. She was so tight. I thought I was going to cum right then and there.

Her hands grabbed onto my back and she whimpered again, tears slowly falling from her eyes. "Please," she whispered, and that was all it took to convince me.

I moved slowly at first until her body relaxed, and then began to thrust harder and deeper, her hips rocking up to meet me every time. I couldn't stop kissing her lips, my tongue exploring every part of her mouth. She moaned my name and I felt her come undone around me. Her walls tightening and spasming , squeezing me, were my undoing. I thrust two more times and tried to pull out before I came but she locked me against her with my legs.

"Katie, relax your legs. I'm going to cum," I moaned, still thrusting hard into her.

"Cum for me, Kai." she whispered against my ear as she held me tighter.

I swear I saw stars, as my orgasm ripped through my body. I pushed into her as deep as I could and came inside of her. My body trembled as my cock twitched and emptied itself.

"Haah… I didn't have a condom, Katie," I told her, realizing what we had just done as my body relaxed against hers.

She hummed against me as I rolled and pulled her to lie on my chest. "I'll trust you, Kai," she whispered against my skin.

How could she say things like that? After all of these years. I laid there holding her until I heard her breaths even out, letting me know that she had fallen asleep again. I pulled the blanket over her body and allowed myself to drift off as well.

I woke up to bright sunshine coming through the window. I reached out for the body that had been next to mine and realized that I was alone in my bed. I sat up and looked around the room. Her clothes were gone.

I jumped out of bed, pulling on my shorts and I went through the house looking for Katie. *She wouldn't use me like that, right?* I found a note on my counter: *"Call me when your phone is fixed. You owe me breakfast."*

I laughed out loud, staring at her neat, bubbly handwriting. This woman was not running back to me. Katie was going to make me work for everything I had done to her. Taking the note with me back to my room, I set it on my night stand and walked to the master bath to get a shower. I was late for work and didn't give a shit, smiling as I stepped under the hot water. *She was back.*

Chapter 29

Katie's POV

For the second time today, I woke up lying across Kai's chest. I pulled away slowly. There were so many emotions exchanged this morning, I couldn't breathe thinking about it. I couldn't believe that I had sex with him. We hadn't seen each other in a freaking decade, and I jumped into bed with him the first time we met. At the same time, everything felt... *right*.

"Shit," I whispered so quietly, as that realization settled in. Sliding out of his bed, I found my bra tangled in the sheets. I slipped on my bra and shirt while I snuck out of the room with my shorts and panties in hand.

We did nothing wrong. I repeated to myself as I pulled the remainder of my clothes on, standing outside his room. I didn't want to just leave, so I left him a note saying to call me when his phone was fixed. I placed it in the center of the kitchen island where he couldn't miss it, before I snuck out the back door.

I walked to the end of his street and then started jogging back toward town. Thank god, I had my phone with me. I called Andie, and she picked me up when I was halfway back.

My face was flushed, and I was sweaty all over when I

climbed into the passenger seat. "Can we stop for some food? I haven't eaten yet," I asked, looking out the window.

"Sure. I'll stop and grab you breakfast," she responded. Suddenly, the car lurched to the right shoulder and she slammed on the brakes; my body jolting forward against the restraints.

"What the fuck, Andie?!?!" I yelled, looking over at her.

"Me? You asked me to pick you up after a booty call with your ex and want to pretend like nothing happened? Ask me to get you breakfast? What the fuck have you done with my, Katie!?" She yelled, staring at me wide eyed.

I was speechless. I just stared at her and couldn't form any words. She reached forward and wiped my cheeks. I didn't even realize I was crying. "Are you okay?" She whispered, petting my hair back from my face.

"I don't know?" I replied truthfully. A part of me felt peaceful, and the other felt like I had betrayed my husband. *My dead husband.* I felt like I was dying all over again, because a part of me really liked being with Kai. He made me feel *safe.*

"I think I messed up..." I whispered before crying harder.

Andie pulled me into a hug. "Shhhh. You did nothing wrong. This is okay. I didn't mean to yell at you. I'm sorry. I wasn't trying to shame you for being with Kai. *I am so sorry, Katie.* Please don't think you did anything bad. You didn't. I don't think anything bad of this at all. I was just teasing," she apologized profusely.

I couldn't stop the meltdown. Hearing her apologize to me, and telling me that I did nothing wrong just broke the dam. The last thing I remembered was Andie pulling me into a fiercer hug. When I woke up, I was in the bed in her guest

267

room; Avery and Aiden sound asleep beside me.

My face hurt from all the snot and tears. I stunk like sex and gym socks. My hair was tangled and sticking to my face. I was a right hot mess, to be sure. I slipped out of the bed and grabbed some fresh clothes from the closet before sneaking off to shower.

The hot steam cleared my head, and relaxed all of the anxiety in my muscles. I scrubbed from head to toe, getting all of the salted sweat off of my skin. When I stepped out of the shower, I could breathe again. Wiping the steam from the mirror, my eyes were still a little puffy but I didn't look quite the same as I did when I woke up the previous morning.

I smelled like strawberries and vanilla, and my skin almost looked like it was glowing. I looked down at my watch and realized it was six o'clock in the morning. *Shit.*

Andie picked me up before ten in the morning. What the hell happened? Memories of Kai came flooding back, and I felt my face heat up. I knocked boots with my ex, and then ghosted him. I literally ran from his house across town before Andie picked me up.

"Oh my god! Andie!!" I gasped. She was pregnant and had to deal with my crazy ass. My eyes were burning as new tears and guilt flooded through me. "Shit. Shit," I whispered to myself, as I dropped to the floor on my ass. I needed to get control of myself. I needed to...

"Breathe."

"That's it. Deep breath. And out again. You're safe here," Andie's voice murmured against my temple.

I looked up to see her concerned face staring down at me. "I'm so sorry," I sobbed, feeling like such a fucking horrible friend. It wasn't her job to fix me, or clean up behind me.

"Stop," she ordered me. "I know what you're thinking, and you need to stop. You cried yourself to sleep in my arms yesterday. Jonas carried you into the house, and you have slept like a baby since."

I shook my head. I knew what I was like. I could be violent and not have any recollection at all. I had seen what I was like in emotional distress, and had no control to change it.

"*Stop!*" She said more forcefully, knowing how my mind was spiraling. "You didn't lose control. You didn't scream. You cried, Katie. I feel like such a horrible friend for shaming you like I did. I have been scared to death that I fucked up your recovery!" She admitted crying into my shoulder as she held me tightly.

I didn't understand what she was talking about. "What are - going on about?" I asked between sobs.

"Yesterday," she sniffled. "You asked me for help, and I just shamed you for having sex. I didn't mean to make you cry! I just wanted to give you shit… Like old times," she admitted, crying harder. "Then you broke down, and I felt so fucking horrible. I am so, so, sorry, Katiedid. You have every right to move on at your own pace, and I was just so happy that you got laid… It felt like old times!" She continued rambling.

I leaned back to look at her red puffy face, snot running down tear stained cheeks, and I started laughing. We were a fucking mess, the two of us. "I thought I hurt your baby!" I admitted quietly.

"I thought I broke your recovery!"

"I felt so bad that you have to keep taking care of me!"

"I thought you would shut me out because I made you feel bad!"

"I could have hurt you and not known."

269

"I knew I hurt you and I wanted to die!"

We sobbed and laughed, confessing all of our transgressions to one another until Jonas came to stand in the doorway of the bathroom and asked us to 'please shut the fuck up.' He hadn't slept because of us. Andie cried all night about hurting my feelings, and kept making him check on me throughout the night.

He looked like a hot mess. "Sorry," we whispered, ashamedly.

"Go away. Take the kids to school, and leave me to sleep," he ordered Andie, as he returned to their room. He glanced at her, asking sheepishly, "Please?"

Andie and I nodded emphatically. Of course we would let him sleep. "Sorry!" We apologized again before he closed the bedroom door.

"Want to make breakfast with me?" Andie asked, standing up from the floor.

"Yeah. What are we making?" I asked, wrapping my arm around her waist as we walked into the kitchen together still sniffling.

"Bacon pancakes?" She offered, looking at me seriously.

I chewed on my lip for a second. "Will that make him less angry with us?" I asked her back.

She squinted her eyes as if she were weighing the options. "We could prep BLT waffles for lunch, and have pancakes for the kids."

I nodded, no idea what she was talking about, but it sounded delicious. "What can I help you with?"

She directed me to prepare the salad and tomatoes, while she pulled the ingredients for pancakes and waffles. I grabbed two packs of bacon from the fridge and set them on the counter.

Thirty minutes later, the sweet smell of pancakes on the griddle was mixed with the salty smell of cooked bacon in the oven. Aiden and Avery came ambling into the kitchen, already dressed for school as we were setting their plates on the table.

Normally, Andie and Jonas would fight with the kids to get them out of bed, let alone dressed and ready to start their day. I looked at Andie to see her just as shocked as I was. "What's going on?" She asked her children when they stopped in front of her.

"We're sorry, mommy. We didn't mean to make Katie leave her bed," Avery apologized, staring at the floor. Aiden was shifting next to his sister and peeking over at me from the corner of his eye.

"Is that why you are up and dressed already?" Andie asked.

"Yes. We're sorry, Miss Katie!" Aiden cried, running for me.

I dropped to my knees and scooped him up, speechless when he hugged me fiercely. Andie pulled Avery into a hug and addressed both of them, "You little sweethearts did nothing wrong. You were such great little snugglers, Katie wanted to make you breakfast and drive you to school!" She lied.

Aiden pulled back from his hug to study my face, "Really? You not mad at us?"

I couldn't help smiling at his little adorable face. "You are so sweet, both of you. We're making BLT waffles for your lunches and mommy made your favorite bacon pancakes for breakfast!"

Avery made a loud sigh of relief. "We tried to ask daddy

where you went and he said you were both mad... and something about punishments- cause nobody was sleeping." Her voice trailed off as she tried to remember everything Jonas had told them.

Andie bit her lips and tried not to laugh. I looked at her and knew exactly what Jonas said.

We were bad. For keeping him up all night. *We were in the kitchen making breakfast as punishment.* Because Jonas was exhausted. *We would drive them to school.* Because Jonas just wanted to sleep.

"Actually-" I started to correct them, but Andie cut me off.

"It's very sweet that you two would think of apologizing like this. I think daddy would agree that this is really sweet, too," she praised them as they shuffled to the table. "I will make sure he knows just how considerate you both are, and there will be a surprise when you get home. Okay?"

Aiden and Avery nodded excitedly. While they tucked in, I poured batter into the heated waffle iron and sprinkled it with bacon bits. It didn't take long to pack their lunch boxes with tomato slices, lettuce, and bacon waffles.

Soon, we were out the door, both kids fastened into their seats, and headed to the school to drop them off. Andie sent me alone and stayed behind to clean up the kitchen. I detoured on the way back, stopping at the car shop to see my folks.

We had made a lot of progress since Christmas, and I wanted to be able to talk to them without it feeling weird. I found my mom tucked in a back warehouse of parts, her glasses hanging on the end of her nose as she counted parts off to two others loading bins for the runners.

"Hey, mom," I called over to her from the door.

She peered over the top of her readers and smiled. "Hey, sweetie! What brings you here? Everything go okay with the storage unit?" She asked.

I nodded and waved my hand. "Yeah. Fine. I just wanted to talk, if you have some time."

She passed her paperwork to one of the two men standing next to her. "Terrance, Miguel, this is my other daughter, Katie."

The two smiled and waved at me.

"Hey."

"This the Marine?" They spoke at the same time.

I nodded and responded, "Hello. Guilty."

"Oooh-rah!" the older of the two men barked out.

"Oooh-rah," I replied, sounding less confident in my response.

My mom saw my reaction and immediately pulled me to follow her to the office. "Come on, I'll make you some coffee and you can tell me all about it," she said as we walked.

"There's nothing wrong, mom," I attempted, but she just stopped me with a fierce side eye.

Sitting in her office with a small cup of black coffee, she sat down next to me on the small two seater sofa. "Okay, spill it."

My eyebrows went up as I sipped the coffee. "I- I don't even know where to begin," I stuttered.

She nodded as if I had spoken volumes. "Let's start with how you're feeling today. What's your happy today?"

I chuckled at her, and pulled a small sandwich box out of my bag. "Waffle BLTs," I said, passing it to her.

"Is this for me?" she asked excitedly.

"Yeah," I smiled, watching her inspect the unconventional

pairing.

"Okay, I accept this offering," she said, closing the box and setting it on her desk. "Now tell me what has you unsettled."

"I ran into Kai," I whispered. She didn't need to hear anything else, and pulled me into a hug.

"Oh, wow. I was not expecting that. Tell me everything you are comfortable sharing."

Chapter 30

Kai's POV

It took two days to get my phone back, and it was filled with messages from work. Even though I had been proactive about having my calls forwarded, it had not stopped the deluge of missed calls and messages.

I started from the oldest and worked my way through every voicemail and text between patients. I didn't hear anything from Katie, which I wasn't expecting; but at the same time I hoped. I hoped that I hadn't scared her off. I hoped that she hadn't felt forced or like she *had* to call *me* back.

Fuck. What if she thought I was just messing with her? What if she didn't know how serious I was? I started to call her and stopped. What would I say? I didn't even know how to ask what I wanted to know.

I threw my head back in my chair and let out an exasperated growl. *Why did this have to be so fucking complicated?*

"Everything alright in here?" Dr. Lee asked, leaning against my door.

I couldn't help but smile. "Hey, man! What brings you to my neck of the woods?" I asked, standing to go shake his hand.

Lee had been the man with me when Heather died. He

helped me put my packet together for the doctoral program. He mentored me through my clinicals, and helped me prepare for my dissertations. He even wrote the reference letter that got me a job with this clinic.

"I was hoping you would have time for lunch with an old friend," he offered.

I took a quick look at my desk, comfortable with the workload I had managed to get through so far this morning. "Yeah, as long as I can get back by one thirty for my next consultation. What did you have in mind?" I asked, grabbing my keys and closing up my office.

"I thought we could grab some wings from that truck over by the fire station," Lee suggested.

My stomach grumbled before I could utter a peep. Lee laughed and clapped me on the back. "Sounds like we're having wings!"

I stopped by the reception desk to let them know I was stepping out for lunch, but I had my phone on me.

"I like the new guy the clinic hired to work the desk," Lee commented as we climbed into his car.

I nodded, looking back toward the building. "Yeah, Marty's a great guy. Super professional. Efficient as hell!" I swore quietly.

Lee laughed. "What happened to the little brunette that was there?" he asked as we pulled onto the main road.

I shook my head. "Hell if I know. I can't keep track of the temps this place runs through," I admitted.

Lee looked over at me. "Oh? I thought there was some other issue going on. You were just running through temps this whole time?"

I caught onto the double meaning in his words and shook

my head. "No. Nope. Never happened. I don't shit where I eat, dude. You know that."

Lee laughed. "I wasn't saying that to you *personally*. I just meant your clinic."

There was a moment of silence before he looked over at me again. "Seriously though.... Not even one?" He asked.

It was my turn to laugh as he parked behind the fire station. "Not one," I confirmed.

"But there was somebody recently," he pried.

I didn't say anything and stepped out of his car. I thought my poker face was good enough, but something must have given me away because he started cackling behind me. "You did!!"

Suddenly, he was behind me and clapping me on the back again. "So the dry spell is over? This mean you can be my wingman?" He asked.

"No."

"Come on! You never went before because you were married. Then you were grieving. Then it was school... What's it this time?" He asked.

As we approached the window of the food truck, he let it go. I didn't say anything and ordered my food. Once we were both seated with our lunches at a picnic table, Lee went back to his questioning.

"So? Spill it," he said, taking a sip of his sweet tea.

"There's a woman I am seeing," I admitted. Then added, "I think. Maybe. I hope so anyway."

Lee stared at me wide eyed for a second. "What kind of shit is that? Have you at least talked to her?"

I rolled my eyes, wiping my hands on a wet napkin. "Yes, I've fucking talked to her. We've known each other since back in school, and just kind of…. reconnected recently."

Lee nodded, following along. "So…. What's that mean? You exchanged numbers? Saliva? DNA samples?"

I choked on the soda that was mid-way down my throat, and started coughing.

Lee laughed at me. "Holy shit! You *really* reconnected!"

I wiped my mouth with a napkin once I stopped choking on my beverage. "When are you this straight forward?" I asked, eyeing him.

He grinned and leaned back a bit. "Eh…. I was afraid to talk when you worked for me…. Now, we're friends; I don't need to be so diplomatic," he said, winking.

"Jesus… Fine. We're friends. So tell me, wise one. What do I do to get the love of my life to give me a second chance?" I asked, staring back at him.

Lee sat speechless for a good two minutes before saying a word. "This the girl that left town?" He asked, quickly piecing everything together.

"Yep."

"I thought she was married. Scary marine or some such other shit, out of state. What happened?"

I bit my lip, deciding what I wanted to share about Katie. "Widowed. Finished with the Marines. Just moved back two weeks ago."

"And you already slept with her?" He whistled, looking shocked.

I looked down at the ground, feeling ashamed. "When you put it that way, I sound like an asshole. But it wasn't like that. She just…. She started crying and I just held her. The whole night," I admitted quietly and told him everything that had happened up to Lacy's house.

"Damn," Lee exhaled. "You're the better man, Kai."

"I don't know what to do, Lee. I don't want to fuck this up. I want to spend the rest of my life waking up next to her."

"Well, try the old fashioned way and take her out to dinner. You got an in with Alex's; why don't you take her there?" He suggested.

My face heated up immediately, remembering our first time. "I don't know how she'd feel about that, to be honest."

Lee laughed at my reaction. "Take her to dinner, and let her get to know you. You've both been through a lot over the last ten years, from the sound of it. Start with dinner, and see where it goes from there."

* * *

Katie's POV

"Andie, can I help you with anything?" I asked, watching her whip around the kitchen preparing food for everyone.

"No! You just sit and relax. I don't want you to be stressed or anxious, Katie. Just try to relax, ok?" Andie smiled at me and gave me a sweet kiss on my cheek like she was placating a child.

"I can't," I whined. I was nervous and stressed. Kai hadn't called me in a week. I knew his phone was broken, but it had been *a week*. My insecurities had completely taken over my rational thoughts.

Andie stopped and stared at me. Her face was a mix of thoughts that I couldn't read. She started to turn away, and then sighed as if in resignation. "I can't do this," she muttered.

She put down the spatula she had been holding and walked over to me. "Kai will be here at 6pm to pick you up for a date. He wanted to surprise you, so he called me. Go wash up, pretend like you know how to dress yourself up in something other than t-shirts and training shorts," she stated, staring at me, waiting for me to obey, but I was in shock.

"What?" Was all that I could get out.

"You're going on a date. Don't look like..." She waved her hands in a circle gesturing at my whole body, "like *this. Try*, Katie. Try to look like a grown woman again."

I didn't have a chance to say another word because she turned my body and forced me out of the kitchen.

"He'll be here in one hour!" she yelled at my back as I walked to the stairs.

"What the hell is this?" I yelled from the guest room when I found a black dress laid out on the bed.

"An intervention!" Jonas yelled from the living room.

What the hell? Jonas was in on this too?

I grumbled as I walked into the bathroom to get a shower and cleaned up. *I could do this.* Why was I so nervous about seeing Kai? We already slept together. He had seen me broken down and a mess and still wanted to have sex with me.

I came out of the bathroom 30 minutes later, wearing the black dress, my hair dried and tamed into a little bob that rested on my shoulders. I hadn't really worn make-up since, well, three years ago. It felt foreign to me, so I just put on some mascara and a little lip gloss.

I walked downstairs when I was okay with how I looked. Andie stopped and whistled, looking me up and down with an appreciative smile. "There she is," she gloated as she walked over to give me a hug.

"I may have lied about the time," she whispered just as the

doorbell rang.

I jerked back from the hug and looked at her wide eyed. "No, Andie, I need more time," I whispered urgently hoping she would cancel this whole thing.

She smiled and shook her head. "No, it's time for you to inch forward, Katie. You don't have to run, but just inch a weeeeeeeee bit forward."

I followed her to the door, and put on my black flats. I refused to wear heels, but they didn't look bad with the dress either. It wasn't form fitted, but it definitely accentuated the few curves that I still possessed. I wanted to turn and run out of the back door, but then I heard Kai's voice.

"You look amazing, Katie."

I turned to see him looking at me and smiling. I looked at Andie with panic again, but she just laughed and shook her head. Again. *Damnit.*

"Hi." That was all that I could muster up.

Kai seemed to understand and looked at Andie a little worriedly, but she just shook her head at him too. Suddenly two sets of small hands were pushing me to the door, and I turned to find Aiden and Avery smiling up at me.

"Have fun!" They cheered together.

"Et tu?" I scowled at them before being pushed out the door with Kai.

"Um, I guess she didn't tell you about tonight?" Kai asked. His face flushed with embarrassment.

"Eh- No. I just found out about 30 minutes ago. So I wasn't prepared," I admitted.

"Well, we are here now, so let's try," he whispered, taking my hand and pulling me toward his car. He opened the passenger door for me and gestured for me to climb in, but then stopped me. "You look amazing, Katie," he whispered in my ear before leaving a light kiss on my cheek.

I felt my face heat up and knew that I must be cherry red. I quickly sat in my seat and let him close the door while I buckled up. As he drove away from Andie's, I finally found my voice and asked what we were doing tonight.

"If I say it is a surprise, will that make you more or less nervous?" he glanced over at me while he drove through town.

"More," I admitted.

He nodded. "Ok. I am taking you to have a relaxing dinner. No stress, no expectations. Just dinner between two friends."

I processed the words he had just said, and all of my insecurities bubbled up again. "Is that what we are, Kai? Just friends?" I asked, my voice barely a whisper.

He reached over and took my fidgeting hands out of my lap and held them while he drove. "Katie, I don't know what we are, and I don't think you do either. But we were friends once, and I thought that would be the best place to start. We can start here and decide where we go next."

I felt my body relax a little. That was fair. He didn't know me, and I didn't know him. We had history, but we didn't know each other *now*. I let the warmth of his hands keep me tethered to this moment. I didn't need to worry about anything else outside of this moment.

"Ok. Yeah," I nodded in agreement. I looked out the window and realized that we were driving outside of town, the roads seemingly familiar. "Where are we going?" I asked him, recognizing some of the farms.

"To a new restaurant that opened up since you left," Kai chuckled and looked over at me again as he pulled down a familiar road and drove toward a large barn now adorned with a huge sign that read, "Alex's".

Alex had turned his family's barn into a restaurant. It started as a small giggle, but then I started to laugh as Kai parked his car where there used to be a field. "I'm sorry. All I can think right now is that song, *'They paved paradise and put up a parking lot,"* I sang.

Kai just looked at me smiling. He brought my hand up to his mouth and gave it a light kiss. "Come on. I don't want to lose our table," he told me, opening his door and returning my hand to my lap.

Kai walked around the car, opened my door and took my hand again. I stepped out and fell in step beside him after he closed the car door. It was crazy being back here, and walking into this building with Kai after all of these years.

As we walked into the main doors, my jaw dropped. It was an actual restaurant built inside the barn. A nice one at that. Kai led me up to the hostess station and told her his name. She smiled and joked with him a bit before guiding us back to our table.

I stared at Kai in disbelief. Our table was basically where we had done it for the first time. My face felt like it was on fire.

"What is this?" I whispered to him. Mortified that we were about to eat over the place we had *sex* the first time.

Kai saw my expression and started to chuckle. "I honestly didn't know *this* would be our table," he admitted quietly.

I stopped staring around the restaurant and looked at my date. His face was just as red as mine, the pink hue having spread up to his ears.

"Do you want to change tables?" He asked me seriously.

I relaxed a bit. His nervousness actually made me feel more at ease for some reason. "No," I responded quietly, "this is fine."

I let Kai order our food, since he knew what was best on the menu. He ordered two house steaks with everything, and a glass of the white wine that came recommended as the pairing.

"Are you hoping to get me drunk?" I asked as the wine was placed in front of me.

Kai looked embarrassed for a moment. "Honestly, I don't drink. I had a bit of a set back recently, and I don't want to fall into old habits," he admitted, he ears flushing red.

I chuckled, recalling his drunken confession and decided to let it go. We had time to share all of those stories. The dinner was nice. The food was delicious and the conversation between us flowed.

Chapter 31

Kai's Point of view

Katie talked about the places that she had been, and I told her about pursuing my PhD. As different as our lives had been, I can't say that either of us really had it better or worse than the other. I found out that she had a bachelor's degree and was a certified master woodworker.

Her experiences overseas were nothing like my life of comfort here back home. But I understood loss the same as she did. Katie was surprised when I told her that I was divorced. We talked about how I had meet Jenny in college, and how we married after she got pregnant. I told her about losing Heather when she was just two years old, and my marriage ending after that.

She seemed reluctant to ask questions so I asked about her life. She told me how she had met her husband, Tyson. He seemed like such an amazing man. Her eyes sparkled when she talked about the man he was, and I couldn't find it in me to feel the least bit jealous. Katie was glowing talking about him, and she was beautiful.

I asked how he passed, and she told me how he died rescuing women and children during a humanitarian aid mission in the middle east. I didn't know what to say. I saw tears starting to well up in her eyes, and I just reached out to hold her hand.

We never revealed more than we were ready to, but we shared more than either of us expected. We lost complete track of time, sharing stories and reminiscing about all of the crazy choices we each made in life. Suddenly, the dining hall in the restaurant was too quiet.

"Kai!" a man's voice shouted across the restaurant startling us both, though Katie more so than me.

We both stood up and faced toward the door. A man with a full beard and plaid shirt was stomping across the dining area toward us. He stepped past Katie, then suddenly he was flying through the air, ass over tea kettle.

Katie grabbed his arm at the last second and pulled hard, spinning him toward her. When he lost his balance, she followed him down to the ground, and locked his arm twisted up behind his back.

He screamed when she pulled it harder, "Kai, I want to close up! Get your psycho off of me!"

Two waitresses ran out of the dining room. Katie's eyes shot up to me to look for guidance, but I was on the verge of pissing my pants laughing. "How can you call the woman who encouraged you to chase your dreams a psycho, Alex?" I asked, sitting back down.

Her eyes widened, looking down at the man under her on the floor, "*Alex*? Is that you?" she asked.

Alex whimpered. "Kai, did you tell this lady I owe you money?!?" he yelled.

Katie jumped up, releasing his arm, and moving to help him up from the floor.

It was obvious that she felt awful. "Alex, I am so sorry. I

didn't realize that was you," she apologized, dusting nonexistent dirt from his shirt.

Alex scowled at me before turning around to look at Katie. His eyes widened with recognition, before he grabbed her into a big hug. "Holy shit, Katie! If I had known it was you I would have just let you two have the whole place!" He laughed, pulling back from her.

"Kai, why didn't you tell me you were bringing *Katie?*" He scowled at me, before turning back to her with a cheshire grin. "You disappeared after High School! You know people thought you were *dead?*" He informed her.

"Well... Here I am. Alive and kicking. Besides you saw me in California," she grinned. Then she looked over to me with a questioning look, "Dead? Really?"

I just shook my head. "Sorry, Alex. Yeah, Katie just moved back to town so we were catching up over dinner. We didn't realize how late it was. I am sorry for keeping your staff," I apologized, shaking his hand and patting his back.

Suddenly, the doors to the dining hall burst open and two armed police officers entered in front of one of the waitresses who ran out earlier.

"That's them! They attacked my boss because he told them to leave. The woman is *violent!*" She yelled, pointing at us.

"Sir, I'm going to need to see your hands?" One of the officers said, looking at me still holding Alex's arm.

I immediately let go of Alex and put my hands up. Katie, a second behind me, threw her hands up as well.

"Who the fuck called the police?" Alex yelled. "Officers, these are two of my oldest friends from high school. I don't know why you were called, but there is nothing going on here."

The second officer holstered his weapon, and approached us. "We had a frantic call that a customer was belligerent and assaulted the owner of the establishment. We responded with appropriate caution," he explained, gesturing for his partner to stand down.

Alex shook his head. "The only belligerent person in the room was me. I didn't realize who this was and came in screaming. I lunged for Kai here, and Katie took me to the ground until I calmed down," he admitted.

"You were assaulted?" The first officer attempted to clarify.

"No," Alex corrected. "*I* was about to assault my friend here for staying so damn late, but his beautiful date reminded me that I owe my business to her, and I should calm the fuck down."

The first cop began eyeing Katie, and I didn't like it. I pulled her behind me. Alex noticed as well, and began ushering the two officers toward his office at the back of the restaurant to clear up the matter. I couldn't hear what was being said, but then Alex started yelling.

"There are no charges to be pressed, *Karen*! I don't care what your real name is! Did you have the police on speed dial? Shut the fuck up before I fire you!"

Alex refused to allow the police to take our information, stating if anyone should be written up, it would be him for verbally abusing a customer. Eventually, they left and so did we.

I promised to come back another night with Katie to catch up with Alex, and then apologized again to the grumbling staff as we left the barn. It was after midnight as we walked out to the car. How did we always lose track of time in that barn?

* * *

Katie's Point of View

Kai opened my door for me again, and let me settle into my seat before he closed it and walked around to climb into the driver's side. He sat there for a minute staring straight ahead into the dark.

"Kai?" I asked not wanting to disturb his thoughts, but wanting to know what he was thinking. We were having a good night, and then I body slammed one of our childhood friends into the ground.

The police were called.

I knew Alex took the heat for everything, but I could have just as easily been arrested for assault. *Then* what? They would see that I was a veteran with post traumatic stress, and lock me up. Or worse, forcibly medicate me. My mind was spiraling, waiting for Kai to say *anything.*

He was quiet for a long moment, before he started the car. As we drove back through the farms and headed through town, the inside of his car remained eerily quiet. Kai was mulling something over, and I decided to let him think it through before pressuring him to speak.

When we were almost back to Andie's, he pulled over on the side of the road and put the car in park. I just sat in my seat, and began to fidget. This was it. I was too broken to make this work. I held my breath and waited for the inevitable heartbreak.

"Katie, I don't want to get married again," he whispered quietly.

I felt my heart crumbling as a tear slid down my cheek. *I knew it.*

I didn't wait for him to say anything else. I unbuckled my seatbelt and got out of the car. I promised I wouldn't do this to myself again. I wouldn't let Kai break my heart again.

"Katie! Wait!" He yelled from behind me.

I didn't slow down or turn back. I just kept walking. When I had just turned up to Andie's house, two arms wrapped around me.

"Stop," Kai whispered.

I stiffened and attempted to shrug his arms off of my body, but he wouldn't let go. I could feel the tears beginning to stream down my face, but I couldn't wipe them away because my arms were pinned to my body.

I heard Kai's breath hitch and he began mumbling against my neck. *"Shit.* I am fucking this all up. You completely misunderstood."

I tried again to shake his hands off of me but managed to be turned around instead. Kai held me tight against him, his head tucked into the crook of my neck.

"Katie, I don't want to get married. I did that before and it was for all of the wrong reasons, and I don't want to do that again."

If he thought this would explain it better, it just made it seem worse.

He continued anyway. "Katie, I have been in love with you for most of my life," he quietly confessed, afraid to look at me as he made the decision to tell me everything in his heart. "I don't want to get married. But I do want to be with you. I want to spend every single day with you. I want to wake up with you every morning and listen to your snoring every night."

I punched his stomach, sniffling, "I do *not* snore!"

290

He loosened his hold on my arms and peeked down at me. I tried to wipe away my tears and process everything that he was saying.

"I knew the moment that I saw you last weekend that things would never work out with anyone else," he whispered, watching my every movement and reaction to his words.

"When you are ready," he said, taking a deep breath. "I want all of you, Katie."

I stared back at him like he was stupid. "What do you mean?" I asked.

"Please don't push me away, Kat," he begged.

We stood there in silence for what seemed like an eternity. I never said a word, staring at either my fidgeting hands or up at the windows of the houses around us. I couldn't even make eye contact with him...

"Can we drive somewhere else and talk?" I asked quietly, while staring up at the darkened windows of Andie's house.

"Do you want to go back to mine?" He asked. "We don't have to do anything. Just talk."

I had been there before, and could get back if I needed to. I nodded my head and let Kai lead me back to his car. I didn't say another word until we pulled into his drive.

"Is it okay if I use your bathroom?" I asked. My mind was a swirling mess of doubts and self deprecation.

"Sure," he nodded as we walked up to the house and unlocked the door. Opening the door, he let me go in first, "After you."

I nodded and walked past him into the house and went straight for the second floor.

Chapter 32

Kai's POV

I let her go upstairs, while I grabbed two glasses from the kitchen and a bottle of scotch from my stash in the pantry for when Bradley watches the games with me.

I poured two glasses, one with scotch and the other with water, and waited at the kitchen island for Katie to join me so that we could talk. I heard her feet padding down the stairs and my breath caught for a second when she came around the corner. She was wearing one of my t-shirts and a pair of my boxers as shorts. *Fuck.* Seeing her in my clothes made me hard.

She had washed her make-up off, and I could see the faintest hint of freckles across her cheeks. I was mesmerized by her. Every movement, every expression, pulled me in deeper and I wasn't sure that I ever wanted to be freed.

"Sorry," she mumbled, taking a sip of the scotch. "I hope you don't mind if I borrowed your clothes."

"No, not at all. Eh-hmmmm," my voice cracked, as I tried to subtly adjust my growing erection.

"Kai," she whispered, "I am not the girl that you fell in love with anymore. I am so broken inside, I don't even know how to function most days."

"You are-" she silenced whatever words were about to come out of my mouth with a look.

"I lost my husband, a man that I loved more than my own life," she confessed. "I don't even know if my heart can handle another heartbreak, Kai. The thought of feeling that loss again scares the shit out of me. I don't sleep most nights, because I have-" she stopped and looked at me. I watched her drink down the remaining scotch in her glass before pouring a second glass and bottoming it down as well.

"I have really bad PTSD. I can hide it most days, but I really am fucked up. I was admitted to a hospital. There was therapy, medications, the whole nine. I couldn't bring myself to care. Not for myself. Not for anyone," she continued quietly. "I can't handle any more loss," she said, her voice beginning to break. "It will kill me."

Her tears started to fall again. I wanted to give her space but I couldn't. Not when she was trying so hard to be open with me. I walked around the island and pulled her into my arms and just held her, caressing her back and whispering that everything would work out. We didn't have to figure everything out tonight. We didn't even have to make promises of forever right now.

This was enough.

Standing in my kitchen, holding her in my arms was enough for me right now. I didn't want to fuck this up. I didn't want to wonder 'what if' any more. I just needed a little hope, and that would be enough.

When I felt her breathing calm down, I pulled back a little to look at her. I cupped her face in my hands and wiped her tears away with my thumbs. I had never seen this vulnerability in her eyes. She really expected me to break her heart. She was scared to let me in again, and it hurt me more than I realized it would.

"Katie," I whispered against her forehead as I gave her a gentle kiss. "I won't rush you. I won't push you unless you tell me to. I won't do anything that you don't like. Just tell me that *maybe, maybe* there is a chance for this. That will be enough. I don't need yes, just *maybe*."

Katie's arms were wrapped around my waist and she hugged me tighter, burrowing her face into my shoulder. I almost didn't hear what she said, so I asked her to repeat it.

"Maybe," whispered out so quietly from her lips but it hit me like a bullhorn had sounded off.

I hugged her tightly and spun her around in my arms. She squealed and slapped my back to make me stop. "Stop before I puke!"

I set her on a bar stool and searched her eyes one more time. She said, *'maybe.'* I couldn't stop myself and kissed her lips. I wanted her so much right now I could devour every morsel of her mouth. She gasped, and my tongue began exploring her mouth and dancing with her tongue. She tasted like the scotch we drank, and I was getting drunk from the feeling of her legs wrapping around me as I feasted on her lips.

I pulled back and tried to control my breathing. "Come to bed with me. We'll just sleep. My dick hates me for saying this, but we can just hold each other tonight. That's enough. Ok?"

She looked relieved that I wasn't going to push for anything further. Tonight had exposed too many emotions. I wanted her to want to be with me, not feel pressured because of sex. I was going to accept my blue balls, and be what *she needed* tonight.

We crawled into my bed, and I pulled Katie into my chest so that her head rested on my shoulder with one arm draped across me. I pulled the blanket up over us and just held her until she fell asleep.

She said, 'maybe.' I could work with, 'maybe.' I closed my eyes and drifted off.

* * *

Warm hands were stroking my cock. It was so hard, I felt like I would burst at any second. I felt a warm wet sensation dragging up my shaft from the base to the tip. It was a tongue licking me like an ice cream cone.

I groaned from the pleasure of it, and reached out to force that mouth down onto my cock. To take all of it in against that warm tongue and suck it dry. I involuntarily rocked my hips against the warmth, desperate for the release.

* * *

Katie's POV

I woke to the sound of Kai grumbling in his sleep. I tried to sit up to see if he was okay, but he pulled me back into his arms so that my entire backside was pressed against his chest, my ass tucked up against his groin.

He ground his hips against my ass, and I felt how incredibly hard he was. He kept rubbing his erection against my backside, and I would be lying if I said it wasn't a massive turn on.

After some quiet coaxing, I got him to lay back on his back and I lay across his body with my legs slightly straddling him. I needed to wake him up. I refused to take advantage of a sleeping man, no matter how erotic his grunting and groaning may have been.

"Kai," I whispered against his cheek and nibbled his ear. "Wake up, I need you."

I ground my sex against his erection and moaned at how good it felt. "Kai," I said a little louder this time. "Please. I need you."

His eyes opened, staring up at me. "You're here, right?" He asked me, sounding unsure.

"Yes, I'm here. Can I finish what you started?" I asked, watching his face as I rocked my hips up and down the length of his extremely hard cock. "Please, Kai? Can I ride you?" I whimpered, so incredibly turned on by the way his body was responding to my every movement and touch.

He grabbed my hips and lifted me off of him so quickly I thought he was turning me away, but he shimmied his boxers down to his thighs before reaching for me again and yanking the pair off of me as well.

"Katie, I swear to God," he growled. "If you don't get your sweet ass on top of me in the next five seconds I won't be able to apologize for what I do to you."

His voice was raspy from sleep, but it sounded so sexy that it gave me chills. I lifted his t-shirt over my head and crawled back onto his body, licking and kissing up his abdomen until I was straddling his hardness against my wetness.

His hands grabbed my hips, raising my ass up just enough to press the tip of his cock against my opening. My hands on his chest, I lowered myself onto him, sucking in my breath and biting my bottom lip as he stretched me out. I kept raising and lowering until I could drop all the way down and just rocked my hips back and forth.

His hands traced the scars across my abdomen, and I stopped moving. I was waiting for the questions. Maybe rejection because I wasn't flawless anymore. But Kai just looked up at me like I was the most precious thing he had ever seen. It took my breath.

"Kai," I breathed out his name.

He sat up, hugging my body and taking one of my breasts into his mouth. His teeth chewed on my nipple causing me to clench down harder on his cock. Kai sucked and kissed my chest, my neck, and my shoulders. His hands never left my body as I rode him slowly.

My hands were wound into his hair, hugging his head against me. This wasn't fucking. He was worshiping my body, like he swore he would. I had absolute control of us in this moment, but it gave me a heady feeling in my chest the way he showed his adoration.

My body was thrumming with electricity, as pleasure moved through every limb and skin cell. I let out a moan when his hands pulled me down harder as he thrust up. The movement caused him to hit a spot that hadn't been touched in what seemed like an eternity.

He felt the difference too and looked up into my eyes, mischief sparkling through his. "I feel like I missed a spot, KitKat," he said and he rotated his hips up to hit the same spot again.

I let out another moan. *Jesus, let this man have his way with me.* My body was overwhelmed with raw feeling, and I couldn't think any more. I didn't want to think. I just wanted to feel this moment with Kai. "Please, please, Kai," I begged him, riding him harder and harder, trying to hit the same spot over and over and not quite succeeding.

Kai smirked at me, understanding what I needed. He flipped us over so that my back was against the bed, and he was kneeling between my legs, still buried deep inside of me.

He grabbed my knees and pushed them wider apart and then pulled out until only the tip remained inside of me. Kai stared at my face for a second, before whispering words that proved to be my undoing.

"God, I love you."

Then he slammed into me, hitting the deepest part of me. My body was rocked as he hit that magical spot again, then I was coming undone. My orgasm exploded and I screamed my release. My head shot back feeling every emotion, every unspoken and spoken promise, every intent between us cascading through my body.

Kai didn't stop. He kept slamming into me harder and faster, and I couldn't breathe. I tried to push his chest away but he grabbed my hands and pinned them over my head. I wanted to protest but when I looked into his eyes I lost my voice. I surrendered everything to him. Kai loved me and always had.

"Come for me again, Katie. Come for me so that I can come with you milking my cock," he whispered against my cheek.

And like Pavlov's dog, I came again. This orgasm was just as strong as the last one, stealing my breath a second time. Kai released my hands and grabbed my face to kiss me as he came inside of me. His release twitching against my sensitive inner walls was enough to prolong my orgasm and leave me moaning into his mouth as he kissed me.

Dear god, what had this man done to me? I felt like a pile of limp noodles when Kai finally pulled out of me and pulled me onto his chest. I couldn't move if the house was burning down, completely spent

"Fuck," he exhaled. "If that is what sex is like now, I think you may kill me, Kat. You may very well be the death of me," he said chuckling softly while holding me against his body. I couldn't even imagine anything more than this.

Sex with Tyson had been amazing, but this was different. This wasn't Ty. This was the man who I had loved for most of my life, even when I hated him. I sighed contentedly and fell back asleep. I had no idea what time it was, but I knew that I could still sleep a bit more. So I did.

I slept without dreams or nightmares. My mind was at ease for the second time, it would seem, in many years. He said he *loved* me. Maybe we *weren't* meant to be back then, because this was where we were meant to end up. Together *after* hell.

Maybe. He said we could start with just *maybe.*

Chapter 33

Kai's Point of View

One week. It had been one week since she agreed to try. She agreed that we could try to make something of ourselves. I didn't want to do this all backwards, so I asked her out on a second date. We met at the library, and I packed us a picnic basket and blanket.

Katie laughed when she got there and I was sitting under our tree. The raised decking around the tree was still there, but the branches had filled out more, giving us a bit more shade.

Katie and I sat on the blanket eating chips and sandwiches I bought from her favorite deli. "This is kind of nice, Kai," she admitted looking over at me.

"Damn…" I muttered. "I was hoping for better than *kind of nice*," I admitted. I couldn't help the smirk on my face when she reached over and hit my arm.

"You know what I mean," she chided, but she was smiling too. "I don't know how to do this," she admitted quietly, sipping her drink.

I tipped my head down. "I have to be honest, I don't know either. I just know I want more… with you."

She bit her lip, looking out over the park. "Be honest.

When you say you love *me*, what is it you love?"

Katie wasn't pulling any punches. She was going right for it, all the hard shit.

"When I woke up with you in my arms, it felt *right.* No sex, no kissing, nothing like that. It just felt *right,*" I admitted, looking over at her. "I didn't even have that with my ex-wife."

She smirked again. "We don't even know each other any more. How much of that is wishful thinking from when we were kids, and how much of it is real?"

I moved the food aside, and pulled her closer to me so that we were sitting side by side, leaned up against the tree. "Do I make you uncomfortable?" I asked, feeling a bit uncertain now of how I had handled things so far.

Katie shook her head. "No. You really don't."

I nodded, exhaling the breath I held. "The only thing that I want is a chance. Even if we didn't have the history that we do, I would still chase you."

She looked at me skeptically. "Seriously?"

"You're gorgeous. I know you don't see it, but you take my breath away every time I see you. When you laugh and smile, and let yourself be in the moment…. Fuck, Kat. You're stunning," I whispered, holding her hand in mine.

"You only see what's outside-" she started but I cut her off.

"Don't do that. Please?" I asked quietly. "Don't minimize my feelings. I'm not some high school kid, and neither are you. I will admit I fucked up letting you go. I was too late to tell you, but I knew then I fucked up."

We sat for a few moments in silence before she started to open up. "I like you. I like how comfortable it is to be with you," she confessed, caressing my fingers. "I am so afraid…. of life. I can't just open up and give you everything."

301

I pulled her into my chest and held her. She was brutally honest from the beginning. All of her reservations, trauma, and hang-ups were put out front like warning signs to avert interest.

I still wanted her though. I wanted to be the one to make her smile. I wanted to be the one who held her when she cried. I wanted all of her pain and hardships shared with me.

"I'm not lonely, Kat. I could find someone to warm my bed if that was all I needed. I want someone to cry with too. Someone to laugh with, or just be myself with," I told her, hugging her against my chest. I kissed the top of her head, and waited a moment to see if she would speak next or if I should continue.

"You can't tell me you had regrets after ghosting me, Kai," she sighed. "You never once messaged me. You never tried to contact me. Not once."

"Your number was disconnected. How the hell was I supposed to reach you?" I asked, chuckling.

She leaned back and looked up at me. "If my number was disconnected, how did you call me from a bar three weeks ago?"

My jaw dropped open. I hadn't even realized that I called *her* number, and *she* answered. "Wait. Your phone was never disconnected?"

She shook her head. "No. I was waiting for you to call me, and tell me you were a fucking idiot. You never did."

My head fell back against the tree. "Fucking Andie...." I grunted.

Katie sat up and looked at me confused. "What does she have to do with it?" She asked.

I couldn't help but laugh at my younger self for being an

idiot. "I showed up at your house, maybe ten minutes after you left. Andie kicked my ass and told me your phone was disconnected. I tried calling, and none of my calls went through... For weeks."

"What?" She asked, looking pale and flushed at the same time.

"I showed up, Kitkat. I may have acted stupid after graduation, but I showed up, and your family turned me away," I admitted.

"Oh my god..." She exhaled, starting to laugh. "My phone was turned off for three months while I attended boot camp. When I graduated training, Andie kept trying to get me to talk about you, but I shut her down."

Katie looked at me sheepishly. "You came for me?"

I smirked. "I did. I was an idiot and hesitated, but I won't do that again," I said, pulling her back into a hug.

"It never occurred to me that my phone wouldn't show missed calls after being turned off for several months," she giggled, tucking her head against my shoulder. "We were so stupid," she admitted, beginning to laugh a bit more.

"I'm sorry, I made you sad, Kitkat. It's a regret I will try to *right* for the rest of our lives. But knowing that you met a man who treated you well..." I choked up trying to formulate my thoughts. "He set a high bar, and I will do my best to keep that standard. *For you.*"

She swatted my chest and sniffled. "Stop saying sweet, understanding shit... You're ruining my resolve!"

That made me chuckle. *I hoped I could tear down all of her resolves one day.*

* * *

"No! Please!"

The muffled sound of someone talking woke me.

"Please! Stop!" Katie whimpered in her sleep.

I turned on my bedside lamp and looked over at her. She was drenched in sweat and shaking, tears streaming down her face while she slept.

A choked sob came out, *"Tyson!"*

I didn't know what to think. It felt like someone had crushed my chest. She was dreaming about her husband and calling his name out in my bed. I got up from the bed and went to the bathroom. *How the fuck do I do this?* I asked the man looking back in the mirror.

"No! NO!!" her hoarse voice called from my bed.

I didn't think about it again. I ran back into the bedroom and climbed in next to Katie. A part of me wanted to be upset, but it was squashed pretty quickly. I reached over to caress her arm, thinking if it would soothe her back to sleep, but she recoiled like I had burned her. I pulled her body against mine, and held her in spite of the initial thrashing.

She calmed down within a couple of minutes and her breathing normalized again. I held her to my chest the rest of the night. Each time she moved, I woke immediately to check on her. I had never experienced night terrors or nightmares like this before.

I would ask Katie about them in the morning, if she remembered. Worst case, I would reach out to Andie... Even though she was on my shit list for lying back then.

* * *

Katie's Point of View

I woke up feeling like I was being cooked in an oven. Kai held me to him so tightly one would think I was going to float away if he loosened his grip. I tried to pull away, but he only tightened his hold and shushed me in his sleep.

It made me smile, but at the same time I needed to get up. "Kai, I have to pee!" I whined, poking his ribs.

He patted my back and shushed me again, as if he were placating a sleepless child.

"Kai!" I said more forcefully. "Let me go, I have to pee!"

His eyes fluttered open, looking at my flushed face. "Are you okay?" He asked, his sleepy voice sounding hoarse.

I shook my head half laughing, "No, I have to pee and you won't let me go. Please?"

His eyes opened wide, realizing what I was saying. "Shit, sorry," he apologized and let go of me.

I quickly rolled out of bed and rushed to the bathroom. Feeling about three liters lighter, I washed myself up for the morning and brushed my teeth.

When I came back to the bedroom, Kai was sitting up on his side of the bed. His feet were on the floor, his elbows propped on his knees, and his head rested in his hands.

I climbed back into bed and sidled up behind him. My heart stuttered when he stiffened at my touch. It felt like I had been smacked. He must have realized what he'd done, because he reached out and pulled me back to him when I attempted to move away.

"I'm sorry," he apologized, quietly. "I had a rough night," he explained, turning to look at me. He pulled me closer and kissed my lips gently. "I'm just a little out of it."

I nodded, looking at his face fully now that he was awake. I caressed his cheek, and felt like crying. I knew that look. I had seen that look on Andie's face. My parents'. Hell, even Tyson's a few times.

"I take it I kept you awake with my nightmares?" I asked, watching his eyes. He wanted to lie. He wanted to pretend that it wasn't me, but this wouldn't work if he lied.

"I just wasn't expecting it. That's all," Kai tried to tell me, but I knew there was more. He didn't want to talk about it just yet, but we would talk about it eventually.

I spent the next couple of nights at Andie's house. Kai had been weird since the other night, and it made me feel like I had done something wrong. I didn't know what I had done wrong, but it was a huge block between us.

I helped Andie clean up after dinner, and disappeared into their guest room. I had been back for over a month, and it was time to start looking for a job. I sat on the bed with my laptop and searched for carpentry and woodworking jobs in the area.

I heard a soft knock at the door. "It's open, Andie," I said, still reading through the various postings.

"If it's not Andie?" Kai's voice startled me, as he closed the door behind him.

I set my laptop aside and stood up from the bed confused as to why he was here. "What are you doing here?" I asked, looking back at the door he had closed.

"I needed to talk with you, and you have been dodgy the last two days," he said, moving to stand right in front of me. "Can we talk?"

I was a little caught off by the impromptu visit, but I nodded. "Um, yeah? Yes," I agreed, gesturing toward the bed. "I was just looking for a job. There's not really a lot of space to-" my words cut off when Kai stripped down to his boxers, and climbed into my bed.

He looked over at me, holding the blankets open. "Come on then."

This was not what I was expecting. "Does Andie know you are here?" I asked, laying down next to him.

Kai nodded and pulled me in a bit closer. "She does."

"What are you doing here?" I asked him quietly.

He let out a stuttering breath and then began to talk. "You had a nightmare the other night. I don't know what I was expecting but it wasn't that."

I stilled, waiting for the rejection that was inevitable.

"You called out for Tyson in your sleep," he whispered.

I never remembered my nightmares. "I-"

"Shhh. Let me finish," he asked, rubbing my back. "When you called his name, I left the bed. I left the room. I was so fucking angry…. No. I was *hurt*. It felt like I was being cheated on," he admitted.

"Kai, it's not like that!" I whispered, feeling my eyes burn.

"I know. That was all me. I realized I was being stupid and ran right back to bed and held you the rest of the night. I was so ashamed of myself, Katie… Of how I handled it, I didn't know how to talk to you about it."

"I can't change what happened before we came back into each other's lives, Kai." I bit my lip, trying not to cry as he continued talking.

"Katie, you have been up front with me from the beginning. You have never withheld anything. I'm trying to say, I'm sorry," he whispered against my hair. "I am sorry that my first reaction was to pull away."

I had no idea. "I didn't even know. I wouldn't know if you hadn't told me," I offered.

Kai tipped my chin up so that I was looking into his beautiful blue eyes. "But I knew. And I don't want us to have secrets or misunderstandings. Will you forgive me for flinching, even if you didn't see it?"

I rolled away from him, sighing. "Why are you being such a good guy? Can't you have one bad quality?" I grumbled, wiggling my backside into his arms so that his chest and legs cradled me against his body.

He nibbled and kissed my shoulder. "I have my own flaws. I'm working on them for you, Kitkat," he whispered.

I snorted. "I have an army of demons, Kai. I don't blame you for hesitating. We aren't so deep that we can't walk away right now," I said, giving him an out even though it would kill me.

We had only been back together a couple of weeks. It would hurt to walk away from him, if I were honest. I liked him more than I was willing to admit out loud. But it was better to make a clean break now, than drag shit out until later.

Kai pulled me back so that his upper body hovered over mine, our legs entangled. "I said I flinched. I didn't say I was backing down. Don't think I won't chase your ass across the globe this time," he swore staring intently into my eyes.

"Don't break my heart. Ok?" I whispered back, softly pecking his lips and turning my back to him again.

Kai curled up behind me and held me until I fell asleep. "You don't break my heart, either," he whispered as I drifted off.

Chapter 34

Kai's POV

I heard Katie crying in her sleep again. It didn't happen often, but she still had horrible nightmares some nights. I pulled her into a hug and tried to soothe her, but she didn't calm down like she normally did. I snapped awake and turned on the light to look at her.

"Katie? Come on, Kitkat, talk to me," I urged her while trying to check to see what the problem was.

"ka-k- call ambulance," she ground out through clenched teeth.

I didn't waste another second and scooped her into my arms and ran for the car. I placed her on the back seat so that she could lie down on her side and raced to the hospital. She was pale and sweating. I parked in front of the emergency entrance and gently pulled Katie from the back seat.

She would whimper for a bit and then get quiet, whimper and then get quiet. It reminded me of when my ex was in labor. I knew that wasn't it, because we had only been together a few months. Katie would know if she were pregnant.

She would know, right?

Thankfully, the hospital got her straight in and started

to work. Her white blood cells were elevated indicating an infection so they opted to run a scan to see what was going on.

I sat next to the bed with Katie clutching my hand while she slept. They had given her an injection of valium to calm her down, and some pain medicine so that she could rest. It was just a waiting game at this point. I had messaged her parents and let them know that we were here. Katie didn't like to share information with her parents, but I felt like hospital trips in the middle of the night were ok.

The doctor came in, and I could tell by his expression that he knew what was wrong. I started to wake Katie, but he stopped me.

"Can we talk outside?" he asked me and I nodded.

I followed him to a private room for family consults, and sat down in the chair that he offered. This was not making me feel any better.

"Katie had an ectopic pregnancy. Her body is trying to abort it to save her life. We'd like to keep her overnight, for observation. With ectopic pregnancies, the risk of complications is relatively high. I'd feel more comfortable with her here in case we need to intervene surgically."

"She's pregnant?" I felt like I had been kicked in the stomach. Why didn't we know?

"After reviewing everything that Katie told us, I don't think she knew that she was pregnant. I can confirm that the fetus was never viable. There was never a heartbeat. Her body is doing its job, but it's slow. I've put in a prescription to help the process along. If she normally has light cycles, she would have thought everything was normal. This happens more often than you think."

I took the information that he offered and headed back to Katie's room. She could have been anywhere from eleven to six weeks pregnant according to the doctor. I thought back to all of the times that we had unprotected sex, and I couldn't know when it happened. We had been seeing each other for roughly four months now.

Things were going well. She swore that we didn't live together, but her things were slowly migrating into my closets. She could deny it, but I just kept moving her things in from Andie's and her parents' houses.

I sat next to her through the night. I didn't want someone else to tell her. This was going to crush her. She had told me about losing her child after Ty passed away. She didn't know that she was pregnant then either. The doctors had told her that severe emotional distress can cause miscarriage. He might as well have told her that she caused it grieving for her husband.

She didn't tell me all of the details, but I got enough from Andie and Jonas to know that she spiraled pretty bad after that. Andie and one of her sisters had driven out to stay with her, or the military would have had to admit her for psychological concern. I would not have believed them if I didn't sleep with her every night.

Katie carried so much guilt that it ate at her every night. She was haunted by it. This would not be easy. I didn't know what to say to her, but I knew that she could get through this with me at her side. The door to the room slid open and the shift nurse came in to check Katie, and brought a small cup with a blue pill.

"Hi, my name is Mary. I am the nurse on duty. Katie, I brought you some medicine that the doctor called in. This

311

will help your body pass the fet-"

I cut her off before she could finish speaking, "Shut up." I was pissed that this woman was going to tell Katie the worst news and I didn't want this to crush her even more.

"You don't say another word. I will give her the medicine when she wakes up and let you know when she has taken it," I growled at the woman staring at me in shock.

Mary's face was flushed. "Sir, you have no right to speak to me that way," she was raising her voice and waking Katie up.

"Get out," I told her. I was not going to explain our situation, nor was I going to tell a stranger about Katie's. This wasn't just a lost pregnancy. This would destroy her.

The nurse tried to argue with me before I stood up. She jumped like I had made a move toward her but all I did was point at the door. "I am asking you to get out, before I push you out the door."

"Kai?" Katie whimpered groggily from the bed.

I was so angry that I couldn't move for a second.

"Kai?" she whimpered again. "I did it again, didn't I?" She started to cry.

Damnit. I hated that nurse right now. Mary set the pill cup on a tray table with a glass of water and left the room flushed and fuming.

"Kai, I ca-can't. I can't," she sobbed.

All of my attention was pulled back to her when she stuttered. I scooted Katie into my arms and sat down on the bed and held her.

"You didn't do anything wrong, baby," I said quietly, trying to soothe her.

"I did!" She cried into my shoulder. "I kill-*hicc. I killed anoth- bab-hicc."*

My eyes were burning with tears. I never wanted her to cry again. She had cried enough. I held her as tight as I could, and told her over and over again that she did nothing wrong. When she finally calmed down, I looked down to see if she had fallen asleep again.

She looked shell-shocked, like her body was present but she had left it. I felt my tears finally fall down my face. I wanted to tell her the right way. I needed her to hear that this wasn't her fault, that these things happen, and now I couldn't.

"Katie? Kitkat, I need you to listen to me, okay? Can you just listen?" I asked, holding her and caressing her back. She made a sniffle noise and I took that as acknowledgement.

"You had an ectopic pregnancy, babe. There was nothing that could be done. You couldn't have done anything any differently. This wasn't you, Katie," I cooed quietly against her hair.

"I didn't know, and you got really sick. I didn't pay enough attention. I didn't notice that you were tired all of the time. Your body was trying to save your life, Katie. You did nothing wrong," I told her over and over again.

We sat like that for the rest of the night. Katie curled into my chest and me rocking her and telling her over and over that she did nothing wrong. It was breaking me to see her like this. I didn't think my heart could handle any more.

At eight o'clock the next morning the doctor came in to do his final rounds before shifts changed. He looked at the empty cup on the table and nodded. I had gotten her to take the medicine that would help her body to abort the failed pregnancy. We stared at each other for a few seconds before he came near the bed.

"Ms. Johnson? My name is Doctor Valdez. I am the attending that has been looking after you tonight. I need to check your vitals and review some information with you. Can we do that?" he asked quietly.

I felt Katie shift ever so slightly, but she wouldn't look at the doctor. I nodded my head for him to continue.

"I was able to get some of your records from the VA last night, so that we could do what was best for you. You had an accident when you were deployed, is that correct? You were involved in a roadside attack?" He asked.

Katie nodded her head ever so slightly. She had told me about the bombing, but she didn't go into much details about the incident and I hadn't pushed her. But now I wanted to know what that had to do with now.

"After you were in the hospital, did they tell you that you had sustained damage to your abdomen, specifically your internal organs?" He asked.

Katie nodded again.

"Ok. Did they tell you that one of your ovaries was damaged?" He asked.

Katie hesitated, but nodded slowly. I felt her body relaxing against me.

"Did they tell you that the right fallopian tube should be removed because it was too badly damaged to function?" He asked cautiously.

Katie's head turned quickly to stare at the doctor. She did *not* know.

"Ok. Let's start this conversation over," Dr Valdez sighed. "When you were injured, you sustained significant internal injuries that nearly took your life. The doctors were able to repair most of the damage, but your right ovary and fallopian tube were nearly destroyed. Truthfully, they could have been removed along with the lower lobe of your liver that was also severely damaged. Does any of this sound familiar?" He asked, trying to coax Katie into the conversation.

Katie nodded, "Yes. I remember a little."

Dr. Valdez seemed encouraged by her participation, "Katie, you are proned to ectopic pregnancies because of that damaged tube. It is causing the ovum to fail to reach the uterus before it is fertilized and attaching itself to the fallopian tube instead. You've experienced this phenomenon before?"

Katie nodded again, "Yes."

"There was nothing that you could have done differently this time or the last time. From everything that your husband has told us, you could not have done anything differently."

Katie and I both stiffened when he called me her husband. I won't lie and say I was repulsed by the idea. It sounded pretty good actually. But that was a conversation for another day.

"I am going to leave you some information about your care for the next 10 days. Just take it easy, don't work if you don't have to, and no heavy lifting. You'll need to follow up with an OB/GYN after 14 days to verify that your body has passed everything. I am including a surgical consult and recommending the removal of the damaged tube. Do you have any questions for me?" He asked, looking at both of us.

I looked at Katie, and she shook her head. "No, no questions. Thank you, Doctor," I responded for both of us.

"Ok. The charge nurse will be in shortly to start your discharge. Come back in immediately if anything feels wrong

315

over the next five days. Cramping is normal with some pain, but if you develop a fever or your pain is a seven or higher, come right back," he advised.

I carried Katie out of the hospital an hour later. Her face tucked into the crook of my neck, I walked us back out to my car and drove us home.

I took a week off from work, and stayed by Katie's side. She didn't want for anything, except privacy, by the end of the week. We talked quietly every night, and she let me in a little more each time. We would make it through this.

I just wanted to protect her from everything that could make her sad. She deserved to be happy again. We both did.

Chapter 35

Katie's Point of View

I sat at the kitchen island of Kai's home, staring at my computer. I had found two companies in our area hiring craftsmen. Both specialized in the restoration of historical buildings, which, in our area, was a super niche industry. I sent both companies copies of my credentials with a resume, and then found myself wandering through real estate sites.

It struck me that I didn't really have a home. In the five months since moving back, I was at Andie's, Kai's or my parents' houses, living out of suitcases and boxes. Before that I had spent nearly two years not really *living*. I had enough money for a decent deposit, because I had no expenses. Not really anyway. I paid for my phone, my insurance, and groceries when I could sneak my card in fast enough to pay for shit.

Otherwise, I had no expenses. Kai walked up behind me and pulled me into his body. He kissed my temple, and then rested his chin on my shoulder, looking over what I was looking at.

"Why are you looking at houses?" He asked.

I closed my laptop and turned to hug him. "I was thinking of getting my own place. I've been a squatter or hospitalized the last two years. I feel like I should try to act like an independent adult again," I explained.

Kai stiffened and pulled back from my hug, patting me on the back twice. "Is it that bad being here with me?" He asked.

I looked up at him, feeling my defenses go up. "I haven't had my own space, or paid my own way in a long time. I can't keep mooching off of you."

"Is that what it feels like staying here? Like *you're* mooching off of *me?*" He asked quietly.

His eyes were guarded like he was waiting for my answer. Waiting for me to tell him that this wasn't what I wanted. I didn't even know what I wanted. Before I could answer he continued, "What if you just moved in here? I can give you bills to pay if that's what will make you feel more comfortable. I didn't think about how you felt, and I should have asked sooner."

There was a long moment of quiet contemplation on my part. *What would it mean to move in with him? What would happen if things didn't work out? What if we had an argument and I couldn't stay here?*

"You already practically live here. You are the only one who doesn't see it. If we have a disagreement, then we will work it out. This is your home if you want it to be, Katie," he softly whispered, tucking a piece of hair behind my ear.

I closed my eyes for a second, trying to stop the burning behind them. I didn't want to cry... "I said all of that out loud didn't I?" I asked him, realizing I had voiced my deepest worries.

"Yep," he chuckled, pulling me into a hug. "This only works if we talk, Kitkat. If you're worried, you can talk to me. I'm not saying everything will be perfect, but we can make this work. If you want your own space, I'll help you look. But don't move away because you think you are *mooching*."

I sighed and felt a weight of tension leave my body with his words. Truthfully, I didn't want to live on my own again. I didn't want to face all of my demons alone anymore. Kai kept me grounded, and kept me from getting too far in my head. I was better with him in my life.

"If we do this, you can't keep paying for everything," I mumbled against his chest.

His body vibrated as he laughed. "Tell you what. I'll let you buy me a new car. Will that make you feel better? I've been eyeing this sleek red mercedes convertible-"

I pulled away and swatted his chest. "I am *not* buying you a *pussy magnet, Doctor!*" My voice came out high pitched and whinier than I intended. I immediately started blushing when I realized I had yelled at him in jealousy.

Kai's face was lit up with joy as he laughed harder. "Holy shit, that was not what I was expecting! I thought you wanted to spend your money!" He chuckled, taking my face in his hands. He tipped my face up to look at him and kissed me softly.

"Seriously. You are not a burden, Katie. No one sees you as a mooch. If anything, I am the one taking advantage. I have a gorgeous woman, who I am completely in love with, tolerating my seemingly unending need for physical contact. I was afraid you wanted to move because you felt *used.*"

I started laughing at that point. "How would *I* feel used? I am so high maintenance, you really are at the disadvantage. Between my nightmares, my weird PTSD triggers, and all of my meds and schedule-" my words were silenced with another kiss.

His lips were soft and coaxed mine. Kai kissed me until I was a pile of goo in his arms. "You are not a burden. I have never felt that way, and I never will. Come on," he said, pulling me from the chair. "We need to iron out any concerns before you decide to move in here. If you want your own space, Amy knows a great realtor who can find you a great place."

I held Kai's hand as he led me through the house to the bedroom. I couldn't help but chuckle a little bit. "Why are we going to the bedroom to discuss all of this?" I asked him.

Without batting an eye, he told me. "Because the only time you are truly honest with yourself and what you want is when you are writhing on my cock or my tongue. Consider this like a truth serum. Now, take off your clothes so we can start this conversation." His voice was low and husky as he pulled me to the bed.

I thought he would push me down, but instead he began slowly stripping our clothes off. He trailed feather light kisses along my shoulders and neck. When we were both naked, he laid back on the bed and pulled me up to straddle his waist. "Take whatever you want, Katie. I'm all yours. Everything I have is yours."

He didn't have to tell me twice. Running my hands down his chest, I knew exactly what I wanted.

Two hours later I was sprawled across his chest, fully satiated and still panting. Kai ran his hand up and down my back, caressing my skin. I couldn't have raised a fight if someone paid me at that point. My energy was completely tapped out. *Pun intended.*

"If you could change this house, what would you change?" Kai asked, softly.

"I like the house. The garden needs some work though," I whispered back, my fingers drawing small circles on his chest.

"What if there was a workshop in the back for you to do your woodwork?"

"Mmm. I'm not sure. I think it would mess up the flow and layout of the garden. I don't need a lot of space. Maybe like a small eight by ten shed in the back corner."

"Nah, you need at least a ten by ten. If you start turning? You'd want that space, right?" He suggested.

"Yeah, I didn't think about that," I agreed.

"Did you hear back from either of the two places you applied?" He asked.

I picked my head up and smiled at him. "I was going to tell you tonight. The one I really wanted? They liked my portfolio, and offered to let me work on their next project as a trial run. I would get paid full rates, but I wouldn't have a contract with them until the project was completed to their satisfaction."

Kai smiled back at me. "What's the project? Do you know yet?"

I couldn't stop the grin from spreading across my face. "They're rehabilitating the big house on Fourth Street. Remember the one with the spires?" I reminded him.

His eyebrows went up a bit. "That blue and gray house you always wanted to tour when we were in school?"

"That's the one!" I squealed.

"Well, shit. That is perfect. It's walking distance from my office, so we can have lunch together if you have time," he smiled back at me, hugging me against his chest. "Or you can come to my office and let me have you for lunch."

"Oh, my god! You really are a pervert!" I giggled, squirming to escape his hold.

"You didn't even think about it before just shooting it down!" He whined, releasing me from his hug.

I laughed and sat up on the bed, the blankets pooling down around my waist. "I'm being serious!" I tried and failed to keep a straight face.

"Ok, ok… we'll table that idea," he said, pulling me back down to the bed and rolling so that he lay between my legs, pressing me down into the mattress.

"You're joking!" I gasped, feeling his erection rub against my clit.

"We're just talking, Kitkat," he whispered, slowly trailing kisses down my jaw to my neck.

"Ah… T-talk," I moaned. How did he do this to me every time? My entire body was on a hair trigger because of our previous activities, making everything he did now feel ten thousand times more pleasurable.

"Do you feel safe here?" He asked, nibbling my collarbone and grinding against me further.

"Mmmm, yes. I feel safe with you," I gasped when he took a nipple between his teeth.

"Do you want to live by yourself?"

"N-n-no," I responded honestly.

He pulled his hips back and slowly pushed inside of me. The feeling of being filled again, had me shivering from pleasure. My legs wrapped tightly around his waist as Kai pulled back and slowly filled me again.

"Do you want to live with me, Katie?" He asked, quietly watching my face contort with pleasure under him.

"Yes-," I moaned, when he pivoted his hips up to hit that

spot deep inside that nearly had me coming after two strokes.

"I won't lie to you, Kitkat. I'm so fucking hooked on you. You have me, if you want me," he admitted quietly, thrusting slowly in and out, kissing my jaw. "I don't want to wake up without you beside me."

"No," I whimpered, feeling my insides tightening up into a ball. I didn't know if it was fear of being alone or my impending orgasm that caused me to cry, but the tears began to slowly stream from my eyes.

"Look at me, baby girl," he cooed softly.

I opened my eyes, not realizing that I had shut them tightly. Kai kissed my tears away and continued our quiet conversation. "I'm in love with you, Katie. You don't have to say the words yet. You don't have to make any promises about our lives together. Just tell me that we can try this. Together."

I couldn't hold back the moan that left my throat. Did I love him? Yes. I always had. Could I let down my guards a little more? I could. *For Kai.* He had earned that much.

"Please," I begged him, feeling like my body was about to combust.

"Please, what?" He asked, taking my hands and pinning them over my head. "Tell me what you want, Katie. What do you want?" He asked, thrusting into me a bit more forcefully and causing electricity to ricochet through my body.

It was everything about him at that moment. The feel of his chest rubbing against mine. The way he filled me and made my body sing for him. "Me. I want to be myself again," I cried out as he thrust into me again.

"Then we start from there," he whispered against my ear, nibbling my lobe.

Fuck. What was this man doing to me?

"Do you want to laugh and be loved?" Kai asked, finding a sensitive spot on my neck that nearly caused me to convulse right then and there.

"Yes!" I cried out.

"Will you let me love you?"

"Yes!" My whole body cried out to his every touch and word. Every fiber of my being was giving him a truth I could not speak before.

"Come for me, baby girl. Let me see you come apart in my arms. Let your walls down, Katie. Let me protect you," he pleaded, thrusting deeper into me each time at the same slow pace.

"Don't hurt me," I cried, letting go of everything. My body exploded with a euphoria that should be illegal to feel. I felt weightless and tied to him all at the same time. My heart felt like it had burst, and I couldn't stop the tears from flowing. "I love you."

Kai kissed me hard. Taking the words from my lips and swallowing them. His body shuddered as he came inside me, the twitching of his cock buried deep inside dragging out my own orgasm. My whole body felt like I had been through hell and back with this man. He let go of my hands and I clutched at him as though he were my life line.

Our kissing slowed down, but I was still crying. I couldn't stop the floodgates of emotions. I was *home* with Kai. I was *safe* with Kai. I was *loved* by him, and I couldn't deny it anymore. I was *in love* with him. I was myself with Kai. I didn't need to pretend, or hide my fears. He saw all of my scars and took me the way I was, without hesitation.

"Thank you for trusting me, Kitkat," he whispered against

my lips. I didn't need to say anything more. My heart and body gave him every answer. Honestly.

He slowly pulled out and rolled over, pulling me with him so that I was again laid across his chest. "Sleep, love," he cooed against my hair. And like an obedient child, my eyes fluttered closed. I fell asleep without worries or doubts filling my head. My mind was in absolute peace.

Chapter 36

"Hey, Katie! The moving truck is here," Kai called from downstairs.

Shit! I was supposed to be out of bed already!

I threw off the blankets and ran to the bathroom to brush my teeth and pull my hair back. Changing into a pair of sweatpants and one of Kai's t-shirts, I hurried down to the front door.

"Where's the truck?" I asked, looking out the door and noticing the lack of a large delivery truck.

Kai snickered from behind me. "They just called and said they would be here in 15."

I looked at my watch feeling confused. "But it's been like 15 minutes. Where are they?" I asked.

"On their way. You were still in bed weren't you?" He asked, sneaking up to hug me from behind and changing the subject.

"No."

"Yes," he corrected. "What happened to the Marine getting up early? You're always trying to sleep in now," he whispered against my neck, causing a shiver to run down my spine.

"Don't start shit you won't finish," I scolded, trying to pull away from him.

Kai chuckled darkly and hugged me tighter against his chest. "I bet I can unwind you before they get here," he whispered as one of his hands rubbed my stomach before dipping into my pants.

"Kai," I whimpered.

"Let me make you feel better, Kitkat."

I leaned back into his embrace and rested my head on his shoulder. He began softly kissing my neck as his fingers slid into my panties and to find my already soaking wet clit. Suddenly, he withdrew his hand and pulled me into the kitchen.

"I need to be inside you. Now. Drop your pants and bend over the island, baby," he ordered in a low voice.

I didn't need to be told twice. My pants were down a second later and I was perched over the island with my ass in the air. I was reminded of my first night in this house, when he promised to fuck me on this very counter.

Why hadn't we done this yet?

"Uh, ahh," I moaned loudly when he suddenly thrust all of the way in. My breath stuttered. There was no more foreplay needed between us. My whole body was humming with the feeling of being filled and fucked each time he bottomed out, pressed against my ass. "Harder," I moaned loudly.

"Whatever." Thrust. "You." Thrust. "Want." Thrust. He slammed into me over and over. "Fuck!" He cursed, picking up the pace. "I will never get used to how good you feel squeezing me like you do."

"Kai, I'm close," I whimpered, feeling that tightness in my stomach. How was I so close to coming?

He grabbed my right leg and opened me up further, and I thought I was going to see stars as his balls slapped into my

327

clit. "Oh god!" I yelled, loving the spot he was hitting in the deepest part of my core.

Kai grunted behind me, holding my left knee half up on the counter. "Come for me, Kitkat. Come all over my dick before the mover gets here," he growled behind me before leaning further into me and nibbling my back.

I felt his cock start to swell and twitch, signaling his own impending orgasm. With my breast stimulated by the friction against the counter, the positioning and the lewdness of possibly being caught by the movers; it was all I needed. Knowing how much I turned him on was the biggest freaking turn on for me.

I came, shivering and convulsing on the kitchen island as Kai grabbed me by the hips and thrust once more before coming deep inside of me. Laying across the counter, I couldn't help but giggle.

"You know I am going to be useless now, right?" I asked him.

"But you won't be stressed, and I won't be blue balled watching you strut around in my clothes," he retorted, pulling out and tucking himself back into his pants.

I slid off of the counter as Kai began pulling my pants up. "I need to go clean up now," I giggled.

Before I could get two steps away, I was pulled back into Kai's arms. "Leave it. I want you to have my cum dripping down your delicious thighs while they move you into our house. And when they leave," he whispered in my ear. "I'm going to fuck you in every room, and on every surface of *our* home."

* * *

I woke up feeling like crap. I didn't want to get out of bed. I didn't even want to brush my teeth, let alone get dressed and drive two towns over to be poked and prodded. Kai wasn't having it though. He *let* me sleep in until eight, but now he was pulling the blankets off of the bed, and dragging me to the bathroom to get cleaned up.

"Come one. You agreed," he reminded me as I stumbled out of the bed and shuffled to the bathroom.

I glared at him in annoyance. "You can't ask me stuff in bed, Kai. I will agree to anything and you know it! It shouldn't count!"

"It's happening."

"We're really doing this?" I asked.

"Yep."

"Can't we just wait another two days?" I whined against his shoulder.

"Nope. I took the whole week off for this. It's happening," he replied.

"But I don't want to. Things are fine right now," I argued back.

"Are they?" He asked, pulling back to look at me. "Do you have the meds you need to be taking? Do you have a doctor you can call when you are sick? Who do you have to talk to about your health? What about all that shit from the IED attack? Do you really know all of the lasting side effects it will have on your body?"

"No," I whispered in defeat.

"You're doing it today. Let's go!" He urged, shoving me into the bathroom and closing the door.

"Rude…" I grumbled, turning on the shower and stripping off my pajamas.

All of this started when I had my address officially changed to Kai's house. Letters held by the post office were delivered in bulk.

Then my folks brought a few boxes from their house, and one was filled with unopened mail. Kai joked that I had a ton of fan mail at first, but then got serious when he realized the majority were letters from the veterans' office requesting follow ups on my health care.

* * *

"Did you send what they needed?" He asked a week later.

"What who needed?"

"Kat. Have you sent your stuff to the VA yet?" He asked, looking annoyed.

"I think I sent it off."

"You think?"

"Well... I meant to. But I forgot it when I ran to the site for work," I lied.

"Where is it? I'll mail it tomorrow when I go to work." He offered. He took one look at my face and knew I was lying.

"Get your laptop, Kat."

"What? Why?" I asked, grabbing my laptop and setting it on the table.

"You're doing this now. What do you need to fill out the medical claims?" He asked, rummaging through a box of paperwork for my medical records.

I stopped moving. "Kai, we don't have time for this. I'm supposed to be meeting Andie in thirty minutes."

He didn't even bat an eye before calling Andie and telling on me. I could hear her screaming through the phone. She was so

pissed, she proceeded to further rat me out and told him she was
bringing the rest of my stuff over. Apparently, there were records
in the boxes of things at her place that I would need.

"How does she know what I need?" I asked defensively when
Kai hung up.

"Apparently, your Doctor Giancolo gave you a nearly completed
packet that just needed to be mailed a year and half ago!" He
growled in frustration at me.

* * *

Three weeks... It took three weeks for the VA to process my
medical disability claims and schedule my appointments.

Today, I was scheduled with a general health doctor, a
nutcracker, an osteopath, and a 'full photo shoot' in radiology.
I didn't want to seem like a whiner and tell someone how
broken I was. There were guys far more damaged than I was,
and it didn't feel right claiming 'disability' when I could walk
around and work.

I dressed in a pair of loose jeans and a sweater. It wasn't
cold yet, but the damp fall weather always left me feeling
chilled. Kai was waiting for me in the kitchen with a cup of
hot coffee and breakfast.

"Don't I need to fast or something like that for blood work?"
I asked him, eyeing the bacon and egg sandwich he prepared
for me.

"They said you can eat. They'll do the bloodwork later
today, so it will be okay to eat breakfast."

I grudgingly sipped the steaming cup of coffee. *How did*
he always make it so perfectly? Kai smirked as a small moan
escaped my lips.

Damn it.

"Now hurry up and eat so we can get there on time," he chuckled, turning to put his dirty dishes in the dishwasher.

Feeling extremely petulant, I ate that sandwich like it was my last meal, and savored every damn bite. Kai didn't say a word and just leaned against the counter with his arms crossed, watching me. When the last morsel was in my mouth, he grabbed my plate and coffee cup and put them in the dishwasher.

I started to grumble, but he passed me a bottle of my favorite raspberry sparkling water. *Damn it! Why was he so fucking perfect?*

"You done stalling?" He asked.

"No."

He walked around the island and turned me to face him so that he could stand between my legs. He pecked my lips and pulled me off the stool toward the front door.

"It will be okay, Kitkat. Time to go," he assured me as we walked to the car.

* * *

I had *even more* appointments after the day-long doctor-a-thon. I was so angry with Kai every time. I didn't mind the dentist, but then there was a gastro, an optometrist, *and* a gyno before my claim was completed. When they said I would be checked "tooth to toe," they weren't exaggerating. I felt like such a broken freak with all of the appointments, health checks, labs, and questions. My god, the questions seemed never ending. It was exhausting.

Kai kept telling me they were just being thorough. Apparently, it was enough. It took a little under two months to get my rating back from the VA.

100%.

I received a 100 percent total and permanent disability rating. My occasional headaches were attributed to the IED. My breakdown at the end, attributed to my time in service. My difficulty conceiving due to loss of reproductive ability was included. Apparently losing an ovary was a bigger deal than I thought.

I was assigned a primary care physician in a women's health clinic, and all of my physicians were other female veterans. It made it easier to share information about my health, and enabled them to adjust my medications and set up a solid treatment plan for everything that ailed me.

I hated it when he was right about everything.

Chapter 37

.

I received the call a week ago that the permits to begin work on the 4th Street house were finally approved. I was dressed in jeans, a loose sweatshirt from up north and my steel toe boots. I wouldn't be able to start work for another few days, as another team would be responsible for stripping the floors and woodwork throughout the interior, but today was the walk through with the contractors to prioritize what needed to be done.

I was so freaking excited, I couldn't sit still. I had packed, unpacked and repacked my tools three times already. Kai just sat back and laughed at me, obsessively adjusting everything in my tool belt.

"Is this a Katie quirk or a Marine thing?" He asked, watching me jump and shift with my tool belt on.

"What are you talking about?" I asked, adjusting the placement of my hammer so that it wouldn't hit the front of my leg if I squatted.

"This," he chuckled, waving his hand at me.

"I have no idea what you're talking about," I said, looking at him like he was nuts.

"Babe, you have adjusted the belt three times, and rear-ranged the tools at least four. I can understand that part. But why do you keep jumping around and squatting?"

I had to laugh a bit at myself. "I look crazy, don't I?" I asked.

"Nooooo," he responded sarcastically.

"Well, Mr. Smarty pants... If I have to wear this belt most of the day, I don't want it to ride or sit funny on my hips. That causes blisters, and blisters on my hips or back would affect how I move. As for the jumping and squatting..." I exhaled, "I don't want anything falling out, or smacking my legs while I work."

Kai nodded, finally understanding the madness behind my methods. "What time do you have to be there? We could drive to work together," he offered, wiggling his eyebrows at me.

I laughed and set my toolbelt with the rest of my tools near the front door. I wouldn't know what I really needed until I got on site, so there was no sense in continuing to obsess over it. "The foreman said the walk through wouldn't be until eleven, but I want to be there by nine to do a walk through before that. I want to have time to check out everything before I get asked questions."

Kai stepped up and pulled me into a hug. I wrapped my arms around him and felt the tension leaving my body.

He kissed my hair and leaned back to look at me. "Let's ride into work together and get a coffee before you head over. We can take yours so you don't have to unload all of your tools, and I can just walk over to the house when I am done. That work?" He asked, kissing my forehead.

I nodded nuzzling back into his chest for more hugs. I was nervous. I wasn't this nervous about joining the Marines. I wasn't even this nervous when I first started working at 15. Yet, the thought of starting this new job and possibly a new career made me anxious.

"Come on. Eat some breakfast and then we can go," Kai urged me.

The ride into town was quiet. I let Kai drive so that I could sit and destress a bit along the way. I hadn't realized I was biting my nails until Kai reached over and took my hand in his. Interlocking our fingers, he pulled my hand up to his mouth and kissed my battered nails. "You'll be fine," he assured me.

I nodded absently and leaned my head back on the seat rest. *Today would be just fine.*

The coffee they served at Kai's clinic was gross. "How do you drink this?" I asked, smacking my tongue around my mouth to remove the taste lingering in there.

He laughed and took my cup from me. "Not everyone's pallet is as refined as yours," he joked.

"It's not even a matter of refinement. When was the last time someone cleaned the machine out? It shouldn't taste burnt!" I argued quietly.

"Don't you have a job to get to?" He scoffed back.

I realized it was nearly nine and panicked. "Shit! I have to go!" I said, jumping up to run out the door. Kai stood just as quickly and pulled me back so that he could hug me.

"Have a great first day, Kitkat," he whispered, pecking me on the lips with a gentle kiss.

I felt my anxiety drop by half. "Thank you," I whispered. "I love you."

"I love you, too. Now go show them what you can do!" He encouraged me with a pat on the ass as I walked away. I squinted my eyes at him as I departed, but made sure to add some extra sway in my sashay as I went out the door. "I see what you're doing, Katie!" He yelled after me, causing me to laugh and jog back to my SUV. I wouldn't put it past him to chase me down for being cheeky.

I was right to get there when I did. The team stripping the wood was not as gentle as I would have been. I stopped one guy setting up a floor sander, and convinced him to change the grit of the paper before gouging the grain away. The floors weren't cherry or oak, but pine. Pine was a softer wood that couldn't stand up to the lower grit papers.

I took measurements and made notes of the different woods in a small book I kept in my belt. The grand dining room had a built-in buffet and china cabinet constructed from black walnut. Black walnut was nearly impossible to find on a budget, but I was pretty sure that I could sister in a few small pieces of maple where the wood had been broken or gouged over the years.

By eleven o'clock I had written meticulous notes on the key areas I would need to work on as well as a modest list of wood supplies they would need to provide to complete the repairs. The foreman gathered everyone outside the front entrance and began the walk through with the home owners and representatives from the Historical Society. This house dated back to the revolutionary war, and had received several well known forefathers in its heyday, chief among them: William Penn.

The exterior was primarily brick, which was common for this area. Unlike the clapboard and shake siding of the northeast, brick was cheaper and easier to acquire in this area. I wouldn't have anything to do with exterior work, so I just followed along and listened to the other workers talk about their plans for rehabbing the brittle mortar.

By the time we got inside it was already after noon. The guy sanding the floors took his lunch break so that we could tour the inside. We started from the main entry and walked room to room. I didn't get a chance to speak once, because of the men discussing bulk supply requirements for electrical and plumbing versus timelines.

"Well, I guess that wraps up the list," the foreman said, clapping his hands together. "Any last comments before we get into this project?" Everyone else was shaking their heads, until I spoke up.

"I do," I called out.

"And you are?" The homeowner inquired.

I smiled politely. "I'm Katie Johnson, your in-house craftsman. I was hired to repair the damaged woodwork throughout the house," I said, offering my hand.

"Oh, wonderful! I was wondering if that would be addressed. My wife would kill me if the integrity of the original structure wasn't maintained," he confessed, shaking my offered hand.

The foreman, named Jack, smiled. "I wasn't sure if this was gonna be too much for you. You didn't say much," he pointed out.

I nodded in understanding. "There are a lot of things that need priority over missing spindles on a balustrade and chipped molding. I didn't hear anything about budget ceilings? I can use maple wood to patch the black walnut, and Caribbean pine to repair the wide baseboards in the upstairs bath," I started, looking down at my notes.

"I would also like to sit with the homeowner to discuss their intentions for the servant doors in the cellar. They could be used to replace the battered doors leading to the kit-"

"This your first time on a site, little girl?" one of the men asked, causing several others to chuckle.

I smiled back at him. "It is. But I know my job. I won't question your ability to patch plaster, so don't question my ability to repair the woodwork," I stated before turning my attention back to the foreman and homeowner. "As I was saying, the doors to the kitchen are damaged and could be replaced with doors from the cellar. I can fabricate new ones for the basement that would be keeping with the style of the home."

I flipped through my notes to make sure I hadn't missed anything, and remembered the spindles. "Lastly, is there a preference for wood to be used for the spindles? Will the balustrade need to be fortified with harder wood?"

"Why does that even matter?" A younger guy scoffed at me.

"It matters if you ever decide to slide down the rail. Once or twice wouldn't be a problem for someone my size. Corn fed fella like yourself, I would insist on something like cherry or oak that won't crack under the pressure."

The young guy blushed in embarrassment, but a few of the older guys chuckled.

The foreman just looked to the homeowner for his input.

"I don't see my wife or I sliding down the banister, but I can't put it past our grandchildren. I will leave it to your professional judgment," he stated, chuckling.

I nodded and looked back to the foreman, "Then I will make sure you have my list of materials for the spindles, baluster upstairs, and trim and new doors."

"We'll make sure it's ordered, Katie," another guy responded. I was assuming he was the project manager, Dan.

Dan and Jack gave me the green light to set up a workshop in the basement, as it would be one of the last areas to be rehabbed. The priority was set on the primary living spaces, which meant I had a lot of turning to do to repair the rickety balustrades. I estimated that it would take at least three weeks to turn all of the spindles. I planned to keep the ends longer and blocky so that I would have room to adjust measurements off each end when they were cut, rather than turning each spindle to an exact length for placement. Old houses were nothing if not asymmetrical after years of wear.

I loved the thought of using a hand planer for the mahogany baluster on the third floor loft area. The bevling was simple and didn't require a lot of work. Not to mention mahogany smelled so much better than the oak when it was worked.

I didn't mess with the other guys too much, and the older ones pretty much left me alone while I worked. The younger ones were a pain in my ass from the first day. I got into the habit of locking my stuff in my car if it wasn't in use, after someone decided to hide my tools around the site. It took three hours to find everything, and, although highly annoyed, I was just relieved that none of my shit was broken.

When the floors were finished on the main level, I got to work on the built-in cabinetry. The homeowner hadn't decided on a stain yet for any of the woodwork, so I could take my time with each task. I repaired the drawers and cabinet doors structurally before adding mahogany veneer to the faces of the drawers. The original wood wasn't unusable, but no amount of sanding and filler would make it look new again. Using thin sheets of real wood gave the appearance that the drawer face was a solid slab rather than an amalgamation of woods slatted together. It was clean and restored dignity to the piece.

One of the older guys walked behind me as I cleaned up the mess I had made of the dining room. "That's some nice work you did there," he commented, running his hand over the cabinet benchtop. "Where'd you learn to do all this?" he asked, squatting down to get a better look at the drawers and trim.

"Mike Gyllenhall's school up north," I commented offhand. He stilled for a moment before looking at me a bit more appreciatively.

"Which course you take with them?" He asked, standing back up.

"I did the full year. Made no sense just taking one class. Mike's an amazing teacher," I said.

"My name's Paul," he introduced himself. "You need any additional materials or have any issues, you just let me know. Gyllenhall only graduates 20 folks a year. You want to shut them idiots up, let them know who certified you as a tradesman."

I smiled softly at the man. "Thank you, Paul. I appreciate the support."

"So what's next on the schedule for you?" he asked, helping to carry my tools out to my truck. "Wait, why are you lugging this stuff back and forth from your vehicle? Didn't they set you up with a workroom downstairs?" He huffed at me.

I bit the inside of my cheek as I tried to decide how to answer that question. "Let's just say, I like my things where I leave them. If they are in my vehicle, I don't have to wonder where they *ran off to*."

Paul looked confused for a moment, before his eyes

wandered over to five guys around my age cracking jokes with each other. "I see."

"I can handle myself," I explained. "As long as they don't mess with my work, I won't have to kick their asses."

Paul immediately started laughing. It was a deep belly laugh that made me want to laugh with him. "Come on. Come have lunch with the old timers. We can discuss how to put those arrogant shits in their places," he chuckled.

"That sounds amazing," I agreed with a giant smile.

Chapter 38

After months of lazing around, four weeks of woodwork was kicking my ass. It wasn't just that the work was grueling, but I had the added effort of carrying my tools *everywhere*. Thankfully, I was done with the first floor, and all of the balustrades between the cellar and the third floor loft area. The owners loved the work I did in the dining room and grand foyer, and that was what mattered most to me.

I trundled into the door of our house, thrilled that I would have the next two days off. It was hard to have so many different trades working one house at the same time. I especially had to work around the heavy lifters who were doing the plumbing, electrical rewiring, and ceilings. The ten foot ceilings were gorgeous sheet metal inlays. However, all ceiling work required scaffolding, which meant that ceiling work stopped all other work at floor level.

"How was your day," Kai called from the kitchen.

"Good. But I feel like I have been worked over," I whined, slipping off my boots. "Whatever you are making smells really good."

Kai came out of the kitchen and stopped in his tracks at the sight of me. "What the hell happened to you?" he asked, eyebrows raised.

I was covered in a combination of wood dust and chimney soot. I was certain that I looked like I had crawled through the chimney before leaving the site. "Couple of assholes ran a sweeper down a chimney while I was working on the mantel. Thankfully, I still had my mask on, or I would have inhaled all that shit. Can you remind me to replace my filters?" I asked.

Kai looked pissed. "Wait. Was this another *accident?*" He asked, his face flushed with anger over the treatment I received on the site. Because I told him everything...

I didn't say anything at first, and just started stripping my clothes off where I stood. "I would like to think the actual guys sweeping didn't know I was there. I *can* say the guys who should have warned me, did not."

"What the fuck, Kat? This is harassment!" He yelled. *Yep, definitely pissed.*

"I don't want to get into it right now. Let me get cleaned up, and then I will tell you everything. Right now, I need to wash this shit off me," I told him, as I walked toward the stairs.

Kai didn't look convinced, but agreed nonetheless. "I just put a lasagna in the oven, so you have about an hour."

I smiled at him. "I would kiss you, but I feel really gross. I won't be long!" I promised, suddenly feeling more energetic than I had when I walked in the door.

After washing my hair three times and scrubbing every inch of skin twice, I finally felt clean again. I hadn't realized how high my anxiety had gotten, until it came down after the shower. I didn't want layers of fabric all over my skin, and threw on a long t-shirt sleeper. It was a soft jersey material that reached my knees that Andie bought for me at some point. When I joined Kai in the kitchen he was standing by with a glass of milk and my evening medications. "What's this?" I asked slightly confused.

"It's one of your anxiety pills and a pain killer. I know you freak out about smoke and soot on you, so I figured you would need it. The other is so you don't cry when I work on your muscles later," he explained.

"I don't freak out about soo-" I started before he gave me a look.

"You don't need to hide that shit from me, Kat. I pay attention. It's okay if you're not okay. Just don't pretend it is with me, when it obviously is not."

I sat down at the table feeling like I had just been chided. "When have I ever-"

Kai halted my next words with a single look. "Labor day weekend. Tried to take you camping, and you were a mess the whole time. I honestly thought it was the company, but Andie and Jonas told me they noticed things before as well," he explained.

"You compared notes with Andie and Jonas…" I trailed off, looking for the right words.

"Sure did," he replied, pulling the lasagna out of the oven.

Wait. What? My boyfriend was discussing my mental health with my friends? "What the fuck, Kai!" I growled. "You can't talk about me like I'm a fucking child. I am not okay with you, *whom I sleep with*, discussing my mental health with fucking outsiders!" I shouted.

Kai sat the lasagna down on the stove and looked genuinely shocked that I was pissed about this. I was yelling at him, and nearly shaking. I was so angry.

He took a deep breath and exhaled, trying to choose his

words carefully. "Two months ago, we had just decided to move in together. There were a lot of things I didn't know, but learned by going through the motions without a guide. I had no idea what a trigger was; let alone that I needed to look out for them.

"Andie chewed my ass out, because, *according to her*, I was going out of my way to keep you riled up the whole fucking weekend. She and Jonas cornered me while you were swimming with the kids, and tore into me. I would never *'discuss'* your shit with anyone without your say so," he explained.

My eyes felt like they were burning. I remembered the first two days of that trip being so stressful, before everything calmed down on the last day. "You didn't tell them about stuff I told you, right?" I whimpered, feeling like my soul was bared before this man.

Kai came across the room in three steps and pulled me into his chest. "I would never do anything to betray your trust in me. I swear. Besides, they already know how you snore and fart in your sleep- Ugh!"

I punched him in the stomach. "I do not!" I said, crying like a baby.

"Ok, ok. You don't fart in your sleep," he chuckled at me. "Come on, let's eat dinner. Then I can help you de-stress. You're off the next two days right?"

"Yes," I grunted petulantly, causing him to chuckle again.

"Do you need another minute?" He asked when I didn't release him from the hug.

"Maybe."

By the time we finished eating I felt like I could sleep for the next two days. I did make the effort to clean up the dishes though, since Kai made dinner. Kai sat up on the sofa, and I sat on the floor between his legs so that he could massage my shoulders while we watched tv.

"Ughh. that. That. Right there," I moaned as his fingers found and worked a knot in my tight muscles.

Kai chuckled and kept working. "Now tell me about your day," he coaxed.

"Well, I am making doors for the servant's rooms in the basement. I glued a couple of boards together and I am going to fit the nicer wood around the outside, but it's a pain in the ass. Every piece slides together like a puzzle, so if the measurements are off, even a little, it's shit. OOOOH, that feels good, Kai," I trailed off at the end as he started into the front of my shoulders.

"I thought you were working on a mantel?" he questioned.

"Oh yeah. Paul asked me to look at a mantel in one of the upstairs rooms. It had beautiful flower patterning carved in the face, but a chunk looked like it was dug out. The mantel isn't original to the house, but the owners love it. Paul wanted to know if I could repair it or replace the whole piece. It's a lot of work, like two straight weeks to hand carve all of that detail in a new piece," I explained.

"So what are you going to do?" he asked

"I think I want to try recreating it. Anyway, I was stripping the layers of paint off to reveal some of the detailing. Paul stepped out to grab the project manager so we could talk materials… That's when the soot came flooding down the chimney. I looked a sight when they came in. He started shouting, and the foreman came running in. The project lead was swearing something. The chimney guys were freaking out, because they were told the room was clear… Within twenty minutes the whole site was shut down.

"The homeowners were called in, 'cause it was a safety violation. Then the big office who has the contract for the project was called in. I didn't even have time to be upset, because so many people were upset *for* me. The little fucktards that have been messing with my shit were fired on the spot," I continued.

Kai stopped massaging and pulled my face back to look at him. "Seriously? They fired them?" He asked, looking shocked.

"Apparently, Paul and Jack had noticed some other shit going on and set up cameras around the house. They hadn't just been messing with my tools. They were going in and messing with my work," I explained.

"Are you fucking kidding me?!" He growled, gripping my muscles tighter than he intended.

"OUCH!" I yelped.

He let go immediately. "Shit, sorry. I'm so fucking pissed-" he started.

"Let me finish…" I whined.

"You're right. Sorry, keep going. But, I'm not going to lie, I want to punch those assholes right now," he grumbled.

"Anyway, they had recordings of some inappropriate conversations. One of the assholes had tried telling the homeowners that I was fleecing them, because he couldn't see where I had done any work," I laughed at the end. "I never saw someone piss their pants in fear outside of a combat zone, but the one dude, Randall… They said they were contacting lawyers because I had a solid lawsuit against the fucking lot."

"So? What happened?" Kai asked, now sliding onto the floor to sit behind me.

I leaned back against his chest and sighed. "They left with their tails between their legs. Turns out everyone was thrilled with my work ethic and the quality of my work. The historical society nutters couldn't stop raving about the turned spindles I made for the master staircase. Anyway, I was offered a full contract with the head company. I am their new go-to gal for woodwork, apparently," I finished, leaning back against his chest.

Kai pulled me back against him and kissed my neck. "That's so awesome! Congrats, Kitkat," he whispered against my skin.

"It gets better," I giggled.

"There's more?" he asked, chuckling.

"They're paying for my workshop here at the house."

Again Kai tried to pull me around to face him. "Seriously??" He asked.

"Well, I told them it's too much traveling with everything I needed from site to site, and they would rather pay for a workshop than me sue them. I'm fine with a workshop we don't have to pay for. We'll need to prep the backyard this weekend," I finished cheekily.

Kai stared at me for a solid second before pushing me on the floor and kissing me senseless. "You are amazing. I wanted to kick their asses every fucking day. Now tell me...." he whispered. "How much of that take down was plotted with the old timers?"

I bit my lips and stared up at Kai. *He knew.*

"Fuck! That is so damn hot," he said huskily, grinding himself against me so that I would know how turned he was.

"Shut up!" I chuckled, swatting at his chest.

"You think I'm joking?" He asked, nipping at my jaw. He

took my hand and guided it down to his growing erection. I grabbed onto it through his pants and stroked him. "Don't tease me, Kat," he pleaded, inching my shirt up so that it bunched at my waist.

"Who's teasing who?" I asked, unbuttoning his pants and lowering the zipper.

I lifted my head up to kiss him. He responded with a ferocity I hadn't felt in a while. My mouth felt like it was being devoured. I whimpered when he pulled my hands away from his body and pinned them over my head. I wanted to touch him too, but was denied.

"Shhhh," he tutted against my lips as his free hand gently stroked my cheek before wandering down my body. He massaged my breast, squeezing it before pinching one of my nipples. The latter caused me to arch my back into him as a moan escaped my lips. His hand continued its path down to my center, where his nimble fingers found my now soaking panties. His thumb found my button, and god, did he press it.

"Please," I started, but was silenced with another devouring kiss.

Between the day I had, the physical labor, the anxiety drop, the massage, and now his ministrations of every *fuck me* hot spot on my body, I felt like I was drugged. I couldn't keep my eyes open. I felt him slide my underwear to the side and then the head of his cock rubbing up against my folds.

"Please," I begged again, a writhing mess beneath him.

"As you wish," he whispered, pushing into me so slowly I thought I would die. I tried to dip my feet into his ass to pull him in deeper. Faster. He stopped me, his free hand hooking under my left knee and pushing that leg up and out to the side. The leg positioning left me wide open so I had the stimulation of him thrusting inside me as well as his pelvis grinding against my clitoris when he bottomed out.

"Yes, like that," I moaned again. My mind traveled back to the first time Kai had me in this position. And the words I had uttered to him. We had had unprotected sex since we got together again. I couldn't imagine not feeling his skin against mine, even deep inside. However, we had been careful since the miscarriage to not have sex when I was ovulating. Until now.

The thought hit me like a lightning bolt. I opened my eyes, and looked at the man looking down at me. There was only love and adoration in Kai's eyes. I wanted everything with him. Everything and then some, but I knew he would never marry me. He had said as much. "I want a baby," I whispered as tears trickled from my eyes.

Chapter 39

Kai's Point of View

I stopped moving and stared at Katie in shock for half a second. "What did you just say?" I asked quietly, unsure if I heard her correctly. *Please, tell me I misheard you, Kat.*

A few tears trickled from her eyes as she lay staring up at me. "I said, 'I want a baby,'" she whispered.

Fuck. I hadn't misheard her.

"Are you sure that's a conversation to have right now?" I asked quietly.

"Well, I'm ovulating so we kinda should talk about this now, or you'll need to pull out," she whispered back.

"Fuck!" I swore, closing my eyes and gritting my teeth. It took *everything* I had not to come. Katie telling me that she wanted to have a baby, *with me,* were the hottest, dirtiest, sexiest words to my ears. When I opened my eyes again, I felt like I was absolutely possessed.

I thrust hard into her, now intent to fill her with every last swimmer I had in me. I continued hard and fast, pounding one set of lips with my hips while kissing the other like she was made of porcelain. When she moaned into my mouth I let her have some air before continuing. My body was humming, but I needed to hear her say it again. I pulled back again, to ask her to repeat herself, but she turned away from me instead.

"Don't appease me, Kai. This isn't just a thing. I want a child. You'll be tied to me for the rest of our lives," she whispered as if giving me a last chance to pull away from her.

I released her hands, and turned her face back to mine. I couldn't help but chuckle darkly, as I continued slamming into her. "Kitkat," I whispered, nipping at her jaw. "Say it again. Tell me what you want from me."

Her eyes were teeming with tears, as she looked up at me. "I want a baby. With you," she confessed, her voice breaking as she confessed her heart's desire.

I swore again, fighting the immense pressure building in my balls. "I need you to come, Kitkat," I growled. "Then I am going to come inside of you, praying to every god I can think of that one of my swimmers will knock you up. Then, tomorrow," I continued, thrusting harder again. "I'm going to fill you again and again and again. *Fuck!*" I cussed feeling her getting close. "Get there, Katie, we're starting right now. We are going to make a baby right here, right now," I promised.

Katie's body shuddered beneath me; her insides squeezing and spasming around me was the last stimulus my cock could take. I slammed into her and shook as I came. I lowered my body and hugged her underneath me. I intended to kiss her gently but she threw her arms around my neck and attacked me with a ferocity I hadn't experienced since our first kiss. Her legs wrapped around my waist as I cradled her head in my hands.

I had just come, but after two minutes of kissing me like

she was, I felt myself getting hard again. I ground against her, feeling her warm soft walls still squeezing me. She looked at me with wide eyes.

"Seriously? Already?" she asked in shock.

"I told you," I said, kissing her nose, pumping slowly in and out of her. "I'm going to spend the next two days filling you up until you are pregnant. You don't have to do anything but eat, sleep and keep your legs in the air."

Katie stared at me for a second before her giggle bubbled up. The giggle flowed into full belly laughter. I could feel her floor muscles contracting and pushing back against me buried inside her.

"Stop laughing! You'll eject my guys!" I half heartedly yelled at her, which only made her laugh harder. I loved seeing her laugh like this. This was the carefree woman I fell in love with nearly 20 years ago. She was it for me.

I made good on my promise. I didn't let Katie go for two days. Everything she did, every sound she made, made me hard. I had her in the kitchen, on the table, in the shower, on the sofa, bent over the sofa. The thought of getting her pregnant made my balls tighten with need. Now we were laying in bed, both of us unwilling to go back to work yet.

"Thanksgiving is coming up," she whispered.

Absent-mindedly, I answered, "Yeah it does that every year."

She poked me in the ribs, causing me to grunt.

"Stop, that tickles," I mumbled, rolling us so that I could spoon up behind her.

"What do you do for Thanksgiving?" She asked quietly.

I chuckled, not understanding where this was going. "I eat turkey?"

Katie huffed, making me chuckle. "I mean where do you go? Do you eat at your parents'? Your brother's place? I haven't been home for Thanksgiving since I left, Kai. Are we eating dinner together? Do you have plans? Should I be making plans?" She rambled.

Ah, now I understood. "I don't really plan anything. I usually stop at my parents', then go over to Bradley's to watch the game. Why? What do you want to do?"

Katie didn't say anything for a while, and I thought maybe she had fallen back to sleep. "Hey, why are you so quiet, Kat?" I whispered against her neck, pecking her lightly.

She took a deep breath, like she was trying to get enough courage for an uncomfortable confession. It actually made me nervous. The thought that she had Thanksgiving plans that didn't involve me did not set well. *At all.*

"What if we had our own Thanksgiving here?" She asked in barely a whisper.

"Okay," I exhaled, realizing too late it sounded like I wasn't happy about it.

She turned to look at me nervously. "Do you not want to have Thanksgiving here?" She asked, searching my eyes.

"Honestly, love, I am happy doing anything that involves us being together. Your parents', my parents'…. Here, Andie's or Bradley's. As long as your plans don't involve ditching me on our first Thanksgiving together, I will do whatever you want," I said.

She had a shy smile. "I want to invite our families over here for Thanksgiving. I mean your parents, mine, maybe my sisters and your brother and his family?"

I couldn't stop the wheels from turning, trying to figure out how we were going to fit eleven adults and four kids in the dining room. Not to mention, Katie and her sister Fiona were barely civil to each other. Katie misunderstood my silence as rejection of her idea, and started getting out of bed, but I wouldn't let her go.

"Stop. I'm thinking of how to make everyone fit. That's eleven adults, and four kids. We'd need to borrow a table and chairs, but we could make it work if we rearrange the living room and make it the dining room for the day. Maybe put all the kids around the island," I rambled off, trying to picture how best to accommodate everyone with the space we had.

Katie looked back at me, the relief on her face obvious. "I thought you were going to hate the idea!" She exhaled, burrowing her face into my neck.

I hugged her and kissed the top of her head. "We could make this even easier and make everybody bring something. We can cook the turkey here, then everyone else brings the sides."

Katie grabbed her phone from the night stand and began texting furiously. She invited our folks, her sisters, my brother, and even opened the invite out to Andie, Jonas, Bradley, and Amy to watch the game after dinner.

"Are you sure you want to have that many people over?" I asked, knowing how she was with crowded spaces.

"Yep," she answered, getting out of bed and walking off as she texted. I could just see her ass peeking from under her shirt as she walked away and my dick twitched.

I smashed a pillow on my face and cussed. Planning Thanksgiving dinner should not make my dick hard. Groaning, I got out of bed and followed Katie down to the kitchen, trying my best to adjust the now obvious boner I was sporting.

I sucked in a breath when I got to the kitchen. She was bent over the island still messaging our family and friends, and her ass was on full display. *Fuck.*

"What time do you have to be at work, Katie?" I asked, walking up behind her.

She glanced at the time, and mumbled something about being there by nine. It was only seven.

That was more than enough time.

I quietly dropped to my knees and lifted her ass, causing her to squeal. I didn't wait though, and immediately went to town feasting on her. My tongue licked between her folds and plunged into her as I squeezed her cheeks to keep her from squirming away.

"Kai," she moaned in a breathy whisper, leaning forward so that I had better access.

My tongue slid forward and rolled around her clit, eliciting another moan. I had spent so much time worshiping her body, I reveled in how quickly I could make her come. It didn't take long and she was trembling through her orgasm against my mouth. I stood up, and pulled my painfully hard cock out of my shorts and pushed into her. *How does she feel this good every time?*

One hand held her hips as I slowly thrust in and out of her, while the other caressed up her back pushing her shirt up to her shoulders. This woman was a goddess, and I wanted to worship at the altar that was my Kitkat every day of my life. "Did you do it on purpose?" I asked huskily.

Her responding giggle turned moan told me everything I needed to know. "You left this gorgeous ass out for me to enjoy. Is that it, Kitkat?" I asked, reaching under her chest and pulling her back against me. I thrust harder as her weight dropped down against my hips. She was so sensitive after her orgasm, her insides were still twitching, milking my cock with every thrust. *Fuck, this woman is going to be the death of me.*

"So close," she whimpered, her head rolling back against my shoulder.

I pulled out, causing her to whimper in protest. I had no plans of staying separated though, as I turned her around and shoved her back against the wall. I pulled her legs up around my waist, and thrust back into her as her arms wrapped around my neck. I kissed her like she had the air I needed. I couldn't understand why hosting Thanksgiving would make me this fucking crazy.

"Yes, just like that," she cried out. "You're going to make me come. Fuck. Yes. Kai," she rambled as her orgasm washed over her.

I pushed harder and deeper as she came, making her scream for me. It was enough to get me there, and I came. Legs trembling, body on the verge of collapsing, we hugged each other and kissed sweetly.

I slowly let her legs down as I pulled out of her. Katie was biting her bottom lip, her face was flushed with the 'just fucked' blood rush. I kissed her nose and hugged her to my body. I was so happy she gave us a chance.

"Kai?" she called quietly.

"Yeah?"

"Is it just Thanksgiving or do you get this excited about all of the holidays?" She asked against my chest.

There was a moment of silence before we both erupted into hysterical laughter. "All of them. You planning anything in our house will get a reaction. You. Just you being here," I whispered against her hair, still holding her to me

Chapter 40

I don't know what I was thinking when I told Katie, 'The more the merrier,' when she asked who to invite for Thanksgiving. Everyone said, 'yes.' Every single one. Andie and Katie decorated and organized the house the night before so that we could seat thirty people. *Thirty.* The island was too small for the *eight* kids, so we set them up around the kitchen table, and decided to use the island like an open buffet.

We had two long tables set up in the living room for all of the adults, and set up more spaces with tray tables in case it got too tight once everyone filled into the house. Katie was up at five to put the turkey in the oven and I was just doing my best to not add to her stress.

I told everyone to dress comfortably, so there wouldn't be any stress about dressing up. Katie was relieved when she heard me confirming with Lacy and Val that jeans and t-shirts would be perfect. It was just after one when Katie's folks showed up, followed quickly by my own. I had to stop myself from rolling my eyes, when our mothers started talking about all of the 'trials' we had overcome to get here.

There were no secrets between Katie and I, but I didn't want her to hear about how fucked I was after she left. I didn't want her to know how far down I fell before hitting rock bottom. I was heading to answer the door when I heard Katie starting to yell in the kitchen.

"Jesus Christ, mom! Can you stop telling everyone that I was in a hospital for depression and PTSD?"

I quickly doubled back and pulled a fuming Katie to greet our guests. "Breathe, Kitkat," I whispered against her ear as we walked.

"I don't know if I can do this," she whispered back, turning into my chest to stop herself from crying. I stopped and hugged her tightly.

"You get the door, I'll take the parents," I offered.

She looked up at me like I had just saved Christmas for all the Whos in Whoville. "Thank you. I don't want bloodshed on our first Thanksgiving," she whispered, giving a quick peck before running to the door.

I stalked back into the kitchen to find our mothers looking like misbehaved children. "You four, out back, please," I gestured to our parents.

Katie's dad gave me a gruff look like he was prepared to go toe to toe, but I didn't give a fuck. We had come too far, to let these gossiping busy bodies fuck up the day. When we were outside, I closed the door and took a deep breath before speaking.

"I know today is all about being thankful, but I will kick you out if you start comparing stories about which child was more fucked up. We're adults. It's taken a lot for us to get here, please don't humiliate either of us by gossiping," I said quietly.

My mother was the first to pipe up, "Who was gossiping? We were catching up, Kai. We haven't talked since you two went to prom, for crying out loud."

The next thing I knew the two women were going back and forth trying to explain (and justify) discussing our shit with anyone who would listen. Ten minutes in, I threw my hand up to silence the squawking. I looked at my mother like I didn't know who she was. "What the fuck does my drinking have to do with catching up? You couldn't think of anything else to talk about today other than the lowest points in your child's life?" I asked her.

She blanched and stepped back toward my dad. Then I turned to Katie's mom. "And you don't get to tell everyone everything about Katie either. You want to brag? You need to catch up? I am a fucking doctor, and Katie is one of 3000 craftsman in the country certified to do what she does. Rather than shaming us by digging up our fucked up pasts, try a little humble bragging. It's what normal parents do!" I shouted the end.

Katie's dad looked at mine and the two cracked a smile. "Let's go get a couple beers while these two sort themselves in time out," he offered, walking toward the house.

"That sounds delightful," my dad replied, following Katie's dad.

I gave our mothers one more reproachful look before walking inside as well. Grown women should not have to be told what was appropriate topics of conversation at Thanksgiving. Katie was beet red when I walked in the door, and on the verge of tears.

The whole house was pin drop silent and everyone stared in shock and horror at something beneath Katie. "What the fuck happened?" I asked, crossing the room as quickly as possible.

On the other side of the island, Andie and Val were dropped

onto the floor holding a steaming hot turkey with towels. I didn't think, and grabbed said hot turkey with my bare hands. I quickly regretted that and tossed it up on the Island. It bounced twice, then slid to the other side of the island and onto the floor.

"TURKEY DOWN!!"

"STRIKE!"

"WE HAVE A TURKEY DOWN!" the kids started yelling.

I turned to look at Katie, horrified that I had just stolen the saved turkey and launched it onto the floor. Not to mention burning the ever loving shit out of both hands. No one said a word. I was regretting ever inviting these people into our house. Family, friends... Didn't care. I swore if she cried today, I would disown every single one of them. Then I threw her turkey on the floor.

Jonas picked up the turkey with oven mitts and set it onto the tray. "Five second rule?" he asked Katie.

She made this weird "Hic-" noise, and looked at me. She bit her lip, and the tears started brimming in her eyes. I saw every emotion that rushed over her face. We started laughing at the same time, and it was contagious. Andie, Val, and Katie had all been splashed with dressing, when the pan tipped. So the floor was a slippery mess.

"It *bounced!*" Katie wheezed.

Andie was now hunched holding her very pregnant belly as she laughed her ass off. "It fucking *bounced! Holy shit!*"

As we were laughing hysterically, my mother came back in with Katie's mom. "What's so funny?" They asked, smiling at all of us laughing.

"Kai just shared his secret technique for tenderizing turkey," Katie's dad quipped, and I thought Katie was going to piss herself.

"Shit, shit, shit!" Andie started hollering. "I'm going to piss myself!"

Jonas moved to help Andie to the bathroom, but sprung into action a little too quickly and slid across the kitchen floor, now greased over with turkey drippings. It looked like a skit from a comedy show. His legs were moving left to right and his arms flailed wildly before he slammed into the island, nearly taking the turkey down a third time.

We got to work cleaning the mess that was now the kitchen, not saying a word about the Turkey hitting the floor to our mothers. They probably figured it out though, because there were only so many ways to get turkey drippings on so many people and surfaces. Katie took Val and Andie upstairs to change and clean themselves up while Bradley and Jonas helped me salvage the punted bird.

By the time the girls returned, we had already started serving the kids. Everyone circled through the kitchen, filling a plate with whichever items they liked best. There were two trays of stuffing, one with cranberries and one without. Various vegetables, potatoes, and finally a gravy that my mother managed to salvage up from the little dressing *not* spilled on the floor. Once everyone was sitting around the tables, I could see Katie physically relax beside me.

It struck me that this wasn't just *our* first Thanksgiving. This was her first for another reason. It didn't really click until that moment. Katie said she had not had Thanksgiving dinner with her family since leaving high school. I reached over and rubbed her lower back as we ate and laughed with our families.

By three o'clock most of the food had been demolished.

Cleaning up the dishes and little leftovers remaining, I was thankful Katie insisted on disposable plates and cutlery. The dishwasher was full, and I really wouldn't want to stand washing all of the used plates and forks after eating. Just as I was about to take the trash out, Katie gave me a wink and mouthed 'I told you so.' I rolled my eyes going out the door, which only made her laugh.

Amy and Bradley were the first to leave, as they had plans to visit their families for a later dinner. Katie hugged them and thanked them for coming, and Amy promised to host New Year's if we were interested. Katie just cackled looking over at me, "Kai said he *loves ALL* of the holidays. I can't wait!" I felt my face heat up which only made Amy and Katie laugh harder.

My brother pulled me into a hug before he left, whispering, "I'm happy for you both, bro." I'm guessing everyone whispered similar things to each of us, because Katie and I couldn't help but look at each other whenever we heard well wishes. Those who knew us, knew what it took to get to this point in our lives. Their happiness for us meant a lot more than I realized it would.

Jonas came up behind me and asked if we could watch the kids for a bit while he and Andie ran out for a bun. I didn't understand what the fuck he was talking about. I looked over to see Andie red faced and laughing with Katie. "What are you talking about?" I asked.

Andie and Katie both looked at me like I was a moron. "Her water just broke, Kai," Katie whispered so the kids wouldn't hear.

"OH SHIT!" I yelled in surprise, looking at Andie in shock. *"Be quiet!!"* The three of them shushed me immediately.

"We've got the kids. Go. Let me know if you need anything," Katie reassured Andie as Jonas helped her out the door.

"Where are they going?" Avery asked, as the door closed.

Katie knelt down in front of Avery and whispered in her ear. Avery's eyes became as big as saucers and brimmed with tears. I thought she was going to throw a tantrum, but instead she smiled and hugged Katie. "He's coming *today?!?*" She whispered loudly.

"We're going to have a big sleepover tonight, and then tomorrow we'll take you and Aiden to meet him. Deal?" Katie offered.

Avery nodded enthusiastically and took Katie's hand to go find blankets and pillows. An hour later, everyone was gone except for Val and Lacy and the three kids. We made a huge blanket fort for the kids in the living room with sofa cushions and sheets draped over the chairs. Once the kids were down for the night, Val and Lacy took the guest room. Katie said she would run by Andie and Jonas's place to grab Andie's 'baby bag', and meet them at the hospital.

"I'm not sure what I was expecting today, but this was not it," I said quietly as we pulled into the hospital parking lot.

Katie held my hand and laughed, "Babe, you gave a whole new meaning to *The Turkey Bowl.*"

"Shut up! We are never discussing this again!" I huffed, failing to be angry as she laughed uncontrollably in her seat.

"This was the best Thanksgiving *ever!* Thank you," she whispered and leaned over to kiss my cheek as I parked in the labor and delivery lot.

Chapter 41

Katie's POV

I found myself wandering around the drugstore carrying a basket full of junk I didn't need. I didn't need the body wash, but I threw it into the basket after the first lap. I didn't need the new mascara either, but it was thrown in there too.. I didn't need the fifteen other things I was carrying around. I just came here to buy tampons, and ended up staring at pregnancy tests. Not really.

My period should have started yesterday. The thought of being pregnant, however, was stuck in my head. What if this was just a false alarm? What if I was getting my hopes up for nothing? I could start bleeding right now, and then what?

I'd start crying like a crazy lady.

I shook my head and grabbed what I knew I came for. When I got home, Kai was still out with Bradley, Jonas, their two boys, and Xavier at some little league meet and greet. He had been messaging me all day with various updates on what they were doing. It was so much more information than I ever wanted to know about kid's baseball. I mistakenly thought the term *little league* applied to all kids' baseball teams below high school. That is *not* the case, as Bradley and Kai had explained before they left.

There was T-ball, Minor League, and Little League. In order to play the Minors, the kids had to play one season of T-ball. As the hourly updates continued from Kai, I gathered there were not enough T-ball coaches for kids to play the required one season, so Kai and Bradley had volunteered to coach a team together. An hour later, he apologized because they were going to be late getting back. Apparently, they were busy meeting their newly established team of tiny tikes.

The thought suddenly struck me: one day our kids would be signing up for T-ball. *Our kids.* I didn't want to think about it, and went out to my workshop in the backyard. I kept a small clipboard by the door to write my start and stop times so that I could log how long it took to work a project. I had been working on recreating the intricate wood overlays for two mantels in the 4th Street house.

There were various pieces around the shop with carved inlays, overlays, and combinations of the two. I wanted to give the owners options between the three. Personally, I preferred the carved mantels. The decorative filigrees were carved into a solid piece of wood that would become the mantle. I played with different stains to create the look of blooming flowers on one of the pieces. I wasn't one hundred percent happy with it, but Kai swore it was perfect. I loaded the cumbersome samples into my wheelbarrow and trudged out to my jeep. I wanted to get these over to the site before it snowed.

Arriving at the site, Paul and Jack had several guys come out and help me take the mantles into the house. I couldn't help but chuckle, listening to a couple of them grumbling about the weight and cumbersomeness of the wood. Paul quickly shut them up by telling them I loaded them in my jeep myself. They at least had a second set of hands to help unload.

Jack wanted to set them up on saw horses so that the owners could see each one and decide which they preferred. Paul didn't like that, and had the guys help me mount each one over a fireplace. There were four smaller fireplaces in the main bedrooms on the second floor, and the grand fireplace on the first. I had already cleaned up the grand fireplace, so it made no sense to have them sit there as comparisons.

Paul had me mount the stained floral inlay in the master bedroom. When I stepped back, it took my breath away. The mantle looked like it was always meant to be there. "You should take a pic and send it up to Gyllenhall. He'll be over the fucking moon with this work," Paul commented, patting me on the back.

I nodded, fumbling to pull my phone out of my pocket. I couldn't see what I was doing because everything was suddenly blurry. I heard Paul chuckle as he passed me a tissue. I blinked a couple times, causing tears to run down my cheeks. *When did I start crying?* I snapped a couple of pictures, and tucked my phone back where it was.

"You did good, kid," he said, throwing his arm over my shoulder and giving me a half hug. "Come on, let's get the other three up before the Craigs get here."

"These were just samples, Paul," I explained, not under-standing why he was having me mount them in place.

"Katie, these are fine. If you are really not happy with your work, we'll take them back down. But I don't think Mrs Craig is going to allow that to happen when she sees 'em."

Fucking dust making my eyes water.

We quickly went about getting each mantle hung in their

369

respective places. I had butterflies in my stomach the rest of the day, waiting for the Craigs to come and decide if they liked them or not. I was coming up from the basement when I heard screaming from the second floor.

"WHERE IS SHE?!? OH MY GOD! OH MY GOD!" Mrs Craig's voice filled the house.

I ran up the stairs expecting for her to be upset with the placement. I was ready to take them down when she barreled into me and threw her arms around my neck. "They're *amazing*. You have a gift, Katie. Thank you, thank you, thank you," she gushed, squeezing me and rocking excitedly.

"So these are okay?" I chuckled, pulling back a bit to truly gauge her reaction.

"You have no idea!" She exclaimed, pulling me into the master suite. "Look at it! It's just stunning! How did you make it look like that? Tell me your secrets!" She squealed, running her hand over the carvings.

Seeing her so happy, I couldn't help but smile. I told her how I created the carvings, and then used various stains to create the colored effects. When Paul asked if she wanted to see the other three *options*, I thought she was going to have a heart attack. He explained that I had intended these to be samples for her to choose from, to which she adamantly chose to keep each in their respective places, as mounted. I lost count how many times she ran over and hugged me before I finally managed to head home.

* * *

I wasn't sure what made me do it. When I got home, it was like I was possessed. Now I was standing in the bathroom staring at the stick on the bathroom counter, and I wanted to vomit.

The last few months were a blur of appointments with all kinds of doctors. Kai had been so pissed when he found out that I never applied for any disability compensation after leaving the military, and set me up with an initial appointment to review my medical history with a veteran affiliated clinic. There was so much in my records that I knew nothing about.

I had been diagnosed with traumatic brain injury after a concussion during my second deployment. I had been referred for psychological evaluation for my PTSD, but no one ever followed through with the referral. I thought I was fucked up because I couldn't cope. Instead I learned that people with TBIs are more prone to depression and PTSD issues than others.

We found out that I had a lot more damage to my body after the roadside bombing than I ever knew about. Maybe I hadn't asked enough questions back then? Kai was certain that Tyson would have known and just wanted to protect me just like Kai was trying to do now. I think Tyson would have done something like that. He would have done everything he could to shield me from anything that would cause me heartache.

Now I was staring at a stick and I didn't know whether to be happy or cry. Could I do this again? Could I go through all of this again?

"Kitkat, you okay in there?" Kai called from the bedroom.

I had been in here staring at the stick for thirty minutes. Should I tell him? Should I wait to see? I felt myself starting to shake and let out a choked sob.

371

The bathroom door burst open as Kai rushed in and pulled me into his arms. "What's the matter? Did I do something? I'm sorry I got back late. What happened, Katie? Talk to me," he murmured while hugging me into his chest and rubbing my back.

He stiffened suddenly, and pulled me away from him. He saw it. He studied my face, before cupping it in both hands and kissing me softly.

"Katie, are we having a baby?" He whispered quietly, staring into my eyes.

I stared back and nodded before bursting into tears and giggling, "I'm pregnant, Kai."

"*Fuuuuck!* You scared the crap out of me!" He hollered before pulling me into a tight hug and laughing with his face buried against my neck.

"I'm scared, Kai," I admitted out loud. Holding onto him as tightly as I could. This was my third pregnancy. I didn't dare to hope. *What if it was another ectopic?*

He scooped me up and carried me to our bed. He pulled me against his body and held me. "You are not alone, Kat. This is not just you fighting everything by yourself anymore. We will take this one day at a time," he promised, kissing me softly on my cheeks, my eyes, my forehead, and my nose. "We will take this one step at a time. And this little *rainbow*," he spoke softly leaning over my stomach and kissing just below my navel, "is enough *hope*."

I threw my arms around his neck and kissed him. I didn't deserve to be this loved. I felt cherished and adored by Kai. "Can we keep this a secret until we know everything is okay?" I whispered.

Kai leaned back a bit before kissing me so tenderly I almost started crying again. "We'll call the clinic on Monday and get you scheduled for an appointment. We won't get excited, or tell anyone, until we know that everything is okay. Does that sound good?" He offered.

I nodded. We laid there together for who knew how long, before I giggled.

It took two weeks to get me in to see the obstetrician and get a first ultrasound. They confirmed that I was pregnant, and then told me to come back in two hours after drinking a lot of water. When we got back, I was greeted by the waiting sonographer. I thought the ultrasound would be over my stomach, and made a shocked expression when the woman explained that I needed to drop my drawers and put my feet up in some stirrups.

Aashilde, as she introduced herself, chuckled and explained that the baby would be too small at this point to see through all of the stomach tissue, organs and other things. "Okay, mommy, let's get a look at this little bean."

I laid back holding Kai's hand like my life depended on it. It seemed like an eternity had passed before turning the viewing screen toward us. "Congrats! You have a baby bean!" She smiled pointing with her free hand to a small spot on the monitor.

"It's okay?" I asked, choking up.

"This is good egg placement," she repeated.

"It's not ectopic? Could you see if it were ectopic?" I asked, not ready to believe what she was saying.

She nodded again. "So far so good, mommy," she repeated, pulling the wand away. She gave me a cloth to clean up with and left to print a couple of the pictures for us.

"We're having a baby, Kitkat," Kai whispered against my

cheek, kissing me gently.

I looked up at him and smiled, my heart near bursting with butterflies. "We're having a baby! You're stuck with me now," I assured him, giggling.

Chapter 42

Kai's Point of View

Katie was officially nine weeks pregnant today, and she had her second scan to confirm that everything was still good. We hadn't had sex in three weeks, because she was afraid of hurting the baby. I couldn't lie, hearing that heartbeat did something to me. I couldn't concentrate on what the doctor was saying. I couldn't even remember feeling like this when I went to the first scan with Jenny.

My mind was filled with thoughts about everything that our futures held as a couple, as a family. It was one thing to take responsibility for a pregnancy, but this one was intentional. We wanted this baby. We purposely *made* this baby. This was *our child*.

"I think he's in shock," I heard Katie chuckle.

I snapped out of it and looked at the two women in the room staring back at me. "Sorry, I'm just overwhelmed. I was afraid to get my hopes up," I admitted.

Katie smiled, giving me a knowing look. We had talked about this a lot over the last month. From the first pregnancy test to the first scan to now, we were both afraid to get too excited before we *knew*. Now, we *knew*; this baby was happening.

"Ok, Katie, your next scan will be after the New Year after you hit fifteen weeks. Your little bean is going to start growing rapidly from here, so some pain is expected," the doctor explained. "If you have any cramping that lasts longer than a couple minutes, call me. Spotting can be normal, but you're at high risk with your health issues, so don't hesitate to come in if you notice anything like that. Do you have any questions?" she asked.

I shook my head, and thanked the doctor as we left.

When we got to the car, Katie stopped me and took the keys from my hand. "Are you okay, Kai?" She asked.

I shook my head, and realized that meant no, and then started nodding which only caused her to chuckle. "Stop. Talk to me," she insisted when I tried to get in the car.

"Are you okay?" She asked again, but this time with more worry in her voice.

I had no idea what to say, I was completely overwhelmed by the feelings in my chest. "I'm good, Kitkat. I'm just overwhelmed. I want to scream and tell everyone in a hundred mile radius that I got you knocked up. I want to tell our families and celebrate, and then I think about the future..." I trailed off.

She nodded and pulled me into a hug. "Let's go home. We can talk when we get home, okay?" She offered.

I agreed and drove us home. Katie was quiet the whole way there. I had no idea what she was thinking, but I could nearly guarantee that it was nothing like I was thinking. When I parked the car, she got out and went straight to our room without saying a word. I let the door shut behind me and leaned against it. There were so many thoughts going on at once, I wouldn't even know how to articulate everything to her right now.

After I hung my coat up and kicked off my boots at the door, I went to find Katie in the bedroom. Problem was, Katie wasn't in our room. I heard a loud crash coming from the guest room and ran down the hall. "What happened?! Are you okay?" I yelled, running into the room.

Katie was laying on the bed smiling in a baseball shirt that read, "Kai Rayburn hit a home run and knocked me up."

I couldn't stop the smile that plastered across my face. "When did you do that?" I asked, walking over to her.

"Do what?" She asked, smiling back mischievously.

"When did you get the shirt made?" I asked, grabbing her ankles and pulling her toward the end of the bed.

"Two days after the stick said I was pregnant," she whispered back.

"You've had that since Thanksgiving?" I asked, running my hands up her legs.

Katie shook her head, and bit her lip. "Nope."

Now I was confused. "When did you get it done then?"

Katie reached up and pulled me onto the bed with her so that I between her legs, my arms on either side of her head to keep my weight off of her. Her eyes were sparkling as she looked up at me and whispered, "Wrong stick, babe."

"Which-" I started, but my words were silenced when her hand trailed down my body and caressed my previously half erect cock.

"I ordered it the day you agreed to have a baby with me, Kai. When you came inside of me," she whispered, rubbing my now full erection. "I knew this would be our baby," she confessed.

How did I ever deserve to have this woman in my life?

I lowered down to kiss her lips. I wanted to tell her everything in my heart, but instead I devoured her lips with mine. My tongue plundered her mouth, danced with hers, and then repeated. I groaned when her legs wrapped around my waist so she could grind herself against me. Katie taking what she wanted would never stop being a turn on for me.

I pulled back, and quieted her protests when she realized I was stripping my clothes off. She started to take the shirt off, but I stopped her. "No. Leave that on. I want to read it while you ride me, Kitkat."

She chuckled and pulled me back onto the bed so that I was on my back across the center. "Do you want me to go down on you?" She asked, trailing kisses down my chest.

A hoarse, "No," choked out of me as I pulled her to straddle my body. "Ride me, Katie. I don't want to hurt you," I confessed my biggest fear.

Katie chuckled again and raised herself so that the head of my dick was pressed against her slick opening. There was no doubt that she was turned on. She braced her hands on my chest and took me in a little bit at a time, coming back up and lowering a bit further each time. It was killing me not to just fill her to the hilt. I wanted to slam into her and make her scream, but she needed to be the one in control.

Then she dropped down completely and there was no more left. I couldn't go any deeper. I thought she would go up again, but instead she just rocked her hips back and forth so that the head of my dick rubbed against her g-spot over and over again. I grabbed her thighs and squeezed, my head tipping back with absolute fucking pleasure.

"You like this, *daddy?*" She asked in a sickly sweet voice, and my head shot up to look at her, as my whole body shuddered.

I just came.

Katie leaned back and giggled, gently riding out the rest of my orgasm. "That was mean," I said, my voice hoarse as my body came down from its high.

Katie laid her head on my chest. "Are you okay with all of this, Kai?" She asked. "I know we have talked about it. Like, A LOT. But I wanted to make sure you are really okay with this baby coming," she whispered against my skin.

I tipped her chin up so that she could see my face while we talked. "I'm not going to lie, I'm scared shitless. You work on a construction site, breathing in all kinds of fumes. Anything could fall and knock you over..." I started. I saw the look on her face and knew where her mind was going, so I cut it off before it got too far.

"I think you should tell Jack and Paul that you're pregnant. Maybe enlist them to help you with stains and solvents? I want to buy you a mask rated high enough for a pregnant woman. Do they make those?" I rambled, feeling her relax against me.

"We didn't even get genetic testing done on *us*. What happens if we've given the baby some rare genetic disease? Are we ready for that?" I continued. "I am so over the fucking moon about this baby, Kitkat, that I am almost sick with doubts."

Katie sighed, and moved so that she was laying beside me but her head rested on my shoulder. "Let's tackle these in order. First, I told Paul and Jack about the bean. They said, 'congrats,' by way. The rebreather I have is already rated at the highest end, because it was needed for my training. I looked for something better, and there really isn't anything out there. As for chemicals, Paul is going to take care of all of that for me.

"I'm not working on the site any more, so they will send guys here to pick up or deliver whatever I need to the workshop *here*. What was next?" she asked, absentmindedly. "Ah, yes…. Genetics. Will knowing any of that change anything at this point?"

"No, not really," I admitted.

"Ok, so let's table that one until they offer to test us at 32 weeks. If this baby is born with a flipper, we'll make sure it can swim. If it can't speak, we'll learn sign language. We don't have to worry about any of that, but if talking through it helps you feel better then we do that. Now, it's your turn," she said, taking a deep breath.

"My turn?" I asked, eyebrows raising. "Ok. Let me hear it," I encouraged her.

"What if I am a horrible mother? What if you decided that I'm not it, and you want me to leave? I'm so fucking scared of losing this baby, I don't know if I could ever recover after hearing its heart beating in there," she admitted, placing my hand on her stomach. "What if I have a fucking night terror and harm it? I wouldn't know what I was doing, Kai. I could kill this baby in my sleep, and it terrifies the shit out of me," she confessed as her voice broke.

I pulled her into a tight hug, and let her relax before I said anything. "I have seen you with Avery, Aiden and Oliver, you're amazing with them. I remember you babysitting your neighbors in high school, and you took care of the baby like you had done it a thousand times before," I reminded her, which elicited a small giggle.

"The amount of patience it takes to do what you do, just tells me that you will be just as patient with our kids. I have no doubt you will be an amazing mother, Katie. None. Now as for you and me? You were the one who got away for ten years; the love of my life, I was never going to get over. Why in the hell would I walk away now? I'm so in love with you, Kitkat, I am starting to wonder if it's unhealthy," I told her.

Katie poked me in the ribs and giggled again. "As for the other stuff? We can ask your doc. You haven't had a night terror in months, Kat. Between the therapy and just us being open with our communication, there hasn't been a build up of shit. But if it would make you feel more comfortable, I am happy to tie you to the bed every night until you feel better. Deal?" I asked, kissing the top of her head.

Katie snorted. "You have been saying you would tie me up since high school. Don't threaten me with a good time, if you aren't going to put your money where your mouth is and follow through, buddy."

I pulled away from Katie and dragged her out of the bed. She squealed when I picked her up and carried her down the hall to our room. I sat her down on the bed and took off her t-shirt. Her face was flushed crimson, when I pulled up a blindfold and ropes from under the bed.

"What are you going to do, Kai?" She asked breathily. I smirked watching her chest heaving as her breathing picked up from excitement.

"I'm putting my money where my mouth is," I said, throwing her words back at her.

She dropped back on the bed and let me have my way with her for the rest of the night. I was pretty sure she blacked out for a minute after her seventh orgasm, so I untied her from our bed and carried her to take a bath. I remembered that she couldn't take a *hot bath* while pregnant, so I carried

381

her into the shower and washed us both down.

As she fell asleep in my arms that night, my brain was filled with thoughts of a different nature. After tonight, I wanted to try so much more with Katie. I wanted my Kitkat mewling on my cock, begging me to let her come. There were so many possibilities, but my mind settled on one. The one I never imagined I would get to do...

Chapter 43

Katie's Point of View

Kai pulled away from my kiss and stared down at me, brushing the hair away from my face. "There is nothing I would rather do than strip you naked and worship you," he whispered, kissing my lips tenderly. "But we have to go meet everyone at Bradley's, and if I don't show up with you *on time*, Amy may kick my ass."

I laughed at his serious expression. I couldn't see why Bradly and Kai were so afraid of Amy. She was all of five feet two inches, and sweet as could be. But they both walked on eggshells with her. It made me laugh to watch. Eventually, I would have a girls' night with her and Andie, and find out what happened to make them so afraid of her.

"Ok, let's get going," I told him while still kissing his jaw and trailing my tongue down his neck.

"Kitkat," he growled at me before rolling us so that he was pressed on top of me. "If you keep doing that, we will be late," he looked down at me seriously.

I had never felt such joy and peace in any single moment since we were 18. He saw everything in my eyes, and groaned a half-hearted defeat. I thought he would drag me out of bed, so that we could leave but he just stared at me for another second, waiting. I didn't leave him waiting for long.

I wrapped my legs around his waist, and pulled him further against me. I tilted my head up and kissed him, my tongue going straight for his. He could blame *me* for us being late to the New Year's party.

Blame my hormones.

Blame my crazy needs.

I didn't care, I needed him right now.

He pulled away from my kiss, his eyes just as dark as mine with lust. "Roll over, Katie," he directed. He leaned back on his knees to give me room to do as he said.

I immediately rolled onto my stomach, my legs parted on either side of him. He reached under my hips, unbuttoned my jeans and pulled them down to my knees. I heard his breath suck in when a red lace thong was revealed.

His hands caressed my ass, squeezing my cheeks before pulling my ass up higher. One hand slid down between my thighs and caressed me through the lace. My breath caught as one finger slid under the material and rubbed up and down against my clit.

I looked over my shoulder at Kai, and whimpered, rocking my hips against his hand. He was biting his bottom lip while staring at my ass and fingering me. "Babe," I moaned.

His eyes snapped to mine, "You brought this on yourself, Kitkat."

Kai's other hand, which had been caressing his cock through his pants, now unfastened the buttons just enough to free his erection. He pulled my thong to one side and pushed into me, filling me completely. A moan escaped me as he leaned forward over my body and grabbed my arms.

Kai pulled back as he pulled my upper body off the bed by

my elbows. As my body arched back, he slammed into me; eliciting another moan from me and a satisfied grunt from him. "Is this what you needed, Kitkat? Hmmm?" He asked between thrusts, slamming into me as hard and as deep as he could.

"Mmm... Yes. Yes," I moaned against his thrusts. I was so turned on by the way he was holding me and controlling every bit of my movement. I trusted him completely and released all of my control to Kai.

He pulled me back further so that my back pressed against his chest as he continued to thrust deeply, hitting my cervix. The sensation was causing my core to spasm and tighten, spasm and tighten, pushing me closer and closer to the edge. "Please, please, Kai," I begged him.

He nibbled my ear, and bit gently at the base of my neck. "What does my baby need, hmmmm? Tell me, Katie. What do you want?" He whispered, thrusting harder and faster into me.

Dear God, this man worked my body like it was a profession. I moaned and whimpered, feeling the tightening pleasure building up higher and higher.

"Come. Make me come, Kai," I gasped out, dropping myself hard against each of his thrusts.

He pushed me forward onto the bed so that my face was on the blanket. One hand held my wrists behind my back, providing leverage as he thrust into me, the other reached around and found my clit again. Kai pinched my clit tightly between his fingertips and pulled on it.

It was the last stimulation needed to send me skyrocketing into my orgasm. My whole body trembled against him, as I came harder than I had in months. He released my wrists, grabbed my hips and pulled me hard against him as he found his own release.

"Jesus, babe," he panted. "When did you start wearing thongs again? Hmmm? Are you trying to kill me?" He asked as his body relaxed against my back and he trailed kisses across my shoulders.

We lay there in bed breathing hard, both completely sated. I would have gone to sleep if Kai's phone had not started ringing.

"Shit, we're late," he groaned, reaching to silence the phone on the nightstand.

I giggled and rolled over to face him. "I love you, Kai," I whispered against his neck as he held me. "Thank you for spoiling me."

He kissed my forehead and swore under his breath as his phone started to ring again. "I will spoil you every day, if you let me bend you over like that," he growled, pulling me up to kiss me thoroughly. When he parted from my lips, I was breathless again.

"Come on, I need to clean you up before we head over to Bradley's," Kai said as he rolled out of bed and leaned over to carry me into the bathroom.

I bit my bottom lip, giggling. I couldn't help provoking him further, "You don't want me to walk around all of our friends and family filled with your cum, babe?"

I swear he tripped walking into the bathroom and almost dropped me. He looked down at me, closed his eyes and took a deep breath. "I don't know what dirty smut you have been reading, but I am willing to buy more if you keep talking to me like that," he whispered into my ear.

I couldn't help but laugh. *He found my Linz Vonc smutty*

romance books! "Just remember you said it!"

* * *

Kai's POV

Bradley was pissed as he met us at the door. We were almost two hours late. I would have blamed Katie, but she started talking dirty as I went to get us cleaned up. I ended up pushing her up against the wall in our shower and fucking her two more times before we actually got out of the house.

"Butthead!" Bradley yelled at me as we walked into his house. "Two hours! Two hours, you dick!"

"Bradley!" Amy yelled coming from the living room. "It's *fine.* They have had a lot going on. Don't mind him, Katie," she cooed at Katie while completely ignoring me.

"Hi to you too, Amy!" I yelled at their retreating backs as they walked off together.

Bradley scowled at me. "Are we doing this or not?" He asked.

I smiled. "Yeah. Let's see if she goes for it," I grinned at him.

"What happens if she doesn't?" Bradley asked.

"Then...we never tell her," I sighed. *I hoped she went for it.* "Is Amy willing as well?"

Bradley snorted, "Are you kidding me? She has been down for this since you introduced her to Katie."

"Well, let's see what happens. Maybe this will be my lucky night!" I told him, taking a deep breath and walking to find where Amy had taken my girl.

"Truth or Dare!" Jonas yelled from the kitchen.

"Seriously? What are you 15?" I grumbled following Katie

out to the backyard bonfire.

"You're a chicken shit, if you don't play," Andie piped up laughing. This was the first time she and Jonas had been out since their little Oliver was born.

The kids had all crashed out in the guest rooms upstairs, so it was just the adults left in the backyard, apparently playing *'Truth or Dare.'*

Katie nudged me with her shoulder, "Are you afraid of a little *dare*, Kai?" She asked while giving me a side eye.

"You too, Kat?" I grumbled. "Fine. For you, I will play this stupid fucking game."

She has no idea what I have planned for her tonight.

Andie passed Katie a glass of wine, smiling. "I bought your favorite. I know you two have had a lot going on, but tonight you should just unwind and see where the night takes you," she whispered and winked at us.

Katie smiled back and pretended to sip the wine before passing the glass to me, "Have you tried this one, babe?"

Our eyes met and a thousand words of understanding passed between us. We didn't want to tell anyone about her pregnancy, so I was going to be drinking a lot of wine tonight. I took the glass and gave it a sip.

"That's pretty good. Not as sweet as what I heard earlier," I said, and watched her skin flush. I smirked and drank the rest of the wine, placing the emptied glass on a table. "Why are you so flushed, Kitkat?" I whispered against her ear as I pulled her into a hug.

Katie pushed me away, looking embarrassed; her eyes scanning the backyard to see if anyone else had heard my comments. I couldn't help but push her buttons a little bit more tonight.

"I thought you liked the idea of being watched, maybe even caught," I whispered in her ear, nibbling on her ear lobe. "Didn't you want to try new things? Huh?"

"How about we start this with an ice breaker. Let's play Never Have I Ever first," Val suggested.

Amy was the first to jump up and agree, "Oh! I love that game! Let me get some post-its to play with," she squealed while running back into the house and returning two minutes later.

"Ok, everyone," Amy announced. "This game is called *Never Have I Ever.* Everyone gets two colored post-its. If you have never, hold up hot pink. If you have.... Green for name and shame," she explained while sticking post-its to everyone as she went around the yard.

I found an empty chair in front of the bonfire and sat down, pulling Katie onto my lap. She leaned back against me and laughed as the games began. This was going to be interesting.

Chapter 44

Katie's POV

I hadn't laughed this hard since Thanksgiving. We were all couples sitting around playing games and just having fun. It was exactly what I needed to take my mind off of everything else.

It was Andie's turn, "Never have I ever slept with two women at the same time." I held up my hot pink post-it and looked around to see who held up their green.

Val and Lacy began to whisper back and forth before looking in my direction laughing when they held up a pink each. Suddenly, Jonas jumped up and yelled, "Kai! You lucky bastard, you have to tell!"

I whipped my head to look behind me at Kai. His face was crimson red, as he held up the only green post-it. "It's not what you think," he whispered, kissing my shoulder.

Clearing his throat, he stared ahead at Lacy and Val. "I slept with two women six years ago. They were drunk and wandered into my room," he told the group.

Jonas and Bradley whistled and encouraged him to tell all of the details. Kai cleared his throat, and I realized that he was making a big deal of this and Lacy and Val were turning redder and redder.

"Well, these two hot chicks, broke into my room, crawled into my bed and proceeded to-" Kai stopped when Lacy cut him off.

"Proceeded to pass out! Don't you dare make shit up!" Lacy shouted.

Kai pretended to be offended. "I do believe this is *my* story to tell, Lacy. You held up PINK!" he snorted at her and began again.

"Now, where was I?" He asked out loud.

Bradley urged him on, "Two hot chicks, your bed, proceeded to…"

Kai's face lit up with that mischievous smile I loved so much. "Ah, yes. They then proceeded to squirm around until they were under my blankets with me. They put their hands all over my body…"

He made this long dramatic pause to build up the suspense, but I elbowed him. "Let me up!" I whined. "I have to pee!!"

"Sorry, right," he whispered, letting me run back into the house. "Potty break, have to wait," he sighed.

Alex leaned back and groaned, "You two planned this out didn't you?!?"

I ran into the first floor bath and got done as quickly as I could. I made sure to dry my hands thoroughly after I washed them so I wouldn't get too chilled sitting outside.

I returned to my spot on Kai's lap and he continued, "They got under my blankets, put hands all under my body, and then they told me their *heat went out* and they just needed to *warm up.*" He made the last part so suggestive that Val and Lacy looked ready to burst.

"Oh for fuck's sake, Kai. Stop milking this shit out," Val interrupted him. "It was me and Lacy. We had come back from shoveling the cars out of the snow. We were frozen and exhausted, so we crawled into Kai's bed, put our popsicle hands under his body and went to sleep for three hours. He was asleep, and so were we."

"Boooo! Val, your version isn't as fun," Amy chimed in with Bradley and Jonas.

"Who's next?" Alex asked.

"Um, you are, Alex!" Amy said, pointing at him.

"Yes! Ok... Um... Let me think... Oh! Never have I ever had a baby with someone who isn't here," Alex smiled, holding up the pink post-it and kissing his wife, Jane.

Jane whispered in his ear, and Alex nodded. "Pregnancy doesn't count. Has to have been a living child ex-vitro," he added.

I watched pink slips go up around most of the group, mine included. I side eyed Kai, and had to do a double take when I saw that he held up the pink post-it and not green.

Andie was the first to admonish him, "Kai, you had a kid with your ex-wife. You can't pull that shit."

Kai's face turned very serious, "What was the Never again? Never have *I ever gotten another woman pregnant who is not here.* There is a reason my divorce was ironclad, Andie."

He was pissed. I was going to tell him it was okay, but then he said all of that.

"She cheated on you?" Andie asked. I had never told her why Kai divorced Jenny. It didn't seem like my story to tell, but Kai was telling them all now.

"She told me the kid was mine because we had been fooling around. When Heather died, I found out she wasn't mine *by blood.* I loved her and I miss her still, but I was not the father who planted that seed."

I threw my arms around his neck and hugged him. "I love you so much, Kai," I whispered in his ear, feeling his arms wrap around me. "Never have I ever loved anyone as much as I love you."

Kai leaned back, cupped my face and kissed me deeply. When he pulled away again, I was breathless and panting.

Bradley stood up, "Ladies and gentlemen, you don't have to leave, but you need to man your stations for this evening's main event. It's nearly midnight!"

I looked around confused as everyone pulled out hats and party poppers. "Where's my hat and party popper?" I asked Bradley, sounding like a sullen child.

Kai tapped my leg and told me to stand up for the final round of the game. Everyone swore that this was how they played the game while I was gone for ten years, so I went along with it.

I was pulled over to Andie, "Never will I ever be happier than I am when you smile," she said before pushing me toward Amy.

Amy smiled at me, "Never will I ever wake to a more beautiful sight than you in my arms." She then pushed me to Lacy.

"Never will I ever ask for anything again, because I have it all," Val said, grinning ear to ear.

I didn't understand this game. They all sounded like they were making overtures to me.

Never will I ever be happier than I am with you; wake to a more beautiful sight than you in my arms; ask for anything again, because I have it all.

I turned slowly realizing that I couldn't see Kai behind me. Someone grabbed my hand and I halted, looking down to see Kai on one knee and holding a candy ring pop. Before I could say a word he pulled me closer to him and spoke.

"*Never* have I ever felt more love than I do when I am with you. *Never* have I ever wished more for someone else than I do for you. *Never* have I ever wanted to spend the rest of my life with someone as much as I want to spend all of my days with you," he told me, staring into my eyes.

I couldn't see clearly as my eyes brimmed with tears. *What was he doing?*

"*Never* will I ever get a woman as pregnant-" there was a volley of gasps and squeals before Kai gave them all a look for interrupting. "-Gotten a woman more pregnant with joy, love, and *hope. Never* will I ever feel more blessed than I do with you in my life, Katie. Never will I ever leave you. Never will I ever make you cry another tear, other than those of joy. Never will I ever-" I stopped him.

I couldn't stop the tears running down my face. My whole body was trembling with emotions. Never *had I ever* felt anything like I felt in that moment. Kai stood up, wiped away my tears, and continued.

"Never will I ever ask another woman to be my wife. To love only me. To be with only me for all of our days. Never will I ever see another woman walk down an aisle unless it is *you*, walking toward *me* on our wedding day. Katie Renee Preston Johnson, I have loved you since the sixth grade. I was an idiot to not tell you for six years. I was an idiot to let you go 11 years ago. I will never make those mistakes again. Never will I ever let you go a day without hearing how much I love you. Katie," he whispered my name.

"Yeah?" I asked, choking back my tears.

"Will you marry me?" Kai asked in the softest whisper.

"Will you marry me, and have beautiful babies with me, Katie?"

I sobbed out, "YES," threw my arms around his neck and wrapped my legs around his waist so that he was carrying me.

The entire group cheered and shot confetti poppers into the air just as fireworks erupted to mark the start of the new year.

There was a loud group chorus of, "Congratulations!"

I didn't care what was happening around us. I didn't want to talk to anyone else. I just wanted Kai at that moment. My heart was filled to near bursting with sweetness, and I didn't want to share any more of this time with anyone else. "Take me home, Kai," I cried holding him tightly.

I calmed down enough to say our good-byes, get hugs from everyone, and finally leave. I stopped suddenly as we were about to get in the car. "Oh my god, I have to pee!" I squealed running back to the house making Kai laugh harder than I had heard him laugh in a long time.

When we were finally home and snuggled against each other in bed, I could barely keep my eyes open. Today had been a roller coaster of emotions. My phone pinged and Kai reached for it.

"You have a message from 'T.Mama,'" he whispered before putting the phone back on the nightstand.

He felt me still against him, and hugged me a little tighter, caressing my back. "You can call her tomorrow. Tonight, I just want to hold *my baby mama,* and maybe rock her to sleep."

Kai turned my body so that my back was against his chest, and I became very aware of his hardened erection pressed up against my ass. He nuzzled his nose against my neck as he pulled up the t-shirt that I wore for pajamas. His hands then slid down my hips and shifted my thong to one side, fingers caressing my lower lips.

A small moan escaped my lips as Kai shifted my left leg up so that he could slide his cock against me, lubricating the whole shaft. He slowly rocked his hips behind me, the engorged head of his cock pressing up against my clit each time causing me to moan a little more. I reached behind me and grabbed his hair, holding his head against my neck.

"I love you, Kitkat," he whispered, nibbling my ear as he pushed into me.

"Ahhhh. I love you, Kai," I moaned, feeling complete as we were as close as we could be in that moment.

Kai rocked slowly against my backside, building our pleasure gradually this time. My whole body felt like electrical currents were running through it each time he thrust into me. "Never-" he whispered against me, picking up speed and thrusting a little deeper.

"Never will I tire of how good you feel, squeezing me inside of you, melting in my arms," Kai continued. "I want to start and end everyday buried so deep inside of you that I lose my mind."

Kai's words combined with his hold on my body while thrusting into me was quickly pushing me to a euphoric climax. "Harder, Kai," I whimpered, arching my ass back into each thrust.

"Roll on your stomach, Kitkat, but don't lose contact," Kai whispered as he started to move with me as I rolled on my stomach.

My legs were held tight together with Kai's on the outside.

He pulled my arms out from under me and used one hand to hold my wrists over my head against the headboard. With his chest rubbing against my back he thrust hard into me, and I felt like I had been shocked. This positioning repeatedly hit the front of my cervix and his cock head just rubbed the same spot over and over and over.

I couldn't believe we had never done this positioning before, and I wanted to do it like this every night. Kai didn't speed up but just thrust harder and deeper each time. It felt like I had fire crawling from deep in my abdomen and spiraling out of my body causing me to tremble.

Kai kissed my shoulders and nuzzled my neck again, "You feel so good, Kitkat. I am not going to last much longer. Come with me."

"Angh, ke-kee-, keep - harder," I whimpered in my pleasure-induced delirium.

I felt Kai's chest vibrate as he chuckled against my neck. "Whatever my baby wants, I am happy to give her," Kai grunted as he thrust hard into me.

Shockwaves started rippling through my body, as he thrust harder and harder, still not picking up the speed. I started whimpering, the pleasure building too high. I wouldn't be able to handle this orgasm, it was too much.

"Too much, Kai," I whimpered as he pivoted his hips slightly upwards with the last two thrusts, and then everything flashed white before my eyes. I tucked my face in the blankets and screamed as my orgasm ignited through every nerve in my body.

Kai continued to thrust through his orgasm, his twitching cock prolonging my own pleasure as he came deep inside of me hitting against my cervix. A second spiral of pleasure ripped through me as I came again.

"Fuuck, Kitkat," his voice labored against my shoulders, his body weight relaxed against mine. "Did you cum twice?" He asked as he pulled out of me and turned my panting body so that I was laid across his chest.

There had always been great chemistry between us, but this was on a whole new level. I couldn't speak anymore, all of the energy to move or speak was gone.

Kai caressed my back without another word. He had felt it too. Our bodies had said everything that needed to be said between us. I closed my eyes, and fell into a deep sleep in his arms. We had every day going forward to talk. Tonight, no more words were needed.

Chapter 45

I woke up in Kai's arms feeling like last night was a dream. I tilted my head back to look at him only to find him watching me. "Are you watching me sleep?" I asked.

"Maybe," he chuckled.

"You know that's weird, right?" I giggled back, still sleepy.

"I was wondering..." He trailed off.

"Wondering what?" I murmured against my pillow.

"I was wondering if last night really happened," he whispered, pulling me from my pillow so that I lay on my back with him leaning over me.

"Really? What happened last night?" I whispered.

Kai peppered my face with kisses. "I asked the love of my life to be my wife, and she said, 'Yes.'"

I couldn't help giggling again. "I had that same dream, you know."

"It was the craziest dream," he continued. "I proposed, but then she ate the ring I gave her."

I giggled again, remembering that he had proposed with a ring pop which I ate on the way home from Bradley's. "It was so sweet though," I attempted to justify myself.

"Well, we have a problem then," he whispered seriously, looking down at the plastic ring still on my finger.

I was curious to see where he was going with this so I asked. "Oh yeah? Are you angry that I ate up all your sweet words?"

Kai shook his head. "Nope. That's not it," he chuckled.

"Did you want me to savor it longer than one night?" I asked suggestively.

Kai chuckled again. "Yes, but not for the same reasons. I guess I have no choice but to give you something you won't eat, huh?" He asked as he held up a sparkling black diamond ring surrounded by small white ones.

"I bought this because it reminded me of us more than any other ring. Most people think a black diamond would be a bad choice for an engagement ring, but I think it best fits where we have been in life," he explained as he pulled the plastic ring from my finger.

I felt my eyes burning, hearing these words come from him. That he accepted me with all of my demons, my past, my baggage....

"See, we've each traveled dark roads to get here. It made us who we are, for sure, and I think we are both stronger for it," he whispered, sliding the diamonds onto my finger. "Finding you again has been a light at the end of the tunnel for me, Katie. No matter how dark things were before, you have lightened my life."

The tears brimming my eyes cascaded down my cheeks. "I love you," I whispered hoarsely.

Kai kissed me sweetly. There was nothing sexual or needy in this kiss, but it made my heart stutter nonetheless. This was my love language. Kai was showing me how much he adored me through his actions. He gave me a place to feel safe, a home to stay rooted, and love to help me through my dark days.

"I love you so much, my heart hurts," I choked between tears.

Kai chuckled and pulled me onto his chest. "I love you, too, Kitkat. More than words can describe."

We were in bed or cuddled on the couch the whole morning talking about nonsense. It still surprised me that we could talk for so long without becoming bored or running out of topics to discuss. Just before noon our phones began to ping with messages from our families. Since we were out on New Year's eve with friends, we agreed to visit our folks on New Year's day.

"Do our parents know?" I asked, coming out of the shower.

Kai was already half dressed in a pair of jeans. My face flushed seeing him standing there smiling at me while he brushed his teeth. I had to make him get out of the shower after he pinned me against the wall and had me screaming through two orgasms. My legs felt like jelly already, and he would have kept going if I hadn't made him leave.

"No. I only told our friends," he said, rinsing his mouth.

I tried to slip past him, but he pulled me back and trailed kisses down my neck again. It sent goose bumps down my arms, and had my core tightening up.

Don't fall for it! We have plans! My responsible side screamed in my head.

I wiggled and squirmed out of his grasp, losing my towel in the process. "No! We are already late!" I yelled, laughing as I ran to find my own clothes.

I didn't make it far before Kai had me bent over the bed and was lighting my body on fire all over again. It should be illegal to feel that good. Every. Single. Time.

"I can't move," I whined laying across the bed after. He had properly rocked my world, and there was no more energy left in my body. This only made his smile bigger, proud that he had fucked the energy right out of me.

"It's not funny," I whined, though I couldn't stop giggling and smiling as well.

"I'm not going to apologize," he admitted, pulling me to sit up. He was standing between my legs at the side of the bed looking down at my best attempt to appear annoyed. It failed, because he just chuckled more. "Seeing that ring on your finger, and knowing you're pregnant with our baby…. It does something to me, Kat. I could go again just thinking about it," he admitted.

He rocked against me to emphasize his *point.* I couldn't help laughing, feeling his dick beginning to poke against my stomach. "We will never make it out of this house, Kai," I attempted to persuade him.

He tipped his head back and sighed, knowing that what I was saying was the truth. "Be a good boy, and I will give you a surprise before we go," I promised.

His head tipped back down, his eyes completely darkened with lust. "Fuck, Kitkat," He cursed as his eyes raked over my naked body. He gave me a quick peck on the nose, and walked away from me grumbling. I couldn't hear everything he was saying but enough to know that he was cursing our parents for insisting we see them today.

I couldn't stop laughing at this childish side of him. He didn't show it often, but this petulant man was amazingly adorable. I got dressed as quickly as my screaming muscles would permit. I had to lie on the bed to put my pants on because my legs were so weak. I tried building a grudge and blaming Kai, but I had brought this one on myself. I needed to stop sashaying my ass when I walked away from him.

* * *

I didn't know who was quicker to notice the ring, my mom or his; but they had both reacted with the same shock and elation. My mom squealed and ran over to give me a hug before hugging Kai. She rambled about welcoming him to the family. Dad told her to stop being so dramatic, and pulled her away so that he could give me a hug.

"Ty would be happy for you. We all are, baby," he whispered softly. His words caused me to stiffen for a fraction of a second.

Would Ty be happy for me? I was moving on with my life. I was marrying another man, having his child. Could Tyson really be happy for me? A sob choked in my throat, but my dad just held me, continuing to whisper all of the things he knew about life, grief, loss, and standing up again after a fall. It was all of the words I didn't know I needed to hear. The small part of me that was still holding on with guilt, slowly let it go.

Tyson would be happy for me. Were our circumstances reversed, I knew I would want Tyson to find love again. I would want him to be happy in life. I forgot that Tyson had a relationship with my parents. He talked to them every day after I was medically evacuated home. My dad, more than anyone else, knew Tyson's wishes for my health and happiness.

"Thank you, daddy," I whispered, hoarsely. When he finally released me from our hug, Kai was ready to hold me up. I didn't know what conversations Kai had with my dad, but unsaid words passed between them when they shook hands.

"Thank you," Kai said quietly.

"Take care of her," my dad said back, smiling.

"Okay, let's eat!" My mom said, pulling us toward the kitchen. She was making our new year's favorite: macaroni and cheese with fried spam and grilled corn. There was something so amazing about the crispy salted meat and acidic flavor of grilled sweet corn that went so well with velvety mac and cheese. My brain was doing somersaults, until my nose took it all in.

I barely had my hand to my mouth as I wretched and ran to the bathroom. I vaguely heard my dad laughing, "I told you!"

There was the sound of more squealing as I am sure Kai, confirmed what they had already guessed. After losing the contents of my stomach, I cleaned myself up and returned to see my dad and Kai tucking food away in plastic tubs and my mom trying to air out the kitchen. I felt so guilty that my hormones had ruined their meal plans.

"Sorry," I whispered.

Mom ran over and gave me another hug. "I am so happy for you, Katie. I am just over the moon!" She gushed. "I'm going to be a Nonna again!"

I was the last of my sisters to have a baby. My younger sister had a little boy who was three years old, and my older sister had twin girls who were almost 10. I had missed a lot of their lives, but it was getting better.

"How far along are you?" Dad asked.

"Two months," Kai answered, coming over to hold me again. "We weren't planning on telling anyone until Katie was past the first trimester. It'd be nice if you can keep this quiet?" he asked them nicely.

My dad immediately pointed over at my mom. "If she says a word, you have my permission to uninvite her from the wedding," he threatened. My mom balked at his words.

"I won't say a thing! I can keep quiet for a couple more weeks!" She insisted.

I shook my head, knowing where her mind was going. She assumed Kai meant we had known for two months, not that I was nine weeks along. "Stop. Whatever you are thinking is wrong," I warned her. "You don't get to tell anyone *anything*, until *we* have announced it. We don't even know if I can carry this baby to full term. Please don't add strangers congratulating me to a list of possible humiliations if I miscarry."

Suddenly my mother looked like I had punched the wind out of her sails. "Have you seen the doctor? Did they give any reason that there may be problems?" She asked, reaching out to hold my hand.

Kai kissed my temple and suggested that we all sit down to talk. With everything that my parents knew about my health, there was so much more that they did not know. Telling my parents everything was not something I wanted to do, but Kai made the argument that telling them some could only help me. I wasn't alone. I was not walking by myself anymore.

I needed my village to help me get through this. To do that, I needed to let down my walls a bit and tell them what they didn't know. Like how close to death I really was after the roadside bombing. I needed to tell them all of the decisions Tyson made to save my life. Because, although I was alive and I would have made the same exact decisions for myself, it complicated my ability to have children. My insides were quite literally rearranged. If Kai wasn't with me, and something happened, my parents needed to know what to do until Kai could get to me.

Facing the past because of this bright and shining future was not nearly as difficult as I thought it would be. There weren't tears or accusations, as I had imagined there would be. My parents asked serious and pointed questions about my health, my wishes, and our intentions as a couple. As if on cue, my phone pinged on the table with a simple message, reminding me that I hadn't faced *everything* in my past.

Mama T: [Happy New Year, Katie. From Annie and Tom]

Chapter 46

Kai's Point of View

"Are you ready?" I asked Katie.

She was nibbling her nails as we sat in the parking lot outside the doctor's office. The last two months were a roller coaster. Just after New Year's, Katie had passed out on the site, and they had to call an ambulance. Thankfully, Paul sent one of the guys to the clinic to get me. I got there just in time to ride with her to the hospital. I won't lie. Seeing her so pale on that stretcher scared the shit out of me.

Paul and Jack assured me that she hadn't been near any fumes or chemicals. She had been talking to the owners and then collapsed. The hospital kept her overnight for observation. She was anemic and her blood sugar was lower than they would have liked. They sent in a dietician to discuss dietary changes, and prescribed her a different prenatal to help with her vitamin deficiencies.

The sonographer at the twelve week scan saw something that concerned her, and refused to let us see the scans. She said the doctor would be in contact with us with the results. Katie cried for two days, convinced that the baby was dying. I couldn't wait, and called the doctor for the results. There was nothing wrong. The baby was healthy, organs developing like they should and all limbs accounted for.

With all of the ups and downs, Katie stopped running. She stopped working on the 4th street house. If that weren't enough, she cut me off. No sex. She stayed in bed and focused on her health. I tried to get Andie to come over and sit with her, but she refused to tell anyone about the pregnancy until we reached the half-way mark. She made excuses for why we needed to take rain checks when we received invitations, and promised to make it all up later.

We were finally going in for the eighteen week scan, and I prayed that this put Katie's worries to rest. Her blood work over the past four weeks had been perfect. Her blood pressure was amazing. Her weight gain was perfect. Everything on paper said we were through the worst, but she wanted to see this scan before anyone could know. I remembered her sobbing when we lost the first baby. I would support anything she wanted to do to keep this baby safe. I never wanted to see her cry like that again.

"Come on," I encouraged her, opening my car door. I walked around the car and opened her door for her. She looked terrified. I tried the most reassuring smile I could muster. "When they tell us this baby is perfect, I am going to take you home and pamper the shit of you for being such an amazing oven," I said, pulling her into a hug.

She giggled against my chest. "I'm being crazy, aren't I?"

"Nope. No crazy here," I swore, making her giggle some more.

Thankfully, the original sonographer was in today and not the last one. They got us in pretty quickly and had Katie's belly lubed up in no time. "Ok, mommy. Let's see how this little baby is doing!" She said excitedly, smiling.

The heartbeat was perfect. No murmurs, and no malformations were visible on the heart. The organs were all perfect. "Mommy you have to tell me your secret! This little girl is a tank," the woman cooed, and then realized what she said. She looked at Katie and I as if she was in trouble. "Did you want to know the baby's sex?" She asked.

"It's a girl?" Katie asked, eyes already tearing up looking at the screen. Her eyes darted to mine. "We're having a girl!" she cried.

The doctor came in to review the scans and then looked seriously over to Katie. "I don't know how to say this…" She started. "You have a perfect baby. The placenta is moved up. Your labs are spot on. As far as this little girl is growing, she's meeting all of the growth markers that we want to see. She is active, and your vitamin levels are stable. I'd still recommend you continue with light duty because of your physical condition, but I feel comfortable saying we're out of the woods."

My eyes were watering up. The baby looked perfect. *She was great.* Everything was perfect. Katie let out a choked sob. "She's perfect?" She asked.

The doctor chuckled, "Yes. She is. I'll see you back here between 22 to 24 weeks. If you have any pains or her activity drops, and I mean no movement over six hours, come in. Don't even wait, just come in. You're doing great, Katie. Kai, keep up the support."

The sonographer gave us a copy of the ultrasound pictures, and let Katie record the heart beat. We couldn't stop smiling the whole way home. I knew she wanted to tell everyone. Keeping it quiet was killing her, but now she wanted to tell everyone.

"Let's invite everyone over for dinner. We can set up a bonfire in the backyard, invite our family and friends over. Make up some bullshit, and surprise them with a reveal and announcement," she suggested, hugging me as soon as we got in the door.

"When do you want to have this grand party?" I asked, chuckling.

"Is this weekend too soon?" She asked, giving me the saddest puppy eyes.

I laughed and kissed her. "We can invite them over tonight if you want, Kitkat. You tell me when, and I will pack the house and the backyard!"

We sat down and sent text messages to everyone. Katie included Paul, Jack and the Craigs from work. They had been so good to her in the time she was at work, that she wanted to include them. By the time our phones died, I think we had invited like seventy-five people over.

* * *

Saturday afternoon and the house was quickly filled to near bursting. We set up space for the kids to play games, color, or watch cartoons in the living room. Her mom brought over a chocolate fountain and surrounded it with tons of fruit and bread bites to dip. It was still relatively cold out, so we ordered thirty pizzas and sorted them according to preferences: cheese, meats, veggies, etc.

It was nearly three o'clock when the last of our guests arrived. We had no idea how we wanted to tell everyone, so Katie's mom suggested putting pink frosting inside of one of the cupcakes. Then we would just wait to see who got the cupcake. Katie's dad had a better idea. He told everyone that we were announcing a big venture, and that Katie's company and a lot to do with it. Seeing the new workshop in the backyard, most thought Katie was starting her own business.

I called everyone out to the backyard and passed around glasses of sparkling apple juice. "First, we want to thank everyone for coming over on such short notice. We haven't been able to see everyone a lot lately, so we thought we would have everyone over. As you can see we've been busy here around the house, and we wanted to share some of our firsts with you all," Katie announced.

"The first time I saw Katie was in fifth grade. She had no idea I even existed, but I noticed her. We didn't have enough people in percussion, and she volunteered to play the xylophone and bells for a concert. She was so focused and energetic, I couldn't help but love her," I said, making Katie tear up.

"That's not true!" She yelled. "I noticed you. But you made fun of me, so I ignored you!"

"Ha!" Andie yelled, laughing.

"Our first kiss was during our senior year of high school," Katie admitted, leaving out all of the details.

"The first time I knew she was the one, was Prom weekend. I always loved you, Kat, but that's when I knew it could only be you," I said.

"Do you remember when we held our little girl for the first time?" Katie asked me.

Everyone stopped talking.

"You can't skip ahead to shit that happens this summer! You'll confuse everyone!" I whined, doing my best to look annoyed.

411

"OH MY GOD! YOU'RE PREGNANT?!?!" Amy screamed and everyone started shouting *congratulations,* jumping and squealing when Katie turned beet red.

"Congratulations!!" Andie said, pulling us both into a hug. "I'm so angry that you didn't tell me, but I am so fucking excited at the same time!!"

"How far along are you? Summer is just around the corner," Alex's wife Jane asked.

Katie laughed and we both started pulling up our super baggy sweaters. We had matching shirts made to show everyone that said, '19 weeks and counting,' but Katie had an obvious baby bump to show off as well. I couldn't take my eyes off of her the whole day. She was glowing. Her eyes sparkled every time she looked at me, and she couldn't stop laughing and smiling.

We ended up ordering a second round of pizzas around eight o'clock, but the majority of people had left by that point. My parents couldn't be more thrilled, and Katie's parents pretended to be shocked so that no hard feelings developed because one set knew before the other.

"So when are you guys tying the knot?" My brother asked, while we sat around the bonfire.

I looked at Katie and she giggled. "Well, we thought we would make that another first. We want to have a proper wedding, and I was hoping you'd be my best man, Reggie."

For a second I thought my brother would cry, but he pulled it together. "It'd be a freaking honor. I cannot wait to roast your ass when I give my toast-"

"On second thought, Bradley are you available?" I cut him off.

"You think I have less shit on you, Kai? I have a fucking

412

encyclopedia britannica's worth of shit I have been saving for a wedding toast!" Bradley cackled.

"Fuck… Alex? Jonas?" I called out before Katie dropped into my lap and put her hand over my mouth.

"Reggie, you can say whatever you want as long as it isn't mean. But I will let you know that Andie is going to be my matron of honor… So this is going to be a bet to see who can give the best speech," Katie informed my brother.

"Oh yeah? What's in it for the winner?" He asked.

"Well I was thinking of gifting some cake, but I'll make a custom piece for the winner and the second place will get a consolation custom piece for Christmas," Katie announced, sticking her belly out like she was bragging.

Andie and Reggie jumped up at the same time, "DEAL!"

"When is this wedding happening?" My mom asked. She hadn't been too happy that I eloped last time, so this was news to her.

"We're thinking of October. Alex is going to let us have it at The Barn," Katie grinned ear to ear, waving at Alex.

"Oh that's so nice!" Our moms said in unison.

"Isn't that where they knocked boots the first time?" Jonas asked, not so quietly.

"OH MY GOD, ANDIE! ARE THERE NO SECRETS?" Katie squealed, hiding her face in my chest.

I couldn't stop laughing as I held Katie in my arms. This was the first girl I ever liked. The first woman I fell in love with. The first woman I had ever given my whole heart to, without any reservations.

"To all of our *firsts*," I toasted, holding up my glass of sparkling cider.

"To the firsts," everyone cheered back.

413

"I love you, Kai," Katie whispered against my neck.

"I loved you first, Kitkat," I whispered back and kissed the top of her head.

Chapter 47

Two years later... Katie's Point of view

"We're here," Kai whispered as we pulled up to the house I had only seen once previously. "You ready?" he asked me, watching the swirl of emotions cross my face.

"Yes. No," I replied, a small smile picking up at the corner of my lips.

"Come on. This has been put off long enough," Kai held my hand to his lips before turning off the car and getting out.

I took a deep breath and let it out slowly. *I could do this.*

I stepped out of the car as Kai handed my bag to me from the trunk. "You take that and I'll get this," he said, opening the rear passenger door. "Come on, baby girl. Time to wake up," Kai cooed at our daughter who was sound asleep in her car seat.

She rubbed her eyes as he unbuckled her harness and lifted her out of the car. "Watch your head, baby girl. Come to Daddy. I got you. Did you have a good nap, hmmm?" he continued to prattle and coo at our little girl. I loved watching them together. Her face lit up in a huge smile as she grabbed onto his shirt.

I never had any doubt that Kai loved us. He had done so much for me over the years and my chest just felt stuffed with sweetness watching him with our daughter. I closed the door as he stepped away from the car. Holding our girl on one arm, he reached out and took my hand with the other.

I didn't know what to expect coming back here. The front door opened, and an older couple stepped out. "Hello. I'm so glad you made it all this way," the woman spoke quietly to us. Her eyes stayed on me a moment longer before looking over to Kai who was holding our daughter. "You must be Kai, you can just call me Annie. This is my husband, Tom," Annie gestured making the introductions.

Kai handed our daughter over to me and shook hands with Tom and Annie, "It's nice to meet you both in person."

"Alright, Annie, let them in the house. They've been on the road long enough for this," Tom shooed his wife back into the house and held the door for Kai and me. "Please," he gestured for us to follow behind Annie.

I walked in first, feeling the comfort and warmth of Kai's hand on my lower back. He knew that I was nervous. Ty's parents hadn't spoken to me in years, then suddenly wanted to reach out two years ago. I refused to speak with either of them because of my own guilt, so Kai had done the majority of the communication via my phone.

I wasn't angry with them. But I didn't want to see the guilt and blame when we began picking at wounds that had healed. I moved on without them because they didn't want anything to do with me. I needed to honor Ty's last wishes, and I couldn't do that over the phone. It was time to face the past.

"We can sit here in the living room. It has the most space for the baby to play. I'm sorry, what is her name? She's just beautiful," Annie cooed, looking at our daughter.

"Tysan. We named her Tysan with an A, but we just call

her Ty for short," Kai spoke up, taking Ty from my arms and setting her on the floor to play.

Tom and Annie froze, sharing a look between them. Their eyes watered up, but they smiled. "That's a beautiful name, Katie. Kai, you have a beautiful family-" Tom choked up for a second, wrapping an arm over Annie's shoulder and pulling her to his side. "Thank you," he said to me after a moment.

Kai smiled back, and pulled me into his arms. "I am sorry for your loss. But I can't be sorry for Katie coming back into my life. Your son was a huge part of her life, and I don't ever want to take that away from her or from you. Katie said that Tyson always talked about chasing rainbows to find your happiness. This little girl is our rainbow," he explained, smiling at Tysan playing with a bear she found in the corner by the sofa.

"You lost another child?" Annie's voice shook.

I felt my eyes burning and I couldn't speak. I just nodded.

Kai seemed to understand everything when I looked up at him and he caressed my back. "I don't know if Tyson ever told you about Katie being severely injured during a deployment, but it did a lot more damage than she knew. I'm sure he just wanted to protect her, so she didn't know the extent of it. She had no idea until after we had reunited a few years ago," he explained.

"Katie, I don't blame you. We don't blame you for anything that happened. I just," Annie looked at Tom, who nodded for her to continue. "Let's sit down and talk. I need to clear the past between us. It should not have taken this long," she added.

We sat a few minutes later around the living room with coffee and a few snacks for little Ty to nibble on. She loved bananas and puffs. So she sat on Kai's lap and ate small bites of soft banana, before climbing down to play with the bear again.

"We knew about you. We were thrilled when you had finally accepted Ty's proposal," Tom started the conversation. "Annie and I were supposed to surprise you and be the witnesses when you eloped, but things didn't work out that way."

He nodded encouragingly at Annie. It was her turn to talk.

"I had not been feeling well, and had had some doctor's appointments and blood work done the week before we were supposed to leave to - for the wedding. I got a call the day we should have left and was told that I needed to come to the hospital. They found cancer, and it was a really aggressive breast cancer. I didn't want to worry you or Ty just before a deployment, so we just canceled our trip," Annie spoke softly, her fingers running around the lip of her cup as she spoke.

She explained that she had already started aggressive chemo and radiation treatments when they notified her and Tom of Ty's death overseas. She had had double mastectomies three days after Ty and I married. Ty never knew how sick she was because they had kept it from him. When the funeral occurred, it was all they could do to stand upright. Annie's body was being ravaged by the treatments, and Tom was exhausted as the only caregiver in the house.

"We didn't mean for you to feel pushed aside, Katie. Lord knows, we were looking forward to meeting you finally. I just didn't have anything left when we finally met. I was given six months to live two days before Ty died. They told Tom to make arrangements, because my chances of survival were 5%," Annie continued, her eyes brimming with unshed tears.

My eyes were overflowing as I struggled to process so much information. "Oh, Annie. Why didn't you tell me? I could have been here to help you and Tom," I offered, reaching out to hold her hand.

Annie smiled at her husband, and held my hand. "Ty was such a great judge of character. He told us that you were *the one* two weeks after you met," she told me as she squeezed my hand. "Three years after Ty died, I was told that my cancer was in remission. I don't know how many times I came close to reuniting with our son, but it was enough to turn Tom gray."

"When she finally got the clean bill of health, we couldn't find you anywhere, Katie. We wanted to tell you everything and let you know that we have always considered you our daughter-in-law. I know we sucked at showing it, but I hope that you can forgive us," Tom pleaded with tear brimmed eyes.

I was overwhelmed. I looked at Kai, fell into his chest and cried. All of the guilt, self-blame and self-hatred poured out of me with every tear. I felt the weight of my guilt lift away. They never blamed me. Ty had told them everything about me, and they knew everything about us. *Fucking Ty, with his secrets and surprises.*

A giggle escaped my lips. Kai pulled me out of his arms and searched my face. "I told you to give this a chance, Kitkat," Kai whispered adoringly in my ear.

I walked around the coffee table and gave Annie and Tom a huge hug. "I thought you blamed me for taking Ty away from you. I had no idea you had such a hard time. I am sorry for disappearing from your lives as well. I was not in a good place for a long time," I apologized to Tom and Annie as the three of us hugged each other and cried.

"BO-BO!" a tiny voice squealed from the floor. "Bo-bo?" Ty cried, working her way around the table to me, before Kai intercepted and scooped her into his arms.

"Mommy is fine. She is crying happy tears. No boo-boos. She didn't hurt herself. It's okay," Kai laughed as Ty stared at Annie, Tom, and me with tear stained cheeks trying to judge if her dad had told her the truth.

We all started to laugh when Ty 'hmmmph'd' and tried to climb from Kai's lap again. She came to soothe and there was no soothing to be done, so she went back to the bear.

Sitting back down on the sofa next to Kai, I squeezed his hand. *This was the right thing to do.* Kai's eyes searched my face before nodding in agreement.

He passed me the envelope from Ty's travel bag, and I slid it across the coffee table to Annie and Tom.

"This is for both of you. When Ty deployed he set everything up so that he left me everything. I never spent a penny of his savings or the life insurance, so it had been sitting there all this time collecting interest. He wanted you both to take half," I told them as Tom opened the envelope and saw the check inside.

"Katie," he breathed in hard, "we can't-"

"You can," I smiled at him. "And you should. Ty wanted this for you both. He worked so hard and saved up so much money to help you both retire early. I am doing this for Ty, because he can't be here to do it himself."

Annie took the envelope from a speechless Tom, and pulled the blue check out. "Oh dear lord! Katie, this is too much!" she gasped, staring at a check for nearly half a million dollars.

"Ty was really good with money. He didn't want the people he loved to want for *anything*. Please. This was his last wish for you both," I pleaded. "This is Ty's last gift for you, Annie and Tom."

"Gam?" little Tysan asked, staring up at Annie.

Annie looked down at Ty unsure what to respond before looking over to me and Kai for guidance and a translation.

Kai chuckled, "Grammy is ok. She likes her gift, Ty. Are you going to give Grammy and Pops hugs?"

"*Hiccc-*" Tom nearly choked back more tears as he opened his arms to Ty barreling in to deliver her hugs.

"Pops!" she beamed at Tom, and patted his shoulder then lunged from his arms into Annie's lap.

"Gam!" she cheered, hugging Annie, and patting her on the back too.

Tom wiped the tears from his face, "She called me *Pops.*"

I couldn't help but smile with more tears in my eyes. "Ty always said that he couldn't wait for our kids to call you Grammy and Pops. We told little Ty that we were visiting Grammy and Pops. She isn't Ty's little girl, but I would like you-" I stopped speaking as my voice broke.

Kai squeezed my hand again and pulled me into another hug. "Ty brought us together. We would like you both to be a part of our lives. Little Ty isn't your grandchild by blood, but you will always be Grammy and Pops for our children. We have every intention of including you both in our lives, if you want to be involved," he explained for me.

Tom and Annie's faces lit up with bright smiles. "We would love that very much," Annie whispered as tears continued down her cheeks.

Ty reached up and wiped Annie's tears away. "Shhhhh-"

she whispered as she placed her head against Annie's chest and rocked in her lap. "K-Gam. Shhhh. Gam k. bo-bo k, Gam," Ty attempted to soothe another boo-boo, patting Annie's arm as she rocked against her.

Everyone started laughing. This child was too stinking sweet for words.

"Grammy is okay, sweet girl," Annie laughed. "Thank you so much for taking care of your Grammy."

Ty looked smugly at Kai and me. "Gam, k!" she informed us, patting Annie one last time before going after the bear again.

Tom looked at me for a moment, seeming like he was at a loss for words. "Do you have other children?" he asked quietly.

Kai's smile at that point was so big it covered his whole face. "Not quite yet, but the buns are rising just nicely as we speak," he laughed, rubbing my stomach.

"YOU'RE PREGNANT?!?" Annie squealed, jumping up from her seat in excitement.

My face flushed bright red. "Yes. We found out I am carrying twins," I told them. I couldn't help but smile seeing the joy in their eyes when we told them.

"Oh, Katie! That is so wonderful!" Annie clapped happily and laughed as Tom pulled her back down to sit on the sofa.

"How far along are you?" Tom asked.

"I am about 16 weeks along. The due date is just before Thanksgiving, so we wanted to invite you out to stay with us. Maybe have Thanksgiving with us and meet our family?" I offered, unsure how they would take the invitation.

Tom jumped up this time, giddy as could be, "Wild horses won't keep us away this time!"

Chapter 48

Kai's Point of View

Once again, we managed to pack the house for Thanksgiving with family and friends, with the addition of Annie and Tom who traveled to spend the week with us. We had chatted with them pretty regularly after our visit in June. Tysan didn't know what to do with herself when they arrived. She was so excited to introduce everyone to her Gam and Pops.

I had never been so thankful that all of the grandparents had different names to her. Katie's parents were called Nonna and Poppop, and my parents were Grandmy and Grandpy. To be honest, I wasn't sure how my parents were going to feel about Annie and Tom staying with us, but my mom took to Annie like they had known each other for decades. I couldn't have imagined our lives like this when I saw Katie that day at the gas station.

She leaned back in her chair with a slice of pumpkin pie resting on her belly. Every once in a while the plate would jump when the babies moved, and all of the kids would start screaming and laughing. "How the hell did we get fifty people in our house," she whispered over to me. Her face was flushed and she was looking around at everyone else smiling and laughing.

"I have no idea," I chuckled back. "Better question is why do we keep doing it?"

Katie started laughing and then suddenly stopped.

"Miss Katie peed her pants, mommy," little Max, Bradley's youngest, announced just then.

I looked down to see water dripping from Katie's chair. "Babe?" I asked, sure of what had just happened. "Did your water just break?"

Katie huffed in annoyance. "I don't know what it is about Thanksgiving at our house that induces labor!" She stated loudly enough that everyone stopped eating and started shuffling tables and chairs out of the way.

"Is she serious?" Katie's mom asked. "Katie, are you in labor?!?"

"Well, I sure as hell didn't sit here and pee my pants in front of everyone I know!" Katie yelled back. Then she leaned forward and squeezed my hand. "Babe, I may not make it to the hospital," she whimpered.

"I told you she was in labor. Did you not see how she was timing her bites of pie?" Andie added in.

"What did you just say?" I asked Katie, but Andie answered.

"She's been having contractions for the last few hours, Kai. I tried to tell you earlier, but Katie pushed me out of the room. She's in active labor."

"Shut up, shut up, shut up, oh oh oh, I don't want to have these babies in front of everyone!" Katie started crying, unable to move.

Annie jumped up, "Gentlemen, we're going to need you to clean up dinner and reset the furniture. Ladies, if you would be dears and help keep the kiddos quiet, the grandmothers have some grandbabies to deliver."

Suddenly, everyone was moving. Mine and Katie's moms ran upstairs to the master bath and started running water in the tub. Andie called an ambulance while she was pulling clean towels from the cabinet. I don't know how Jonas and I got Katie up the stairs without her ripping our limbs off, but we made it to the bathroom just as the tub was ready.

They all stepped out as I helped Katie strip off her pants and underwear and lowered her into the tub. I quickly stripped down into my boxers and lowered into the tub behind her. We had been prepared for early babies with her carrying twins, and attended all of the home delivery classes *just in case.*

Annie knocked on the door once I was in. "Are you ready, Katie? I'm not sure who you want with you."

"I want moms! OUCH Oh-oh-oh- it hurrrrrts," she whined.

"Breathe, Katie. Come on, breathe with me," I coached her until she got through her contraction. As she relaxed against me again, we heard what could only be described as three women playing rock paper scissors to decide who would come in.

"She meant all three of you!" I hollered out to them, making Katie giggle.

The three of them burst into the bathroom with smiles. They had changed into t-shirts, and took up positions on either side of the tub just in time for the next contraction.

"That's it, Katie! Breathe. HUU-HUU-HEEEEEEE," my mom encouraged her, while Annie wiped a cool rag on Katie's forehead. I had no idea how long this was going to take. I was just doing everything I could to keep her calm and focused.

I heard the sirens just as Katie began to push. "That's it, Kitkat. You're doing so good," I cooed, helping her pull her knees back.

"I don't know if I can push yet," she cried.

"Just listen to your body, Katie. Do you want me to check?" Katie's mom asked.

"No! I do not want your hand in my vag, mom!" Katie barked back. "Shit! Shit! I want to push!"

"Ok, Katie. Deep breaths. One. Exhale. Two. Exhale. Good. Next contraction, you push with everything you have, okay?" Annie coached her.

"Okay, mama," she whimpered.

Annie sucked in a breath, and her eyes watered. Katie's mom reached out and side hugged Annie. "Let's deliver these grandbabies," she said.

Minutes passed before the first baby was born. As soon as they had him out of the tub he was screaming. I was in awe of these three women working together to deliver our babies. "It's a boy!" Katie's mom gushed.

Someone knocked on the bathroom door, and Annie stepped out with our boy. As she stepped out, a paramedic stepped in to assist with delivering baby number two. Two minutes after her brother, our little girl made her entrance into the world. Katie sagged back against my chest, and I just held her.

"You are the most amazing woman I have ever met," I whispered against her temple. "Every time I think I couldn't love you more, you surprise me."

She smiled, exhausted. "I love you, too," she whispered.

↤〜⟵※⟶〜↦

Tom's Point of View

It took the ambulance 45 minutes to get to the house because of an accident on the highway. The paramedics came in to find a house full of people between eating Thanksgiving dinner, and pacing the floors. I took them straight upstairs to the bathroom that Annie had taken Katie into.

The first paramedic opened the door just as the wail of a baby cried out, followed by three women cheering. "Annie the paramedics are here. Let them check the baby," I called into the room without looking.

Annie came out with the baby swaddled in a towel, and passed it to the paramedic. "It's a boy," she said proudly.

The paramedic smiled down at the little fella and set him on the stretcher to check him out. He made sure the umbilical cord was clamped and checked all of his vitals, before swaddling him back up in the towel. Kai's mom came out next and went straight to a bag on the floor.

"There's some diapers in here. Katie wanted to make sure he is decent before he meets everyone," she chuckled.

I left them to it and went downstairs to announce the first arrival. "Baby boy has arrived!"

There was a loud cheer of congratulations before everyone quieted down again and waited for the next announcement. I remembered when Tyson was born. I had been two towns over on business when Annie went into labor. We didn't have the communication devices we had today, so she had no way to reach me directly. I didn't know how she did it, but she did get the message to me. If a cop had clocked me on that drive home, I was certain I would have been locked up. I got to the hospital just in time to hear Tyson's first cry.

Annie was smiling at me from ear to ear when I came into

the room. *"He knew you were coming. He wouldn't make a peep until just now. He knew his daddy was here, and he hollered."*

"You okay, Tom?" Katie's dad asked, taking a seat next to me.

"When Tyson died, I never dreamed I would experience this," I admitted, fighting back tears.

"If it helps, I wasn't sure I would either a couple years before that," he admitted. We didn't need to say anything else.

"IT'S A GIRL!!!" Annie yelled down the stairs a moment later, followed by another round of cheering through the house.

Knowing that both babies were good, and the paramedics were checking on Katie, the guests started to leave. I stood there with Kai and Katie's fathers and thanked everyone for coming and supporting the family. Kai's dad promised that Kai and Katie would let everyone know when they could make the rounds to meet the twins. Tysan had fallen asleep on the sofa, so I volunteered to put her to bed.

Katie and the babies were taken to the hospital. Everything seemed good, but because of Katie's health issues they wanted her to stay overnight in the hospital to make sure she didn't have any complications. Katie's parents left shortly after the ambulance, and Kai waited to make sure that Annie and I were good, before he left to join his wife. I promised to bring Tysan to meet her baby brother and sister in the morning, and assured him that we were good.

Holding Annie in my arms later than night, I found myself thanking God for bringing this family into our lives. Annie and I had been so lost after Tyson died. Between the cancer and the grief, we hadn't *lived* since she was diagnosed. Being with Katie this past week filled a hole in both of our hearts.

"Annie, you still awake?" I asked.

"What's the matter? Are you okay?" She asked, turning on the side lamp.

"How would you feel about moving out here?"

"Hic-I was afraid to ask," she admitted as tears filled her eyes. "I want to be here with Katie and her family, too."

I nodded. "Good. We can talk about it tomorrow," I whispered and pulled her to me. We'd start planning everything else tomorrow.

�👈←✲→→👉

Katie's Point of View

We decided to name the twins Andreas and Amanda. Amanda was named after Kai's grandmother who left him the house and also the name of the woman who helped me get back on my feet when I left the Marines. Andreas was named in honor of Andie, a woman who had done more for me since high school than I could say. Kai and I had not discussed names before they were born. We didn't even want to know what we were having this time around. We had planned for so many other things, but baby names weren't among them.

Then again, we never imagined delivering the twins in a bathtub, let alone being surrounded by my mom, Kai's mom, and Tyson's mom. Three years ago, I was certain that Tom and Annie hated me. Now, I couldn't see how that would have ever been possible. Tom and Annie were two of the most selfless, loving, and honest people I had ever met. Getting to know them made me love Ty a little more for the man that he was, and miss him a little less at the same time.

It's not that I didn't miss him, but having Annie and Tom

here made it feel like Ty was with us. Kai and I had talked about moving closer to the midwest to be nearer to Tom and Annie. They had about fifteen years on either of our parents, and I felt like I needed to be nearer to them. It was just a feeling, but I couldn't quite shake it.

Kai was asleep on a small pull out bed, next to two rolling bassinets. At just after seven a nurse came in to check on me, and a pediatric doctor checked the babies over one more time. As soon as the little bassinet shifted, Kai was wide awake, causing me to laugh.

"They look good, mom," the doctor said. "Usually with home births we see some issues, but these two look perfect. You must have had a great doula to help with the delivery."

"We did," Kyle smiled at me, standing up from his cot.

"Well, as far as my decisions are concerned, babies can go home as soon as mom is released. I'd like to see them back in three days to check their bilirubin levels, and make sure they aren't jaundiced. This isn't your first, but have you decided to breastfeed or formula for them?" he asked.

"I want to try nursing for as long as I can," I told him.

"Okay. I'll ask the nurses to send the lactation consultant to come talk with you," he continued.

"We've got it covered, Doc," the nurse chuckled. When the doctor made his exit the nurse chuckled. "He's new here. I don't know if you have a pediatrician set up, but Doctor Cambrey is amazing. He did his residency and fellowship at a children's hospital in Texas. I'm surprised he chose to work for us, to be honest. He's too good for this hospital, but don't tell anyone I said that!" She whispered the last.

Just after ten o'clock our parents arrived to meet the new additions. I kept looking out the door for Tom and Annie.

"Did you tell Tom and Annie where the hospital was?" I whispered to Kai.

Kai's mom heard me and chuckled. "Don't worry, they followed us over with Tysan. They just stopped to get 'suprises' for the new babies," she said, pronouncing it just like Tysan would.

A few minutes later Annie and Tom joined us with Tysan busting in the door. "I'm big sister!" She announced, proudly showing off a t-shirt that they just bought for her.

"You *are*, baby girl! Come sit with me, and we'll hold the babies together!" I said. She ran straight for the bed and climbed up next to me. Once she was settled at my side and the safety bar was up, Kai passed Andreas to me. "This is your little brother, Andreas."

Her eyes watered up as I placed him gently on her lap and positioned her arm to support his head. "Hi, baby. I'm Ty-Ty," she quietly introduced herself, making everyone giggle and tear up. Then she leaned forward and gave him the softest kiss on his head. "He's so pretty," she whispered.

Andreas started to fuss a bit, so my mom took him and Kai helped Tysan hold Amanda. "This is Amanda, your baby sister," Kai introduced them.

"Hi, Amanee. I'm Ty-Ty. You can't wear my pretty dresses, cause they're too big. But when you are all growed up I will give you pretty dresses. Okay?" Again the adults chuckled at her adorable interactions with her new brother and sister.

My parents didn't stay long because they had to get to work. I hated that people had to work the day after Thanksgiving. The retail and repair places made lots of money on Black Friday, but the craziness of *people* wasn't worth it to me. Kai's parents left shortly after.

431

Tom and Annie looked nervous once it was just us. They kept looking back and forth at each other, having some secret conversation that I didn't understand. "Everything okay?" I asked nervously.

Annie looked at Tom one more time before elbowing him to speak. "We've been talking about selling the house. It's too big for us, and maybe finding a smaller place. You know, downsizing."

Kai smirked, "That sounds like a big step for you guys. Where were you thinking of moving to?"

"Well, if you don't think it's too weird, we'd like to move here," Annie admitted, looking at my face for anything that would suggest I was opposed to the idea.

I dropped my head back, and laughed. "Kai and I were talking about moving out west to be closer to the two of you!" I chuckled.

"What? No. You have all of your family and friends here. It's just me and Tom, we'll come to you, if you're truly okay with it," Annie insisted.

"Gam and Pops can live in my room!" Tysan said excitedly, causing everyone to chuckle.

"You would really do that?" I asked, looking at Annie then to Tom.

"We would," Tom said without a moment's hesitation.

I ended up staying two days in the hospital just to be on the safe side. Although everything turned out well, the OB was pretty honest and said that repeating a home birth with my condition was not advisable for future babies. Kai's eyes had sparkled, remembering how we made these two babies. I could only shake my head at him. He was not getting in my pants for at least a month, if not two!

Tom and Annie returned home a week later than planned, but in that week we found a few cute apartments not far from us and a realtor to help them sell their house. Kai and I offered to come out in April to help them pack up everything and move here, but our parents beat us to the punch saying they had already planned to help instead. We just needed to stay home and wait for good news.

By the time Christmas rolled around, I had forgotten my pledge to keep Kai away from my pants. I couldn't deny him any part of me. Not my body, and surely not my heart. Everything about him caused some crazy chemical reaction in my brain that made me love him more. *And I was here for it.*

Epilogue

Five years later... Katie's Point of View

"Katie?" Kai called out from the back door. He paused as he stepped outside, seeing the kids running around under the sprinkler. "What happened to not getting wet before we go?" He asked, laughing at the chaos.

I didn't feel guilty about this. "It was so hot outside, it didn't seem fair to make them stay in their nice clothes. We'll be quick. Is it time to go?" I asked.

Kai nodded, trying his best to look like he was annoyed. Unfortunately, his eyes sparkled when he was happy. "Ok, kiddos. We have to get dressed now!" Kai said, turning off the water.

"Why can't we stay home?" Andreas asked, plodding over to the pile of towels I had set out for them.

I kissed the top of his head as he passed me. "Because it's time to go and see Pops," I reminded him.

"Did he get moved?" Tysan asked, now wrapped in her own towel.

"Not yet. But we're trying to convince him," I said, turning as Kai came up to hug me.

It didn't take long to get the children dressed. Tysan was so independent, she was dressed before I could get our youngest,

Ivy, out of her wet bottoms.

After having the twins, I hit a low. We miscarried three times, before I decided I couldn't do it any more. The hope and joy that ultimately ended with loss and sorrow each time were too much. I got back into running, and just dedicated myself to our family and growing my woodworking business. Then it happened. I found out that I was pregnant after collapsing on a job site. *Again*. Paul had joked at the time that it was a baby telling me to take it easy. I swore that wasn't possible, but sure enough, I was pregnant.

My pregnancy with Ivy was a struggle from the beginning. I was sick all of the time, and had to be hospitalized twice for dehydration. As if that wasn't scary enough, Ivy was previa the whole pregnancy which meant my placenta remained over my cervix instead of shifting to the top of my uterus like it should have. Kai was terrified that I would bleed out if I went into labor, and the doctors agreed. I spent five months on bedrest before the OB did a C-section at 32 weeks. Kai convinced him to remove my tubes while he was in there. Four babies were enough for us.

"Ok, here are the rules," Kai started as he put our minivan in park. "Manda and Dre, you need to stay with me. Ty, you stick with mommy and Ivy. There will be no running off, understood?" he asked, turning to look at them.

"Stick with mom…" Tysan groaned, unbuckling her seat-belt.

"We get daddy!" The twins cheered from the third row.

This of course made Kai chuckle. "Did you think one sprinkler run would earn their favor? HA!" He whispered, and got out.

He was such a shit sometimes. It was one of the reasons I

loved him, but it was so obnoxious. "Just wait to see what I have up my sleeves, Mister!" I scowled at him.

Kai got Ivy strapped into her stroller while I got the twins out of their seats, and grabbed the diaper bag. "Is there going to be any food here?" Tysan asked me, as we walked toward the apartment complex Tom and Annie had called 'home' since moving here..

"Not here, love. But after, you're all going to eat at Nonna and Poppops. Do you want a sucker until then?" I said, showing her one of the soft mints hidden in the key compartment of the stroller.

Tysan palmed the mint and quickly put it in her mouth. What the other three didn't see, they wouldn't ask for.

Tom was waiting for us at the door of the building when we walked up. "I know it was expected, but I'm always happy to see you, sweetie. Hey, kiddos!"

I felt my eyes burning and tried to brush away the tears as quickly as I could. "Thank you, Pop."

We lost Annie two years after they moved here. Her cancer relapsed, and she made the decision to live her days to their *fullest* without chemo or radiation. When Annie wanted to dance, we went dancing. When Annie wanted to drink and sing off key, I didn't need alcohol for that, so I drove. When Annie asked to try marijuana, my mom was there to give her her first ride. When she was ready to go, she went quietly in her sleep that same night.

"You know you can come live with us, Pop," I whispered, giving him a hug.

"Well, that's kind of why I wanted to invite you out," he admitted, giving Kai a knowing look.

"What are you two hiding?" I asked, squinting my eyes and

looking back and forth between the two.

"Pop wants to take you to look at a house," Kai confessed.

I pursed my lips at the two. "Where is this house?"

Tom smiled, "It's just down the road from your place. Come on, let's go take a look!"

We shuffled the kids back out the door and loaded up into the van again. I sat in the back with Tysan and Ivy until we got to my parents' house. My mom was outside waiting for the grandkids. Our parents alternated taking the kids one night each week so that we could run errands or go out on the occasional date night.

I handed her their bags and gave them all kisses and hugs before we were back on the road. When Tom said the house was just down the road, I didn't realize he meant it literally. Three blocks to be specific. My jaw dropped when I saw it.

"Tom, this place is huge! What the hell are you going to do with this much house?" I asked, laughing. I had looked at the listing when it went on the market. It had five bedrooms, three and half baths and sat on a huge two acre lot.

"Well," Kai started. "What if we moved, too?"

I couldn't stop my jaw from dropping. "Seriously? Kai, that was your grandmother's house-"

"And I wouldn't be selling it," he cut me off. "My brother wants to move closer to us, so they would obviously take it over."

"What about the workshop?" I asked. My workshop was my livelihood.

"Leave it. Paul and Jack already said they'd help convert the old stables into a workshop and I could use a portion for a home office."

"I thought you couldn't have a home office because of

zoning," I reminded him.

Kai nodded, remembering the discussion we had had several years back. "I can't see patients *in* our house. That is true. But if we use the stable for our respective business fronts, it's not a problem."

He knew I was wavering as my eyes scanned over the massive barn-like structure behind the house. "The noise, Kai. My equipment is loud."

"Soundproofing," Tom interjected. "They make material now that could hide a drum corps in the next room. Stop fighting it, Katiedid. You don't have enough space with the one you have, so this is a step in the right direction, either way."

The two of them guided me around the property. It was a gorgeous house and it had a lot of potential, but there was a lot of work that needed to be done for us to make it ours. There was an inground pool and hot tub behind the house (both of which needed serious servicing), a bocce ball court and weathered horseshoe pits.

"What is that?" I asked, pointing to the tiniest house I had ever seen outside of a television program.

"That would be our one and only tenant. The electricity, water and sewage are all separate from the main house, so they are responsible for that," Kai explained.

"What happens if we buy the property?" I asked, not wanting to be someone's landlord, literally or figuratively. "Are they willing to move?"

"No. Not only will they not move, but they're the seller. So if they don't approve the conditions, no one can even rent the house," Tom whispered.

I looked at them in shock. "What are they asking that no

one has been able to buy this place in ten months?"

"Well, first, we'd have to guarantee access to whatever food we have in the fridge..." Kai said.

"WHAT?!" I half yelled.

Tom pulled me under his arm. "That's not even half of it. That old som a gun wants to play with your kids and teach 'em how to swim."

I lost my shit. "HAVE THEY LOST THEIR DAMN MIND?!?" I started screaming, as the realtor came out the back door.

"Oh! It's you Mr. Johnson. I heard hollering and I wanted to make sure there weren't any issues. Are these the buyers you were talking about?" The man in a suit asked, smiling at first Kai and then me.

"Close your mouth, Katie. I can't help that I have such high standards for neighbors. You don't know what kind of *crazy* could be living next door," Tom said, shaking his head at me.

"You?" I sucked in a breath when it all clicked.

"Me," Tom confirmed, nodding smugly.

"Since when do you own this place?" I asked, now trying to figure out the timing of everything.

"Well, Annie and I bought it about five years ago. We had planned to get it all fixed up, but things always happened. She designed the tiny house herself, you know. Made it so the grandbabies could come visit and we'd have room for them. I know it's a lot to ask, but it's yours if you want it, Katie." Tom explained.

I burst into tears. It wasn't just a little sniffle, I was sobbing and hiccuping. What had I done in this life to be surrounded by so much love? "You want us to be your neighbors?" I asked between hiccups.

Tom and Kai were both misty eyed holding me. "I know. It's a lot to ask, Kitkat, but I'm willing to cook and grocery shop for him if it will make this house ours," Kai offered.

"HAHA!" I burst out laughing, and then finally settled down. When I realized the realtor was still standing there, watching all of my crazy on display, I composed myself.

"You two are in so much trouble," I whispered at them before turning to walk back toward the car. "And don't think about talking to me before those keys are in my hand, Kai Rayburn!"

Kai and Tom laughed and walked into the house to finalize the contracts with the realtor. On paper, we bought the whole property for ten dollars and unlimited access to our fridge. In reality, Annie and Tom had used Ty's money to buy this house for all of us when they moved here five years ago. It was such a bittersweet surprise.

Paul and Jack showed up the next morning to discuss *my* plans for the property. It turned out the new project they had been heatedly discussing over the past month was the house down the street, and *I* was the new *VIP* client. Kai and Tom were insistent that I had my dream home. Needless to say, I burst into tears again.

After everything that had happened, all of our heartaches, sorrows and losses; our family still found its way to laughter and joy. Nothing went as we planned, but we did our best to make everything work. I couldn't imagine our lives together any differently.

I had no idea what the next chapter held for us, but I was looking forward to whatever came our way, with Kai and our growing family.

About the Author

Cave Marie is the pen name adopted by an American immigrant living her best life in Norway. While writing is her passion, it's not everything about her. She holds degrees in Education, Latin American Studies and Organizational Leadership, speaks three to four languages, and will honestly admit that she's hopelessly addicted to coffee in all of its forms. She is a combat veteran, advocate for women's rights and staunch supporter of victims of sexual assault and domestic violence. "People should support people."

You can connect with me on:
🔗 https://bsky.app/profile/cavemarie.bsky.social

Also by Cave Marie

I write books inspired by the world around me; spilled tea over coffee and wine and all the drama you just can't make up. My books are a mix of contemporary, science fiction, paranormal and fantasy genres with a little romance and smut thrown in for the thirsty. I like to create emotional journeys, filled with examples of life's hardships: loss, fertility, death, abuse, and mental health. I don't pull punches. Not everyone gets the happily ever after we wish for. Grab your tissues and coffee, and settle in for a good read.

La Llorona: Rise of a Mafia Queen
"The first installment of the Weeping Women Mafia Series hooks you from the prologue and keeps you reading until the last page."

Anastacia wants a life of abundance and love, two things she never had growing up. When a crisis threatens her family, she enters into the world of exotic dancing to provide financial stability. However, her aspirations take a complicated turn when she encounters Domenico, a man who ignites her passion while threatening to break her heart. Navigating their tumultuous relationship won't be easy. Anastacia must decide if she loves herself enough to let him go, or if she is willing to trade everything she knows to stand beside this Syndicate King.